GLIMPSES

THOMAS G. MORGAN

MINDSTIR MEDIA

Work previously published: "The Outrider", Mindprint #7, 1988;
"You Have Such Pretty Breasts, he said"
"To Hold Death Still", Mindprint #8, 1989;
"The Bulls of Berja", "Succubi", "Cold Morning Years";
Not of Our Time 1989 Glenn Hill Press
"Abortion and Borgeois Feminist Debate"
IN Center on Law and Poverty Review
Restoring Traditions: Mid America Harness News

Published by Mindstir Media, LLC
1931 Woodbury Ave. #182 | Portsmouth, New Hampshire 03801 | USA
1.800.767.0531 | www.mindstirmedia.com

Printed in the United States of America
ISBN-13: 978-0-9975435-7-5
Library of Congress Control Number: 2016909651

for Wendi

Glimpses; A momentary shining; a flash. Arch; glymps> the earth by night. A faint and transient appearance. An occasionally perceptible resemblance; a tinge or trace of glimmering vision.

The Oxford English Dictionary

This life with its glimpses of goodness, is still a terrible probation.

The Koran 3/85

But what of the living garment that the Earth Spirit weaves?
Is it laid up in Heaven as fast as it is woven, or can we, here
on earth, catch glimpses at any rate of patches of its ethereal web?

Arnold Toynbee *A Study of History*

Contents

Preface 8

Introduction 10

I   Echosuite 36

II   Croatoan 102

III Intinction 203

IV The Outrider 252

V   Portions of Wrath 329

VI A Proper Caliber 403

Epilogue 610

(Editorials, Articles, Political Action Report, Ads, Five Funerals and Farewell)

Preface

THE NEW GENRE

"…a new genre has sprouted… scattered acro: many sub-fields… on the front tables of bookshops a: required sectors for college courses. The genre takes the form short works on dramatic events… Serious penny dreadfuls that d sire an appellation controlee… the best name I can come up with 'incident analysis'!" [It Happened One Night New York Review of Book June 24, 2004]

These words of Robert Darnton naming the new cent ry's genre on love and madness, history and politics in his revie of some twenty titles for the New York Review of Book "The new genre," he continues, "seeks to understand the wa people construe their experiences" rather than construct the: Akin to the Italian micro-storia, it focuses on small unit ordinary people's constraints and their improvisational strat gies. It is distinct, however, in that it deals with the concentr tion of events rather than merely the events themselves. It attemp to find their meanings… "to provide a 'cognitive jolt' whic 'ignites the imagination'."

Mule strong hybridites are attempted here. As in the equine ep sodes of Apuleius; a desultoria scientia leaping from steed to steed, sti to gracile styling style. Pulp non-fiction poetically and politically astric two centuries… to re-enchant through the fait divers of experience. my opinion, American free verse has been struggling toward such a for ever since the post-war beatitudes of Kerouac, Corso, and Ginsburg. B the war, I mean of course, the "great generation's" war; that last time the nation had a fairly decent excuse to turn its patriots into gun fodder.

A war baby myself, I've glimpsed life on both sides of the "great generation's" Popular Front, seeing national and global life get better and worse at the same time.

The Holy Koran teaches "this life with its glimpses of goodness, is still a terrible probation." Surrounding evidence indicate it is not difficult to violate probation. As there is no escaping the trials of this life, we plead our case with the stories we tell. Here are some of mine. -- Drawn from the Aquifer of my existence, those underground lakes that slake the limestone pastures and hidden valley ridges of Western Indiana.

Held in the foliage of hardwoods older than the genocide of our Prophet's[1] people. This country aches with a broken hearted beauty of pastoral toil. Life bred and reared to please His natural law – betrayed by sin and the profit motive. A Yeoman farmer[2], I've had the good fortune to live with livestock – equine, ovine, bovine, feline, canine and avian. These creatures I have known, loved, birthed, trained, buried and/ or butchered live without personal sin or grace. The latter provided and partnered by Immortal Power and mortal work conserves in peace that revolutionary hope on Earth to be "as it is in Heaven". In the eye of the storm, like my stock dog's eye whose restrained stalking – herds his flock to safety. Happiness in such caring contradiction cheer my days, kin and friends. To abbreviate the Beatitudes of Jesus, "Blessed (i.e. Happy) are those who do the right thing and are not surprised when it fails. It still counts. I pray these stories count. The meaning from which these glimpses were distilled.

TGM

1: Prophet: Tecumseh's brother martyred upriver in a place now called Battle-ground in Tippecanoe County, IN.
2: Yeoman farmer: (No Kulak) small freeholder who farms his own land alone and has another job.

Introduction

Glimpses is part daybook, part scrapbook, and mostly a volume of collected free-verse poetry and non fiction prose, including vignette dialogues, letters, homilies, elegies, and a few obscure news clippings and publications. It is a mercurial series of efforts "to provide a cognitive jolt" which "ignites the imagination"-- the cultural critic Robert Darnton is quoted in the "Preface"—throughout which Tom Morgan displays venerable literary skills: attentiveness to detail, alertness to context, and hunger for larger meaning. Yet Morgan, who describes the volume in his own words as "pulp non-fiction poetically and politically astride two centuries" (9), is a man with a fiercely unconventional personality. Hell-bent on a quest for authenticity, he will brook no white-washing of the past keep no damper on simmering differences with those who have violated his sense of ethics; and make no effort to conceal his own aching humanity as he brushes off depression and humiliation with a self-mocking humor (see "Uses of Cruelty," 364).

He also has a rare gift: The literary equivalent of preternatural bat-like sonar that senses how to address readers in a voice possessing both immediacy and retrospective wisdom. Sometimes this uncanny flair comes in the form of his heat-seeking eye for the selection of apt quotations ("This life with its glimpses of goodness, is still a terrible probation," The Koran); definitions ("Diffraction: when light passes by the edge of an opaque body or through a new slit"); or titles ("Intinction," referring to the sacrament of Catholic communion as bread is dipped in wine and both are given to the communicant). Mostly we find it in his crafting of hauntingly introspective lines: "My life was grinding to a halt. I could hear it...like a lame horse in heavy gravel ("The Comely Widow," 411). Occasionally it suffuses an idiosyncratic description: "Terre Haute in the cold is a dreary ass place. Its dark and wintry soul succumbs to the shade of an old noir film. Sinister, sore and still ashamed with a wanton working class preference to be insane, never inane" ("Love in the Environs of Lee Avenue," 418).

Then there is Morgan's uncommon political history undergirding many of the references, narratives, and values. He is an unrepentant 1960s revolutionary sympathetic to Trotsky and Castro yet genuinely religious and harboring conservative views about sex, feminism, homosexuality, and much of the youth culture. To clarify this aspect from Morgan's perspective, the best place to start might be "Need for a Neo-Comm. Manifesto: A Conservative Case for Communism" (548) or "Revolutionary Recluse" (558). Having moved from activist to witness, he aims to converge what he sees as the best from the Far Left and the Far Right, driving out the worst. In my own reading, there is an unpersuasive döppelganger relationship between his puritanical convictions and the medieval church that won't work any better as a radical program in this century than it did in the last.

Nonetheless, I admire that he never seems to have thought of Marxism-Leninism-Castroism as a special wisdom that trumped everything else, and he is refreshingly free of the reflexive contempt for erudition that one can still find in sections of the Left, Old and New. One detects some hero-worshipping when it comes to Eugene V. Debs and James P. Cannon, but mostly he is commendably devoted to free inquiry, a spirit of skepticism, and reliance on evidence. Such people (I count myself among them) are always going to have a problematic relationship to homogenizing political organizations, even before such groups go entirely off the rails.

Morgan's time in outfits like the now-defunct Young Socialist Alliance and the probably moribund Socialist Workers Party was short compared to the long shadow the experience cast on his life. Still, this volume documents that Morgan never forgot how liberals teach about fairness and compassion while being interlocked with forces of oppression. On some burning issues of our time—racism, imperialism, class oppression—he is on the Left of the Left.

Writing may have been a way of saving his life. Glimpses has aspects of a reconstructed coming-of-age story crafted from psychological necessity, a journal that is fragmented but especially evocative in references to a progressive loss of innocence—the kind of loss one can spend the rest of one's life seeking to restore. Paramount for Morgan was the fantasy, inspired by his parents, of one long-lasting love in the form of one marvelous person. From first page to last of this book, lurking like a bad dream at the back of his mind, are the traumas of marital infidelity and abandonment. Yet I would never shelve this book amid those rows of self-consciously therapeutic and often narcissistic memoirs; there is too much else here that vigorously conjures other times, places, and emotions.

To be sure, Morgan is far from a Jane Austen or Theodore Dreiser in their ability to orchestrate thick descriptions of a social milieu, but he does have an astuteness for the telling visual particulars, an ear for small talk and the emotional subtext beneath, and a notable knack for story-telling. At first the discrete segments of Glimpses might suggest an all-over literary style similar to the art of a Jackson Pollock abstract expressionist painting in which the compositional details are to be given equal weight. But gradually we see how he structures his reminiscences and meditations as a series of vignettes that add up to often taut scenes from a mid-Westerner's life in mid-20th and early 21st centuries—some occurring in Europe, Mexico, and California.

The job of Morgan's writing is not to act as a reflecting mirror of his experiences but as a lens through which we catch views of an alternately baffling, exasperating, and mesmerizing search for some fixity by which to oppose the chaos of daily living. (Spoiler alert: Morgan finds stability in rural living, nature, and a loyal third wife.) There are intoxicating concentrates of pure beauty ("'Pathetic Fallacy' John Ruskin," 502), but more often the tone is prickly and wild ("Left Americana," 156-176). He is astonishingly well-read and usually exhibits a verbal sure-footedness (an exception is "Not By Way of Sport," 357). He has access to a munificent store of language (keep a dictionary handy), endless quotations (Ferdinand Celine, F. Scott Fitzgerald, Umberto Ecco, Robinson Jeffers, Heinrich Boll), and characters from every movie from the last six decades (Carrie and Grizzly Man were two that surprised me). In the end there is victory: The dead can return but they can't stay. What remains instead is the spiritually intense presence of the author. Morgan has become the kind of character you think about long after you finish the book.

Alan Wald
Febuary 28th, 2016

I   ECHOSUITE

ECHOSUITE

COMRADELY CORRESPONDENCE

TERRE HAUTEUR

FIRST LIGHT

COLOMBOS WEATHER

UNQUIET WOUND

HARNESS

SPOT

T.V. SETTS

BOYS RHYME

SPLIT EFFECTS

AS VIOLET

COLOR AND LINE

SOUTH YARD

WHERE THERE ARE VIADUCTS

DEAD SOLDIERS

MASTER SAWYER

PARTITIONEDNESS

TESTAMENTS

BALLS

Ballad of Red Brogan

Mumps

Cold Morning Years

In Desperate Kindness

Snowfall

John McCool

The Last First Punch

Fin-De-Siè-Cle F.ing Fusion

The Clean and the Carport

Labor Day

We'd Ride in Limousines

Ever Homeward

Rust Belt Raga

After the Fair

Old Light

On the Avenues

My Father and the Robins

Native River Riff

Aisle of the Heart

II CROATOAN

CROATOAN

BULLS OF BERJA

SUCCUBI

GABLES

ALPINE TRUTH

DIRTY THIRTIES

NEARING

DROM

MY FRIEND MIKE

LABOURS LOVE . . ALMOST LOST

PARTICIPATORY INCORRECTNESS

PROBATIVE EVIDENCE

BAD ASS GENTILE

KURDISTAN AT SEA

SOLARIUM

STERLING RESISTANCE

L.eft A.mericana

Under the Vultures Eye

Silencers

The Byzantine

Beat Regional Spaces

Miners Code

Quit Claim

White Negros

Luggage Rack

Uncommon Denominator

Détente

Eternal Revolution

III   INTINCTION

Sable Dawn

A Toast to Perfection

Adagio for Uncle Tom

Geese

Conatus

Torso Murderer

September Skies

Shepherds Quake

Galen

Ourselves and the City

Cats of Rome

Chaos Theory

The Lot of My Relation

Papa, I'd Prefer a Kinder Stable

Me and my Shark Attack

SHADES OF ST. KIRIL

WEATHER FOR PACKY PAHL

JUDY DUKES (TERRE HAUTBOIS)

THE TERRIER MAN

RUMIS BETTER PAST

HARDER TO KILL

HANDS OF THE SHEPHERD

RAPPORT WITH THE FISHES

RABBIT ON THE LAWN

DEOCENTRICITIES

TOAST TO SAINT CATHERINE

THE FALL OF LIGHT

GULLS IN GARY

NOON WINE

INTINCTION

IV THE OUTRIDER

THE OUTRIDER

PENNSYLVANIANS

BOTTOM LAND

FREEZE ETCHED

WITNESS TO THE WOLVES

PURITAN IN THE WINGS

HE IS RISEN

TO ORESTES

THE DIABLO RANGE

OLD PRIEST GRADE

WAITING BECOMES SAM BECKETT

CHARGING THE CONDOR

BAD WEATHER

"YOU HAVE SUCH PRETTY BREASTS," HE SAID

ERRANT NIGHT

MISSING THE LOCAL

WARNING TREES

DULL ROOTS

NO STROKE NECESSARY

BYE CHINESE CAMP

ONE PEOPLE

THE PROPHETS ENNUI

Between my Teeth

The Humanist Hag

Indians and Cowboy

Burgos

Stalin in Wales

Second and Cherry

Consider the Raven

For Lope De Vega

C.P. Time

Raging Sighs

Summers Over

Rough Swallow Moon

Adversary and Answer

The Niche of Night

Not an Albatross

Dairy Hand

Keep from Falling

Fado

New Priest Grade

Brave Country

A Pass at the Season

To Hold Death Still

Cheerful Defiance

V   PORTIONS OF WRATH

DAVIES COUNTY SALE

AUTHORITY QUESTION

BABOON MACHINE

WHITE MAN

YOUNG MAN

OLD MAN

MIDDLE OF THE ROADER

DESIGNATED CLUSTERS

UNDULY FAMILIAR

LITTLE DEATH

SOCIALIST STENOSIS

THE CHURCH IS SOLD

UNCLE TIME

PEOPLE

LILAC WINTER

THUNDER FACTORY

SNIDE AND CREDULOUS

SHANGRILA IN WINTER

PONY EXPRESSIONS

¿RESTFUL SENTENCE?

LAGGARD DAWN

ABANDONMENT ANXIETY

THE BEGINNING OF SORROWS

TO CELTIC NATIONALISTS

LEGERDEMAIN

Remembrance of Rats in the Wall

Libertarianism

PZ Pivot

A Female for Some Seasons

Anti, Anti, Antis

Gaza

Seasonal Dirt

Shades

Film Review

Coulombs Law

Scarcity

The Autumn Follicle

Exconversation

Redoubt

Not by Way of Sport

A Catholic Child . . . Defiled

Anglo Saxon O.D.

Collider

Even Lincoln Had to Get Over Indiana

Anus Envy

Campus Banter

The Penumbral View

Fascinators Funeral

Uses of Cruelty

Seasons Jostle

Emoting Edna

Overcomers

V PORTIONS OF WRATH

DIFFRACTION

N.Y.C.

COLLECTIVIST

DISCOURAGE

MANHOOD IN MANHATTAN

STORE POEM

MISTORY

THE CITY IN WINTER

GOYOPLA

KURASAWAN

MEET THE PRESS

WET ETHNICS

WINTER WREN

SUPERMARKET

PUPILS

HALLOWEANED

RE: THE QUESTION OF WOMEN IN COMBAT

. . . OR SENSE OF COMFORT

PEDRO IN OUTER SPACE

NO SIGNAL FROM MARS

TIC TAC PTO

BIRDWATCHING

PROBATIVE EVIDENCE 2

U.S.♀ SOLDIER

HITLER'S BRIDGEWORK

THREE POSITIONS

WANTING OUT

COMRADELY BANTER

NEO UNCON.

GERIATRICOM' ON BABY

HORSE HAULING

ANATOMICAL APPRECIATION

POST BLIZZARD MUD

CALENDARS DISORDER

CLASS REUNION

ROBINS IN BAGDAD

THE KINDRED SHADE

FRIENDS INTO AUTUMN

PLOWSHARE

SEX VS. VIOLENCE

LOOSE CARGO

LIONOPHOBIC

UNION HOSPITAL LOBBY

A TREMBLING CUP

JANUARY

EPIGRAM AGAINST COMRADE BARNES

VI   A PROPER CALIBER

A Proper Caliber

Anno D.

The Comely Widow

Love in the Environs of Lee Avenue

While I Wait For Her

Our Time

Adumbrare

Turkey Run

Crazy Eights

Love is not a Reality Achieved, but Endured

From my Window

Barnswallow

No Place to Die

In Clover

Caress

My Foals in Far Pastures

Fledgling

Teamstering

Tender Pastures

The Shepherd Boy

Womb Envy

TEEN TIME

FACTIONS

OUTSIDE MODESTY

THE DEATH OF STALLIONS

SWANS

THE BLACK HEM

HEATHER

FUNERAL RAIN

BOILER PLATE

NO SURPRISES

NEARER THE DUST

DEATH OF A WREN

WREATH

THE PENTECOSTAL BOMBER

BREEZE AT OUR BACK

THE GREATEST ELENGENESS

GREEN ON THE GROUND

OZARK COFFEE

OPTICAL ALLUSION

EGYPTIAN WELLS

LOCKING THE DOORS OF DARKNESS

NOVEMBER SUN

VI A PROPER CALIBER

NOT SO LITTLE DEATHS

GENTLY STUPID

INDIAN GIVER

GRAY PUDDING

PLAIN JUSTICE

PRAIRIE MINDED

AMISH PRISONERS

HEAVY WATER

EVERYTHING MATTERS

YONDER

SYCAMORES

POLLACK

OLDE BRUSH WOLF OF THE WABASH

BRAVE KID

INJURED BUCK

COLD CONVIVIALITY

MULES ON THE ROAD

APOSIOPESIS

HIGH DENIAL

COLDSTREAM GUARDS

VAN GOGH YELLOW

Koranic Haiku

Comely While Leaving

Pathetic Fallacy

Two Kinds

Beyond The Pale

Bison

38th St. Smoke

New Made Bed

Mexican Frowns

Three Jakes

Ancien Regimes

Clouds on the Ground

Breaking Severities

Red Grey Evenings

The Furthest Turn

Holy Saturday

The Full Loaf

Permutation

Imperanent Pasture

Winterior Seiche

Calico Coyote Hounds

Sluice of May

VI   A PROPER CALIBER

FIST OF TTHE MOON

A NATURAL SMILE

BROTHER HOUNDS

THE OTHER TIME

INTO THE RAIN

DYING MEN DON'T DRINK BEER

LONG JOHNS IN JUNE

SPRUNG

CONSOLIDATION

TRUTH AND COMMOTIONS

NO GNATS IN GOSHEN

THE AUTHORITY OF FAILURE

FIREWAKE

NEED FOR A NEO COMM. MANIFESTO

BALLAD FROM A STILL POND

THE TALKING POND

STABLES

THE YEARLING MULE

SWEET FURLOUGH

EMBALMED EVENING

A Hearts Tack

Wholly Holy Picture

A Muggy Day in Manhatten

Revolutionary Recluse

Sunsigns

Hope for Audacity

Negritude

Hard Light

Synchronicity

Rain not Fallen

Terre Hautesprit

Les Vestiges de Terre Haute

Conditional Love

VII EPILOGUE

EPILOGUE: EDITORIALS, ARTICLES, POLITICAL ACTION REPORT, ADS, FIVE FUNERALS AND FAREWELL

EDITORIALS TO THE NEW YORK REVIEW OF BOOKS AND THE TERRE HAUTE TRIBUNE.

MARCH 1997   RE: PHILOTYRANNY

MARCH 1998   RE: FINTAN O'TOOLE

APRIL 1999   RE: COLUMBINE

JUNE 2001   NO SATISFACTORY RETRIBUTION

JANUARY 2007   DEFUNDING WAR

SEPTEMBER 2008   RE: HILLARY AND GERALDINE

EASTER WEEK, 2009   RE: IDEOLOGUE BAYH

FEBRUARY 2009   RE: GUANTANAMO

JULY 2009   RE: BLUEDOG DEMOCRATS

SEPTEMBER 2009   RE: OBSTRUCTION OF HEALTH CARE

OCTOBER 2009   RE: McGENERALS

JANUARY 2010   RE: OBAMA AND THE BANKSTERS

JUNE 2010   RE: BILLION DOLLAR COKE BOTTLE

DECEMBER 2010   RE: RECENT SUPREME COURT
DECISIONS, ELECTIONS, &
DEFICIT COMMISSION REPORTS

January 23, 2011   Revisiting Facts of the Rotten
                    Tree

February 2011   Re: D.A.D.T. repeal

August 2011   EMPIRE INDEED

Spring 2015   Letter to Editors Re SAE racism
                    Terre Haute Tribune 8 Indianapolis Star

                    Indiana Daily Student 8 Bloomington Herald
                    Indiana Statesman
January 2016   Trump Check

Articles

Restoring the Traditions (Midamerica Harness News)

Abortion & Borgeois Feminist Debate
(IN Center on Law and Poverty Review)

Political Report:

Hands Off Unions and Horseracing

ADS: 'Swimmer', Shadowgaits Standardbred Stallion at Stud
        Swimmer's issue

American Night: Response to Allen Wald

Leroy McRae: Obituary and Responses

Five Funerals . . . . and Farewell

"Of the most things therein, I am no Compiler by hearsay, but have beene a reall Actor; I take myself to have a propertie in them: and therefore have beene bold to challenge them to come under the reach of my owne rough Pen."

Captain John Smith,
(The Buried Truth William M. Kelso)

Yet . . .

*"Memories are like movies.
We do with them what we want"*

Bobby Cassotto Darin

*"A well devised story needn't try to be like real life.
Real life is only too eager to resemble a well devised story"*

Isaac Babel

I   ECHOSUITE

"What gives a man worth is that he incorporates everything he has experienced. This includes the countries where he has lived, the people whose voices he has heard. It takes in his origins, if he can find out something about them. By this is meant not only ones private experience but everything concerning the time and place of ones beginnings."

Elias Cannetti   "Play of the Eyes"

Echosuite 41

Comradely Correspondence 42

Terre Hauteur 45

First Light 47

Colombos Weather 48

Unquiet Wound 49

Harness 50

Spot 51

T.V. Setts 52

Testaments 55

Boys Rhyme 58

Split Effects 59

As Violet 60

Color and Line 61

South Yard 62

Where there are Viaducts 63

Dead Soldiers 64

Master Sawyer 66

Partitionedness 67

Balls 68

Ballad of Red Brogan 74

Mumps 75

Cold Morning Years 80

In Desperate Kindness 81

Snowfall 83

John Mccool 84

The Last First Punch 85

Fin-De-Siè-Cle F.ing Fusion 86

The Clean and the Carport 87

Labor Day 88

We'd Ride in Limousines 89

Ever Homeward 90

Rust Belt Raga 91

After the Fair 92

Old Light 93

On the Avenues 94

My Father and the Robins 98

Native River Riff 99

Aisle of the Heart 101

Terre Haute General Strike 1935

The States's response

ECHOSUITE

Where is the sound
between our voice
and its echo.

It is out there . . .

where my verse begins

in an older place

than perception.

More softly we repeat our style

and fade . . .

and fade softly

into the echosuite.

COMRADELY CORRESPONDENCE

Comradely correspondence between Terre Hautes Eugene Debs and Theodore Dreiser tell us a bit about the place and region. Ted wrote Gene in October of 1922 re: the Dreiser family's desire that his brother Paul (Dresser) be buried with a monument in Terre Haute where he was born, not in contending Chicago, Lafayette or Indianapolis. Ted thought Gene might get the governors help. Indiana's soon to be criminally convicted governor McCray denounced Debs as "the arch traitor of America" and was not helpful. Debs felt that "Terre Haute, Paul's native city, 'On The Banks of the Wabash', which so ardently and lovingly claims him should have the honor of his burial site and memorial."

The Terre Haute Tribune and New York Times entered the fray. A New York Times editorial on December 20, 1922 notes "the squabble over a Memorial for Paul reflects his brother Theodore's book, 'Hoosier Holiday' which is an indispensable document for study of the *Peculiar Hoosier Civilization*." Paul was buried in Chicago.

Letters of Eugene Victor Debs Volume III

*"Terre Haute, Indiana would undergo decline after the 1920's . . .
railroads . . .coal mining. . . local manufacturing relocated to other parts
of the country where unions weren't as organized or other parts of the
world where wages weren't as high"*

Tom Roznowski "An American Hometown"

"Terre Haute . . Child of the River . . entered the 1940's optimistically."

Mike McCormick
"Terre Haute Queen City of the Wabash"

"And . . . this ain't Terre Haute"
(Small town bartenders response to under aged women)

James Jones,
1950's novel "Some Come Running"

Wedding Picture: John Paul & Violet Maureen Morgan:
My Parents wed September, Friday 13, 1936
I was born on their anniversary September, Friday 13, 1940

Terre Hauteur

"If childhood is a lie of poetry" [William H. Gass "In the
Heart of the Heart of the Country"]
then its neglect is abusive:
empirical non poetics neglect and abuse
the nurturing of life.

In the Heart of this broken heart land
TerreHauteur treads close
to the still nights waking
magnified in windshields that upholster sleepy eyes.

The other world is like that . .
furtively imagined;
a childs extended view of color
from a truck cab

Where the weather is one way
and visceral presence less
neuropathic to foregone reality;
a reticent and seemly post consciousness.

Reinsman Tommy Morgan, Sister Barbara, Pal, and Katina Terre Haute IN 1944

FIRST LIGHT... (AND THE DREAMCROSSED TWILIGHT BETWEEN BIRTH AND DYING.) T.S. ELIOT, ASH WEDNESDAY. 1930

I was a glint struck in my fathers eye

while he worked as brakeman

for the high grounded Pensy.

Old tracks cross chording a dark and wintry carol

alone as the deep and dissonant night sings

he worked all the while high balling Terre Haute

and the idea offsprings to see

his black and gray lantern hallowed

the place he slept in the crumie

and rose at smoking dawn

where tramps and gandydancers point out his goatee

before he rode the Harley home; making love to my mother

they brought about me.

Through utero nineteen forty

I breathed the dark industrial night

by a bend in my mothers birth canal

toward my fathers gray lanterned light

exploding from the forceps

into Doc Redmans hands and abandonment

upon newspapers on the floor

until I bawled "the Baraka is with me

I ain't dead yet."

I've been living and dying ever since.

COLOMBOS WEATHER

"I want to get behind the weather"
Christopher Colombo to his son.

Jagged glass in the gutters water tore my toddlers flesh like a gator and I healed in the heat of sand piles, lying with my sorrel pony Katina, named after a war horse, I think, by the back alleyed Roosevelt shit house; near black neighbors with small dogs . . we shared a darker countenance looking at each other like we'd done before.

My mother blanched to find me lying with the little red mare before we'd visit the round house down the hill to watch the trains and fires from the coke plant that came at night. There was an Airedale in the neighborhood, a fine tavern, and one poor wretch who lived alone in a gray shingled place amidst catalpa trees we were sure was a witch. We'd spy on her before fighting departures from friends who dared to leave. My pal Bobby Carmichael (who grew up to be a flying ace) never understood why I whupped him whenever he wanted to leave. I loved his company and just wanted him to stay. A bad old habit of mine.

And I learned the sounds of certain death . . . my Pal hit loud by Hulman Streets heavy traffic.

My fathers gray lantern and mothers off white radio with a woman dressed in white on its dial; "mother as bride" I thought before I could stand or speak.

An old photo frames the evening with a pointer pup, on the saddle of Dad's Harley.

He looked so seriously at the beast and the machine.

'Childhood wounds in each writer lead them to become the writer they are'

A paraphrase from Edmund Wilson's Wound and the Bow...

UNQUIET WOUND

Terre Haute as child in sun grounded sidewalks down the pavement with Smokey colt into the sale and commerce off horse flesh. Technicolor terrors of sellers and traders . . an obese woman carelessly nursing her child . . in the eye of the colt who sees little color and threatening strangeness on all sides.

My fear . . my failure – all for technologies trip on a bicycle toward false promises of fraternity. I crashed my bike at Jims Fishman and Callahan; erred through the authorized cave of my fathers disdain.

GRAITH [1]

My father in whose hands

were held the reins

I favor unadorned

never adored me

except for my own fifteen minutes

almost . . . successfully

I'd hold his shirts from the laundry close

to smell neats foot oil and new mown Timothy

from the block barns he'd build

in the backyards of my childhood

where there too, I fought an English bulldog

driven mad by brain tumors

to a bloody standstill.

His mother in her slip and poison oak,

his wife, my mother . . .

alarmed to know

their little man was destined to fight . . though

not more than others

but wyrdly [2] so . . .

1: Graith: Irish for Harness
2: wyrd - wyrdly: Celtic for fate; the preordanied shape of time

SPOT

My cousins had a dog named Spot. Probably part Blue
Tick and Terrier. He'd bite a stranger or maybe kin if you weren't
careful. He got more protective as Aunt Kitty got more ill. I'd
bicycle home on Poplar and drop in on them. Spot would bark and
someone would come out. There were a lot of them; cousins I
mean. Seven altogether from the oldest, my age, to the youngest,
my namesake, still in diapers. When I'd stay over on Saturdays
we'd go to Mass in shifts to share the Sunday shoes. Uncle John
was my godfather.

Spot kept barking that day and no one came out. I talked
to him for a while 'til he growlingly allowed me on the porch.
Keeping an eye on Spot, I moved slowly toward the door, looking
in before knocking.

My aunt was sitting alone in the kitchen. Her head on her
arms, on the table. She wept. I reckoned she wept for John, all her
babies and all her life she loved and was leaving. I could not hear
her weeping yet her silent trembling still reverberates through all
the life and death I've known.

She sensed me at the door, gathering herself up with such
braveness and beauty beyond any cues of expectable bereave-
ment, that I shall never lend mortal countenance to any less grace.

T.V Setts

*"A percentage of the snow on static T.V. is
from the big bang creation of the universe."*
Theoretical Physicist
Michio Kaku

My father's milk route began at 5 am. He liked the morning when it was fresh, he'd say, breathing the new days air before anyone else did.

I never liked the whole cold dark idea of it. Especially at Christmas and Thanksgiving. The milk customers' homes would be moving slowly toward warmth and celebration. We would be running up and down the street delivering cold bottles of milk. The oven scent of turkey, dressing, and pumpkin pie wafted everywhere and there was increasing numbers of the new T.V. sets and their shiny antennae's up and down every street and unpaved road.

On porches I could slightly hear the muffled tones of this new phenomena comforting and informative; softly lulling attention from all other sectors of consciousness. I'd see children through the windows cuddling under blankets in front of that snowy reception of the one possible channel.

On Saturday mornings they watched hours of 'The Big Top' (or tried to through the snowy static), a three-ring circus that came right into their homes with liberty horses, big cats, and beautiful women. Some of whom were trapeeze artists.

I watched once at my Grandmas who thought believing what you saw on this new contraption was more than slightly idolatrous. She'd scoff at me for believing people could fly through the air or do anything else with the greatest of ease.

"No, come look now Grandma," I'd appeal. She'd glance up at the snowy screen, then practically spit in contempt, "Puppets!" she'd say, "just puppets."

My own idolatry grew until I realized I was worshiping the Godchaux Sugar commercial. Consciously I was only intrigued in following the hazy animation. Unconsciously I was beginning to believe the answer to the mystery of human community was on the other side of a clear signal reception to that commercial.

How I envied those other kids on holiday or Saturday mornings. I thought if we ever got T.V. I would get under a quilt in front of it from the a.m. test pattern to the p.m. star spangled banner and then I'd know everything that went on in the world.

Sometimes still when I'm up early or getting in late the lull of soft flickering light will draw me toward the tube. Thank God for hundreds of clear, fragmentary 24 hour channels. Such access is less seductive. Gone is the fascination of connecting the dots on that one snowy channel to find the heart of human common ground.

That certain shatteredness clarifies the cold heart of propaganda and the bull roaring truths we learned when dancing cigarette packs with majorette legs first irritated our attention.

It is all irritainment* and easier now to get up and go to bed or to work.

* "Irritainment": John McFall's word

TGM & Jim Fishman 1948
(with Shadow; an Irish X Louellen setter bitch)

"Wheres a boy a-goin an' whats he goin to do

When the world bu'sts through

Co'se he ain't no bragger, des a-rippen an' a-rarin

An' a-darin all de beestus an' a-des a double darin"

James Whitcomb Riley' 'When the World Busts Through'

TESTAMENTS (LIKE RILEY)

With sun on the sap of the trunks of our youth
we clumb the trees and toured the trenches
of new basements near Sugar Grove School
whose playground was ten acres of weeds . . .
and that was it . . where we'd chase the girls
at recess and noon not knowing what to do
once we caught 'em.

On weekends we'd catch bumble bees there . . .
(who could catch the most in a bell jar without
being stung or crying about it if you did) around
the trees of the ten acres he'd organize air
rifle fights assigning his old Red Ryders to
us gentiles . . taking the high ground with
his new Daisey Pump.

I evened the score with swordplay, poking
out part of his eye with an old battin board his
mother never forgave me for that and persuading
him to jump off their garage in the genuine
World War II parachute he owned and bragged about.

He was my pal Jim Fishman who looked like a
little John Garfield. He was my pal even when Dean
Aberman and him beat up on me for "making
fun of their religion," they said, when I thought
I was just expressing envy at their Hebrew lessons.

Then they drafted me into spin the bottle with

birthday party girls which scared back my social

development for several seasons.

    I wuz backward with women, he said, and

he showed me dirty books and decals kept under

his bed. My Gawd! . . what awful feelings got

aroused for me to fight and I couldn't blame

him cuz I wuz the one feeling them, knowing

they weren't right when I glimpsed in his

half wounded eye, a look more naïve than even I could ever bleeve

'bout Seminary boys, cousins, and kin.

My jewish friend didn't know 'bout sin!!

Sure as he and half his family had an inside track

to those Bible guys . . Jesus, Joseph, Abraham, Moses

and God . . . I sensed just then . . .

his religious education was salvifically thin,

compared to my clan who knew all about sin!!

    "You want one of these women tonight?!"

I dramatically gestured toward one of his

pictures of slinky maidens being molested by monsters.

If you pray to the divil he'll deliver alright;

jest give him your soul forever and you can enjoy

illicit licentious pukertude (terms from my catholic

cousins) all the way to the burning

lakes of fire (images from my Baptist grandma)

    I had him goin now. He looked skeered

and confused. Confused?! – about this awful stuff.

Confusion was for math but not for morals.

Why even my masonic Dad going through the chairs

had to agree with Priests about this activity.

"Never . . never trust what defies gravity!!!"

Jim was reeling now with sensual temptation.

I could see him struggling with his mind making

deals with the divil . . . to have his own

slinky maiden to molest until morning.

"I wish you hadn't told me that," he said,

and sadly walked away.

Going home on my bike I thought, "He's

not outsmarted me today."

I never saw him much after grade school.

We heard about him and onry girls. I wrote

him a letter to find one good girl and love her alone.

He married a beautiful gentile right after graduation,

and began carrying a gun. I fought along side

him against some bums at the bowling ally once

and worried he'd pull it. I think he almost did.

He worried I'd give jews a bad name talking so

much about Trotsky. I worried about my friend

and the gun. He went into the Army and had

marital trouble.

I read his obituary in my new wife's old house.

BOYS RHYME

The bigger boys ran loud in taller stride;

my smaller peers and I

scattered, we scattered wide.

Thump! Chuss! Pump-Thuss! air rifles report

one hour of spoorless sport

behind Rushes grocery store.

Finally a sparrow careens in an arc towards the alley;

the skies no shelter when you're shot.

It huddles between mud puddles on the ground.

Blood flecked the little bird looks me in the eye,

and I will tend the terror

of that dying sparrow

until the day I die.

TGM 1950

SPLIT EFFECTS

Somewhere between 1946 and 47 at 6 or 7 I saw "Duel in the Sun" with my parents at the Indiana Theatre. The film was heralded as Hollywood's first Freudian western. Its split in sexual cause and effect disturbed me.

. . All those erect cacti around maiden head rock where Gregory Peck and Jennifer Jones finally and fatally penetrate each other with a death wish of threatening sexuality. . thanatological hard-ons proving a hormonal pentecost for the gender gapped tower of babel.

After they dueled for days and then shot each other in a traffic jam of emotional, class and racial confusion; loving and hating each other . . . killing each other in the hot bleeding gravel . . .

I knew then that boys and girls could have communication problems.

"Like an evening evoking the spectrum   Wallace Stevens
AS VIOLET."

Violet was my mother.

We sang to her that song.

Now the April lawn is covered

by wild violet that comes

with the wet moon . . .

answering the question her life

and mine were asking,

that lace and lancet of nature

build grace as the redbud

holds up the edge of hope

for summer nights as Violet

as the nearer dawn is born.

"Line and plane are combined in a gyre which must expand or . . .
contract according to whether mind grows in objectivity or subjectivity"
                                                                    W.B. Yeats 'A Vision'

"Let art confine itself to the disposition, pure and simple of
COLOR AND LINE . . .
                                                                    Clement Greenburg

There is a blue gray point of pencil lead
in my sixty nine year old knee;
the color and line appeal to me.

It was put there by Billy Dello or Jim Callahan
in a fifth grade sharpened pencil fight at Sugar Grove School
where all classes caroled around a huge Christmas tree;
the color and line appealed to me.

Outside fighting and carousing we'd watch the girls stand on their hands
revealing panties, white, blue, and pink.
I liked blue the best, the white was not interesting, pink too embarrassing;
the line and color excited me.

As they stood then fled across acres of unfinished playground
we, of course chased them. Some ran very fast,
zig zaging across the grounds weedy sea;
the color and line appealed to me.

After we'd catch them, we had no idea what to do with them.
They would catch their breath, smile and zig zag run again.
Breathlessly we all ran and are running still;
the color and line no longer appeal to me.

The bell would ring, we'd come inside to our lockers;
burnished wood, gabled and dark inside.
Sometimes I'd rest in mine and hide;
color and line itself confined.

SOUTH YARD

I left a note for my son to trash wrap the dead mallard found in our south yard. The Pyrenees pup had killed and dragged it from the pond.

The south yard . . I said to myself. It was an old term for me. I grew up with a south yard in nearly two acres of terrestrial time. Looking out west from it across a vacant lot I imagined that far shore of the Wabash becoming prairie . . becoming the Great Plains, and over the Rockies to California and the Pacific. All that cowboy country I would travel someday. But for then, I was content in the south yard.

I mowed it without a machine and weeded my parents flowers with a wood handled weeder about four feet long. Then I would practice with it as a javelin, spearing the air from our driveway to the neighbors hedge. When retrieving my "javelin", Duke the neighbors red cocker would challenge me. I would growl back at him. Actually I was always a little afraid of Duke.

There was a paddock and block barn by the alley at the east end of the south yard. My father built and fenced them both. They were for our welsh pony and her offspring . . all of whom were only "honorarily welsh." They were really Shetlands . . originally from my Aunt Ferns farm. Dad groomed, gaited and dreamed them into being Welsh. They looked Welsh.

My grandmother helped us put in a huge garden in the south yard . . one year . . maybe it was two or three years . . it was grand but so very much work. Potatoes, sweet corn, tomatoes, green beans, squash, strawberries, raspberries, and steel posted grapevines for the foxy concord; me, my pals and the sparrows would raid through August.

I worked hard in the garden, but would never admit liking it... which amused my proletarian father and mortified my peasent mother.

WHERE THERE ARE VIADUCTS

Dick Haymes recorded sounds like Uncle Leo did . . .

attractive, ignorant, placid;

a veteran compulsion of talent toward squishy wonder bread,

his bakery truck in coastal motion

pictured in my head

where there are viaducts

for the darkness in our dreams

passing through lives life forms

a frame outside whose edge

I've stood . . . just a kid by the window

seeing his loved ones as another song

too white and too involved in their time.

"Muses sometimes form in those low
haunts their most lasting attachments."
W.B.Yeats

DEAD SOLDIERS

"If you don't plan to f. or fight; stay out of bars and taverns at night," was one of my fathers slogans. Where Jesus preferred to speak in parables my father liked lines that rhymed. It was the way he wished to dispense advice.

When my young wife and I first set to housekeeping he advised, "Whether you rent or buy; you pay for the house you occupy."

Not that these rhymes should in any way suggest my father's nature was poetic. He was not. Indeed he was radically concrete; preferring interminable quantitative descriptions free from the slightest conceptual effort. Conversations with him were like being lost in an early Dreiser novel; turgid, factual, and may I say, more than mildly uninspiring.

"Hi Dad, how's it going?"

'I took your mother to see aunt Edna Sunday. We drove out Fruitridge, past Poplar and took Hulman east to 46 all the way to Ellettsville. We made good time. I pulled out from home at noon and up their hill not a minute after one . . . and on and on . . .'"

Though it was less paternal analysis than the cultural significance of that first slogan that led to this glimpse I do not like bars or taverns nor plan to f. or fight in them anymore, yet I remain attracted to their abrasive proximity. Those joints with an air of alleged depravity are particularly appealing. I used to covet their atmosphere from the sidewalks of my childhood, near the end of my first decade walking West on Wabash Avenue from the safe civil districts toward the lumpen effluvia of the court house. In this old town of Terre Haute I walked to my horn lesson past Cinema Marquees called The Lyceum, The Fountain and Savoy where boyhood gossip alleged the floors flowed with chawed tobacco spittle and vermin. I'd duck into Quinlans Feed Store to look at the rabbits and then slowly peruse the alley bar across the street, which seemed radiant with low life adventure.

Near the end of my second decade I braved entrance to the place. It was after the races at the county fair and carnies grimly sat amidst dead soldiers.

MASTER SAWYER

My snow gray uncle took me fishing before my youth
. . . an outdoorsman with diamond sawyered expectations that
I befriend his child; that I befriend his child's child as his clan had
kindled ken and kin in me.

To expand the heart's deliverance, from high minded
negligence; in failed and failing experience! . .

His sawyer's jaw set wide, as a valley's smile of
approval he expected this little all from me; getting into places
he would never be . . . delivering my aunt's pecan pies to ivy
gabled academic spaces . . . college peers pretending not to
notice his Mexican bad building blue buicks he'd drive after
they quit making Nashes.

For I will do it now in our hearts new places . . . the way
I never promised and he always justly expected. I will do it now
in my last paces and he will approve by the boats bright shining
waters and all the outdoor places.

PARTITIONEDNESS

Partitions devise . . .a layering . .

in angle bricked sun bright by Sycamores

from heights . . where the air . . can be held.

Where . . the sight of remembrance is

layered in high angled light to how the ground

smelled by buildings pluraled sites tending

yards aside cream colored milk truck traffic. Divco's

disengaging the curb to promise Lady Borden

in the windows; chocolate and cold as

the dirt deep down in basement foundations

cement around outside the forms of faster

recollection to peacefully devise . . .

partitions of the wise.

BALLS

His was a pink and white Ford Fairlane with a see through fiberglass sunroof. It even had pink and white leather seats. A hot car in 1952. He stocked bottles and boxes of veterinary medicine and equipment throughout the trunk and all over the back seat. The car reeked of iodine, ether, worming concoctions, horse liniment, and calf boluses. He was Dr. Odell Archer D.V.M. graduate cum laude of the defunct Terre Haute Veterinary College. I was his assistant my twelfth and thirteenth summers and every Saturday in between.

There was public acclaim in being with Doc Archer. You could sense it in the sunny smiles and nods from people in Terre Haute traffic and the great hospitality we'd receive from Vigo County stock farmers. Not just a pill roller or knife man Doc Archer was the virtual renaissance man of livestock savvy. He knew how to handle, rope, train, set, break, harness, feed, castrate, whelp, calve, lamb, kid, foal, farrow, drench, float, trim, worm, and comprehensively care for every critter in the county from show dogs, to trail hounds, gun dogs to game terriers, guard dogs, lap dogs, mad dogs, game cocks, wild hawks, range poultry, racing pigeons, rabbits, caged quail, beef and dairy cattle, breed bulls, bad goats, swine barns, barn cats, saddle horses, draft horses, race horses, and mules; every canine, equine, bovine, feline and ovine problem you could think of . . from lost kittens to crazy cayuses.

I'd ride with him along back country brown graveled roads til the sun dried dirt caked over his pink Ford turning into a shade like coral; in my kids mind a preview of the 1955 car color of my fathers Oldsmobile. Then, I thought a lot about cars as well as critters. We'd drive with the windows down in hot humid weather with road dust settling in over the dash, leather seats, and veterinary supplies. Sunlight seared through the fiberglass sunroof and I would doze as the radio droned on announcing every play of a Cardinals or Cubs game. Doc would gently laugh when I'd bang my head on the dusty dash.

As a 'large and small animal practitioner' Doc responded to every farm call request. My first was across the Wabash at a river bottom swine farm.

"What are we doing?" I asked.

"Cutting pigs!" he replied.

I had no idea what "cutting" meant. We arrived at the farm in the heat of the day. The farmer here was practicing Purdue's post war advice to raise swine in pastures like cattle. It was cleaner and aesthetically more pleasing to scent and sight. However the pigs were wilder than those raised in pens.

This farmer had convened several hundred, hundred pound boar pigs into his rickety old barn. Our job was to make them barrows i.e. to castrate them, "cutting" off their testicles. Early adolescent boys are unusually sensitive and imaginative when it comes to that area and I was no less when instructed to grab the young boars by their back legs and wrestle them into position with their scrotum presenting frontally. At twelve I weighed about as much as the pigs and was just tall enough to peer directly at the scrotal positioning. When Doc Archer quickly splashed the first scrota with disinfectant it also splashed in my face. Even quicker Doc grabbed the bulging sac with one hand, his scalpel flashing in the other . . . cutting it open lengthwise, pulling out the offal looking blue and white ball until it tugged at the cord, then jerking the cord out completely. Accelerating his speed Doc repeated the process on the second ball, then splashed more disinfectant on the slashed and bleeding sac and into my face again instructing me to drop that pig and catch the next one.

"Whoa . . ! . hadn't expected that!" I thought, walking gingerly and awkwardly to the next pig still thinking of my own testes as the farmer pitched the extracted pig nuts for the older swine to eat . . . Oops!, I walked with even greater difficulty. Doc asked the farmer to please not feed the swine that way . . out of sensitivity to me I thought at the time.

The farmer collected dozens of testicles off the ground putting them into a galvanized bucket. I didn't notice Doc put this bucket of balls into the trunk of his pink Ford. It took us the rest of the day and next to finish the job. And still I was not desensitized to this "cutting" work until the end of the summer after we'd cut stallions into geldings, ram lambs and bucklings into wethers, bulls into steers, and even roosters into capons.

After many of these jobs Docs nephew Gene Riker would go to the tavern next door and bring back the best deep fried tenderloin sandwiches imaginable. One day he brought us the sandwiches in what I finally recognized as Docs galvanized bucket.

Around the fourth of July Doc went on a diet. He was small-framed but had a huge bay window. By Thanksgiving he'd lost most of it and a hundred pounds besides. He ate only steak and tomatoes for six months. . . always followed by a La Fendrich cigar. Fred Campbell, the handsome traffic cop at Seventh and Wabash, impeccably uniformed like Ron . . in Dick and Jane's Reader, would stop "Crossroads of America"[1] traffic to consult Doc about his Bantam Hens and also inquire about the progress of Docs' diet.

Through Doc I discovered the black farm families around Burnett just north of Terre Haute. Some of these "Persisters" had held on to their land with ante-bellum deeds since the 1820s. Indiana's black population had grown at the slowest pace of any Northern state mainly due to the hoosier-racist "constitutional convention" convened in the fall and winter of 1850-51 which restricted black ownership, barred "newcomer negroes" from settling within the states boundaries, and prohibited free blacks from entering the state after November, 1851. Thousands of disillusioned black farmers fled Indiana for Canada and beyond. "African-American (fugitive slave and free) out-migration away from Indiana then out paced in-migration by a significant margin".[2] Frederick Douglas called on Indiana's Prince Hall Masons, African Methodist Episcopals, and Black Baptists to defend themselves with force, place all northerners on notice and to persist. Balls! Those who heroically held on were called "Persisters". I still think of those heroic beautiful black "Persisters" around Burnett; especially one pretty 14 year old tending her jersey cow.

Old Doc Archer reckoned the extreme humidity of the hoosier state produced such extreme heroism and villainy.

Doc was definitely a resourceful thinking man. Somehow he managed to appropriate three or four discarded malt cans from Franks Restaurant down the block. These chrome milk shake canisters were perfectly matched to most Dog's muzzles. We'd mash wads of cotton to the bottom of the can then pour dollops of ether over the cotton. At that point I'd usually cough and gag a bit before placing the malt can over the dogs muzzle or cats face. The canine or feline patient being spread-eagle and tied down on the operating table. Gene Riker and I would be the crude anesthe-siologists. Most patients would resist at first, but soon breathe in enough fumes to faint away. Doc, of course was always in charge directing when to place on and when to take off the malt can . . . all the while chain smoking La Fendrich cigars. We never lost a patient to the ether and he rarely got cigar ash in his incisions.

After several surgeries however, the anesthesiologists would feel a bit lost and woozy. One afternoon, following four surgeries; two bitches and one female cat spayed, then the removal of a large tumor off the back of an old Doberman I was a little more than disoriented. Our fifth surgery patient was this large male raccoon. Another neuter job!! By mid operation I was less conscious than the coon. He snarled the malt can out of my hands writhing up on one elbow to untie his opposite paw like a monkey. Rearing up on his hind legs like King Kong of the operating table he roared his guttural roar. That roar began like a dozen, then grew to 100 mad squirrels and ended as loud as a Grizzly Bear. All the while looking straight at me; his gaze following mine as Gene Riker and I climbed three shelves 6 foot high half way up the wall to escape his rage.

Ol' Doc laughed til he had to sit down. Gene and I never climbed down til Doc managed the coon back to his cage. Since school I've maintained two livestock farms. I've sent my bull calves, ram lambs and bucklings to market entire.[3] I still prefer to ride a Stallion or mare . . and I don't allow anyone with those modernist malt cans of male bashing close to me.

1. "Crossroads of America"; old US 40 & 41. Seventh & Wabash

2. See Stephen Vincent's "Southern Seed Northern Soil"

3. "entire" i.e. not castrated.

BALLAD OF RED BROGAN

Up from breaks
of the Busseron bottom
came red Jimmy Brogan
with bottom enough to perdure
against the patriarchal horsewhip
against the clone for a conventionally conscious corpse
against the state
against the lawmen he shot.

He was not . . . unloved
this son of Thomas
and sweet Katie Brogan
with the strength of a section hand
and the tenderness of a mother's tear
he raided banks from the Wabash
to Manhattan where . . .
in . . the words of his time
'he got the chair'
'Never seemed fair' to the Dreiser boys
his childhood pals
who remembered wandering as boys
through the Busseron bottom land
I now hunt as an old man
my hounds projected thoughts
into the forested swamp
less threatened now by the gaping wounds of mines
baying mystery up from the scent on sandy loam
those moments of boyhood
with the Dreiser boys
and our dear brigand
the magnificent Red Brogan.

MUMPS

In 1952 I had never heard of homosexuality. Of course, I'd heard rough talking peers at sandlot ball games call people queers and cocksuckers. Epithets whose ugliness I presumed were extended beyond reality.

I had however heard of and been frequently warned about sex maniacs. Mother would read aloud from the Tribune sordid accounts of sexual crimes in New York, Chicago, and worse in West Terre Haute.

One story in particular caught her attention with such infective images that it terrified both her to tell it and me to hear it. A sex maniac had captured a youngster in a public restroom and with a razor had cut the boys genitals to pieces and flushed them down the toilet.

The warning was clear, look out for sex maniacs! 'Any image I had of them was not clear but I figured any one capable of such hideousness ought to be recognized a mile away.

Mother often swore like a sailor, especially while doing laundry. She'd once caught her breast in the Maytag wringer and had a personal animosity toward the appliance. Never, never . . however did any sexual swear words pass her lips. Sexual swear words indeed most sexual words were proscribed from household usage. My parents were frank working class survivors of the Depression and not prudish but they were serious about sexual boundaries so "vulgar talk or behavior" was not allowed.

At a seventh grade band contest Jim Fishman and I (1st and 2nd trumpets) discovered the word *fuck* drawn on a sidewall blackboard. It was drawn on first with lead pencil, then colored chalk.

As militant gentlemen (me more than he I recall) we were aggressively trying to erase this vulgarity from public sight. Mistaking our action for application Mr. Foosier, our band teacher, attacked us verbally. Volubly asserting our innocence we gave him the eraser and left the room.

There was still time before our first rehearsal and we were expected to go to our respective practice rooms. "I gotta go to the bathroom if I can find it," said Jim. "Meet you at the brass practice room." Our practice room was supposed to be 115. We were in the lab school on Indiana State's Campus. This lab school seemed labyrinthine to me. Hall after hall of numbered rooms . . . that didn't seem in logical sequence like the addresses on twenty sixth street. And it was crowded today with band contestants and college students.

None of us were very sure about college students. Our bias against them was just above Illinois drivers. In fact many of them came from Illinois and Indiana "hick towns" that surrounded our 'Crossroads of the Nation City'. My father worked at a Creamery near campus. I'd watch them from his truck. They walked funny. They'd kind of amble. They walked with less purpose than our people.

Nevertheless . . . this was their turf today so I asked one directions. "Scuse me," I said, "Can you direct me to room 115?" A big stocky guy, he studied me for a second (they're in the habit of studying, I reckoned) then said, "Sure, I'll show you the way."

We made one turn and I followed him down a long hallway when he said, "Pardon me but I need to go to this restroom. It will take just a minute. Come on in." He held the door open for me to follow. We entered the empty room where he went over to a urinal while I leaned against the white tiled wall. He then made a face like his zipper was pinching and said . . still matter of factly, "Wow these shorts don't fit right . . what kind do you wear?" Now he was staring. I mumbled something about, "boyville briefs I think . . my mom gets em' at Sears."

Walking straight at me he was saying, "I don't think I've seen them, how are they made?" He grabbed my fly and looking over his shoulder backed me into one of the stalls trying to unzip my pants.

It was the monster maniac for sure me mother had warned me about. All reason abandoning panicked mute, unable to cry out, and blocked by the big students bulk I braced myself for the razor blade when some other boys boomed in the bathroom door. Then he panicked backwards out the stall and ran out of the place.

Perplexed and traumatized I tried to think through what had just not happened to me. I found Fishman and described the ordeal.

"It was a queer man!" he said.

"You're kidding! What about the razor?"

"Did you see one?"

"Nope"

"Uh huh .. he was just a homo. There's lots of em' around. Yuh can't always tell."

"Damn!" I didn't like Jim Fishman minimizing the danger I'd just escaped. And if there's lots of em' around and you can't always tell .. how can you tell them apart from the real razor blade maniacs anyhow!?! I knew one thing for sure; that there was a whole lot about this I did not know. After we finished the brass section of 'Deep River', before my pals in the larger group were done I headed straight home. Half afraid of every adult stranger on the bus I was glad to find my Dad getting home the same time I was.

Hey Pop, I gotta speak with you. He was headed toward his tool bench in the garage but he dropped whatever he was doing and walked with me into my room. My Dad was like that .. he'd always hear you out, listening with those steely gray eyes and when he spoke it was always something you could count on. This evening he spoke the most profound insight and the dumbest explanation of homosexuality the world has ever heard.

After I'd told him my story, he shook his head, those eyes asquint and said, 'Mumps! . . . they say it's caused .. by mumps'! Incredulously but respectfully I protested, "Come on pa, how could that be?"

"I dunno . . but they say young boys get the mumps . . infection in their testicles . . . then the infection spreads up to their throat glands then down to their balls and back up to their throat again. Sometimes through this infection the function of the glands get confused . . . you know between their privates and their throat latch."

"You believe that Pa?"

"Nope. It's just what they say . . kinda scientifically. I'll tell you what I think son whatever they say scientifically."

'What Dad . . what's the deal?"

"It's onryness son, I think it's mostly onryness. You've seen dogs in the yard and street humping fire hydrants and each other if they couldn't find a bitch. Onryness!! Some of em' can't get enough bitches, fire hydrants, or each other. A good dog, a dog with a purpose has got more control of himself. A good man keeps it zipped up until he's married . . or pert near so."

I wanted to ask him about the pert near so part but that was another subject. The day's fears and mystery was solved. My old man knew how to shut the door on a subject. I knew all about onryness and was resolved to keep it at bay.

Cold Morning Years

I remember freshness that came from the fields, and even off the pavements in those early morning neighborhoods, riding in my father's milk truck down the brick streets of Terre Haute. The city quiet and not yet smelling. The Center Street houses looming white and brown as the old Divco started and stopped again at their porches. We stood on a thin corrugated metal floor with holes left in it from older discarded parts. I used to watch high earth fly by beneath the holes in this floor. There was an arched hump between us for the axle and the engine hummed up through the floor to your knees.

I remember my father driving that truck like a ship's captain, standing before the wheel, steering, braking, shifting gears and enjoying it. The truck's number was 14, there was no 13, and the wooden cases in it used to rattle with glass bottles. It was usually cold and the side hinged folding doors slammed open and shut at each stop. In spite of all the dust, metal, glass and wood, the old truck always had a kind of dairy odor, probably from the broken bottles and spilt milk of the day before.

When I grew tall enough, I used to stand holding the hand grip of the overhead door lever. I could balance myself that way and it made it easier to slam open and shut the doors as we started and stopped and started again down those Terre Haute streets in the cold morning of my years.

IN DESPERATE KINDNESS

From the porch swing . . my dear aunts,

my fathers sisters dreamed in Currier and Ivesian

for all our hallowed ground. A generative issue

after they married men to fight in the

silent night of Europe whose evening light

I only glimpsed before they brought

the red flag down . . before the lights went out

again and before it didn't matter . . . before

collective frailties fell so very far from

their smile in desperate kindness.

"The Swinea" review band Thornton In Winh 1055 ... from right Tommy Dunn, Tony Mill... Bill Britt, TCH, L.... Wh... ... right ...

SNOWFALL

He was not my regular barber. I'd gone to school with him. He'd quit college, went to work, and was getting married. His name was Eddy Snow and he talked softly; wistfully, almost in a whisper. His quiet words fell like Claude Thornhill* sounds and you remember them years and decades later.

"A man is always under a woman" he said. Accustomed to different geometry I protested. "No, think about it", he continued, "first its your mom, aunts and grandma, even the neighbor ladies, then it's your girlfriends and finally it's your wife."
"Don't forget your nurse", somebody laughed.

"Think of the deer," Eddy even more quietly explained. He was a deer hunter and not the kind that now shiver in stands. Back then they'd stalk the deer, "You can get right up on the buck who just thinks he's in charge. But the does, they never miss a thing . . not a twig moves or snaps or even a cricket chirps that don't trigger their alarm. They save the buck and herd most of the time!" "Yeah and the rest of the time", quipped a fellow hunter, "they're just a pain in the ass over twigs and crickets".

I hear Eddy has been married several times. His present wife is a psyc-patient and suffers fugue states and delirium. She insists on lots of trips; not occasionally but daily. Eddy is said to be worn out and worrying about gas bills. But, I'll bet he is comforted by his dreadful wisdom.

*Claude Thornhill, big band leader from Terre Haute had Quincy Jones as arranger; their theme was "Snowfall."

JOHN MCCOOL

John McCool's Dad ran a doughnut bakery late at night. Located between St. Josephs and the Saratoga Cafe we'd visit at the end of our weekend prowls in the wee hours of the morning. Harry would grab some finished dough from the hot oil and throw it at us like a line drive. We'd catch them in the sweet relief of those Saturday nights.

Johns mother was known in collective affection as Big Red. Near the end of his first decade she announced to her son he had an Auntie Reel who lay dying in Greenup, Illinois and that they'd be going there soon to meet her.

John had just negotiated a big haul in baseball cards, sticking a dozen squares of bubble gum into his mouth when Big Red announced they were off to meet Aunt Reel. Sure, and he kept that great chaw of sticky sweet gum between his teeth all the way there.

His mom led him through the crowd of well wishers in the yard and on the porch directly through the doors right into Aunt Reel's room. While being introduced, John noted the slight choking sensation as his teeth stuck to the expanding ball of gum treacleing to close his throatlatch. Unhinging his jaws enough to speak, he said, "they tell me you're dying." Aunt Reel, her wizened little face among pillows replied, "Yes, I am." Young John then earnestly asked "Why?" There was a brief silence John remembers breathing through his nose, his mouth now totally full of the matter.

Aunt Reel finally answered in profound and jocular wisdom "... I swallowed my gum!"

THE LAST FIRST PUNCH

He was a quiet, Anglo-Catholic boy who wore a red nylon jacket over his t-shirt and holy medal. Pock-marked, he looked at me pokerfaced cool, and never gave an inch. We were sixteen and I'd been fighting a lot. The bad asses we worked with were friendly now . . . let's just say they deferred. I was famous amongst them for my quick first punch. Reputations had to be protected . . . now no one messed with me.

Yet this new guy stood up... and did not defer. After work I followed him home. When I knocked at their kitchen door his dad looked up but did not follow us out into the street. Past his parents view, I whacked him.

He reeled, rebalanced, spat blood and stared at me. His cold eyes scolding me for calling him out in front of his father. His fear was less than his resolve. He told me this was . . . unjust.

I shrank back to my car. It was the last time I threw the first punch.

FIN-DE-SIÈ-CLE F.ING FUSION

I'm from f.ing Terre Haute . .

Ware; high grounded blues man

of note has not written but said

on poetic occasions.

Ware Smith has been led

like Django Rinehart with his knife

fighting the Wabash Sessions

ending the century's riff with a life

from where, for us, it all began.

"I'm from Terre . . .

I'm from f.ing Terre Haute, Man!"

THE CLEAN AND THE CARPORT

The garden hose would hiss against cement as mother would murder her mortal enemies of filth and dirt in the carport. She was a clean old girl and valued godliness as close to cleanliness. Once she scrubbed all the enamel off the bathtub and nearly crippled Dad by cleaning his slippers with formaldehyde.

My father had built the carport and she would keep it clean. Everyone walked through it to call at the kitchen door; even the stray Jehovah's Witness or neighborhood dog. Heresies against her clean carport! She cleaned it more times than a mass murderer mows down victims.

Mom and Dad died within months of each other and both their funeral receptions were held in the carport . . . which now gapes open as property defiled. An open wound against all my mother fought against. Decency uncleanly exiled.

LABOR DAY

We had no tomatoes of our own until labor day. Gallons of water on the plants beside the house brought forth no bloom. Little hard green nubbins slowly turned up toward the sun but did not ripen red and pink until the long weekend.

I washed them under the spigot and cooled them in the fridge. I'll eat 'em with cold beer and radishes then study the picture of who I think is my Dad in the Terre Haute Tribune. His back is turned in a crowd at the stamping mill. He's in shirt sleeves and wearing a white dairy flat cap.

The picture is with an article on the General Strike. My young father militantly stands at the edge.

WE'D RIDE IN LIMOUSINES
(AN IMPERFECTLY FRANK RECALL)

I was not thirty five

nor was it a very good year

but, we'd ride in limousines

and meet secretly in matching convertibles;

forbidden in the blow of the weather.

Her mothers bonneville; my fathers rocket olds

touched bumpers in sacred glades of doom

through that glass darkly fallen askew

in the time foiled foliage of our lives.

Their chauffer would not drive . . .

and I was never thirty-five.

EVER HOMEWARD (FOR DAVE RUSH)

The panel truck was green . . . panel truck

green, driven along the design so structurally

sullen; shored up from the Xosphere

and the dead dust of my childhood.

Forearms burnt tan in the sun; the green trucks

window rolled down and reminiscent life

blurs from the paneled tones of an old

friend witness to the drawn purpose and

shunned as the herds increase . . .

We kneel in the fire.

RUST BELT RAGA

Environs of the post proletarian

are decadent in a peculiar way

for toilers who've lost their chance.

A brothel ambience –

for intimate fraternizing

with their keepers.

Rather like the lunchroom

was at school; boiled eggs

brown bags and old wax paper

reeking of class envy

to please the bitches

who were our teachers.

After the Fair (with Thomas Hardy)

The barely choired claybank is sentried by a

cottonwood for all the changinglessness yet to come.

Is promise lost? . . . or simply no longer needed.

Glades of time enacted softly as

sunlight in late July; a midsummer's wake

of what is not likely to last . . .

Prairie breezes caress the garden; perennial

as grass fires on Gods brow.

> *"Light seen with our eyes open and that
> seen when we rub our closed eyes is light
> coming from the soul itself."*
> Plotinus

> *"Light as the collective act of a universal
> self dwelling in all selves."*
> Yeats

OLD LIGHT

An older light
is languid and never known abruptly
not even in the morning
of that cold house where I was born
steel eyed to mothers screams that flashed
near the frame of the lost cabbie, my fathers embrace
and the grace of her fighting dog, Chico.

That same light streams through Saint Benedicts
and stays in some of the taverns; an old brick light
like Brocksmiths up the street from the switchyards;
a red pony light, flaxen maned and lovingly remote.
A Gene Deb's porch light where letters from Lenin were read
and Cannon covered his funeral for the Labor Defender;
a dimly celebrative light like dinner at Louisa's and the
softshoe Kelly and Carsey did.

The faltering light around fir trees decorated
with annual financial abandon; wintersett
and never quite going out in cold hope

for better light that will not come til spring
except in the laughter and kindness of reckless
and careful smiles that gently banter
in the old cold light.

On the Avenues

He signed my yearbook, . . .
" to the guy with the cool
Plymouth". He was charitable.
It wasn't easy being cool for me or

Plymouths in 1957. But we were easy on each other back then unless a female was involved.

He was a pale, wild Irish tough transferred in from the Catholic and the technical school. We were impressed he'd had trouble in both.

He drove a souped up Ford. It was black with a mean red top. My Plymouth's paint was squarely suburban blue and white. His car was lowered with glass packs. Mine . . was bull nosed with fender skirts. He was frequently and aesthetically smudged with mechanics grease. He knew a lot about cars. I didn't. We both worked nights to pay for them.

We both liked a big-eyed Welsh girl who lived on Garfield Avenue. She was the only girlfriend I ever had whose parents liked me. They were as sweet and kind as she was ill tempered. She came to prefer this other guy.

That was OK. I was beginning to prefer a Jewish girl away cross-town. This other guy soon preferred a friend of mine. She was a dark complected Alsatian number who lived on one of the avenues. I think we'd worked together. I know we talked a lot together. We saw each other in respite from our respective romances. We'd meet on Sunday afternoons at the jukebox joint, share cokes and dance. We were just pals.

Never more than a good night kiss. But she became to him . . an issue of war.

He'd see her Saturday night and we'd talk about it Sunday afternoon. She liked him but less than he desired. He blamed me.

At one weeknight mixer when I wasn't working, I dropped in on the crowd at the Wassel Inn. More stags than couples I said hello around and then danced with my friend. She'd been dancing with this other guy. He'd been drinking and she'd had it with him. Near midnight I drove her home . . . on the avenues.

He followed. He followed with a carload of drinkers deciding to be bad. I knew them all and liked most of them. There was Lace riding shotgun with Mac, Larry, and somebody else I can't remember in the back seat. Lace was the most interesting. A good- looking Roumanian . . . Roumanians were always the best looking people in Terre Haute . . . he was renown for his coolness, anticipating all Fonzie like depictions of the fifties for years to come. A hoodlum genius who contemned academic effort, excelling in a kind of criminal composure pivotally poised for every existential moment. That was Lace.

Now what?! I thought, what's the Lace doing with this scene of awkward ugliness?

'Can't hold their liquor from this loss', I reckoned while walking her up to the porch. We could hear their muttering and see their cigarette ash across the dark avenue.

Those avenues . . . a perfect set for proletcult passion and pissing contests . . they were lain out in the early 20th century for industrial barracks becoming modest but tastefully comfortable working class housing . . stretching from West of third St. East to 25th and beyond. They tied the slim and unslim waist of Terre Haute together like fingers clasped in prayer doglegging across Lafayette around Sacred Heart and Saint Ann's Parish West to the little black churches East behind St. Andrews Clapboard Orthodox Onion Dome.

Terre Haute had been a muscular, proletarian place in the spirit of Gene Debs and Teddy Drieser; the little city of the big General Strike when these avenues were being settled. There were too many Nursing Homes here but there were great Taverns . . . "Baltesus" on the back street between the C & EI railroad tracks and 8th avenue, the Dew Drop and Little Havana by the Steelton Avenue tracks and nineteenth street crossing W. of Hungarian Hall and the Jack of Diamonds by Elm Park on to the Whiskey Barrel by the tracks on 25th and First avenue. Sometimes these avenues . . . like that night seemed finger marked fists clenched separately to knock you silly as those drunks out in the car. Synaptic clefts compelled to cross!

I whispered, "Linsel lets show him what he came to see." Eu-*daemonically* kissing began . . quickly reaching what was then called 'making out.' As we lay down, he lay on his horn announcing angrily it was time for us to lay into each other. Equally angry I was eager to oblige him. Hustling to my Plymouth I started it and drove into the first side street off the avenue. He followed . . tires screeching to start and stop as his accomplices piled out. Grumbling, they assumed a formation to face me like so many B. movie "rumble" positions. Nothing was said. My blood was up to get a piece of the primary causer. It was clear four of them weren't going to allow it.

The fifth however was Lace who had in seconds boozily reconnoitered the situation . . uncool to bully or futilely defend anyone . . he pivots to the right then hits Mac to his left with a haymaker so hard . . Mac goes down holding his jaw and shrieking like a stuck hog. The other three join in with a loud cacophony of shouting complaints at Lace who winks in my direction and coolly nods for me to go. Bedroom and porch lights are coming on up and down the block from all the commotion. I drive away out from the avenues . . amused and guilty how some things did and some things did not matter.

We had only retained the form not the content of working class heroics. Factionalized free enterprise affection would embarrass our socially conservative, politically radical predecessors.

The other guy with the cool Ford left Linsel alone, married the big-eyed bad tempered girl and killed himself in his garage.

Pro Forma Sine Substantia

International Relations Club Garfield High School 1957

My Father and the Robins

Dad loved the robins

and it saddened him

when they came too early

dying huddled on the winter pavement

trying to be warm.

NATIVE RIVER RIFF

Reverie is riverine after the rain in refracted remembrance along points in a stream . . like traveling the Wabash between Notre Dame and Cayuga where Nicole's brother found her body in the logjams then downriver past the falls of Montezuma, the Vermillion County Islands and Eli Lilly's' hot water violations of Prozac spills in the public stream of unconsciousness. Past the viaducts and bridges of Terre Haute, my nephews fish ranching, and spooks of Valentines cattle heads and horns afloat . . over channel cats as big as sharks in the shallows before Vigos water treatment plant . . past the Federal Prison executions as crows on its lawn fly miles to Ted and Pauly Dreiser's house then back again to the Fairbanks of fishing camps on stilts in groves near Hutsonville past Graysvilles' ghost of a purged girlfriend whose rear revolved like a sail before the mast of her fathers democratic eyes. I remember leaving her before the afterwards of leaving. Prayers repair and prepare us for the flavor of our departure where on school grounds Jerry Roberts unpersuasively admired Gene Autry by a wagon wheel on a comic book cover who when fifty years later as awkward orderly for my olde hearts surgery I explained my preference for Roy Rogers even before I knew he kept blue tic hounds. Whitney directed him through Saturday afternoons at Republic Studios to our BEST theatre where next door Max made hamburgers my bad sister loved before she was bad while Dick Seybold was shoe/cobbler on the other side spawning a dixiecrat denial of another Stalin-ist temperament cobbled half way 'round the world memorizing scripture for the madness to follow. My father would leave the DIVCO milk trucks engine running for Masonic grips and proletarian wisdom that ill tempered men were probably morphodites across from drugstore cowboys who spied me steal bubble gum from Mr. Wright and never let on for Protestant explanations at Dean Ave Christian that it was as bad as the worst depravity there being no hierarchy of sin between Wayne Bovenschean's basketball court and Butch Buckner's gaze at the Tavern across the street whose comraderie I coveted in Community Theatre Players on breaks with Puccas as certain as Harvey. We shopped at Kimballs Variety Store by Withrows Poultry House near Paul Duckers who'd lost his mother and planted a tree for her in Israel, he said. One year we bought only wash cloths for each other during the Teamsters Creamery Strike at Christmas. Joe Withrow and me shot craps for comics and marbles behind his familys business. His Uncle Jim had been my fathers friend and was dead. His other Uncle was jolly and delivered the turkeys for slaughter. The place always smelled of blood, feathers, and big women. It now houses a "Christian Counselor" proving there is more than one way to skin a chicken. The Clareys furnace exploded in Farrington Grove and they briefly rented on our street bringing tales of German genius brewers and the appearances of beauty and bourgeois civility. When I misbehaved in these third grade days my weary Irish mother would threaten me with the wish that I grow up to marry "a broad shouldered German woman to beat the hell" out of me. In the fourth grade Carol Kassabaum was transferred to the desk in front of me . . examining her lovely shoulders . . . and the rest of her I told me mother I was ready to sign on. But no matter how many Pontiacs there was no measure for the voices of the Kassabaum females. They spoke with sounds you hear high in the trees if you're not afraid to climb them.

"God probes the inmost mind
and depths of the heart"
Psalm 64:6

AISLE OF THE HEART

Sitting in the aisle of Sacred Heart
where Skinny Welsh had fallen
after his confession he'd done everything but
kill a man . . my cousins and I . . . pallbearers
for this guy who taught us to fish and explore
unknown country places; faith and knowledge austere
before and after every new glade and meadow
we found trust in a wisdom first darkly then clear.

He spoke the word "leaving" as young priests speak
of post vocational careers, but without their
naïve lusting for another soft job.

With brave faith he engaged deaths country
and all of its dark angels without the slightest trace
of entitlement, defiance, or servility.

As I dream now of joining such company . . .
I see them with their sleeves rolled up, sand colored
forearms matching the wet claybank of evening light.
Darkening brite as Saturday matinees film
from the fifties dream of death as corrupt
as the film of life they came wearing
double breasted suit coats over their bib overalls.

They came for the burying but I was not dead yet
Their collectively murmured conversation
sounds like the engine of an old airplane.

Leaving . . . apparently is about as peaceful as birth.

2   CROATOAN

*"The connection between truth and power
is important since power is above all
the ability to define reality in ones own
terms and impose that definition on others."*

Mohameden Ould-Mey
"Global Restructuring and Peripheral States"

*"The true hallmark of the proletarian is neither
poverty nor humble birth but a consciousness —
and the resentment that this consciousness
inspires — of being disinherited from his
ancestral place in Society"*

Arnold Toynbee
"A Study of History "

Croatoan 104

Bulls of Berja 111

Succubi 112

Gables 114

Alpine Truth 115

Dirty Thirties 121

Nearing 122

DROM 123

My Friend Mike 125

Labours Love . . Almost Lost 128

Participatory Incorrectness 131

Probative Evidence 138

Bad Ass Gentile 139

Kurdistan at Sea 152

Solarium 153

Sterling Resistance 154

L.eft A.mericana 158

Under the Vultures Eye 182

Silencers 185

The Byzantine 186

Beat Regional Spaces 188

Miners Code 189

Quit Claim 190

White Negros 191

Luggage Rack 192

Uncommon Denominators 194

Détente 195

Eternal Revolution 201

CROATOAN

I had been slipping into Spain.

For months now . . . cold torsoed winter months where you only stayed warm from the waist down. Hot coals were placed under the table and we'd wrap its felt covering around our belts. Then, half embalmed I would leave the Pensión at noon and walk the streets funereally.

Lottery chants and the intercourse of busily, barely bathed throngs were little company. The Religious sisters and the whores and all the orphans in their care further depressed me. Soldiers were everywhere with smiles the color of their cheap coats; young underlings who refused an angry consciousness of their own history. Castanets like skeletons clattered from gypsy caves, along marble bars to brothel courtyards . . always near a Roman altar.

I had lived two decades and Granada was the morgue of my youth. I was particularly attentive to the black feathered, horse drawn hearse on Calle de San Jeronimo.Harness horses always give me pleasure; these didn't. Fed a bit more grain the four in hand hitch of black horses would have looked stylish but they didn't. Instead they seemed sour and resistant to pulling that frosted glass black buggy of death. Even their oiled leather blinders appeared indecorous, mere, methods of control.

-Aye- control . . . how that was talked about at Coffee House Centro. El control.. bajo control.. descontrolarse.. controlando...whether I was with anarchists or the opus dei;

whether we spoke of corridas, civil war, basque poets, or the omnipresent statue of the rearing horse, whatever words we used . . . thought and talk centered around the concept of control.

It was 1960 and El Caudillo Franco was strongly in control of everything. My own ideas on control being somewhere between King Solomon and Prince Kropotkin I mainly listened to the others.

Anarchists did most of the talking. Indeed it was hard to shut them up. They railed against Franco's control, the church's control, the commissars' control, the bankers control and ultimately their mama's control. I didn't like the anarchists much. Their disheveled displays of ideological license seemed to deform their spirit. And more than a few of them loved their fellow man a bit too erotically. Having known them however helped one anticipate hippies and libertarians, their later counterparts who like them were full of gas and so against all authority they were a threat to none.

The quieter men of the opus dei were as secretive as the anarchists were threatening. Between the trenches of Church and State they maintained an austere if corruptive calm. Their less secretive, less Spanish, and least quiet spokesman was named Rooney. He'd once been red haired and once taught in Boston. He disliked Eisenhower and Bing Crosby. He liked Kennedy and George Santayana. He'd pick out strangers around the bar and build a caffeine-induced myth about their purpose in existence. I liked listening to Rooney.

But today I met someone more like myself and was shocked to hear the myth that Rooney identified for him. I was watching the black horses pull the hearse again when someone asked, "American?" That was an inquiry I sometimes refused but this inquirer seemed pleasant enough so I answered, "Yeah."

He was a goateed instructor from Carbondale and we laughed out loud when I located myself by pronouncing the s in Illinois. His name was Robert Alden. I invited him to lunch at my pensión back at Sierpe Baja Calle. He laughed at the name of the street. He was enjoying Spain. He wasn't staying long.

There were three Puerto Rican law students also living in the pensión. They were on the G.I. bill and never went to class. They were just sobering up and joined us for lunch. Luis, the Indian, Sammy, the European, and Sal, the African had become good friends of mine. Alden said something about their representing the full range of Puerto Rican ethnic types united by the imperial U.S. army. Sal, Sammy, and Luis had fought in Korea and they hit it off with Alden. They talked about the crush of finding themselves so quickly drafted away from their tropical home light into the snowy mud around Seoul. Luis hated the killing, Sammy hated the languages he didn't know and Sal was afraid of the Turks.

Bob Alden also spoke to the Puerto Ricans in Spanish and English about a lot of things I barely understood. There was a lot about Cuba and the new U.S. administration. We were surprised that Alden was not impressed with the recent inauguration. Hell!

. . .even Hemmingway had been there!

Six years my senior this Alden was intellectual without being dispassionate, as ascetically serious as the opus dei yet apparently ... in some ways . . . more radical than the anarchists. I'd never met anyone like him. He made a great impression on the Puerto Ricans too. They stayed completely sober the week he was with us; never missed a meal and never tired of asking him rapid fire questions.

He urged them to start studying or go home. He spoke of the Alhambran mysteries. He urged me to forget about bullfighting. He warned all four of us to quit the smuggling trade.

The latter advice was particularly hard to take. We'd been collecting mad money from our frequent trips to Gibraltar (or the Golden Goose as Sal called it) and it was safe enough to do so. The La Guardia Civil backed up from our passports and everyone knew Franco tolerated the national sport of smuggling unless it involved something he was trying to manufacture himself.

Recently however Rooney had introduced us to a distinguished little abogado who proposed we move into the major leagues. Spanish Morocco was closing and automobiles were being smuggled from Ceuta back to Spain with fake legal papers. Drivers with American passports would be so much added security.

With Puritanical judgment in his eyes Alden insisted that the little lawyer was either (a) dishonest and we'd lose our money or (b) naively honest and Franco's men would kill us at the border.

¡¿What did he know?! We were the old hands on Spain. After all, he was a tourist. And we had planned on the money. But, somehow we couldn't move without his approval. His disapproval we resented as prudish and controlling. We kept arguing otherwise. In the mornings we'd walk down the cobblestone streets for mojicone breakfast cakes explaining to him how simple we thought it could be. During afternoon beers at the Café Torinos we'd poke fun at his 'very American moralizing'. But like the Spaniards we did most of our talking at the coffee house.

That's where Rooney met Robert Alden. The five of us approached him at the marble bar. He started at the sight of us with Alden. His alarm did not alarm me but I stumbled over my English words introducing them. Over compensating for my awkwardness the Puerto Ricans grew animated in Spanish and English insisting to Rooney how important we thought this introduction.

Rose gray wisps about his balding skull shuddered with the rest of him. They shook hands, muttered mucho gusto's . . and, it began . . .

"Here we go again," he sighed with a kind of fathers regret to see sons too much like himself. "Rein up lads," he wailed at us and Alden . . . mainly at Alden. "You'll mount the rearing horse with the likes of him . . gaahd . . what a terrible ride . . until you break your bad asses, up against reality. I've done it! . . we've you should know . . Read Dos Passos he jabbed . . we've all done it before.

To us . . Rooney was now even breathing strangely.
He seemed . . . out of control. "Gaahd , . . Americana arcane . . ."
he intoned . . "tough and apocryphal . . . darkly marginal . . . the
underground American."

"And midwesterners," he went on. "Heartlanders who
read and wear what they see at the movies. Like Sutherners . . .
and the cult of Mitchell's Cavaliers . . Gone with the Wind?!" . . .
he nodded at us eyes bulging. Then quickly aside, "I had a drink
once with Thomas Mitchell."

"Your propensity for lost causes . . !", he rather partially
announced, then gasped, halted, and almost mildly now exhaled,
"You nits will be blownin in the wind till the next century.
Not even . . ! not even with their stance, their . . too early and too
late to learn from Eliot," he said into his cups . . then back at us . .
"their agrarian stance against wage slavery and industrial tecnick-
ery . . . you'll call part of it the Caps and you'll struggle with your
class envy as the more righteous and vulgar part of the worlds
industrial plight; raging on the days and whoring the nights for
lost causes. Where is your locus of control . . . your own perception of responsibility . . . your perceived (he spit it out) ability to
respond??"

We stood chastened and unresponsive. Sal touched
my arm asking, "how does this mick get drunk on coffee?"
"Beats me," I grinned, "but yeah I've wondered myself."
I had learned Rooney's private language . . .

following the elliptical images and letting their meaning settle in. Pictures in motion referred to each other. His mind in conversation was a motion picture of the secret cause careening into time again. Since Spain . . pictures and sounds stream interiorly.

We encountered Alden and Rooney in the spirit of its essential contradiction.

Our locus of control became our ability to respond.

BULLS OF BERJA

(In the winter of 1960 I studied in Granada for the
coming village corridas. My first and last was in Berja.)

The bulls of Berja, I did not fight

Are in my mind tonight

Breathing in the sounds and shapes

Along the wet pavements of Spain

The air of Easter's eve and the brave lameness

Of the small brown girl

Laughter of dark young men

On bicycles eating grapes in the rain

Getting ready for the giant Colorado*

And his rolling brutal eye

My kind of thing, to die between his horns

In a sixth size small stupid suit of lights

My cowardice contained, saved by bad weather

And an old man on a donkey who brought the cancel news

We hitchhiked down the mountains

Delivered by the rain

*Colorado: roan fighting bull

SUCCUBI

Down the late afternoon hill light

Near the gypsy caves outside Granada

Through the white frocked picnic girls

altogether ignored, by their laughing solemnity

Andalusian spontaneity is for the tourist season

And I no longer looked like a tourist

More like a ghost walking

Sick, and pale, and feo

I lived on Lower Serpent Street

Studying the muleta

Staring at the living queues

Becoming Las Calles De Abuelas

Reading Gorki

Every night

And giving Hell and Hemingway

Back to the Puerto Rican

Friends who were persuasive

About smuggling

From Ceuta and Gibraltar

Invited me to join them study Roman law

This day, I had been to church and to the brothel too

Unable to pray or think at either place

Obsessed with the haunting

Of her hand in mine

I came upon a wall of the Alhambra

It was easy to scale

And I climbed quickly

To the other side

Of paradise it seemed

The harem gardens I had toured before

But stealing here alone

I found the succubi

Among the veiled dark women looking up

There was the astral germ

Of all my spiritual wives

Small, but like a desert lion

Aging fast into a fountain, the elemental one

Is drawn gleamingly

By winter's gold alhambran sun

Bristling like Lev Bronstein's cacti

Saguaran retainer of male tears

Resilient to the draught

Of all these exiled years

GABLES

My best moments at University
were those walks off campus
where I made friends with certain gables
imagining home within them.

Time, better than seminars at the Kinsey, or
comradely talks at the tavern
were those walks
I dreamed with gables.

Now I know
I've been where I am going
but then, I didn't appear
four times in a stanza

. . . and the gables beckoned nye
strong, permanent, and peaceful
coming my way I reckoned . . .
they were purpose passing bye.

> "Lies are more revealing than non lies"
> Alberto Moravio

ALPINE TRUTH
(For Joseph Ratzinger)

Hitching south of the Oktoberfest in München, I first caught sight of the Alps. Looming otherworldly and icy pale with the promise of a newly heightened vision of the world.

Truth was another matter. It belonged to the position that paid the most, the girl or the professor that gave or graded the most and increasingly the views that best accommodated my viscerally ambitious future.

A twenty year old Americanisch war babe; I was an offspring of the conquerors. As students visiting the PX or the officers club in Mannheim we were remotely accepted as sons of the empire.

The last swastikas were blown off buildings in Berlin a decade and a half ago. I'd grown up in the popular front film culture of the forties. My parents had been New Dealers . . .but that was more than half my lifetime ago. It seemed ancient history to me. It didn't to the Germans.

My half German cousin Tony loved southern Deutschland and Austria. He'd written me of pastoral places and described countryside's of flowers, music, and prayer. Tony was a Franciscan Priest. People find what they're looking for, I thought. I kept finding falcons on buildings and in people's faces; always ready to swoop down for a fight. Still more principled than pragmatic on some issues I argued with the Germans. I did not believe every veteran I met fought only on the eastern front. I did not like to hear how "Hitler had been good in some ways", how the Polish obsessed French had declared War on the Third Reich and thrown half the world to bolshevism. I did not believe so many could maintain ignorance of the holocaust and I tired of the Konkret refrain "Why didn't (and why don't) you take our brave soldiers and march east against Slavic communism."

Arrgh . . . these defeated ubermensch. They all talked the same. Students, postmen, trainmen, bartenders . . . everyone we drank with sang the same old song.

I set out for the Swiss border. Into the free cantons of Switzerland I would seek out and speak with the Jungian left wing of the Reformation.

I had one more lay over in Austria, a town called Löefer. Earlier I'd perfected the art of finding accommodations in German speaking villages. I would approach the farm house introducing myself as an Americanisch studenten and ask to spend the night in their hay loft. Sometimes it would take a while for them to understand. Then without fail a smile would break formality and they would invite me inside their warm homes for the night.

Two hours passed in Löefer and still no ride. Dark came with an alpine chill. Many vehicles stopped but none were headed toward the Swiss frontier. All were friendly and curious. Several asked if I knew Hans Rightinger of Löefer who studied in America. I inquired where the Rightingers lived and was waved on to a large farmhouse near a truck terminal at the edge of town.

I approached the Rightingers household making my same pitch for shelter, shivering a bit for good measure, adding that "Ich vas un froind uv Hans Rightinger studean im America."

At first Frau Rightinger appeared a stern and suspicious soul. She stood stiffly glaring at me shivering in my rough and unclean clothes. But, predictably with the light of understanding came a light smile upon Frau Rightingers stern brow and she invited me . . . only half way into the house. She went to get someone (an employee I think) from the adjoining garage. Returning quickly with a nervous husky man who attempted few words in English . . basically grunting," froind uv Hans . . . uv froind Hans . . yes OK.

Her employee said OK to Frau Rightinger who then said it several times to him and to me. She led me down a dark corridor, opened a door and flipped a switch to light up a magnificently large bedroom with a proportionally large bed adorned with gleamingly clean white sheets and ample featherbedding. "De Zimmer uv Hans. Hans zimmer. Nicht? OK?" "OK!" I gratefully approved. Across the narrow hall she flipped another switch to show me the adjoining bathroom. Quickly turning the tubs hot water faucet on and off she nodded knowingly at my dirtiness. I replied yes ma'am in English she understood. Back in Munich my mates and I had paid more attention to drinking than to dirt.

After a hot bath I found cold milk and warm cookies on the night stand which I inhaled, brushed my teeth, stowed my rucksack and was drifting off to sleep in that wonderful featherbed when a ruckus erupted on the other side of the house. Three male voices, one especially loud, was contending with Frau Rightinger whose voice now seemed unhinged with fear. While congratulating myself as the most clever hitchhiker in Europe I made a colossal error as to the time and location of Hans Rightinger. He had been a student in America years ago. Now he ran a trucking business with his family in Löefer and he was protesting sleeping on a couch for somebody in his room he didn't think he knew! Damn, I thought aloud while hearing several angry footsteps coming toward the bedroom. The door swung open, Hans Rightinger leading his entourage into *his* bedroom. Springing from his bed, extending my hand I exclaimed with all the familiar emphasis I could muster . . . Hans! Hearing his name he stumbled, shook my hand and quizzically asked,

"Do . . . do I know you!?"

In poor Deutsch and Sneakend English I began mentioning every German student I'd ever met, could think of or imagine attempting a confused impression that we had mutual friends who had referred to Hans and Löefer.

He wasn't buying any of this but smiled broadly as I was running out of breath. I think he found my predicament entertaining. I think he also liked hearing about Wolfgang Schall and other names at Citie Universidad in Paris and all the Dutchmen in Amstelveen who belonged to the CORE fraternity. He asked if I knew students at the University of Wisconsin ten years ago. Of course, I did not but I'd heard stories about Madison so I prattled on about the lake, the bicycles, and beer in the cafeteria. Finally with his hands in the air, he turned to his mother and his men saying in german and english for me "It's alright I know him", he lied. With relief and something akin to shame I turned back toward the bed. Hans was grinning and very much in control now. "I'll wake you early", he said, "and one of our drivers will truck you to the border." I heard him laughing as they walked away down the hall. It was more or less good-natured laughter I thought, and they were hospitable and being damn nice about it. I went to sleep.

True to his word, Hans woke me early indeed with a loud knock saying " We will take time for breakfast. It's ready in the kitchen." Into our large cups - big as bowls - Frau Rightinger first poured warm milk then a small shot of coffee. I tried to tell Hans it tasted good as a brown Swiss cow. He didn't understand. He wanted to speak of more serious matters. "My father was killed in the war," he began . . ."in France during the retreat from Normandy. The German army fought a brilliant retreat as you know (I didn't) but he and many others were killed . . . (his voice trailed off) we were defeated by Eisenhower not by the Soviets, and with your help we could have defeated them."

Finally I was hearing a western front narrative . . . but not as confession, more like an accusation. "Why have you come to our German countries, he asked. "For the fencing and frauleins in Heidelberg," I honestly answered. My answer didn't please him. I added jokingly, "and for the bier". I tried to speak of Professor Morganthaus' saber scar, Theodor Dreiser and WWI dachshunds set on fire. He ignored me and continued, "After the war my family sent me to study in yours (I let him think my name ended in en) and Eisenhower's' country. Your people defeated mine. I needed to learn from them. But I didn't," he continued "the truth is I merely confirmed what I had learned from my own people . . . Br(rr)eeding-(he rolled his r's like a Castilian don at Oxford) it's breeding mein herr. I was studying engineering and science but traveled north and south America. European leadership! Wherever there was united European leadership . . from the Maritime Provinces to Chile . . there was progress wherever diluted from Mexico, Miami, to Brooklyn . . . backwardness." Now enthusiastic . . . leaning and reaching out over the table, his big blonde head disheveled and fanatical, "We are uniting Europe! If European Americans unite with us we will out progress the Slavs and backward third world."

It got worse. He spoke openly of eugenics. American traffic engineering had inspired him. Spermatozoa like other vehicles had to be managed. My god, he must imagine little clover leafs in the sperm bank, I groaned to myself. When he got around to sterilizing the indios and blacks in the south, southwest and Latin America I began to experience a kind of loathsome paralysis. Not so much self-loathing for the web I'd weaved but for the compromise I'd created. I'd made myself obliged to listen to this shit. Not that I haven't heard worse since but never in a situation where I thought I had to.

After what seemed like hours we took our leave . . . then the Rightinger driver and I climbed up into his Mercedes truck. All the way to Switzerland I pondered anew this truth and consequences business. I remembered a sixth grade history lesson where the teacher told of some goody two shoes puritan who never lied being confronted by the Redcoats about her two patriot sons hiding in the basement. "We know you never lie Goody so if you tell us your sons are not hiding here we will believe you and go!" "What should Goody tell the Redcoats?", our teacher asked us. My classmates . . . unbelievable to me . . . actually had different opinions about this.

Long before reading Clausewitz I knew truth was the first casualty in war and that you didn't . . couldn't owe truth to your enemy. It was necessary for Goody to deceive the Redcoats to save her sons from an unjust firing squad. And yet necessity is not in itself a virtue. No nihilist me, I knew that wrong and repentant was better than wrong justified yet I accepted no specific glimpse as true, only the whole mural was truth and one always had to be doubtful of the adequacy of any specific vision of it. I never hesitated to act on the felt grain of truth in any specific but tempered that action knowing the specific couldn't possibly be the whole truth. That is to say there is no literal truth only little labyrinths of the dreams of truth.

And yet, since Hans Rightinger I've taught my children that "While not everyone deserves the truth; rare . . . rare is the occasion that requires a lie."

DIRTY THIRTIES

Those terrible times we escaped

because we were not yet born

when the men looked and talked like Bogart

and leftist temperament made sense

in all environments.

NEARING

"Not now; not again," he thought against the pervasive sense of life's test acuity. That space between the right and left lobe seemed to be collapsing again.

"In every crisis there's opportunity," he'd taught others. But he'd plenty enough of both . . . now, he'd prefer some peace.

That lateral pass to the left he always resisted. The big picture, what he called 'the mural' was his natural inclination and yet, stumbling into this new century none of the pieces fit . . . easily.

Buckley's "autobiography of faith", "Nearer, My God" was just out. He'd read "God and Man at Yale" in the late fifties. Like Brother Buckley, that lace-curtain conservative he agreed with its two major points; (1) "that the duel between faith and atheism is the most important in the world" and (2) "that the struggle between individualism and collectivism is the same struggle reproduced on another level."

Except! . . I saw God on the collectivist side. "Gods omnipotence belonged to no individual or corporation and was alien to the very notion of capitalist property."

1960 DROM

We saw them on the roads from Spain til we crossed the Neckar; from Granada caves to camp grounds on the Wahnsee. Gypsy wagons that traveled daily while we hitched as best we could across the continent. One night their camp was close to ours and they sang like the motion of cobras.

One waggoner with an Andaluz X Westphalian looking horse would wave as he recognized us in passing cars. I studied his grizzled face and how his eyes panned the horizon like a camera surveys all that surrounds it.

We may have glimpsed them in the Ukraine and there were wagons near Novgorod but I saw him for sure on May 2nd. A post celebrant in Red Square like me; his eyes panning the restricted horizon hoping it was more like it promised to be.

Michael McNaughton & TGM in Morelos

MY FRIEND MIKE

Spring chills ache through the plate in my arm
from the old knife wound I've lied about
memories of time and place overlap
like some far fetched novel I'm beginning to believe in
the way weathered boards nail us together.

Folios editor said I should drop the narrative description
right through the screen door; Dostoyevsky
drew Mike up from the Dexedrine reading of Crime and Punishment
against the screen with an axe in his coat
he moved in with a Japanese girl called Moscow.

I visited with a Birch Bayh Beauty Queen unable to imagine doing else
with Democrats. Mikes friend Gil would visit in between stays
at the State Hospital. He was asked to be Mikes best man 'cause
my feelings were tougher' than his tender ones that tended
toward schizophrenia. After the wedding Gil died in State
Hospital. I was slightly glad about it.

I saw Mikes adultrous wife under the marquee of
'Zorba the Greek'. She'd just seen it and was smiling
like the big fish who later ate her in the Pacific.
Mike stormed through Mississippi
as we made it to Morelos.
Two Zapatistas with one lame shoe.

They'd called for his hide at Showalter Fountain;
a greater defector than the rest of us
he was principled in financial and personal ambitions.

We avoided fencing scars in Heidelberg
and drank with drunken mongol officers
in East Berlin . . smashing goblets
against the mantel of a smugglers economy
helping bring about the building of that wall.

We'd budget student soup and crackers
on Ku-dam by the zoo. A chimp threw
excrement in an ex nazis face
for what I thought must be a racial slur.

We haunted the beer halls and more than once
exorcised old Hitler's Ghosts that always
wanted to see Miami. Mike had been the
prospering merchant Marxist even while in school
he'd work two jobs and lived on Russian Hill.

The summer of flowers when his wife was
eaten after a hippie boat crash and her consorts
hand made craft went down we'd walk down
Russian Hill and dine like the general staff of an
outlawed army smoking cheroots late into the North Beached
evenings.

Critical illuminati of what was happenin then.
We met Maoists at the pool room,
Social democrats on the street,
friendly Trotsky factionalists everywhere
and C.P.ers cheering Johnson against Goldwater at the movies.

Post politically he took a Dutch wife from Stockton
went boar hunting in the hills and stayed
to run a ranchers school in the San Antone.
He starts his engine with a breathalyzer and plans to move
to Mexico on Danny's yacht from Seattle to the Sea of Cortez.

Maybe . . on to hospital in Havana to make
medicine with the best damn docs in the hemisphere. "We have known
a love embattled" in nearly fifty twenty sixths of July, this grand
widower, my brother Yevgraf* who helped me survive this system.
We now covet hospital care instead of Revolution in Havana.

*Yevgraf: Zhivagos' salvific bro.

"The gift is good in those
when it is acute"
The Bard

Labours Love . . almost Lost

(Left Open Lament for London)

"In times of labor quiescence, radical youth

adopt the cause and style of the lumpen."

(If Rosa Luxemburg did not say something like this..

she should have)

There is nothing left

of London

That in my mind kept left

Mortal months of sunlight

Keep Left signs for spring

And the easy glare

Of youth in 1960

London left

Morning pubs

Opening

Comradely, serene

Churchlike

Our culture secured

This side of the saloon

That ubiquitous divided bar

Had thundered solidarity

Like emissaries

From some grand and distant country

Socialists announced themselves

As 'from the working class'

'From the working class', like me

Not to be overcome, but asserted...

Something I was became something to be

Not a base to become something else

But to be

Here, everywhere

And at home

My family, my kind, my international countrymen

The brawn and brains of the century

Were waiting in the wings

For that moment when ideals of youth

Would brave their marxist cue

Burst center stage

And make sobered liberation

Of the Everywhere

And Everything

Thirteen Years pass, the youth

And not so young are still in center stage

By Christ, they bloody fill the stage

The script is abandoned though, they ignore the wings

And play to the gallery

Pandering to the lumpen, they invite them on stage

They become the lumpen (for the length of the play at least)

They abuse, drug, and sodomize

The holy citadel

Their nakedness goes unbathed

Wit turns to seed, and

Decay steams up from the floodlights

The Partisan

Is now a porno pit

Harold Laski's hostel, a Gayfere dormitory

Giggling off Great Peter Street

And the pubs . . . desacralized

Fancy charicatures of their former selves

Democratically bourgeois, pretty

And in the round

A fashionable mod freak confusion

Without destroying the worst of class distinction

Soho's den of third world plots have evaporated

Into massage parlors, for hyper genital tourists

Percy Kruger was last seen years ago

In a new plastic alpine place

And Frank Hirschfields' in the nick

Yet worse - - -

The Mandrake Club has prospered

Participatory Incorrectness

It was 1961 and I was home from the Soviet Union.

I was mainly home from a year of hitchhiking through Europe . . . but being home from the Soviet Union seemed to matter the most. It mattered radically to me, to my family, and to almost everyone with whom I spoke.

My father was a union man. He'd experienced the Terre Haute general Strike. He backed all organized unions of working people in the country . . . no, in the world. After all, his union, the International Brotherhood of Teamsters and those of his pals, the International Brotherhoods of Electrical Workers, Steel Workers, Iron Workers, Auto Workers, Mine Workers, Craft Plumbers, Carpenters etc. were all world wide in perspective . . they said. It didn't take much to persuade Dad to back my new discovery of the Soviet Union.

Not that it was perfect. Like all the unions we knew there was corruption, cruelty, bureaucracy, and heavy handedness with too many hard ass portraits on the wall but it was what we had against the company men who ran the country and caused mega death wars in the world. All unions needed to be reformed; especially the Soviet Union, but in the meantime they were our common front against upper class privilege and arrogance.

Now, I never mentioned it much throughout the sixties but Soviet Russia rather reminded me of Terre Haute and vice versa. At least Terre Haute in the Forties where I grew up.

The poor ass parts of the world could be developed like the USSR in 1960 or Terre Haute in the Forties . . . not like what both were becoming. The fifties anywhere I barely remember. They were an adolescent blur to me where I looked and thought more about girls than anything else in my environment. Now coming home to an America building gas stations on every corner, sneaking into a disastrous war and with bourgeois cosmetology dangling sex but not respect in front of youthful loins I was ready for a Revolution.

I was also tired of camping out. My parents' hearth and home did so appeal to me. To this day I am still patriotic about American Plumbing. I was not eager to return to the student life at I.U. [1] I settled into part time jobs and two twelve hour semesters at I.S.U. [2] in Terre Haute. Grade credits would all transfer to I.U. as C's so there was little pressure to study hard. I would be free for what in the sixties was called activism.. that euphemism for being an agitator, propagandist, and mind blowing consciousness raiser.

Within weeks at I.S.U. I had organized the New Left (Liberal) Forum. The parenthesis was mainly for young democrats whom I personally tried to keep there. Due to my undefined ambition and later embarrassment I was elected president of the Young Democrats that same year. But I was committed like the Teamsters, and the United Mine Workers in my family not to be sucked into the maw of democrat party moderation.

1: I.U: Indiana University in Bloomington
2: I.S.U: Indiana State University in Terre Haute

That summer I had written an article for the Tribune and spoken at several churches around town. Marvella and Birch Bayh took me for a New Frontiersman. (I was really more a roan if not red unreconstructed New Dealer.) They invited me to accompany Birch to Knox County the night he announced his bid for the Senate seat of Indiana's Senator Capehart.

U.S. Senator Homer Capehart made great T.V. sets and was an extreme right wing windbag. Birch would be better. He wanted me in his organization. I think old Doc Archer (DVM) recommended me as well.

Birch spoke a lot about the New Frontier, J.F.K., his and my political future. Old party hacks were not encouraging him. They thought Capehart unbeatable. I wanted to encourage him. My first and last campaign assignment was to write him a speech against the U.N. Of course, I declined and never saw him again for the next sixteen years. With Hulman money he released a hit song, "Hey Look Me Over," won the election and perpetuated a political career at that relative depth.

Meanwhile back at the New Left (increasingly more radical and less Liberal) Forum we recruited fifty some members at $5 bucks a head, purchased library subscriptions to the New Left Review from London, Studies on the Left from University of Wisconsin, Progressive magazine from Minnesota, U.S. Farm News from Iowa, Dorothy Days Catholic Worker from Chicago, I.F. Stones Newsletter from Washington, Huberman and Sweezys

Marxist Monthly Review and the National Guardian from New York City. More enterprising than our conservative opponents the Y.A.F. (Young Americans for Freedom) we received volumes on consignment of the above publications and sold them at literature tables in the commons. This provided for hours of proselytizing conversations with the student body and faculty.

We formed a central committee and appointed co-chairmen of our issues committees open to non members which were 1) CORE Committee on racial Equality: for civil rights against racism and racial discrimination; 2) Students for Peace: anti war efforts against unjust imperialist war; 3) Students for Labor: committee of correspondence with labor party youth in other countries and speakers bureau for local unions. Out of the latter came our most successful 4) Committee to form a Eugene Victor Debs Foundation.

Red faculty began coming out of the woodwork. Many had been chased west by McCarthy the last decade. At I.U. the majority of my teachers had been graduate student instructors. Students at I.S.U. in those days were totally taught by full professors and most of them quite accomplished ones.

Professors Howard Hamilton, Ron Elperin, Woodroe (Woody) Creason, Jack Stephenson, Gene Dyche, Bob Constantine, and others were grand supporters of our efforts. By the spring of '61 we had de-segregated several restaurants, and a skating rink. We'd influenced the Wabash Valley Labor Council to adopt positions against racial discrimination in hiring, job sites and housing. We raised thousands of dollars through correspondence with many organizations and anyone person who might have even heard of Gene Debs. We pledged to buy his family home on Eighth Street from the Theta Chi fraternity. As I recall the most surprising contributor was Albert Schweitzer. He was famous for receiving but never contributing to anybody. The most significant and least publicized contributor was the Communist Party of France.

We purchased the big house for $7,500 and envisioned a student labor center and educational foundation to promote Debs' socialist doctrine. Many think over the years this project has degenerated into keeping a museum. I think it is better than that.

We also managed to get ourselves expelled from I.S.U. that spring. Until then we had been controversial. Afterwards we were heroic. We had led a delegation of students to the "Turn Toward Peace" demonstration in D.C. Tilford Dudly of the AFL-CIO National Education Council and a personal contributor and supporter of the Debs Foundation put us up and saw us around. He introduced us to IF Stone who'd made an appeal for Debs Foundation funds in his newsletter. The "Turn Toward Peace" demonstration protested 1) the build up toward more war in Vietnam, 2) the proliferation of nuclear armaments and 3) the phony missile gap crisis created by J.F.K. We were gone three days and expelled in abstentia. Students from every major university in the Midwest had been there.

The Forum's central committee consisted of more milieu than membership. Joe Sherman from New York City, Barbara Arzett from Indianapolis, Maurice Rogers from Gary, Hiram Padron from Venezuela, Allen Johnson from Terre Haute, Muhamed Arouzi from Iran, Yuske Kataoka from Japan and "Himself" i.e. . as Dean Jones referred to me and the rest of us as "Morgans Raiders or Morgans Foreigners." We anticipated Tom Hayden's participatory democracy and invited him to speak on campus. Also while temporarily banned on campus we had Peter Camejo come and speak on the Cuban Revolution. The faculty Senate supported us, as did the Labor Council. We quickly prevailed over the aging administrators and the expulsion was dropped.

Emboldened by our victory, Yuske Kataoka became a kind of manicy "Zenga kurin".[1] He called on Mayor Tucker to endorse our existence. An endorsement he of course did not receive but through this meeting began a relationship with the mayor that resulted in Terre Hautes sister city arrangement with Taijimi, Japan, another historic coal mining district and Yuskes hometown. The arrangement still exists, I think, with semi-occasional visiting delegations. Yuski published an account of our activities and the U.S. Civil rights movement in a Japanese student magazine. However he also wished to decorate his article with a photo of me kissing Juliet Brisco the campus African American Beauty Queen. We both considered but decided her boyfriend in Memphis would not approve.

Then Yuske hit the Benai Brith speaking trail. He became the beloved no longer officially Aryan and could of would of been former fascist but now a liberal darling of Jewish ladies banquets. He ended up a houseboy at the Bloomberg Estate.

During this time the central committee convened at my parents house to draft a press release about our re-legalization. My mother was hospitable as always but as wary of foreigners as Dean Jones. In timid reserve she paused as I went around the table introducing her to all these foreigners from Latin America, Africa, Asia and New York City. Yuske was last. Not waiting for me he stood, clicked his heels saying, "Yuske Kataoka from Japan," then bowed . . . as if waiting to be petted. Ritually expectant of praise he was taken aback to hear my mother exclaim, "Japa . . Japan! My God, you're a jap! You stabbed us in the back at Pearl Harbor!"

A very brief silence . . . . . . (Yuske literally fell to his chair and halfway to the floor) . . . then that raucous laughter which conflict between an inflated ego and innocent outrage always deserved before the plague of non participatory political correctness.[2] How we laughed together that evening. Even Yuske . . he mimicked a bombardier looking down his target sites at the ARIZONA, he'd say loudly. Mother laughed in spite of herself.

1. "Zenga kurin": radical student group in Japan

2. The "politically correct" rarely have a history of participation in those struggles they so preciously wish to protect.

PROBATIVE EVIDENCE
(Response to Walt Whitman's Democratic Vistas)

When the shadow of all those clouds

move across our mid wintry minds to

totally settle in the sun drenched fields

of our being we might imagine the people

in probity.

BAD ASS GENTILE

At least one member of our crew was a clotheshorse who insisted we make pilgrimage to Ben Becker's store window to gaze at an utterly unaffordable $40 pair of alligator leather shoes. We'd shoot the breeze with shoe salesmen we liked. Especially two of 'em. One was a brother of our math teacher, Mr. Lybold . . a gentle soul whom we admired for finally losing his temper and rabbit punching Joe Sparks right in class. Joe was also a pal of ours but he really deserved that rabbit punch. The other shoe salesman was Ron Stover. He was only 'bout 10 years older than us, but married and "settled down". He was curious to us. Some of the guys would ask him about 'marriage' and he'd just laugh . . . but very knowingly. Later Ron became a police officer for the Terre Haute Police Department.

A decade later, at dinner with my parents at the Shrine City Club he joined us to tell a tale I'd caused but barely heard about. "So you're the bad ass gentile?," he joshed. "Do you realize?," he continued eyes twinkling, "that me and a dozen of my brother officers were called off beat to surround and protect Temple Israel from . . . . you!" He laughed loudly, scooted his chair closer, and went on quietly in a kind of cops confidentiality, glancing around at the near by tables and noting Mom and Dad talking with friends at one of theirs; he spoke more directly to me.

Mayor Tucker (the last mayor in America to wear spats or shoes that looked like them) had selected Ron (because he knew me) to lead a heavily armed security swat team to guard my girl friends wedding to another. Her family and the Temple congregation feared I'd be there "to object."

"They feared the terror of your wrath 'ol boy", Ron teased.

"They feared the wrath of Yahweh. I was and am simply his messenger," I half joked back.

139

In fact, I had threatened to object.

Leaving the Canal Street local in Chicago for L.A. I knew it was her weddings day defection. I was a bit blue about it, but not too bad. Earlier I'd been depressed . . unable to put one foot in front of the other . . to eat or sleep. Now I was trying to make peace with it.

Her parents kept moving her around . . to avoid me. She no longer resisted. She loved her parents. And . . she loved me. We loved each other but she grew ambivalent.

I had admired her parents. Good looking, hard working, post war liberals who wanted the best for their children . . . the best for their daughter. I certainly didn't appear like the odds on favorite for the best of anything. They had patiently tolerated my being her only serious suitor for six of her seven teenage years. They endured our excessive necking, quarreling break ups, and passionate make-ups.

During our brief break ups we both would libidinally shop around (what mid century Americans called "dating"). I preferred jewish to protestant girls. Catholic girls were far too chaste for my adolescent appetites. My fellow proletarian females I related to more fraternally than erotically. Upper class females demonstrably personified what I wished to expropriate . . . provoking a passionately predatory interest.

When separated from me she would tend toward dating Syrians and under age Sephardim . . . making my Celtic personae comparatively (almost) acceptable to her parents. In the end we always preferred each other. A peaceful co-existence between tenderness and predation.

Still . . I knew 'conventionally' with most "mixed couples" goyim[1] got dumped. I saw that over and over again with my Jewish pals and their shiksas[2]. My pal Steve was shot down over one of the Kassabaum girls. He dumped her anyhow. I enquired why? He replied like a disassociative pre-recorded slogan ". . . blood is thicker than water."

"What about love?", I asked. He looked grieved and acted like I was enticing him to Eden's forbidden tree of knowledge.

"I don't know about that," he lied.

My friend Lonnigan told me if I didn't break up with my girl friend before she got much older I would soon be as gone as the Kassabaum girl. As she turned sixteen I did initiate a break up to pre-empt my own purgation. I did so explaining all the above. It wounded her. She wept . . and said, "you might as well call me a dirty Jew!" – Gak! I was being accused of anti-semitism. Protesting my innocence I started naming all the Jews I liked; our peers, their parents, then John Garfield, Edward G. Robinson, Edith Stein and Lauren Bacall. How I loved knowing Jews whupped the Brits in Palestine better than us Micks did in only half of Ireland. How Trotsky led the Russian Revolution, wrote its history and organized the Red Army. That Irish Greg Peck made the "Gentleman's Agreement" movie and how black Irish McMarxist Gene Kelly[3] played the perfect Noel Ayrman match for Marjorie Morningstar. And finally if she herself was added to the list with Einstein, Jesus, and Moses I not only did not dislike Jews I probably loved the whole damn bunch!!

Her tears comforted; her eyes brightened as she asked, "Would you be proud of jewish children?"

"You mean . . our children?!"

"Yes . ."

"Hell yeah . . of course! Whaddaya think!"

"Then why not marry me?"

It was settled. I had to finish undergrad and grad or law school . . .(as well as start the American Rev.) She had to further integrate me into her family's acceptance and go to University of Wisconsin. We would tie the knot somewhere along the way. Too young for such plans? Consult the Montagues and Capulets. My catholic relatives would be glad her parents weren't divorced. My baptist relatives would be glad she wasn't catholic.

In all the chaos of the following years, I think we both felt an underlying and faithful contentment that we'd be together. And another thing . . she was so spoiled, so totally indulged by her parents I couldn't imagine them denying her anything she really wanted. Even if it was me! Why she so wanted me was a bit of a mystery. Parking my ego strength I frequently pondered the question. Why I so wanted her was no mystery at all.

Terre Haute has always been famous for its beautiful women. I've heard it has something to do with riverine humidity. In my generation there were and are far too many to mention. However, there were more than a few of nerve shattering arche-typal significance. All four Kassabaum females set the standard.. the Farmer twins shaped it; Carols Spiller and Boness, Peggy Purcell, Susan Templeton, Diane Stein, Elaine Einstandig, Tehrese Tartaglia, Barbara Blackmore, Loretta Taylor, Sandra Hartman, Geogias Jenkins and Thompson, Kathryn Geary, Judy Rassie, Ann Swander, Marie Baltesu, RoseAnn Baltesu, and Joann Yeager's design complied. Polly Wright recalled the mythical 'Helen' whose face launched a thousand ships (Polly's launched lunacy in half a dozen of my pals), the Ennis girl suggested Elizabeth Taylor, the Nehf girls Kim Novack, and my Sharon, the Russian-Jewish American Princess Natalia Nikolaevna Zacharenko better known as Natalie Wood. After seeing her like-ness in West Side Story I went days looking for someone to duel.

And that old tragedy seemed to play itself out in our lives. That every other season or so we were denied . . forbidden to see each other made us mutually more crazy about each other; roaringly and receptively eager to sensuously over invest in each other. We were also caught in an emotional traffic jam between two distinct cultural crosscurrents. I'd heard all my life to protect marriage goals you had to restrict pre-marital intimacy or "Don't get 'em pregnant boy O." She was beginning to hear from females slightly older that to protect her rights of intimacy she had to restrict her marital plans or "even if you sleep with goyim; do not marry them." The latter joined with the former made us both very, very crazy. I wanted her angrily. She wanted me guiltily.

Had we precociously. . prematurely . . . recklessly invested in each other both emotionally and sensuously? Was class and ethnic bigotry trying to tear us apart? Or was she just another rich girl who liked being around something a little dangerous? If the latter I obliged her plenty. Soon my life in that regard went too far to the left for her or her parents. Even old comrades at Temple Israel who had confided to me they first came to Terre Haute inspired by the life of Gene Debs and the writing of Theodore Dreiser . . . turned away.

After the holocaust had come the flaccid fifties. Overcompensating Americana an assimilated lack of consciousness prevailed. Glands and wallets were in alert dominance. Souls intellect slumbered. Conscience was hard to arouse.

At historic moments like that train wreck between the fifties and sixties patriotism displaces loves pristine loyalties. To this day if I encounter her younger brother (who was always fond of me as a kid) across the street or room he involutionally stiffens with the Star Spangled Banner radiating silently forth from his forehead.

143

My pals, the Berlinowitz twins had put in a good word for me (for us) . . telling her parents they thought, I "could make it", i.e. college, career, and high income. That is to say, lift myself up from my genetic stock of economic also rans. They had no idea of the dignity and value of labor or the morality of doing without.

Such non-dialectical materialism fell dully on my deaf ears. I was interested in working for "Justice". Later . . after I'd exploded with the civil rights and anti-war movements . . Mom, Dad, and daughter all exclaimed at me, "but we thought you were going to be like Birch Bayh!"[4]

Merchant Liberals love to keep company with kept politicians and celebrities. Her parents loved to tell how at the Ambrosinis reception for Jack Kennedy the future president told them their daughter looked like his Jackie. And she did. She kept a photo of J.F.K. I kept one of Fidel.

As an officer of the Y.S.A. (Young Socialist Alliance) at IU[5] I was indicted with Ralph Levitt, and Jim Bingham for violating the Indiana Anti-Subversive Act. A rich ne'er-do-well stone quarry heir and idiot Prosecutor claimed we were conspiring to overthrow the Indiana State Government. He also accused us of having a running gun battle with the state of Kentucky. We had run supplies and organized support for the United Mine Workers strike in Harlan County. We faced two to six years imprisonment for our ideas.

An International Defense Committee was formed with Bertrand Russell as chairman. U.S. east coast chair was Norman Mailer; west coast chair was Sterling Hayden. Leonard Boudin, the famous left wing and foremost constitutional lawyer in America (also jewish) volunteered to take our case. These celebrities did not impress her parents. They once again and finally forbid her seeing me ever again. I think she agreed. When my infamy hit the front page of the Terre Haute Tribune my father was immediately fired from his job. He'd driven the route 14 retail milk truck for Model Milk and Ice Cream Company for twenty-three years. He immediately called on his Teamsters Union Local 144. President Bill Cokely personally acted as business agent threatening to strike and shut the company down if Dads firing was not rescinded before dark. Management folded.

Tip Kendall from channel 10 called Dad with a lot of questions including, " And what do you think of the Viet Cong?" Dad militantly, loyally, and innocently replied, "I believe everything my son does!"

Class lines were drawn. Her tribally indentured wedding process began. No University was considered safe for her because the movements' popularity was too strong at all universities. They ensconced her a job at the appropriately named 'Covenant Club' in Chicago. I found it by phoning the 'Playboy Club' and enquiring where would wealthy jewish parents be likely to hide their daughter away from a working class gentile obsession and accessible to well heeled jewish bachelors. She'd accessed such a bachelor, and was to be married today.

Celebrated on college campuses and in intellectual circles but a pariah for the Indiana Press (e.g. the Indianapolis Star) I felt like Ralph Ellison's "Invisible Man" at home. Suspended from school, old friends turned away and not a few relatives. Some neighbors actually looked away to avoid eye contact.

The 'Red Scare' was on . . . and not because people feared "Stalinist", "soviet", "secret police spies"; but because many were threatened by the U.S. political police. F.B.I. agents came to call on many of my teachers, previous employers, and relatives. They tried to frighten my parents suggesting possible immigration irregularities. My fathers' family traces back to Dan Morgan in the American Revolution against the British; my mothers' mother came from Ireland. My parents showed them [F.B.I. agents] the door. Others weren't so sure . . . what was right.

Now this . . . my love sent to Siberia. Heart broken and angry . . . my emotions ranged somewhere between the tragic and the childish. After all . . any child will bawl if his lolly pop is yanked away . . . but this was more than personal. Worldly powers were violating my personal life for wrong . . dead wrong political reasons.

I had intended a straight forward (and forgiving) "Congratulations" as I approached the Western Union Desk. Then I thought perhaps a polemical telegram whose irony would suggest its own response. - Naah . . I decided on a straight forward negative message. I sent her a telegram that said, "Congratulations [stop], I plan to be there to object. [stop] Then I went on to California.

Back in Terre Haute, according to Ron all Golgothan Hell broke loose. Snot and tears from the bride. Heebie Jeebies from the groom, and hysteria from the parents, their friend the Mayor, and all the reconstructed anti-subversive patriots of Temple Israel.
"We had to escort them all the way to the airport," Ron said.
"Not all the way on the honeymoon?!"
"Nope."
"Too bad."

Nonetheless my objection was received and proved Prophetic.

Notes

1. goyim: Yiddish for gentile

2. Shiksas: Gentile molls

3. McMarxist Gene Kelly: Mr. and Mrs. Gene Kelly were prominent
"reds" in radical Hollywood

4. Birch and Evan Bayh: Strong holders of the hoosier tradition of kept politicians.

5. IU: Indiana University

Socialist Youth Fight Frame-Up Indictment

By Charles Gardner

Choosing May Day to make it sensational and symbolic, a grand jury in Bloomington, Indiana, directed by a witch-hunting prosecutor, indicted three college students for subversion.

The indicted students, all officers of the Young Socialist Alliance chapter at Indiana University, are James Bingham, 24, Ralph Levitt, 25, and Thomas Morgan, 22.

The indictments were a new stage in the campaign of Prosecutor Thomas Hoadley against the militant student organization. For months he had pressured university authorities without success to revoke their recognition of the YSA as a legitimate campus organization. Simultaneously he undertook to inflame local public opinion against the young socialists with false statements about them and their activities.

The indictments were brought under Indiana's Communism Act, a 1951 "anti-subversive" law. Conviction under it would put the students in the state prison for one to three years. The law is considered by many to be unconstitutional since comparable laws in other states have been struck down by the federal courts. However, this will be the first time the Indiana law has been tested.

The indictment charges that the three students assembled on March 25 "for the purpose of advocating or teaching that the government of the United States, or of the State of Indiana, should be overthrown by force, violence or any

unlawful means, voluntarily participating therein by their presence, aid or instigation, and as officers of a Trotskyite communist organization called the Young Socialist Alliance, the youth group of the Socialist Workers Party."

The reference to March 25 had to do with a meeting sponsored by the YSA on the IU campus at which Leroy McRae, YSA National Organizational Secretary, spoke. His subject was the Negro struggle for equality. McRae, who is a Negro, spoke in support of his people's right to defend themselves from racist violence. Hoadley made McRae's statements the basis for his charges and the grand jury made them the basis for the indictments.

In a May 6 press release, Barry Sheppard, national chairman of the YSA, stated: "The Young Socialist Alliance does not and never did advocate the use of violence

tain, Says HUAC

STATE NEWS

Subversive Activity Charge Confronts Indiana Socialists

Grand Jury Indicts Three I.U. Students Over YSA Activities

Hoadley Tries YSA

Outside Courtroom

Prosecutor Calls Action 'Courageous'

Say D.A. Violates Jury Secrecy To Disrupt YSA Stand

DAILY STUDENT

YSA's Levitt and Morgan surrender to county sheriff

NDICTED. *Ralph Levitt (left), 25, Tom Morgan (center), 22, and Jim Bingham, 24, on the Indiana University campus. Three students face jail terms because they are socialists.*

May Day INDICTMENTS

Paul Ann Gronninger was the diligent chair of our defense committee CABS (Committee to Aid Bloomington Students). She and her husband Bill worked tirelessly organizing (in Socialist Workers Party tradition) a united front support network across North America.

According to Paul Ann (Aug, 2013) this network Jim, Ralph and I implemented became the SWP framework for organizing hundreds of thousands who marched in the "Mobilization against the War", persuading America that the farmers and workers of Viet Nam deserved the victory they were winning.*

* See Barry Sheppards pol. Memoirs vol 1 "The Party"

The Defendants

Young Socialist

George Saunders, Editor

Thedd Beebe, Circulation Manager

"A World to Win!"

SUBSCRIPTION PRICE: $1.00 a year. Bundle rate: 10c for in
$5.50 for each additional 100. The YOUNG SOCIALIST is publish
P. O. Box 471, Cooper Stn., New York 3, New York. Phone GR 7-5
expressed in signed articles do not necessarily represent the views of
SOCIALIST, which are expressed in editorial statements.

Official organ of the Young Socialist Alliance

Vol. 6, No. 6 [54]   ⬥345   May–Ju

Ralph Levitt

Ralph Levitt, one of the three students indicted in Bloomington, Indiana, was born in Indianapolis, Indiana, July 5, 1938. He attended Shortridge High School in Indianapolis and graduated in 1955. He also won a Merit Scholarship the same year.

The University of Wisconsin was his choice for his college education and he graduated with a Bachelor of Arts in 1960. While he was at the University of Wisconsin he was in the Pi Lambda Phi fraternity. He went to Indiana University graduate school and in 1962 he received his Master of Arts from that school.

He is presently working on a Ph.D. on history at Indiana U. During his studies at I.U. he was awarded a University Fellow for 1962-63. He was also a Phi Alpha Theta History honorary. In 1962, he received a grant from the Russian Institute of Indiana U. He has done extensive research on the Scottsboro Trial of 1931-36 and on Eastern European History.

During all of this studying, Levitt found time to travel and during his travels he learned a lot about the world that the universities didn't teach. He visited Canada, Mexico, Cuba (pre-revolution), Ireland, the United Kingdom, France, Spain and Italy. Other countries he traveled to were Switzerland, the Netherlands,

Belgium, Cyprus, Israel and the United Arab Republic.

A former member of the Young Peoples Socialist League, Levitt left this organization in January of 1961. He has also been a member of the Fair Play for Cuba Committee and the National Association for the Advancement of Colored People. Because peace is a vital question to his generation, he belongs to Students for Peace and the Student Peace Union.

After questioning, probing and acting with other groups, Ralph Levitt finally chose the Young Socialist Alliance as the one with the correct outlook and program for the students of America. He is the chairman of the Bloomington chapter of the YSA.

* * *

Tom Morgan, 22, was born in Terre Haute, Indiana, the home of Eugene V. Debs, the famous American socialist leader. His father is a milk truck driver and a Teamster unionist.

Two years ago Tom Morgan went on an eleven month hitch-hiking tour of Europe, the Soviet Union and North Africa. The result of this travel was a radicalization process. After bumping into many neo-fascists in West Germany, he became disturbed about U.S. military aid to a not-too "reconstructed" Germany. While in Spain he witnessed the brutal fascism openly supported by the U.S.A. and became suspicious of the U.S. role in world affairs and of just how free the "free world" is.

In Britain he found stimulating young people who referred to themselves as socialists. While there he became active in the 1960 anti-apartheid demonstrations in London. The same year he participated in the Aldermaston peace march.

In May 1960 he visited the Soviet Union and was amazed at the difference in what he saw and what U.S. propaganda had pumped into him for 20 years. He was impressed with the Russian people's overwhelming desire for peace. Although critical of much of the Russian political apparatus, he was very impressed by their economic gains and welfare and cultural programs available to the Russian working people.

Morgan had left the U.S. as the president of a liberal Republican student club but upon his return he was a convinced

but independent socialist with illusions about the Democratic party. He became the president of the Indiana State College Liberal Forum, and vice-president of the Indiana State Young Democrats. Besides this he was the national secretary of the E. V. Debs Foundation which succeeded in restoring Debs' home as a museum. He was active in the local SPU, ACLU, and CORE.

He was a Delta Sigma Rho De-

bate honorary and his first contact with the Young Socialist Alliance was at I.U. where he had a public debate with an Indianapolis newspaper editor at a Fair Play for Cuba Committee meeting.

After learning that neither of the two major parties represent the American working people, Morgan became convinced of the necessity to build an American Labor Party. After examining groups that were in agreement with this idea, he became convinced that the YSA was the only youth organization theoretically and practically capable of working toward such an end. He is now the treasurer of the Bloomington group.

Tom Morgan plans to become a professor in the future but in the long view, like many of our generation, he wants to participate in labor organization and political work.

* * *

Jim Bingham

James Bingham was born in Indianapolis, Indiana on February 2, 1936. He spent most of his 25 years growing up in a conservative Republican family. He attended the Shortridge High School in Indianapolis and graduated in 1955, the same year as Ralph Levitt.

In 1962 he received his Bachelor of Arts degree from Indiana University, Bloomington, Indiana. Before this he had attended the University of Florence, Italy in 1958-59 and the University of Perugia, Italy in 1959; he speaks and reads fluent Italian. He is presently working on a Master of Arts degree in Modern European History at I.U.

Bingham traveled to Spain, France, England, Switzerland and Mexico. Like the other two students indicted, Bingham's travels gave him a new insight into the real world and its problems.

Upon his return from Europe he joined the Young Peoples Socialist League. He resigned from this group in January of 1961. The most decisive thing in recruiting him into the Young Socialist Alliance was its policy toward Cuba and the entire Cuban issue.

Bingham has been involved in many activities. He was Treasurer and Chairman of the Fair Play for Cuba Committee in Bloomington. During the summer of 1962 he was active in the Indianapolis NAACP Youth Council's struggle to get discriminatory signs removed from the Riverside Amusement Park. The struggle was successful.

He is presently a member of the FPCC, Students for Peace, Student Peace Union and the NAACP. He is an active supporter of the Committee to Aid the Monroe Defendants and helped to organize the CAMD in Indianapolis.

Jim Bingham is the present secretary of the Bloomington Young Socialist Alliance.

FUPI Attacks NSA Stand

The Pro-Independence Student Federation of Puerto Rico, FUPI, has begun publishing a monthly *International Bulletin* to help spread the cause of Puerto Rican independence. The first issue, printed in March, includes a complete report on the decisions of the Seventh Congress of FUPI.

NSA Wrong

The Puerto Rican students, through their bulletin, protest the treatment of their movement and its just cause by the U.S. National Student Association (NSA). At the Tenth Conference of the Student International the NSA opposed Puerto Rican independence. The FUPI bulletin points out that the French student movement supported the independence movement of Algeria.

The YOUNG SOCIALIST agrees with FUPI that NSA should follow the example of the French students and support independence for this nation colonized by the U.S. All those interested in contacting FUPI or receiving the *International Bulletin* should write to: Federacion de Universitaria Pro-Independencia; Apartado 1873 —U.P.R.; Rio Piedras, Puerto Rico.

...3 Indicted

(Continued from Page 1)

ment (see page 8) which characterizes the defendants as officers of a "Trotskyite communist organization, and the youth group of the Socialist Workers Party." Cohen also stated his intention of filing a brief to quash the indictment on the grounds that the law is unconstitutional. Similar state laws have been struck down by federal courts.

The Emergency Civil Liberties Committee's General Counsel, Leonard Boudin, has entered the case as a constitutional expert. The Indiana Civil Liberties Union is filing an amicus curiae brief in behalf of the defendants.

THE DEFENDANTS SPEAK

Speakers will be [...]
from the Young So
liance and the Commi
the Bloomington Stud
plain the case and hel
defense work in [...]
Where possible the
themselves will br a
speak. If your local
tion wants a speaker
the Young Socialist A
P.O. Box 471, Coope
New York 3, N.Y.
Committee to Aid [...]
ington Students, P.O.
Bloomington, Indiana

Help Us Fight Ba

Since the arrest of the Bloomington socialist studen
struggle for free speech, for a free exchange of ideas with
dent movement, is focused on the Young Socialist Alliance
or defeat for the YSA in this battle will be a victory or de
freedoms and rights of the American people as a whole.

The YSA is the only nation-wide student organization
not receive funds from adult organizations that finances i
from its own members and sympathizers. We have no R
Rockefellers supporting us. What we do have is the wi
young workers and students to sacrifice

We need funds desperately to answer the slanders whic
spread by Hoadley through the major press.

We do not only want to beat the charges leveled ag
"subversion" but to set the witch-hunt and its conservati
phere back. You can help by sending us a donation no [...]
small.

Below are the donations we have received so far this s

The score board:

Area	Quota	Paid
Chicago	$250.00	$334.50
Boston	200.00	262.60
Madison	50.00	50.00
Baltimore	50.00	50.00
New York	350.00	320.50
Berkeley	225.00	198.50
Detroit	75.00	65.00
Minnesota	125.00	165.00
Seattle	75.00	45.00
San Francisco	150.00	50.00
Philadelphia	50.00	13.00
Los Angeles	75.00	17.00
Bloomington	150.00	25.00
Others	175.00	133.00
TOTAL	**$2,000**	**$1,606.60**

's who were vastly his superior both
edge of the law and in their under-
mocratic rights. The defense argued
a Anti-Communism Act was uncon-
l in violation of the rights of free
bly and association, and superceded
gislation. The court upheld the de-
law was declared unconstitutional.
now appealed this decision to the
me Court. If he should win at this
would again hold the club of this
over not only the YSAers but all

voices of dissent at Indiana University. Witch-
hunters all over the nation would be given a pre-
cedent and stimulus.

The Committee to Aid the Bloomington Students
is preparing to fight Hoadley's appeal at the
Indiana state level, to go through a trial and to
fight the case if need be up to the United States
Supreme Court.

Help stop the Bloomington witchhunt, and
strike an important blow for freedom by supporting the CABS. For more information, write
to CABS, P. O. Box 213, New York 3, New York.

MINGTON COURTROOM. Although barred from the courtroom, a local photographer
picture of the three defendants through the glass door. Ralph Levitt (left), Jim Bingham
Tom Morgan anxiously await judge's ruling on defense motions March 20.

EET YOUNG SOCIALISTS IN YOUR AREA

SA, c/o Kathy Winston, Antioch
llow Springs
OAKLAND: YSA, c/o Mary Alice
793 Oxford St., Berkeley
A, c/o Horowitz, 1 Linden St.,

SA, Debs Hall, 302 So. Canal St.
: YSA, c/o E. V. Debs Hall, 5927
ve., Rm. 25
rdue, 1890 Race, Apt. 1

LOS ANGELES: YSA, 1702 E. 4th St.
MADISON: YSA, c/o Leonard, 508 W. Johnson St.
MINNEAPOLIS: YSA, 704 Hennepin Ave.,
   Hall 240
NEW YORK CITY: YSA, 116 University Pl.
PHILADELPHIA: Ted Fagin, c/o Chertov, 2708
   Sterner
SAN DIEGO: Lud Carter, 2837 M. Ave., National
   City
SAN FRANCISCO: YSA, 1580 Fulton

KURDISTAN AT SEA

The crossing was on an Italian ship. There was a Turkish girl aboard who had marvelous haunches. "Hips like a Percheron," Taras Bulba promised. Yet etiquette required an engagement of minds.

She was a medical student and daughter of their embassy's staff. Attaturk above Islam, she held many opinions . . . mostly about Kurds. "They have tails you know . . . ," she wondered out loud, stating her half-believed and bigoted superstitions with emphatic tentativeness. Fearfully dreamy eyed, she would describe them as "primitive, strange, unpredictable and predatory." Arrgh . . . I was libidinally disenchanted; this was no exotic escapee from the harem, this was the very picture of every beyond the pale bonneted and cluelessly breathless Southern belle boning up on bigoted fantasies of Nat Turner, Bigger Thomas, Stokely and Malcolm.

I left her imagining pesh mergas coming through her porthole.

SOLARIUM

She was as bare of guile

as her back I held outside the solarium

warm against the even chill

and long was her flesh responsive

to that longing in me

already becoming our loss

the revolutionary tyrant

inpsyde my love for what was

missing . . .

"America may be an occupied countr
but today I met a young man from Indian
There are pockets of resistance
Sterling Hayden 19(

STERLING RESISTANCE

First met as scowling horse farmer

flank shot and trying to get home

for the black colt across the asphalt and the Ohio.[1]

By then he'd gone from footballer to O.S.S.[2] operative

parachuting into Titos Partisans to aid the allies

in anti-fascist Balkan forests.

Before I saw him next in my father's TRUE magazine

he'd rescued/kidnapped his children from domestic courts[3]

and hit the high seas as Jack London's idea of himself

Brave Wanderer[4] he greeted Asher[5]and me in the Wheelhouse of his

office boat in Sausalito's waters.

Big fisted defender of the Quakers[6],

he loved my stories of Indiana violence

and made his famous quote to the papers[7]

telling me and Asher of Dr. Strangelove[8]

and General Jack D. Ripper

"I play the Birchite, you'll get to fight," he said.

Big hearted actor, who never went to the movies

helped us cast ourselves

accurate enough

to slay the century.

Notes

1. The Asphalt Jungle (Warner Brothers film)

2. Sterling Hayden fought with Titos Partisans as an OSS operative

3. S.H. was the first celebrated defier of US custody courts

4. "Wanderer": title of Memoirs by S.H.

5. Asher (Harer): Longshoreman leader of Socialist Workers Party

6. S.H. was called on to protect his children from right wingers hazing them on their way to a Quaker School.

7. "I've just met a young man from Indiana. America may be an occupied country but there are pockets of resistance." Sterling Hayden

8. "Dr. Strangelove" S.H. plays General Jack D. Ripper fighting for his" precious bodily fluids"

Los Angeles City College 1964 "TGM Second Best Street Speaker of the Sixties"   157

L.EFT A.MERICANA

"There is nothing more difficult
to manage, or more doubtful
of success, or more dangerous
to handle than to take the lead
in introducing a new order of things"

". . all armed prophets have conquered
and the unarmed ones have been destroyed"

Niccolo Machiavelli's
The Prince

I'd been half way 'round the world, but it was L.A. that felt like the future. Triple autobahns in everybody's backyard. Disconnectedness. Glitz. Prosperity. Women. And . . working class privacy. Multiple little places where you could imagine living your own life separate from theirs i.e. the rest of this so-called city. You never felt owned by it . . you moved around in it.

In Echo Park I had Jewish comrades and Mexicans with smiles for neighbors. Nobody bothered you. Nobody knew you except at a respectful distance. Anomie[1] with friends beats the hell out of anomie without them.

The cops all seemed terrible tall southerners[2] but easy to avoid. We'd been dodging their cracker equivalents down south (and up south in Indiana)[3] for the last three years.

The Ruskies patronized Latins as revolutionary tourists in the tropics and blather on and on about feces freezing Leningrad . . . but I must admit a certain guilt about the pleasantness of southern California back then, especially after the locals in Minneapolis and Chicago. There was a certain comfort about the Canadian border in Detroit, but here in L.A. we were over the border in all directions . . . Mexico, the Pacific, Baja, mountain snow and the desert. Even hard bitten politicals became insouciant or as my Ashkenazim-Afro-Italian friend Julio said, "Pococurante man, its pococurante!"

Midwesterners like me were as welcome as coastals. Leftist Americana! It never occurred for someone to be told they "didn't belong here" . . . no one did.

My mentor here was a big Norwegian named Oscar whose father had fought in the 1934 Minneapolis General Strike with the Dunne brothers, Farrell Dobbs and Jimmy Hoffa. Most of those guys had gone on to guard the old man (Lev Davidovich Bronstein a.k.a. Trotsky) during his last days in Cayoacan. Oscar grew up amongst them. He was wise beyond his years (having a decade and half on me) wearing his trenchcoat over his shoulders like 'Grizek', party secretary in the Polish film "Ashes and Diamonds". He was a party leader in southern California and worked as union carpenter in the studios. He said he could get me on there.

I was still working with the student faction of the party. Another faction favored sending us all into the factories. When this Proletarian vs. Student orientation was debated at convention I got a big laugh from the old timers and much enmity from the youth by saying "It matters less whether our young cadre be in unions or on campus . . what's important is they be out of bed by noon."

Martialing marxoid categories I criticized what I saw as the coming "lumpenization"[4] of America. This was years before the Panthers [5] declared their "revolutionary suicide" as the vanguard of the "revolutionary lumpen." And before the Hippies idolized a mid-sixties mood swing of "Hells Angels" as an acid inspired preference for Peace.

Only us olde leftys knew the brief mildness of the Angels was not inspired by drugs but from having their collective asses kicked by the Teamsters for being strikebreakers at a warehouse in Oakland. Breaking the lumpen strikebreakers legs on waterfront curbs brought a certain serenity and civility to these fellows for at least a season.

One afternoon a group of them came swooping down on me like a murder of crows. I was riding a 1938 Ariel [motorcycle] purchased from a "peripheral" supporter (That's what non member friends of the party were called) who owned a junkyard. They surrounded my lane on the freeway forcing me quickly onto an exit ramp. It was broad daylight so I stayed cool enough to coast into a crowded gas station as they roared around me making fancy stops.

After a tense second or two they joshed loudly with each other, ignoring me but examining every detail of my bike. They were especially interested in the old Ariel's engine and wheel mounts. As they left they seemed pleased I'd been scared but disappointed I was not grateful they hadn't bothered me. For . . I had been bothered a bit because I had places to go . . I was looking for work.

Oscar wanted me to wait for a job in the studios to open up. They were making a movie called "The Great Race" and many platforms had to be built. He was sure they'd be hiring soon. Friends and comrades in the 'proletarian orientation' faction insisted I settle for nothing less than an industrial union, not a craft union career. I'd been a Steelworker in Chicago . . . but I was still not favoring either disputed faction over the other . . . I just needed a job.

One opened up in the Plumbers Union. As an apprentice I'd be working construction outside and that suited me. I liked working outside in the fresh air. No one mentioned in

Los Angeles' smog filled basement digs there is little fresh air and sometimes no oxygen at all. One day in a deep basement, I was digging a trench with a power drill spade when I realized I was no longer breathing. There was no air down there to breathe. I ran like swimming underwater to the sidewall, scrambling up, as if surfacing out of a pool of that dead smoggy non-air. Air to breathe is, after all, a minimal requirement!

I had transportation problems too. The first day I bungee strapped my lunch pail to the Ariel's handlebars and banged it all the way to work. I could have drunk my lunch that day with a straw. My old Ariel was becoming impractical. It was also pointed out to me that riding my girlfriend on the back fender with her feet perched on the rear sprocket may resemble Marcello Mastriani and Sophia Loren on a Vespa but was qualitatively more dangerous. I needed a car.

Bill, the junkyard man lived way out east on the periphery of L.A. county and way out on the periphery of our politics but he was game to trade a 1956 Chrysler for my 1938 motorcycle. I arrived at his junkyard about dusk on a Saturday night. He knew I was coming. Oscar had phoned and told him to treat me right. But . . . our peripheral comrade had forgotten his seasonal "Parents without Partners" social and gone there instead. He wouldn't be home until well after midnight. I knew none of this but was determined to stay however long it took to get the Chrysler.

The path that led forty yards through smashed cars to his motor home was guarded by two growling junkyard dogs; big, loud chow shepherd crosses. Bill called them his deterrents. The other three dogs tied randomly throughout the yard were quiet and Bill called them his landmines.

I parked the Ariel behind an old Studebaker close in by the dogs and walked several blocks away 'til I found a Chinese restaurant and a movie theater. After ordering Mongolian beef and beer I called my girlfriend from a corner phone booth. "Bills probably out for the night," I told her, I was going to wait however long it took to bring us home a car.

She had been crying. Sometimes I made my girlfriend cry. At first I thought her sobbing was a remnant of some earlier spat. She then spoke more clearly about its source. Friends of ours had been assassinated in Detroit. Three Guys! Two of them I knew well. Both students at Wayne State! Comrades! Jan and Walt were bookish, bespectacled skinny ass young socialists who were no fighters . . . gunned down by some red, white and blue anti-communist bigot.

Overcome with sadness and anger I had to sit down and couldn't sit down. An attack like this had happened back home a year ago. I'd been there! We'd all been sprayed with buckshot, some of us more than others by right wing shot gunners up close. Three blasts and no one killed. Now this! Almost a year and still no defense arrangements. Oscar was talking about it last week. "Chicago [the Chicago leadership] can't get past being campus activists," he said. "Oh there's lots of 'em sure . . and they're probably the smartest college radicals in the country, but they should not be the model for cadre in our movement."

"They're Carlton College clones alright," I added. "Can you imagine . . allowing gusanos[6] to break up and beat up women at a public meeting on Cuba. With all those Chi town Steelworkers and Great Lakes Stevedores willing to form defense committees . . . instead they post a few boys and girls with rolled up Sun-Times to stand by the door."

"Tell Oscar about Bubbles?" one of the guys asked. We were all sitting outside on the street after our local meeting and Oscar already knew the Bubbles story, but he nodded for me to tell the rest of them.

In Chicago I'd helped recruit a youth named Bubbles. He didn't know his last name and Malcolm had inspired him not to care. He was a marginally employed 20-year-old slum kid who lived with his mom in the south side black ghetto. He didn't know much. He'd just been hanging around. While I was in Chicago I took him to the educationals. He was learning. He and my ironworker pal Joe walked with me down Canal Street to the train station when I left. Later it was Joe's Polish girlfriend who told me what happened to Bubbles.

An official gala get together was being held in Hyde Park on Saturday night for and by the revolutionary youth. Mostly students and mostly white they warmly welcomed Bubbles and some of his friends to the party. As she described it I could imagine alternate cuts of Ray Charles, Bob Dylan, and Miles Davis as background sounds before the hubbub at the door.

The hubbub outside was a gang of hostile strangers demanding entry to the party. They were all young black men and they were very drunk. Most were hooting insults around the half opened door at the mixed racial couples dancing. Things quieted inside the door. Outside the door threats escalated to demand that white people at the party pay a tax to stay in the neighborhood. This demand elicited much laughter on the stair well and a kind of choral chanting of Dues, that's right Dues brothers Dues!

Joe and the Polish girl tried to schmooze them at the door for a friendly entrance but it was impossible. "Pay the tax, pay your dues with your cash, your liquor, or your women!" Much cackling followed that one. The door was slammed shut and double dead bolted. Then the outside of the door started to sustain double hits . . two bodies at a time bashing into it with enough force the hinges began to give way. Joe stopped Roosevelt University students from calling the cops.

Soon the door splinteringly gave way completely and

everyone scattered. Except Bubbles. He sprang screaming through the fractured door like a leopard whacking drunks to the floor, then kicking them down the stairs. He never looked back. Of course, he thought he was not alone. No one followed him. The Polish girl got a dozen guys piling on Joe to prevent his following.

The jitterbuggers quickly rejoined the fray against Bubbles when they saw all his integrated, educated comrades cowering behind their shattered door. They mobbed him, dragged him, busting his head on the stairs until they pummeled him unconscious in the gutter, leaving him with a concussion, broken jaw and ribcage.

Joe took him to the E.R. Neither Joe nor Bubbles came back to the revolutionary youth. Joe's Polish ex-girlfriend takes the leadership's side entirely. "Come on!" she protests. "We are not a gang. We can't be brawling like the Blackstone Rangers[7]. Bubbles should have known that. You and Joe should've had him understanding better."

"Better than what?!" I began to speak and thought better of it. My God, she was a wage earner herself and a Steelworkers daughter . . still she hewed to the campus activist line.

Like a pack of veteran hounds baying toward a correct line all these L.A. comrades grunted and growled their collective affirmation of my story. That is, what we'd call the principle in and of the story.

Julio interrupted that Vince was still in touch with Joe. Our eyes turned to Vince. He was an older guy who'd made friends with Joe at the National Convention. "Joes coming back," He said. "It'll give Chicago an out if he puts in for a transfer. Those hard ass baby Bolsheviks will say he's retreating to the softer circles of southern California." We all laughed.

Vince had been a schoolteacher. It would be great if Joe

164

came west. Vince said he'd put him up til he got work. Vince also said that Joe told him another Chicago story the last time they were on the phone. It was about us and the "Fruit of Islam."[8]

Joe and I had rented upstairs rooms in the old Morgan House on Woodlawn. The place was two doors down from Elijah Mohammed's Mosque no#1. The "Fruit of Islam" stood guard. A slightly mixed neighborhood . . . non-blacks and non-muslims were wary of disturbing them. They had a fierce reputation. No one wanted to bother them. We read (their newspaper) "Mohammed Speaks" and hoped they'd get over their extremism and become moderate incendiaries like ourselves.

When my parents came to visit they weren't sure of our house. Dad parked his old vulgar Cadillac (there was a fezed shriner's bobble head in its back window) in front of the mosque and went in to ask directions. There was no white devil nonsense. They treated my father with great courtesy and walked him down to our front door. Dad thought they were some kind of Prince Hall Masons. Joe and I had a laugh about that.

A few weeks later we had a similar but more dramatic experience. We were hosting a barbeque for the 'F.P.C.C. Fair Play For Cuba Committee' in our large backyard. Some of the same students who'd later be at the Bubbles party were there. This time it was the anti-Castro Cubans who raided us. Everyone was eating when they burst through the back gate. Batistianos! Gusanos! The U.S. kept population of cutthroats exempt from prosecution in their open season pursuit of us reds. Joe and I, Ed Heisler, and even the Carlton crowd fought back . . . a little. We weren't tested long when the 'Fruit of Islam' was over the fence, through the gate and effectively neutralizing our enemy. In teams of two our eight rescuers quickly knocked senseless more than twenty anti-communist Cubans. The ones they didn't drag out to the alley volunteered to run. What had been quite a racket turned to quiet as we approached the Muslims to thank them for our rescue and congratulate them on their "revolutionary solidarity with the Cuban Revolution and our multi ethnic support" of the same. Their leader was friendly, appreciative of our gratitude and not sectarian (expressing no hostility toward our racially mixed group). He didn't however have a clue what we were talking about. "We just wanted to keep the neighborhood peaceful . . .," he said. They knew we were neighbors. Our guests looked like us and the gusanos didn't. The community made safe! They weren't interested in hearing any more about it.

We all laughed again. Some of the guys were leaving; their wives and girlfriends picking them up when Bill spoke, "The Party needs to physically defend itself . . . the youth need to defend their work . . . it is the sacred duty of every individual and every human collective to defend itself. It is shameful otherwise." "But how?" he asked with a peripheral twinkle in his eye, "how do we do it?"

Like I said, Bill was out there on the periphery. He sure talked different than we did, sometimes more directly, sometimes like a preacher frequently using the editorial "we". Vince, Charlie, Julio, David and others immediately protested that 'we' had done something about it and some of them began pulling out their Berettas to prove it. Bill grinned. Oscar looked grieved and I thought the scene was more like a bunch of 'blue painted Celts on a hill'[9] than the "Fruit of Islam".

Oscar broke in that 'we' needed a nod from the leadership or a new convention vote to properly organize defense squads. Clearly irritated, he also said, "And you guys make sure those guns are legally registered . . trouble in that department is the last thing we need."

I was glad I hadn't bragged on my weapon . . it was probably illegal. I'd carried a knife, a small pig sticker in my boot for years. I'd never heard of anyone stabbing themselves or anyone else to death accidentally.

Julio agreed, "Any burglar will tell you . . pull a gun and he knows he can't outrun the bullet so he'll come at you. Pull a knife and he's more apt to run away."

Bill wasn't through. A non-member he was under no discipline to shut up between conventions. Leninist democratic centralism. Everyone voted. Then loyalty to that vote as policy was required until the next convention. Internal debate and discussion was allowed but not with non-members. Bill said, "defense organization must take priority." He talked on about the dozens of assassinations. Not just the media covered Medgar Evers, Lincoln Rockwell, Kennedy Brothers, Martin, and Malcolm but all the little people through out the entire country, Canada, and Mexico. North America was polarizing and we sought to be on the cutting edge of its conclusion. "Defense organizing must be comprehensive," Bill was saying. "From the local meeting hall to the parking lot, to comrades homes. From their car to their front door, to their rooms. I've thought a lot about it."

No one liked hearing Bill brag like this and we were collectively inhibited to say too much in front of him. Still and all I found him interesting.

He went on . . "I not only have two junkyard dogs between the front parking area and my home but three more secretly tied in the western, northern, and eastern quadrants of the place. I don't need firearms. My first two deterrents, female and male I named Da-neice and Da-nephew." Not all of us had heard the joke. He was in full stride now. "Da-neice and Da-nephew are loud alarm dogs. The other three are registered and silent Pit Bulls. My land mines. They can bite through a predators knee before he knows what hit him." David and Charlie wanted to argue. "No way, how could you keep 'em silent and dogs can't bite that hard."

Bill was in his element talking about his junkyard. Oscar, steely eyed was viewing him contemptibly as a peripheral petty bourgeois property holder. Bill explained that the pit bulls were not completely silent but quieter than most dogs "cause they're confident in their jaw power. A German Police or Doberman has about 75 pounds of pressure in their jaws. My Pit Bulls have close to 1500 pounds."

Oscar rose and made sighing sounds. We adjourned. Julio and I rode with Oscar back to Echo Park. It was on my mind so I asked him about the famous defense project . . . the one that failed. He shook his head. His own father and the best and bravest of his home local . . the very leadership of the Greatest American General Strike failed to protect "the old man" . . Trotsky himself. The Minneapolis men joined with loyal Mexican Trotzkos chosen by Diego Rivera to guard his every move . . . and yet his enemies struck him fatally with an ice axe. The old genius struggled violently but the blow killed him. Struck down by a Stalinist agent stooge. And Oscar said he saw it coming. "The old man thought if enough people want to kill you – you're gonna be dead."

"His children, his friends and comrades executed and assassinated . . . yet he faithfully continued in a kind of political piety to think and act in a principled way, that History would absolve. Of course he knew that history is propaganda of the winners and he expected that someday socialist justice would win out over capitalism and socialist tyranny . . . his people over Stalin's, but not through short cut cheap ass gains. The true revolutionary's way is the long straight road of personal sacrifice and principled struggle on behalf of the toilers of the earth".

Oscar made him sound rabbinical . . . kind of religious and I liked hearing him described that way. Too often too many of my secular comrades sounded more solipsistic than socialist anticipating the puerilities in Cormac McCarthy's Road, "There is no God and we are his prophets." Whereas the old man Trotsky as a Prophet outcast[10] no less than armed was faithful if not categorically to God nonetheless to His justice and His-story.

"Live a principled life and keep a respectful sense of humor," was Oscar's motto. He also liked to say, "Never trust a businessman!" He said it that night as he was letting us out. Then he said, "that Bill is a bullshitter. He not only sics dogs on poor people trying to rob him . . he hires drunks for nothing as night watchmen. Sure! Give 'em a bottle, an old car seat and a title so they'll work all night for nothing . . . or almost nothing. I knew from Oscar's wife Della that he coveted Bill's junkyard.

My mind racing over the Chinese food I ordered more beers. Every violent episode in life I'd experienced, seen in the movies, read, or even heard about intercalated in my memory. I felt sure there was "just violence" or at least necessary violence as well as "unjust violence." I reckoned you needed one to defend against the other. (The most violent natured human being I knew was a pacifist professor.) I loved the Amish and Quakers but nonviolence was not an option. And yet, here we were . . . significant leadership of the civil rights and ant-war movement considering ourselves the vanguard alliance of the American Rev . . taking the lead introducing a new order . . the only Socialists with an effective plan for workers power and we couldn't seem to defend ourselves or our friends. I was planning to write an internal party document titled "Port Arms" (the order to take up arms to the left.)

I thought of the kid we called 'Wingey'. He was an undergraduate from Hofstra who had a crippled arm that looked like a chicken wing. He thought he might be a Maoist but came to our convention out of curiosity.

The N.S.A[11] had convened at I.U. that same year. We'd met him there with Todd Gitlin of SDS[12] and Stokely Carmichael of SNCC[13]. I think Clark Kissenger of SDS introduced him. He was a serious, petulant, very youngish kind of guy. Likeable but loud. He met up with real Maoists at our convention. A fraternal delegation of tall black men down from Detroit. They immediately quarreled. Wingey was annoying. But he was also a little crippled guy . . . so when he pushed a particular point about Maos' "Contradictions Among the People" poking his few good fingers into the Maoists chest they slammed him up against the wall.

Rolphe who'd been watching was across the room like a streak into their midst. I wasn't far behind him. Rolphe rabbit punched two to their knees and was choking the third into a chalk rack allowing Wingey to scuttle off to the restroom to repair his torn clothing when Peter Camejo led the charge of several people who separated us and sternly ordered us outside. Pete Camejo was that part of the national leadership we admired. Outside we couldn't believe he was scolding us like a school marm. "Personal fighting with a black man in public now" he said, "was tantamount to fighting Union men on a striking picket line thirty years ago." "It wasn't personal," Rolphe protested . . "they were bullying the crippled kid." "You'd smack a picket pushing an old lady around wouldn't you?" I asked . . . or I guess kind of timidly alleged. Pete and Rolphe looked at me critically. Both always thought me too oblique. I shut up and let the scolding continue. It was mainly for Rolphe anyhow. But I didn't agree with it anymore than Rolphe did. Pete Camejo . . . the most gifted political of our generation towing the line of campus temperance. Sad. And then, there was Germaine, the jeweler. A World War II vet who'd fought the Nazis on skis in the Alps. He taught classes on Das Kapital in English, Spanish, and German. I attended the English one, of course, but couldn't follow a full paragraph and not because of his

Austrian accent. Neither me nor Mike Geldman could get it . . . could follow the turgid universal and inevitable economics narrative. Labor theory of value . . yeah! Surplus value . . . OK, but the independent development of the relative form of value and of the equivalent form . . . ? . . bearing in mind that the latter is only the expression and result of the former . . . ???

Mike claimed Fidel couldn't get it either and quoted him as saying "I gave up on Das Kapital but I think I'm a good revolutionary socialist anyhow!" That's all I needed hearing to stop attending class.

Shortly after that there was an attempted robbery at his jewelry store. Two thugs tried to stick him up. He took the gun away from one and in what was reported as a mortal storm of bravery and bullets fought off his lumpen assailants expertly wounding both in the knees as they tried to assault him. The leadership accused him of alienating the community. Germaine was no mere petty bourgeois, property obsessed shopkeeper. Maybe no one is. Germaine would have defended his home and family, or party branch for that matter as fast as he did his livelihood. I was beginning to think Marxists underestimate the superstructure.

I finished my meal of Mongolian beef, vegetables, and several beers. Surveying all those dead soldiers on my table was satisfying. I felt better. More calm and tired of thinking, I thought . . maybe I'd go to the movies.

Typically mid-century modern-Marxist or not I accessed no spiritual tradition, offered no prayers up for my fallen comrades. In reflective anxiety I was unconscious of the questions I needed for the answers I sought.

It did occur to me that personalities seemed to be informing politics as much as politics was shaping personalities. Reading Sartres "Search for a Method" I was trying to understand the old nature ↔ nurture dialectic from my own experience.

I'd not gotten far . . except . . to realize however heretically that the superstructure (its conscious culture) of socialist Cuba distinguished the nature of its revolution from say China as much as any material analysis.

Again the superstructure; that culture of collective psychology i.e. the souls aesthetic and moral consciousness determining (dialectically) our responses to material conditions. To think otherwise arrests the dialectic reducing analysis to the mechanical. As war is but the extension of politics . . culture is the prescient forms of its (political) possibilities.

And our political culture was suffering deformations. We'd become a 'combat party' of 'incombatance'. Disciplined Bolsheviks preparing to be the prevailing catalysts for a social democratic mass that did not exist. Leninists with an increasingly lumpen base of merely proletarian memories. 'Combat Party' organization only made sense with access to a politicized mass, as in the labor parties of Europe and Canada . . . and the undismanteled Communist (3rd International) Parties where survived or in power. That is, to be the left revolutionary nuclei determining the central success of the whole larger, general effort.

Post McCarthy America offered no such opportunities. Leftys had lost themselves in larger liberal forms or smaller sectarian ones. Trotsky had argued against the former, resisted the latter and satirized Stalinist pretensions at both. Still and all... without severe industrial crisis and consequent labor militancy, mid-century Marxists and American Trotskyists in particular became isolative-sectarian failing to directly address the 'organizational question'* degenerating into parade marshal activism and the subterfuge of police spy deformations. Morality remained.

*always suspected as a mask for political differences.

172

A militant "ist" not an "ite"[14] . . . no personality cult
. . no psychologizing I was nonetheless beginning to think that
moral bearings in"the old man" and in all those old men from
Minnesota and Mexico even when they failed was fundamentally
important. Trotsky's most ruthless arguments were enliv-
ened and civilized with humor. The existential pivot requires a
cheerful moral defiance.

I finished my tea and refused the fortune cookie. "For
fortune is a woman," I joshed the waitress paraphrasing Niccos
'Prince' "who didn't give me enough judgment to understand her
early nor enough time to overcome her" . . . lately. The waitress
smiled. "Whats it mean?" she asked. I explained, "Good luck or
bad depends upon the women." Another Asian smile. I went to
the movies.

The feature I misremember was one of the last Hollywood
black and white productions. I preferred black and white films as
more serious than technicolor. "The Courtship of Eddie's Father"
was a Glenn Ford character narrative about the choice of certain
female archetypes. An awesome subject for me! Second only to
politics! I was twenty-three!

The film too simply condemned women to categories.
Not that some women and men do the same to themselves . . but I
was learning that in every being there is a natural cast of characters
in variant types and moods. Dependent upon cultural influences,
genetic, and nurturant conditions . . one, some, or the other get
emphasized. Not inevitably, not universally but naturally imaginable. It seemed to me that any man and woman of natural, even
minimal attraction should be capable of caring enough for each
other to bring out the best in their beloved. People are versatile . .
capable of being brutes, bitches, or productive partners.

As revolutionary puritans of the sixties we needed
traditional defense mechanisms. All the women available and I

mean completely available was distracting. I had decided any one incapable of being satisfied with one partner had no imagination. I had and have no patience for infidelity or disloyalty in love, sex, or politics. "Failure in one leads to failure in all," Jim Cannon[15] told me with tears stinging his old eyes. He'd been over the line in one and overcompensating in the other for half a century. I'd sit on his floor listening to him for hours in his house down the street from that blue collar bar that reminded me of my fathers. In stellar moments this grand old Mick would regress to a Kansan Catholic mode and the realization would hit me that I was serving as confessor to a Father of American Communism. "The only member of the American Left who wants to remember" is how the Draper Bros. described him in their 1963 opus "History of American Communism." Debs[16], Reed,[17] Cannon, Foster,[18] VR Dunne[19] and Jack London[20] were embedded in the hagiography of my political conscience. Old Jim and I used to joke that only he, however was truly canonized.

Jim Cannon liked me. He liked hearing my moral and political critique of the Leadership. And he liked hearing how we bought the Debs house in Terre Haute and formed the Debs Foundation. Jim had known Gene Debs and covered his funeral for the Labor Defender! He told of trading quips with Riley[21] and quotes with Debs. Over and above his rational thought he seemed to sense a nearness of what Riley called, "the jedgement seat." And he seemed to have a conscientiously wounded, almost remorseful good humor about the limits of his life and ours. He was partisanly supportive and hopeful regarding my political career. I disappointed him.

Walking back to the junkyard I tried to focus on more practical tasks while enjoying the evenings slight breeze. Enjoying anything got scarce when I found Bill . . . still not home. It was midnight dark with one small security light over the whole damn junkyard. The hulks of damaged steel looked spooky. The alarm dogs were barking and I decided to seek shelter in his motor home. Even periphery people would have books by Trotsky and Cannon.

I managed to mince carefully around the rubble away from Da-neice and Da-nephew. I got inside with a key from under his doormat. I turned on the lights and found his book cases. The alarm dogs quieted and I settled in for my wait. I remember finding a review by Cannon of Norman Mailers "Barbary Shore." Dozing for awhile before I heard . . .CRASH!!!! Wha thee hell? . . . had come through the large windshield. It was a brickbat, rather one and a half brickbats globbed together with old hardened mortar. It looked like a piece from the crumbling brick building on the far side of the lot. But, it was too heavy to have been thrown that far . . . except maybe by a catapault. It had to have been thrown by someone up close. I switched the lights off. Three more! bangs! hit the motor home. The first one sounded like it might be gunfire if it hadn't hit the top of what served as a roof. The second shattered what sounded like a headlight and the third almost got me sailing through what was left of the windshield. It was a smaller rock. I thought of getting in the water closet when another rock hit that window. I thought of the phone and quickly rejected the idea since cops and right-wingers go together as more rocks pelted the roof and side windows.

If this was some dumbass assassins looking for a red they were going to get more than they bargained for from me. I was less afraid of them (whoever they were) than of handling this badly. I sure as hell wasn't going to be like Walt and Jan or Steve and Shel dying with a book in my hand. I grabbed my boot knife and then felt ridiculous pointing a pig sticker at what was like distant artillery as more rocks slammed into the place.

Over on Bills desk was an old leaded style blackjack he

used as a cigar holder. I put the knife down, pocketed the black-jack and figured I had to get out of the motor home and out far enough in the junkyard to get away from the security light. I could hide in a junked car, listen, and think through my next move.

Remembering my calvinist Grandma who'd say something like . . when your time is up . . . go for it, don't fret about it. Malcolm . . and all those Muslim way of God warriors we'd hear about would probably check their conscience and decide it was a good time to die. Well . . . mine was clear . . except for those tears of my girlfriend and my not helping enough to correct a confused sibling. I'd been on the 'just' side of the main issues of my time. I'd been a good son and comrade. As good a time as any, I reckoned, plunging out the side door and through two and a half rows of junked cars to get beyond the light.

Rocks kept smashing the motor home so I knew they hadn't seen me. If Bill had just kept one firearm I could have at least fired it in the air to scare them off. But then . . I would have located myself. "Nope," I thought, "better to keep out of sight." I slid into an upsidedown old Chevy sedan. It was a late forties model with a torpedo back. Feeling safer I almost relaxed for a second when I swore I heard something close by. I mean it was hard to hear anything . . hard to hear yourself breathe with all the racket of barking dogs and rocks smashing, but it sounded faintly like . . someone else's breathing.

I'd forgotten about the pit bulls. Damn! I reached for my boot knife. I'd left it back in the motor home. Double damn, I hate forgetting things. There I was combatively compromised, scrunched down in an overturned car unable to move my legs in front of a land shark. I was trying to get my shirt off to stuff in its mouth (I'd forgotten about the blackjack in my pocket) when the breathing noise rasped louder and I saw its shadow loom out from the wrecked Chevy in what little moonlight was left of this night.

Then, turning on its vertical axis the shadow reached a perpendicular height, embodied itself and physically fell on me. It was a man! . . lying on his back on my lap!

"Excuse me," his voice held the moment. "I'm the night watchman."

He grinned a gold tooth grin and reeked of stale clothes and tequila.

"Would you like a drink?", he rather begged for a civil reply.

"Yes sir! Si Senor! I would celebrate it." We helped half drag each other out from under the old car and sat in the sand. Rocks were still bashing into Bill's vehicle and scattering around the wrecked ones now as well.

He nodded his head up toward the flying rocks as he passed me the tequila saying, "Mis ninos . . my boys. They want me to come home."

"Good idea!" I said, grabbing his belt and shirt collar . . assisting him to stand. With paternal force he cried out into the night, "Bastante boys, bastante. I'm coming home now, mi amigo, glancing at me . . my friend here will drive us home."

Immediately five boys between ten and seventeen I'd say came flying around our row embracing and kissing their padre. They left just as obediently believing more than I did that this night watchman was on his way home. "Good boys," he said to me, "their mother sometimes upsets them."

Holding up the bottle, "a few more, por favor" and he sat down again. I did too. We more formally introduced ourselves and talked through a few more drinks. We talked about Mexico, Cuba, and California, and I talked about Detroit, Walter, Shel and Jan. About the time I was deciding sand and night air were as complimentary to tequila as salt and lime . . Bill drove up.

His dogs greeted him as joyously as the ninos had their father.

We greeted him. He apologized about the time and handed me keys to the Chrysler. I gave him keys to the Ariel pointing to where it was parked. He noticed the blackjack sticking out of my pocket.

"Their mother upset the boys again tonight," the night watchman reported.

"Oh shit . . .," Bill yelped and went worrying around the damaged periphery of his property.

I drove the night watchman home. Arriving at his house he sighed and said, "ah my wOman . . . young man you should have a wOman. Marry soon and forever. Marry a young wone with few bad habits who loves Dios mas que . . even more than you. You weel not . . . none of us do. You weel not stay fascinating forever. Dios does!! If she loves heem she will put up with you. Be true to her and she will give you sons to chase away the devil even if he's drunk inside of you."

Leaving, he stayed on his feet and said, "Buenos Noche, Companero."

Since then my thoughts have stayed not inevitably but universally fatal.

Since then I've tried never to take advantage of tomorrow.

Notes

1. Anomie: Emile Durkheims term for alienated social condition caused by degenerating societies disintegration of accepted conventional codes.

2. tall southerners: had been targeted for recruitment as policeman by L.A. county administrations since the twenties. They were generally thought to be recruited in order to keep all those people of color in line.

3. "up south in Indiana": Martin Luther Kings term for the Hoosier state.

4. "lumpenization": prevalent influence of slothful undisciplined criminalized lumpen underclass culture.

5. Panthers: Black Panther Party

6. gusanos: Cuban revolutionary name for anti-communist Cubans worming their way into North American corruption and violence.

7. Blackstone Rangers: a well known south side Chicago black youth gang of the time.

8. "Fruit of Islam": Trained and disciplined bodyguard retainers for Elijah Mohammed's Black Muslims.

9. 'blue painted Celts on a hill': classic image of pan Celtic temper tantrum that always scared the Romans but rarely harmed them.

10. The Prophet Outcast third of Issac Deutscher's famed biographical Trilogy on Trotsky. 1. The Prophet Armed. 2. The Prophet Unarmed. 3. The Prophet Outcast.

11. N.S.A National Student Association: Nationwide student delegate assembly. Later exposed as CIA subsidized against leftist influence.

12. S.D.S. Students for a Democratic Society: Some of whom thought they lived in one.

13. SNCC: Student Nonviolent Coordinating Committee. Leader Stokely Carmichael was founder of first Black Panthers Party in Lowndes County, Mississippi. Black Power advocate forced to seek exile in Africa.

14. A militant . . "ist" not an . . "ite": Trotskyist connotes a follower of Trotskys revolutionary analysis, ideas, and program. Trotskyite connotes a mere follower of his personality.

15. Jim Cannon: Celebrated Grand Old Man of American Communism and Founder of the 'Socialist Workers Party'. Early spokesman for Trotskys opposition to Stalin and critical supporter of the Soviet Union. Author of many books and articles including "Notebook of an Agitator" and "The First Ten Years of American Communism".

16. John Reed: All American Red, Freemason, Journalist and Revolutionary Communist who wrote "Ten Days that Shook the World". His honored remains still lie buried in Moscow's Red Square. Stalin's do not.

17. William Foster: Pioneer American communist. Peer of Jim Cannon. Reported to have returned from Moscow with the famous line "Trotsky has the program but Stalin has the power." Foster followed the latter; Cannon the former.

18. Vincent Ray Dunne: Labor leader of the Minneapolis General Strike. Founding member, Leader, and significant strategist of American Socialist Workers Party; second in command to Jim Cannon. Possible kinsman on me mothers side.

19. Jack London: yeah that "Son of the Wolf" (1900) . . early twentieth century American writer (1876-1916) who also wrote "The Call of the Wild" (1903), "The Sea Wolf" (1904), "White Fang" (1906), and "The Iron Heel" (1908). He founded The Communist League of America in between books.

20. Gene Debs: (Eugene Victor Debs 1855-1926) American Labor leader from and of Terre Haute, Indiana. He led the Great Pullman Strike of Chicago and led the Socialist Party USA. He received the highest record of third party votes for President while in Sandstone Prison for anti war activity.

21. Riley (James Whitcomb Riley 1849-1916): Internationally known Indiana Poet who frequently wrote dialect celebrating the virtues of common people. Comrade, friend and drinking pal of Gene Debs.

> *"The erotics of definition making is a special human pleasure."*
> Diane Ackerman, *An Alchemy of Mind*

UNDER THE VULTURE'S EYE

My months in Mexico were like Spain . . . and North African dysentery . . . only worse. I couldn't stay on my feet healthy for more than three days. I might have cried around about it like a tourista but for the stench on this mountain bus . . . a revelatory stench from the shit stains on these peasants' pajamas. We were in yaqui high country and they filled up the bus, these indios, these men of native soil to this place, not an alien lefty like me and yet their G.I. tract did no better than mine here. We broke bread together, sharing broken bowels, broken Spanish and a crepitant breaking of days.

Headquarters were in Cuernevaca. We lived and slept in the shade near the statue of Zapata. The priests . . . there were many, said they prayed for me. I saw them all becoming Camillo Torres![1] They saw us as peculiar psyches, I think . . . American remnants of leftist re-enlightenment.

Trotzkos were crowding consciousness onto the streets of Mexico City and we spoke to them, no siempre[2] at the Universidad, but in slum apartments, in old cars flying around the mariettas and at the bullring watching Cordobes. Sometimes we spoke to muralists memories of General Villa in courtyards with the sound of caged green parrots in our conversation and sometimes in swank Haciendas with flamingos on the lawn . . . and we would listen to the words of Father Czeslaw, as dark and quiet as the seminary ambience of our dorm barracks. No one . . .can damn the upper classes like a quiet Dominican.

We spoke of Cuba and liberation theology; and how Dom

Helder Camara's notion of the 'New Marx' was to be a collective mentation of labor, intellect and prayer led by guerilla students, clerics, and family men who loved the people as their Lord loved them. Transcontinental Revolution[3] had begun! There were to be one . . . two . . . three Vietnams.[4] Che's army was in the South Central jungles and coastal cities trembled. We knew ourselves to be in the vanguard cadre verging toward some elusive future because of the words we used. They held above all other powers (including the Angels) dominion over our thought.[5]

In natural law, as volcanic as Mt. Popo[6] the revolutionary tide was rising and we would lead the people to power, and prevent them from being too brutal to their fallen brethren. We heard from nuns in Nicaragua and were lulled by Destiny removing her bra in the waves . . . and yet, there was another kind of weather, too.

A glum dome in humid skies still fenced our future. It hung above us like the disapproving smile of Ivan Illich,[7] and those vultures that hunt the stench of dead horses in the suburbs . . . stifling our senses as the putrid whiffs of poor ass supper brought up the hill in galvanized bathtubs in the trunks of taxis because the rector insisted we eat the peoples food.

You are what you can't eat because you think too much about it. As Che went without salt in the rain forest we began to note our losses. In route, we retreated back across the border for penicillin, pasteurized cold milk, norte plumbing and . . . cheeseburgers.Later Illich visited Indiana and never held us as clones of a previous season. To him all souls were deciduous . . . we were and are changing foliage that somehow stay the same. A topiarius[8] of new, old, new words may yet define our future . . . beingness.

UNDER THE VULTURE'S EYE: NOTES

1. Camillo Torres: Diocesan Priest in Columbia who became a revolutionary leader and martyr.

2. Siempre: A comfortably removed and generally popular Mexican leftist magazine.

3. Transcontinental Revolution: a slogan of Revolutionary Cuba.

4. One, two, three Vietnams: (Che) Geuvarrista slogan.

5. Wordsworth "Words are too awful an instrument for good and evil to be trifled with; they hold above all other external powers a dominion over thoughts!"

6. Mt. Popo: Volcanic peak near Cuernevaca in Morelos.
That same mountain of Malcom Crowley's "Under the Volcano".

7. Monsignor Ivan Illich: Priest of Austrian Jewish origin conceptualizing "reverse development" and "deschooling society." Founder of CIF, Center for Intercultural Formation in Morelos.

8. topiarius: The art of training trees, shrubs, and hedges.

SILENCERS
(Serious about Henry David Thoreau and Walt Kelly)

The old black citroens swung low

on the leafy boulevard

making hydraulic sounds

as it started to rain.

I loved those old cars, they were the kind

that bullfight promoters drive outside Granada,

but they were not fast enough for the work today

and I worried more than a little about it.

We were to intercept them high

above the curve on the embankment

they would be coming fast, but accelerating

into the downhill slope.

I was a Silencer,

but we were all leading lives

of disquiet . . even noisey desperation.

THE BYZANTINE

His mind was a battlefield. He'd woke to the civil war sounds of 1916 Mexico. Robert Mitchum and Gilbert Roland were blowing up mexican masses on the late show. He did not wake with a start, rather a resigned acceptance that his senses were receiving yet more of the same to come. These summer months his synapses had become battlements to record little but stress of the seasons.

The concept of God used to be a projectile he'd try to watch himself from . . "from above that point where all the waves crash", he'd said. Now he thought the concept, even if true, to be an unhelpful one. "Too much akin to drugs and idealism", too close to obliviousness when "they" are trying to cave in your head. Nothing is ever resolved. Steinbeck had said that a hundred different times, and best through Brando in the old Zapata screenplay. Keep your strength, pace your raids, and never expect to be left alone. Not for long anyhow. Maintain the guerilla's dignity of a constant offensive. Never whipped . . just in retreat; never resting but recuperating for another go at it.

Depending upon the degree of internal stress and the particular style with which it is coped . . people are said to have 'nervous breakdowns', 'mood disorders', 'drinking problems', excuse me 'substance abuse issues', ill tempers' and/or unpleasant personalities. Of these consciously considered options he preferred the latter.

Clancy Sigal, the writer who gained great mileage from the most publicized left wing psychosis in history notes that, "Marxists, however lapsed still require theoretical justifications for their behavior."

BEAT REGIONAL SPACES

Not since the Shawnee saw miles of rain cloud

darken storms along the Wabash

when scouts of their prophets pierced eye

with his interiorities perception

has the weather so beatified our region; whose

complete beauty brings terror to imageandnation.

Moderns in no rational peril run for cover

knowing its more than their car windows they've let down.

Harsh angeled weather; come hush the country in time.

Put out its lights and the techniques that whine

away from the weathermen whose tribes stayed true

to interior tears which still brave the cheeks . . .

of rain in our faces.

Miners Code
(Ghosts of Genesis County*)

The sound of silence made itself known to Ted

in the crowded café at the end of Jordan Avenue. In

graying divisions of silence all the way to Jasonville's

back bar they planned the wildcat strike and

blew up a convoy of trucks with dynamite he hid

in gift wrapping under the Christmas tree. Robin

was deported and Jim bought the farm in Fresno.

The rest of us still go to work in the morning.

*Genesis County: from Lynne Doyles' "The Riddle of Genesis County",
 Jasonville environs.)

QUIT CLAIM

I think it was about the assassinations.

That and Kent State.

The National Guard shoots some students and the so-called student rev. retreats into insignificance. Malcolm, Martin, and the Kennedys get whacked . . . to say nothing of us little guys getting set up and shot from Detroit to the Delta . . . even after Westmoreland's troops are defeated on the ground by Giaps . . . American consciousness continues its rout . . . cadre become consumers of F.B.I.-Gurued medication . . . females become a supra class phenomena and 'white male oppressor' rhetoric ridiculously replaces 'Imperialist Class Enemy'!

At which point masses of otherwise conscious human beings . . quit being and/or respecting men.

I for one quit being white.

White Negros

We read Norman Mailers 'White Negros' in the fifties.
We became white negros in the sixties. And when black people
quit being negros we were still stuck with it.

Wary of the ugly white majority we brislte for a fight
whenever they cross into the ghetto of our consciouness. Hoods
of lost context we haunt the periphery of post modern political in
corectness.

A glimpse of Julian Bond, a picture of Stokely, a memory of Bob Moses sustains our words as Malcom spoke in the
brave contradictions of Dr.King as right on as a Robert Williams
rifle club and radio cast from Cuba, we recall Ray Charles in
those friday night sounds from the steel mill towards a future out
in the streets becoming home we would overcome and overthrow
all those powers we still put up with... segregating our souls.

LUGGAGE RACK

Staying at the Mayflower in '76
I looked directly at John Connolly
near the luggage rack.
He had airport eyes and was concerned about his stuff.
He saw I recognized him, started to smile then saw I was looking
at him unlike a District hack.

His censors signaling I was far from regular here,
in an instant knowing I looked as if I knew
about Boss Clark, Bubba Justice, Mulekillers, and the
assassination of Presidents.

His eyes fumed away from the luggage
and bore upon me;
calling upon retainers I could not see.

With capacities of cruelty I could not know
furious with my existing at the Mayflower
or anywhere else on the globe.

This moment at the Mayflower luggage rack
was worth volumes from then on
I've always watched my back!

In the morning Letelier* was assassinated
by a car bomb
below our window.

*Orlando Letelier: former minister with Allende assassinated
by 'Operation Condor' i.e. Pinochet and the C.I.A.

UNCOMMON DENOMINATORS

The only common denominator shared by the 'civil rights' movement and so-called 'WIMMINS' and sexual rights rhetoric of liberals is the way they talk about them.

After sitting out the violent and non violent confrontations of unarmed people against armed racist power, liberal rhetoric now overcompensates with politically correct prattle equating history they missed with history they invented.

DÉTENTE

I loved the Soviet Union the way Solszhenetsin loved Russia. I knew its history better than he did . . . I thought. He'd had to live there, putting up with the present, hopeful from and for the past. I got to visit intermittently with conflicting sympathies for the present, hopeful for the future.

My hope for its future was somewhere between Trotsky's Prophecy and those of the Portuguese children at Fatima. Similarly my wife's interest was academic and critically sycophantic.

My first visit was in 1960 as a twenty-year-old. From London I'd hooked up with Aussie campers on their way to 'May Day in Moscow'. We damn near froze in the April snows of the Ukraine but made it as far as the suburbs of Moscow our teeth rattling together and salvia freezing against the zippers of our sleeping bags. A rough time we'd had of it when the Komsomol[1] visited our camp. Some of us were coming down with the flu.

There weren't many tourists back then. Technically we were considered "Guests of the State". It was also considered bad form for us guests to freeze to death while visiting for May Day.[2] The Komsomol rescued us into luxury hotels with attendant physicians to treat our influenza. My first experience with socialized medicine was sure better than paying for it. My doctor kept thinking I was 'Cubansky'[3] because of my beard and seemed delighted I was reading Trotsky's "History of the Russian Revolution." Marvelous hospitality!

Returning later . . . Soviet atmosphere was officially hospitable but edgy. No upper class arrogance, no racist remarks, no liberal whiners, no freaked out free market fascists, just a solid sea of Proletarian . . . rudeness which perplexed me. I associated rudeness with class snobbery or lumpen lack of what my mother called "home training." I'd hear people muse it came from being such a big country. The opposite say, of little England where Brits mumble "sorry, so sorry," incessantly in a crowd afraid of touching one another. That made no sense to me.

An American . . . my country was almost as big, and I came from its hinterlands, where working people would look you in the eye respectful and polite. Crowded cities anywhere were another thing altogether.

A Marxist . . . of midwestern extraction I did not and do not tolerate rudeness.

This time at the Hotel Metropole, a short walk from Red Square where I would pray for Lenin's cause beside Saint Basils, Rusky rudeness and me met head on.

My wife and I entered the dining room from a mezzanine area to find no private tables . . . just larger ones and most of them taken. We approached a table where guests were leaving. It was next to an even larger table that was completely taken. I pulled out a chair for my wife walking around the departing people . . . the long way around our table. Before I could seat my wife and scoot her chair in some son-of-a-bitch at the next table jumped up and practically pulled it out from under her for his table.

I spoke no words in English, nor attempted any Russian. I simply walked to their table and knocked him out of the chair returning it to my wife where it belonged. Once seated she convulsed to join the loud abusive sounding Russian from the other table. I stood and instructed her to tell them in her fluent Russian that it may be their country but it is our chair.

Silence ensued as they listened to her. Then slowly . . . raucous laughter from their table ordering us one bottle of Georgian Champaign after another all evening. Tensions eased and we concluded our Chicken Kiev and sweet Georgian wine . . . departing as good comrades in our collective cups.

During this summer of '09 there is much media attention given to the rudeness of "birthers", "deathers" and other (right) wing nuts disrupting "town hall" meetings regarding national health care. The usual list of suspects i.e. Power Elites are all playing the process. Pharmaceutical and Insurance Companies, money, medical doctors, Hospital Corporations and assorted networks of free market idolaters are terrorizing attempted civility here.

On the other side Federal Community Organizers are using the town halls to (a) allow the paranoid, rabid right-wingers to burn themselves out like the George Wallace Presidential Campaign of 1967. And (b) to expose and graphically illustrate with them that is, to blame them for their own [the Obama Administration] failure at achieving nothing more than a health insurance reform (and insurance subsidy) rather than a public national health plan. The liberal media (c) hyping outrage at the hysteria and ignoring completely the lefts case for single payer socialized medicine. Town Hall civil discussions of the same (Rep Elijah Cummins of Maryland has mentioned several) were never mentioned in the managed news.

In fairness to those miserably misled and mindlessly rude right wingers . . . they are merely acting out the anti-communist, anti-socialist, lies of mainstream American propaganda over the last half century. Educated liberals have known better. They've tolerated the outright and embellished lies as they could intellectually budget their disbelief. Simple patriots could not. The mindless militia member with crypto fascist convictions is the Frankenstein monster of liberal duplicity.

Any serious attempt to eliminate right wing rudeness would include invitations to every union local in the area. A significant presence of union men would inhibit rudeness by threatening a fuller explanation. That is to say, the organized working class would splain it to em'. Calibrated violence can be justified. Rudeness cannot. Frequently one is required to correct the other.

Notes

1. Komsomol: Young Communist League

2. May Day: For 100 years celebrated world wide except in post McCarthy America as The International Workers holiday.

3. Cubansky: Cuban

Comradely Conversation 1974
at St.Basils, Red Square, USSR

"Revolution is eternal!"
A banner in Havana.

"Only eternity confers upon existence complete integrity"
(W.B .Yeats)

"Eternity though motionless is in motion"
(Hermes in the Asclepius dialogue)

ETERNAL REVOLUTION

(September 2006) The old man of our revolutionary youth lies in his hospital bed. Thank God the socialist rev. of the Americas is no longer officially atheist. No longer the need for comradely knees to bend only in communist privacy. We republicize our prayers for him. That God forgive his sins and finally comfort his struggle for justice.

Fidel can now afford to see his brother as a family man. Orthodoxy is orthodoxy including natural law and clan.

We learned from the big country of Rabbi Bronstein that revolution is permanent.

Only little Cuba taught us it is eternal.

Gloryville

GLORYVILLE ROAD, FREEDOM, INDIANA 47431

DEDICATED TO PRODUCTION
RESEARCH OF QUALITY LIVESTOCK

Intinction:

*"The action of applying bread to wine at communion;
so that the two kinds are administered conjointly."*

SELECT PRODUCTION AND STUD IN: WELSH BLACK CATTLE ● MORGAN HORSES ● SUFFOLK SHEEP ● MAMMOTH JACKSTOCK ● ENGLISH SHEPHERD STN

3 INTINCTION

Sable Dawn 206

A Toast to Perfection 207

Adagio for Uncle Tom 208

Geese 209

Conatus 210

Torso Murderer 211

September Skies 213

Shepherds Quake 214

Galen 216

Ourselves and the City 225

Cats of Rome 226

Chaos Theory 228

The Lot of my Relation 229

Papa, I'd Prefer A Kinder Stable 230

Me and my Shark Attack 231

Shades of St. Kiril 234

Weather for Packy Pahl 235

Judy Dukes (Hautbois) 238

The Terrier Man 239

Rumis Better Past 239

Harder to Kill 241

Hands of the Shepherd 242

Rapport with the Fishes 243

Rabbit on the Lawn 244

Toast to Saint Catherine 244

Deocentricities 245

The Fall of Light 246

Gulls in Gary 247

By Way of Requital 248

Northern Imam 248

Noon Wine 248

Intinction 249

SABLE DAWN
(A tri-color morning, like the collie's coat)

It was our first year of marriage and my last year at I. U. We would drive the sixty miles to my parents home at least once every month or so, where it always seemed like Christmas when I think of it now. A family at rest in the lovelight of sit down dinners and color TV.

One Monday morning, we rehearsed our fateful drive down old 46 to get back early. Traffic slowed around the elbow curve near that place with a white brick farmhouse and Charlaise cattle in the yard. A school bus had stopped and we smiled at the waiting children and their collie; it made the morning sable. That is, lustrous, clear . . . and oblique. We smiled at these school kids and we smiled at each other for there was promise in life and wreckage yet unborn with so many good things still left in the country.

Two children of our own later, we crashed on that same road.

A TOAST TO PERFECTION

There was this scent of Autumn in the dust when the drought hung on and made you sweat from the inside out if you worked in it. Me and the dogs worked 200 head through the heat of the day, because of the Vets morning call and meetings that night.

The cold brown bottle glimmered up out of the basement ice box and I really set to that beer . . Cleansing spirit through the earthbound dust . . cold grain comrade for a million busted hearts. I carried it low like a nightstick into the bedroom and found them all asleep.

My wife, brown as an olive branch with snows of the abruzzi in her veins and a small earring resting on her face . . resting on the pillowed white beside my infant son whose exorcised saints name is burnt into his frowned nursing. His lips now still upon her quiet breast.

More than half the great bed taken by the crown princess memory of some ancient celtic race. Three feet of captured beauty, the Renoir ringlets of my daughter tumble recklessly about her perfect face. I kiss her splendidness. I touch the boys furrowed brow and bend upon their mother. She wakes with a little squealing like a mare resisting season. She was startled and didn't like it. I liked it fine. Strange . . how I've always been drawn to females who are close veined and jumpy.

Quieted, she drifts back into the picture. She is a wife whose tawny beauty grows with weight and age and whose mind regains precision; like a scholars orange is ripened by the evening sun. Not the darkened anima of youth whose pain and thundered structures remain to plague my soul, but an olive leaf of wonder whose hips and heart have saved me from myself . . . with children who are the flesh and bone and blood of love resacrificed above this plundered plain of Sharon.
Humility concedes perfection
wife, daughter, infant son.
Amen

ADAGIO FOR UNCLE TOM

My Uncle Tom was called a Wobbley,
among other things,
he'd been a hobo raider
in that continental riot
of the unemployed
where I.W.W. men carried red cards
in their shoes
and leaned on Chinese waiters
who'd scream, "Here comes the I. Wobbly Wobblies."

He worked on chain gangs
as a guest of the South
and organized for the U.M.W.
in the coal fields of Western Indiana,
then became a tenant farmer
for the last of his life
dying the same season he finally
paid for his own equipment.
My mothers sister was his wife.
On the fourth of July, he'd explain to neighbors
how flag waving was a remnant
celebration of the pharaohs naval cord
causing feed salesmen to fly off the handle.
He'd fight them to the ditch in town and win.

GEESE

Trebled notes in a cloudbank
sky written sound
seen through charred March pines

I call to them
they come near
then into an updraft . . . and are gone

Fading scar upon the brow of tomorrow
gone upon prevailing drafts
or possibly

to brake toward earth's
availing streams

CONATUS

There were two gaggles of geese on the pond.

Seven striking adults of grey and white and black

next to nine goslings from the spring hatch.

One youngster had the color of a bright leaf upon its breast.

Closer I could see the crimson was a raw shot wound.

I pondered the nature of this injury and its cold wet rest.

Were lice gathering from the fleet of warmth yet

still afloat . . could its flight come on to match

interior flyways of its thought to get

to the hunter who botched his shot

into pangs of keen spasm from his natures not

even keeping the company of a dog?

I'll never hunt geese without a retriever.

Who says I can't be a moderate believer.

TORSO MURDERER

[In the early 70's a killer was wanted in Central Indiana who allegedly scattered his victims body parts around the country. A torso was found in the white river near Freedom. I became a brief . . chief suspect.]

She was our first foal and boys were we proud. Gray as a mouse she had that Blackhawk Morgan look of eagles in her eye; a memory of Justin's' race and Brigadier Dans cavalry envelopment.

Her mother was old government bred, full uddered and . . . the placenta passed quickly. We questioned what to do with all that afterbirth. Our neighbor who raised Arabians advised not to bury it with all the dogs around; "better to sack it for the dump in town".

It was near dawn, I went to sleep but first I gunny sacked the boiling bloody pulp into the Oldsmobile's trunk. I stacked it on car tools next to a set of army harness I'd gotten from the Amish.

While I lay sleeping a boy from the garage came to get the car. I'd forgotten it was scheduled to be painted black today. I woke in time to catch him heading out our lane. "You'll have to remember," I said, "to go by the Dump, take the bloody sack of afterbirth out of the trunk and put it in the fire. Please don't forget it."

He popped his gum, it made a smack switching the tuner through radio stations, he said, "OK man, don't sweat it!" then drove straight to the garage. He did forget it.

. . . and I became chief suspect as the torso murderer.

After no one in the town looked at me for two weeks;
(God forgive me I enjoyed it)
the matter was cleared up the more it bled
everyone grinned and slapped my back,
"Wodn't that silly!" they said.

Belltree atop Gloryville Farm

SEPTEMBER SKIES

The red wine of september skies

drives one inside

for evening pleasure

tannin promise

of comfort from life scrimmaged lies.

"There are no more dreadful revolutions, than revolutions of the left carried out by men of rightist temperament"
Jacques Mauritain
Peasant of the Garonne

"The opposite however need not be true"
TGM
Shepherd of Freedom

See Samuel Palmers *"Moonlight, a Landscape with Sheep"*
circa 1830's
and Dorothey Wordsworths *"Moonlight Lay Upon the Hills like Snow; the glittering silver line on the ridge and backs of sheep"*
circa 1790's.

I was called back at midnight from the Chancery meeting to my farm in Freedom, Indiana. The flock had strayed.
The flock was out!

SHEPHERDS QUAKE

Into the humid earth; moist and sweet smelling, like the warm cool flesh of a young wife. The earth was a woman; a mother and wife, more mysterious than both wrapped in a loose garment of mist . . the odors of dew and the flock bobbing, then floating ahead.

We were the night and earth, slopes and swells . . my eyes and the flock reached the back fence mid point of the hill after we had come up one side along the corn field, then wound down the summer trail into a bottom, heard deer, circled, and turned back again. The back fence we faced was full of briars and small brush.

Before I pressed the flock closely I heard the sound of fence straining posts, and soft landings of hooves as each sheep jumped through the middle strand leaving a wooly necklace on the middle wires. Rachel jumped last. She was bigger and got tangled a bit . . grunted, fell, made a little panicked sound and then trotted clear.

I pressed through the thorny dew with briars against my legs . . checking the old dangling wire for signs of sheep, then grabbed the wooly post, using the middle and top strands to step on to and over the fence.

Looking up . . . Aggoriamento!

I hardly recognized a single line of the sloping canvas . . . crossing the fence much farther east and stunned by the beautiful strangeness of unexpected presence in my own hill pastures, saw how slowly, the bell shaped tree on the ridge loomed up under muted light, the small thorn tree grew near the silver maples down the hill and the great almost cosmic expanse of sloping pastures between this, and the point where I knew the house to be . . . finally appeared.

Reconnoitering, I found the sheep looking toward me . . . waiting . . . got behind them and started down through the mist toward the maples. The four big silver trees rose from each corner of the house like great sentinels granting shade, even at night.

There was sound like a winged unicorn in the trees, quietly galloping along the branches, into the leaves, the air, then down to the grass . . . the sound converged in a wide arc, a smiling dark spectre of speed as Abel dog came under the gate.

Not a sound in our joy we greeted each other while the sheep strung out like a caravan at night watching us . . . trustfully.

GALEN

Galen was what in Owen County is called a backward number. A Purdue graduate, but like his brothers he returned to the hard scrabbled home place, that was forty acres out near the gypsum ground. They'd run a trap line, a few cattle, some sheep, chickens . . . then hunt and fish year round. They'd also take an odd job or two.

I hired Renos for my first shearing. Ben and Kenny helped me build a barn. And Art helped put up hay. Galen did it all. They were all reliable, honest, and hard working. Galen was the middle child of six and excelled at everything he intended. He played the guitar, and liked to sing; . . was sensitive, tough, and very intellectual in his own country way. He read the local papers and farm magazines, knew the Gospels and Old Testament chapters and verse; if I mentioned a book he'd ask for it, read it, return it, and talk about it. He could fix pumps, applicances, and do wiring.

Militantly loyal to his family, he stayed out and lived out in the woods with them most of his life.

They rarely bathed. They wore hand me down, good will, and home spun not regularly laundered with a more than slightly sour smell about them. They didn't like town, didn't go to the dentists, and herbal home remedies were preferred to doctors. They excelled at school but refused regular jobs. They didn't go to ball games or school dances and never crowed about being veterans. Conservative poor country people they were patriotic about the land but not its governance.

Their mother would tend the truck garden and can in the fall with the girls while the boys went occasionally with their

Dad, a master plumber who was "on call for service work." Most of the calls he'd accept, but primacy was time with his family. They loved each other; cared and provided for each other. Theirs was a self reliant, self-isolated, unselfish family unit.

One sub zero night in Christmas week when they were all huddled around the tree or gone to bed, a fire broke out within the walls of their old drafty, ramshackle house. Earlier that evening, the boys and their Dad had thawed frozen pipes with a blowtorch. The homemade insulation of corncobs, creosote, and varnish had kindled for hours and then quickly ignited in several sections. A conflagration followed seen for miles around. They hustled out into the snow, carrying Christmas gifts to watch their home and worldly goods be destroyed by fire.

The very next morning my mother was there with sacks of warm used clothing. Galen quietly thanked her but then with his accented mid-central vowels added . . . "What we really need is money!"

Outraged by such assertive honesty, Mom raged for days about "ingrates and ingratitude!" I tried to assure her he was simply telling the truth. Indeed like my mother Galen was tactlessly committed to the truth.

He truthfully told the draft board he opposed the war in Vietnam. Years earlier I had bluffed the draft that my opposition to the war would require my shooting any commanding officer who ordered me to harm or bomb innocent people. A friendly black sergeant winked and said, "Man they won't even draft you for the next war" [as if they already had one planned.] Draft boards got tougher and more desperate for gun fodder. They processed Galen quickly, trained and sent him to the front. Ambivalently on patrol he spotted a sniper who didn't see him. Galen wouldn't shoot a man unawares nor would he signal his own location. He stayed secluded and silent just watching the sniper scratch and doze. Galen hoped he would go to sleep completely so he (Galen) could crawl off and away. It didn't happen.

What did happen was Galen's hunter sharp eyes spotted a tiger about forty yards behind the sniper. It became clear the tiger was stalking the snipers tree stand. Galen prayerfully thought his Christian duty was to shoot the tiger and save the man. He also knew it was his military duty to shoot the sniper. Instead of either he went home in his mind to a hundred coon hunts where he'd had to let go the idea of his presence making any difference to nature. Willful hunters were always impatient and unpleasant at the tree. Galen had learned to keep the night pleasant by not hollering, throwing or shooting the coon out of the tree . . . rather he would allow its attempt to another tree wherein it would fall and be dispatched by the hounds or make it escaping into the night which was always full of more hunting.

Galen watched the tiger take the man. "First the mans lower right leg, tearing his harness then munched his mid section, rib cage and finally his head." This was done quickly and pretty quietly he said. Galen waited til the tiger dragged "most of the man" away in an opposite direction before crawling off.

Galen was as pleasant as an old timer even in his youth. I remember him smiling his approval when I shared Elwood Dowd's line from Jimmy Stewarts "Harvey"*. "My mother always said that in this old world you have to be very, very smart . . . or pleasant. I've been smart . . . I'd recommend pleasant." And like Harvey the Pucca . . Galen had that uncanny knack of not only "overcoming time and space, but any objections to it."

* "Harvey" authored by Mary Chase. The movie directed by Henry Koster.

When I moved back to Indiana, my second wife split with my third child. Another autumn follicle![1] Winter was moving in. I was depressed and my roof needed repair. I called Galen. He drove the hundred some miles after church and we inspected the roof together. It was three stories high gabled and dangerous. I'd bought the pitch and other roofing materials. I was eager . . maybe even jumpy to get started. Galen demurred. "Not today. I'll be back . . later."

Later . . turned into three weeks . . damn near a month! It was almost too cold for us to work the hot pitch but we managed. After a long hard day on the steep precarious roof we retired to beers in the kitchen.

"I'm sure glad you're feeling better," he said.

"Whaddaya mean?" I kind of protested.

"Last month you were so depressed . . you didn't give a damn. I thought you might fall off the roof."

"I might have . . ," I had to lamely admit.

My wages were being garnished. I started private practice to dodge the damages. One new patient was a big, lovely young gal so alone and depressed she hadn't slept for six months. She had some suicidal ideation. I contracted an anti-suicide agreement with her including encouragement to phone me night or day if in crisis. Crisis management led to many phone calls at all hours. She got better, but kept calling.

One early dawn when I was preparing for a Galen visit to help me worm my flock of Cheviots[2], she i.e. Peggy phoned and wanted to talk. I hadn't time to talk . . but listened. I listened so long I almost went to sleep when I heard Galen's old truck. Looking out I saw him stumble from the truck, turn and try to adjust its broken door handle. I told Peggy I thought she was qualitatively better . . that more than a counselor she needed a husband. And . . I had one for her!

I would arrange for him to call on her this afternoon and recommended a matinee at the old Indiana Theatre. Galen and I discussed the situation as we wrestled the Cheviots. "She is a jilted, big but lovely gal who is feminine, sweet tempered, traditional and ready . ."

"Ready for what . . ?" he asked.

"Ready to be courted! Whaddaya expect?" I tried to describe Peggy realistically and attractively.

As we finished our livestock work Galen leaned on the head gate and announced, "She sounds like my sister."

I knew that meant go. I directed him to the shower . . giving him scissors for his overgrown beard . . telling him I'd loan and lay out one of my grey suits, an old Packard shirt and my regimental tie. He wouldn't fit in my boots so we shined his up as best we could. Then we swept years of trash out of his truck cab. I thanked and paid him for his work explaining directions to Peggy's and sent him off by noon. It was Galen's first [conventional] social engagement.

He politely called at her door and they were immediately and mutually attracted. On their way to the movies they communicated easily. That is, until there was trouble at the ticket window.

"It was strange," she reported how Galen insisted the tickets he was buying be "tickets together . . so that for sure we'd sit together." Holding up the line, after receiving his ticket, he insisted again that the clerk double check the ticket numbers to insure they were tickets together so they would for sure sit together. Galen had come to town!

Soon Galen was staying in town. Peggy quit needing to call me .. and they were married within the year. It was a beautiful wedding at Sugar Groves Free Methodist Church. My parents old neighborhood .. they were fond of Galen and gladly attended. So did Galen's extended family, Peggy's family and others. One other was a beautiful bridesmaid I married the following year.

Galen and Peggy's first child was born eleven months after the wedding. A perfect little boy they named Christopher.[3] The newborn developed lung complications and was rushed by ambulance from Union to Riley Children's Hospital in Indianapolis. Enroute he was unconscious for more than an hour. Riley pronounced him severely brain damaged and it was months before they discharged him. Months before Peggy and Galen could take their baby home. The infant could not breathe or eat without tubes, could not utter any sound and whose life expectancy was only a few more months. He was sent home to die.

Galen wasn't having any of it. "There's an opportunity in every crisis" was a credo of Galens. "You have to deal with every hand that Providence dealt," he'd say. He had sadly thought for years he might never have children. Now, he not only had a son; but a son that required extra care, extra effort and work in parenting. And Galen knew that extra work created extra value. This opportunity for extra care would produce an extraordinary child and valued parental situation. He dove into the work of caring for his needy, needy child.

Months turned into years. The child did not die. Everyone reported the "miracle" and the incredible rapport Galen had with his little afflicted son. Mom, that is .. Peggy . . . was happy too. And she was pregnant again. They came to visit as the boy turned two.

Peggy was sickly and having a difficult pregnancy. She worried about Galen and Christopher. Galen was as always confident and optimistic. The doctor's prognosis kept announcing their son's life expectancy in months. Galen knew doctors didn't "know half of what they carry on about or bill for" and defied their predictions. Peggy confided to my wife she prayed Christopher would die peacefully in his sleep instead of agonizing through all these months. In between construction jobs Galen was putting away part of his unemployment check for Christopher's college fund.

At dinner we lay little Christopher down on the floor by our table. They had to watch him carefully at all times. When a silent tear appeared on his cheek they knew he was uncomfortable and would check his feeding and breathing tubes. He was never able to utter a sound, stand, or walk. His arms and hands became a bit more coordinated. Throughout dinner these ever so tried parents would have to jump up and jiggle his tubes.

I had to lie down after dinner. The arduous struggle and suffering of this family overwhelmed me. Galen had energetically said good night. Peggy was silent. In a few months she successfully delivered a healthy daughter. Christopher's condition did not change. It neither worsened nor improved the next two years. Galen continued to indefatigably defy the doctors these last two years. Then his big heart busted. Galen died.

We buried him grief-stricken to know Peggy would have to institutionalize their son. When she left Christopher at The Home she also left a fifteen-minute videotape. A small T.V. screen was arranged by the boy's bed with his own remote replay button. The video was of Galen saying goodbye to Peggy and Christopher. Just an ordinary going off to work goodbye . . . cept 'ol Galen knew how to milk an exit. There was serious talk about the weather, some joshing, and many "love yous", and kisses.

The Home hospital staff soon complained that Christopher was obsessively replaying the tape several times every hour of every twenty-four hours he was conscious. This was discouraging to the staff. They asked Peggy to remove the tape. She refused. And in that institutional darkness of professional smiles and purchases of friendship little Christopher kept watching his Dad for the next and last four years of his life.

That we all should have such sacral memories . . . I recall when my own good memories fade a little and I think of this child and his brave replaying of his fathers image.

1. Autumn Follicle: veterinary disease mainly in mares and bitches causing interminable heat cycles. (see p.354)

2. Cheviots: fine woolen sheep originally from Scotland.

3. Christopher: The Christ Bearer

"Cities were from the day of their first construction, incapable, because of the motives behind their construction, of any other destiny than that of killing the country, where God put man to enable him to live his life as best he could. Solidarity with the city is the solidarity of the captive with his keeper. We must unceasingly proclaim Gods curse and judgment on the city; but we must also pray that it will not happen. Our accomplishment of this act shows we are not captive like the others. This is the exact line between ourselves and the city."

Jacques Ellul
"The Meaning of the City"

"Who else can cause a prayer to peal
From the Wintry bells of Moscow
Or harder still, to cause
A single, dialectical, thought in Indianapolis"

TGM
"The Peoples Poet", *Not of Our Time*

OURSELVES AND THE CITY

(Indy 1967)   Russified revolutionary solidarity was gigging my maverick tendencies. Traveling black ghettos through developing Mexican corridors on the west side to the lily white countryside was perverse political geography.

Corridors of consciousness from Morelos to the Naptown races made me the "Intellectual vs. the City" rejecting Pasternak's urban recommendation for Gueverra's rag tag rural romances. The only thing good about the city I thought was its cinema and churches, the horse track, and people of color.

One Sunday afternoon break from studies . . . in sunshine and fresh snow, on into the near suburbs . . . not the pretentious fox hunter farms far north but the one step above working stiff suburbs of the west and near north side . . . between trips to the airport and the inner city we'd glimpsed them. Now arriving in skiffs of snow surrounding the grey wolf uniformity of the huskies . . . we saw them kenneled and tied out in well kept pens . . . racing sleds lashed on to outbuilding sheds and displayed like snowshoes above mantles with one odd ½ X Airedale . . wry, rusty brown, rough groomed and mud game . . . a dissident to the sleek Siberian racing teams.

I was the X Airedale.

CATS OF ROME
(A RESPONSE TO SCANDAL)

There are … cathouses in Rome,
but ol' puss on the prowl is of much greater interest,
roaming the ruins and rubbing every stone
that's been part of a prayer to heaven.
Long and rangy, more like whats seen in Amish barns
than the Dubonnet of european store fronts.
Some .. kind of mangy, killing mice in the catacombs
they stalk their own ancestry which witnessed
legions parade tribute and slaves past
their pails of cream and feline poverty;
gladiators, lions, martyrs, and the firestorm
catching Barabbas in the streets.

Perverse crucifiction of Peter bringing Palaces of Prayer
built from Constantines guilt with serious stones from the
Abrruzzi; pirates den of priestly grandeur, magisterial
power to conserve the truth and enforce the good.
Open city cats in black shirts, but some with red flags
mewing through the omerta of mafiosi and … moderation.

Secret squalls of Silone as Revolutionaries
becoming police spies who were revolutionaries;
they've sunned themselves in the radiance of
John the 23rds smile and sheltered
in the Celestine chill of Paul the Sixth.

They witnessed the wisdom of J2P2, the incredible
consciousness of Woytiwa convening the American cardinals,
Gregory, McCarrick, and Stafford; cats who need not
hold their tails in the air . . . We know
 that Jimmy Stafford would hold them
the way Don Corleone did. And yet
they remain remote in their cat-like
lack of confidence in holiness and/or
hypocrisy. More is at stake here
than protecting kittens. The very nature
of the beast is at issue.

    And yet, I join their remoteness;
the trouble with us cats
is ... we only once were lions!

CHAOS THEORY

No visceral cue required, no melting clocks from mad
Spaniards for a queer friend on the sidewalks of Saint
Georges . . . Matins rang, but so has Vespers.

Memory prefers the shade of answers temptation to em-
bellish microbial chaos instead of breaking prayers straight-
forward and fast as the weanlings gait across dawn pastures.

Shadows race in peripheral vision. One is part of His
great palette or one is not . . refracted uniquity in a wasted
paint can rational and irrational desire be defeated?

Always! By the limits of unlimited weather.

THE LOT OF MY RELATION

Drudgery with dreams attached

Is the lot of my relation

Whose minds fly faster through the fields than deer

But, the matter of act is held

Within old scarcity's will.

An auctioned, one eyed, foundered, pinto horse

And thoughts of racking beauty

To race the Friends for church

With enough mornings, standing in the creek

And hours of driving with good blinders on.

Yet he'll be bought and left forever in the muck

A knawing pain of non actualization

A spotted flaw in timeless imagination.

PAPA, I'D PREFER A KINDER STABLE

The cold

that darkly waits

in barns dark corners

standing stiff and cluttered

for the cruel new month

clots an anxious drudgery

that even blooded horses can age,

but not dispel.

Ideas excel racing gaits

and the sorrel strengths of intelligence

require, organized tack

and a clean well heated place.

ME AND MY SHARK ATTACK

Peter Benchly's "Jaws" was published, and first filmed years ago. I had satisfactorily frightened my nephews by taking them to see it. Its theme music almost scared them out of the theatre before the show started. Later my infant daughters first alarm at television came during that same theme music for "the land shark" episode on 'Saturday Night Live'.

Five years later we're at Fort Walton Beach in Florida for a family vacation. We tend the kids and swim in the pool. The ocean of white beaches and surf seem limited to some wading but mostly for just looking at.

One morning instead of swimming laps I'm running on the beach and hear about how at a certain sand bar reef you can walk for miles out into the gulf in two to four feet of water with only an occasional ditch of deep water to swim over. It's perfectly safe I hear and stay to watch several vacationers walk way out there, only occasionally swimming across the deep places.

When I try the next morning, it is spectacular. More than a mile out, the deep places were no more than waist or chest high. You could wade through them. Standing erect surrounded by miles of open sea was quite a sensation.

Over an outdoor lunch of fair Riesling and fresh grilled dolphin I was talking about it while assuring my daughter we were eating fish not Flipper.

Of course, my ever-brave little girl wanted to walk out into the ocean with her Papa. How could I refuse, even though the Jaws movie theme was now beginning to softly play in the periphery of my senses. "Most shark attacks occur in two to three feet of water" someone was saying from the screenplay to my subconscious, as I carried Bethany on my shoulders to the sand bar reef. No one else was around.

We walked through the surf together until it neared a foot deep; about half my daughter's height. Then I carried her the rest of the way. The deep places seemed a bit deeper to me now so I stopped about 100 yards out. The water was less than 2-½ feet here. You could see through it to the sandy bottom. I had turned, shifting my daughter's carriage position a bit when I saw it lying perfectly still on what I think is called my starboard side. Six feet long and stealthily pointing toward my legs. I did not move. Neither did it.

Afraid to alarm my daughter by shushing her angelic babble about how pretty everything was my mind raced as to how I could protect her from the ugly brute beside us.

Paralyzed with fear for another twenty seconds I thought the less movement, sound, or water disturbance might allow something else to distract it, but from the corner of my eye its undistracted focus seemed clearly honed in on us.

There were two deep water "ditches" between us and the beach. Maybe if in crossing them . . their current or the slight undertow out might distract him away from us . . . at least long enough for me to hurl my daughter to safer water shallow enough for her to run ashore. I'd take my own chances with the God damned shark remembering to hit him in the nose but not remembering exactly where a shark's nose is located. "Right above the front teeth!" I decided, while taking long steps toward the first ditch. It was about fifteen feet away.

Glancing behind me I could see it moving steadily toward us. Even if it followed us across this first ditch, I thought I could get Bethany across the second closer ditch whether or not it nailed me. I began to worry about a second or third shark.

We plunged through the first ditch and at first I thought

we'd lost him. I couldn't see him in the deeper water. Wading uphill to more shallow surf, he was immediately back and directed toward us . . his target.

To hell with it! I started galloping, my feet and legs above the surface as much as possible toward the last ditch. Somehow I made it to and through the ditch. Charging up out of it into the shallows I stumbled twice. The second time I threw Bethany as far ahead of me as possible. No time to stand and offer up my legs, I turned on my side in the water to face that fish. Bethany did not cry and he did not surface. I could not see the shark. Scooting backwards in the water toward my daughter I still couldn't see him.

I yelled for Bethany to go on to the beach. She didn't. She remained motionless. I remained motionless. Nothing. I worried it might be flanking me toward her, so I stood to see better. There it was . . right in front of me again. I took a step toward it this time and it retreated a step but stayed on point. Steps to the side were the same. Gratefully embarrassed I turned and allowed my shadow to follow me and my daughter all the way back to shore.

(1978) SHADES OF ST. KIRIL >J2P2

Ireland, Wales, Moscow, and the Abruzzi
Land of my fathers and sons
by blood, tripe, and spirit
The World in all its places change
But, seldom for the good

The tories grow confident again
Welsh hounds collaborate
running wirehaired and cob gaited
to thoroughbred monarchists
leaving another generation to stutter
in the hated language
with impotence and insistence
on the dragons tongue
instead of its color

The fascists show their teeth again in Rome
While everyone else gums their way to obesity
Never more than two hours from the table

Oritual paralysis is exorcised
only by the din of tecno-frenzy
swarming, lip smacking
sucking up to the Vatican
great swollen, surpliced pirates den
of pompous eunichs
its special stores and special whores of grandeur
are Destroyers of the centuries

Yet the lonely father there
haunted by old Peters crypt
and the tomb of smiling John
might convert all his enemies for St. Kiril
if he were delivered from his friends

WEATHER FOR PACKY PAHL
(CANADIAN HEAVYWEIGHT CHAMP)

The tanned wind of Albertan accents
lilt high and wide between jaws of
Bessarabian strength for great seas of
buffalo grass.

He'd gone twelve rounds with
Tommy Farr from Wales who'd survived twelve
 with the Brown Bomber in Chicago. Vicariously
surviving the best of Joe Lewis he drilled
for oil near Riyaddh and retired north of
Calgary with his young wife's cows. We feigned sparring on
his ranch and he sold me a son of "Dugoed Lyr" who
became "Wesh Nation" the biggest 2 year old
black bull in the world. We kept in touch . . . vicariously
sharing each others weather.

oryville Farm's Welsh Black herd with 'Welsh Nation' IN State 1976 Champion black bull
o thousand lbs, before two years old

Receives Trophy

Ann Case receiving a trophy from Tom Morgan, Gloryville Farm, for showing the first Welsh Black heifer in Indiana State. Ann purchased the heifer with the money she had earned from five years of showing livestock for 4-H. She plans to show the heifer again this year at the Sullivan County 4-H fair and the Indiana State Fair.

Crossing: Maternal Characteristics and Productive Efficiency

The rapid improvement of his brood cow herd is the fastest and best way for the commercial cow-calf man to improve his profitability. The use of large, rapid-gaining terminal sires has become commonplace, and there is little doubt that their progeny are more efficient in the feed lot.

Gloryville

GLORYVILLE ROAD, FREEDOM, INDIANA 47431

hyllech Memi 9th

Dugoed Derwyn
[Welsh Nation]

QUALITY

The most celebrated cow in Britain, Canada and the U.S. and the highest valued bull in North America are the foundation stock of the Gloryville herd.

Dedicated To Production Research Of Quality Livestock

ct Production and Stud in: Welsh Black Cattle • Morgan Horses • Suffolk Sheep • Mammoth Jackstock • English Shepherd Stockdogs

PAGE 3

Marketing – Welsh Black Cattle

I assisted the Benedictine Order import some of the first Chianina Cattle from Italy to Indiana. With the influx of New European breeds (Chiania, Limousin, Simmental, and Main Anjou) and their rapid gaining terminal bull sires in the Seventies a need arose for improved brood cows with adequate pelvic width and milk production to bear and raise this new beef.

We imported from Canada and Wales the first and finest Welsh Black Cattle with the families of David Fender, Jim Case, Jim Thurston, LeRoy Philips, Wayne Gobel, the Rev. Richard Holiday, and Emanuelle Packy Paul.

Won grand Champion with 'Welsh Nation.' Initial success at marketing the breed stifled by divorce and corporate calumny toward horns.

237

JUDY DUKES* (TERRE HAUTBOIS*)

In what yearning
her voice resounds
our every darkness.
Vast as the hidden sea
she .. sings tribute
beyond the measure
of incarnate times'
inchoate pleasure.

And our lives quiet a bit
to hear her
husky rivers of regret
move past the standards measure
and our lives quiet a bit
to hear her

to hear her sing it!

*Judy Dukes: Eloquent jazz singer from Terre Haute

*Hautbois: An organ stop giving an oboelike quality

THE TERRIER MAN

I was put off by Bud Halyard when I first met him.
I thought he talked like a game show host.

And his politics—you couldn't avoid them—seemed
somewhere to the right of the Dowager Empress.

Shod in expensive English boots he talked a lot about being an old fashioned American. I had him marked for a salesman
and it amused me when he called it marketing. But, he was one
hell of a stockman and proved to be the greatest friend I'd known.

RUMIS BETTER PAST

As horses remember Indiana perfectly . . .

one hundred years pace through the hardwoods

hymn of dappled shade; the sinew of energy

strains to be forgiven for hope whose time is past.

100 lbs so-called Hoosier Coyotes. Considered wolves anywhere else in the world.

HARDER TO KILL

I had become we ... and we had settled into the farm. Return of the native I felt before there was a funeral for my closest Aunt. And then there were children ... around the first Christmas. They came to visit. Half Hawaiian kids whose anglo mother thought her vagina transistorized. Their aunt brought them for a farm holiday. We loved them and hated .. hated to see them leave. Vicarious preview for what life is all about.

Not art nor politics, not careers or money but the intensive co-parenting of human issue in natures autonomously collective family units. I knew it as I was beginning to know about death and life on the land.

I would achieve it, lose it, and post-traumatically pursue it. Like the 'coyote' who affluently overdevelops, producing smaller litters to lose the careful cunning ways of threatened coyotes who produce larger litters becoming wiser through their parenting skill and are much ... much harder to kill.

HANDS OF THE SHEPHERD

The sting of cold inside the barns

is scalding; old winters lambing

is here as if I had nothing else to do.

Stressed hands in hot placentas;

cysts like inside wire buckle icily

above the snow as warm colostrum

in old Guiness bottles bring on new

life in the lambs bleating eyes.

RAPPORT WITH THE FISHES

The lake, loop, and lawns were hot as the top of an asphalt stove. Jazz in the afternoon taste of Chicago sweat toward the cool of the aquarium. We stopped on the way to hear Hindoos argue with Christians about reincarnation. Hare Krishnas and soft Evangelicals dueled in the sun. The main Hindoo claimed to be an ex-marine and spoke of ancient incarnations in modern agitation. Earnest and desperate, he spoke of human disregard for those souls in other creatures. This ex-marine was nervous and mincing a bit, in a gown too warm for India.

Leaving their argument to view the beaded waters of the aquarium was cool refuge to our senses. Rejecting the preposterity of the ex-marine's rhetoric, a fish surprised me with eyes; so wise he pleaded immediate rapport. I knew that fish to be . . . more than me and the Christian's had ever planned to see. It's immediate rapport still swims along the banks of my memory.

RABBIT ON THE LAWN
(FOR HARE UPDIKE)

The old neighborhood stays dignity with decay;

strange place where growth equals ugliness

and the semblance of beauty saved by yearnings

barely held relic of uselessness.

I kick a piece of sidewalk into the rain

to stay! Unlike the rain to stay! Duplicity

. . half evil twin of time and the otherness ages

things and drops the body down. It stays

in ways unknown. Forgiven love upon this

sacred lawn.

TOAST TO SAINT CATHERINE

He raised the jug of cider
on his forearm.
Speckling his face
he watched the cider colors
coming into autumn.

But, couldn't name the nestling hawk
he'd seen high in the nave of
Saint Catherines . . .
The apocalypse never comes,
the crisis never ends.

DEOCENTRICITIES

Skythicket brushpiles, high rabbited

trees color the sticks at wintersdawn.

Glown forestry stricken descriptedness

and straugn cavisan

stretched interminalbly and spadethrushed

motherbard assuredness.

We need a central account!

THE FALL OF LIGHT

In late summer
the hoosier morn
so usually hot
comes suddenly cool,
soothing the melon workers
in their August sweat
and kills off the tick season.
An iced liniment
for the old season's weather.
It is explanatory weather.
Shut up!, it explains
to all litigants of humidity
bringing even the doves
off the ground
where just this side of resignation

sad they sound
marginal to the wind
and any old weather
it sounds the trace
of ancient longing.

To be . . . no
from where we've seen
to where . . .
we ought to've been.

GULLS IN GARY

There are seagulls now in Gary

half way past Holy Angels . . by the statues

of Jesus, Joseph, and Mary.

By the Baptist's St. Paul on Grant Street

still seaworthy while sedentary

they hang out around blues and barbeque joints

glad God has given them Gary.

No longer white these kick ass gray gulls

hunt the souls hintermost area

in Hoosier groundedness

glad God has given them Gary.

They are the pale horses of our Baghdad

flying no coast riffs that carry

freshness under the sky way as

Gods sea creatures now in Gary.

By Way of Requital

The horsemen of Khalid
 dialectically steadying distress
that we might stand the test
by way of requital

Northern Imam

He was reading "Raising Angora", the northern way
and held his book with the chapped hands
of a muslim in winter.

Noon Wine
(Thanks to Katherine Porter)

Strong red wine tastes so
good in certain weather
that the day should be
set aside for it.

I comforted Bill Roan
by comparing his Alzheimer's
to such strong wine
at noon.

INTINCTION

In the fall of 1980 I attended mass at St. Als in Detroit. That is, when I found time between convention sessions of the C.P.U.S.A. There was new confidence in the Communist Party of the United States that season; welcomed by Mayor Coleman Young and proclaiming its presence from the marqee at Cobo Hall. The Helsinki accords allowed fraternal delegates from around the world, and I liked meeting with all those Communists, there by the river, looking across to Canada.

In the evenings we'd dine in Greek Town and after that retire to the track for harness racing and comradely conversation. At least, that was the plan.

Our dis-ease began in Hazel Park. It was cold there and the standardbreds—all seemed off their pace. The dark gloom of the paddock was not brightened by the cartoon colors of the clubhouse where we glutted on steaks and drinks and televised betting. (For the Laikon had been crowded and the mafia joint had no air conditioning.) Comradely banter was also—not possible. A strangness had set in—and I began trying to make it out.

That brought me to church. St. Als was special to me. She had ventured there and years ago I'd made an important confession at the place. Now descending toward communion, the priest began to panic at my presence. He became visibly shaken as I grew near him. "The body and blood of Christ"—Intinction—then, "Amen."

Maybe it was my delegates badge. No matter how subtly redesigned, the sight of a hammer and sickle still upsets some people. It is upsetting to upset people and it bends the time. As then, intincted moments held sway over the place disrupting any normal sense of time.

He'd preached from the psalter of humility and success; on the necessity of being brought down in order to be raised up. I'd aimed too high yet below His mark. The very stones tumbled through the arcs in my mind. Gaping shadows of the valley of death loomed before my insides. Gears of Providence meshed as giant obscure stones; greyweighing on me to fall the full depth and face those fiends on their own ground. Final flight depending on longsuffering kindnesses. Not martyrdom but victory; a transfigured metamorphosis the other way from Prague.

Our composure slightly recovered we turned away as Celebrant and Communicant are supposed to do. Daylight along the straits[1] joined communicants and delegates with Detroit's throng. There is also an Islamic conference in town. The American land now occupied by Asiatic cities. This evening land, dying toward the lumpen night which prowls against Christian, Muslim and Communist alike.

Penalties of Patmos clear Ionian mists.

Responsibility-----for recruiting others toward the right places is inescapable. Breaking pace brings the whip and redirectedness. Each training heat a little stiffer is still Wayne[2] Smart.[3] Plunging toward the prescience of loss and repair I have dialectically floundered there; even melled. But, gaited to include both kinds I've held the pace.

Later ... streets were filled with dawn-toned children who flew around dark and pale parents in a kind of prophetic hegemony. Intinction assures—meliority.

Notes

1. The straits: Detroit, French word for name and description of the place.

2. Wayne: Detroit is in Wayne County, Michigan.

3. T. Wayne Smart: Delaware Ohio horseman known for stiff training in Detroit.

4   THE OUTRIDER

"Consciousness is the poem of matter"

Diane Ackerman, *An Alchemy of Mind*

The Outrider 255

Pennsylvanians 257

Bottom Land 257

Freeze Etched 258

Witness To The Wolves 259

Puritan In The Wings 2561

He Is Risen 266

Errant Night 267

To Orestes 268

The Diablo Range 271

Old Priest Grade 272

Humanist Hag 273

Waiting Becomes Sam Beckett 274

Charging the Condor 275

Bad Weather 276

"You have such Pretty Breasts," He Said 277

Missing the Local 280

Warning Trees 281

Dull Roots 282

No Stroke Necessary 283

Bye Chinese Camp 284

One People 285

The Prophets Ennui 286

Between my Teeth 287

Indian and Cowboys 288

Burgos 293

Stalin in Wales 294

Second and Cherry 295

For Lope de Vega 296

Consider the Raven 297

C.P. Time 298

Raging Sighs 299

Summers Over 300

Rough Swallow Moon 301

Adversary and Answer 302

The Niche of Night 303

Not an Albatross 304

Dairy Hand 305

Keep from Falling 306

Fado 307

New Priest Grade 308

Brave Country 309

A Pass at the Season 310

To Hold Death Still 312

Cheerful Defiance 313

The Outrider

His muse like his horse was all a'lather. He'd been forcing them on to new terrain again.

As the outrider, he was free to do that.

Point to point races require an outrider to judge the propriety of inside turns. He rides the edge of the racecourse, observes the whole event but is minimally involved with the milieu of the meet itself. As outrider he was free from that busyness of the staff. Indeed his mind was increasingly free from the activity that keeps most men sane.

He began to notice things. His mount habitually spooked as the field thundered by the downside flat. While calming the big horse he began to notice how the light made things appear. Calm or not his horse still tried to join the field as it flew by in the following race. In order to discipline the beast he rode it hock deep into a long mud embankment. Rearing and charging he rode to tire the animal before returning to the course. Even still it leaped toward the passing riders and race horses. In the midst of this struggle he experienced light, or rather "shafts of light," he said, "emanating from the riders." "No not illuminating them," he'd say, "emanating – coming right out of their skulls toward the sky."

'Shafts of light seemed to be falling upon other people too.' Dismounting, he realized the thought more clearly.

The shafts of light did not fall; they were still and arily ubiquitous between the minds of people and the infinities of heaven.

Drunk with the beauty of it he now surveyed the land-scape for the first week of December's painting it appeared to be. Drawn around the clubhouse it was cast upon gently rolling ground becoming a canvas the color of all seasons. Autumnal coats of hounds, horses, and hunters shown warm near the cold clouds of their breath. Cantering across the lawn tended green were patches of dapple matched by badger pied skiffs in the kennel and white breeching worn against tunics in the field. A vast continuum of varying light played upon the picture. Striated columns of light refracting from the minds of those putting themselves into the picture.

He rode home alone that night after loaning his stopwatch to the Master of Hounds. He mused that being an outrider fit him. 'Being on the outside, judging the orthodoxy of insiders,' he laughed. The big horse stumbled, kicked out a no. 2 road rock and trotted on. 'Yes. Judgement respected, but acceptance unsure.'

Through the heavy timber, the light grew less. "Don't worry about trees old horse," he said, "we've too many forests in our mind."

Pennsylvanians

Chopin plays in the rain of Pennsylvania. A Cadillac slides through an oil spill; I ignore it hitting a truck. A woman is holding the ends of her hair. She wept.

Chopin plays after the rain in Pennsylvania.
The turnpike now dry, and scaly hot athirst for what it's not.

A couple quarrel in ROAD CONSTRUCTION, outside their car and fat in vacation clothes they fume. A Buick full of blacks slow down to grin at them. Pennsylvanians glutted with afternoons of asphalt . . . are soon to erupt.

As Chopin plays in Pennsylvania, I am stuck in their pain and rains disaster. So whats it to ya, if I escape to the peace of Lancaster?

BOTTOM LAND

I have yearned and I have grieved
through darkness's
that occlude my heart

Where light is shorn from life
when end shear . . . insures
the tastes . . . of gloom.

FREEZE ETCHED

It was a sub zero morning with no power and my truck would not start. We walked one hundred yards to where the school bus should be coming. It did not come.

One hundred yards back to a freezing house or one mile west to our nearest neighbor? It was hard to look into the wind but I saw woodsmoke rising from our neighbors chimney. That cinched it and we began walking into the western wind.

They faltered at the bridge. It was so cold my little ones wanted to rest. And the ol divil wanted them to die in such rest. I harshly barked orders for them to keep on. And my little girl and boy clutched my bare hands and marched out over the road deep in snow, one eye on me, the other tightly closed.

Witness to the Wolves

It was a cold spring day with scant promise of sunshine. Galen and I were building a coop for racing pigeons above the cement block smokehouse. At noon break, little Eliot burst in the kitchen saying, "Hey pa! come look at this." I moseyed out ahead of Galen and was stunned by what we saw above the pond.

They lay by the water trying to sun themselves. About fifteen of them. Seeing us see them they remained still. In fact they looked right at us; holding our gaze in theirs. At first I thought they must be escaped malamutes from a sled dog team. Each one looked over one hundred pounds and uniformly grey. Galen and I glanced at each other as 'Yonder' our greyhound bitch roared and took after them. Slowly and I thought almost smilingly they rose and loped away. When they saw Yonder put on some speed they did the same and disappeared over the hill. I called Yonder back. She was pregnant and I didn't want her hurt.

My children Bethany and Eliot were both on the porch now and asked us, "Were those wolves?" Galen and I had sat down on the old porch pew, and he answered, "yes." Thank God Galen was there to witness the wolves. Otherwise no one would have believed me and the children as we were collectively seeing too many things that season.

It was almost 1980. The last decade on the farm had witnessed a virtual explosion of wildlife in the countryside. Deer, coyotes, quail, turkey, woodcock, all kinds of waterfowl, songbirds, bobcats . . . and rumors of wolves.

I hadn't believed wolf stories anymore than the perennial and legenda
Indiana Panther stories. I was in the back woods too much not to ha
noticed. I kept two brace of sliver (Duke of Beaufort strain) English F
hounds. I occasionally rode with the 'New Britton' Registered Hu
Their lanky Walker hounds and my big silver ones were occasiona
whupped bad but we all attributed that to the infighting of blood sport
to a mama coyote with pups. But . . . wolves here in the hoosier state w
hard to believe.

What an encounter! The essence of which still range in my ima
ery. Life aloof from modernity. Both ancestrally old and creatively ne
they survive and prosper beside and within the margins of modern ign
rance. The D.N.R.[1] still does not recognize these creatures existence.

Jungian Depth Psychology teaches that animals are represent
tives of our unconscious. Of course, the unconscious, like consciousne
itself is easily depleted. The sight of these wolves beside our farmhou
stimulated some primordial part of my imagination. I became aware
what Jean Huston[2] refers to as the "lure of becoming" outside the se
Witnessing those wolves became a valid signpost for the rest of my life

A transpersonal kind of experience; an archetypal po
er I've tried to manifest more consciously. These totem messe
gers have taught me over the years that only relentless pursuit a
persistence wears down the divil and brings peace.

And if a situation doesn't smell right . . to run for cover.

1. DNR: Department of Natural Resources whose undefined
responsibility and excessive authority, continues to confuse
improvisational degeneracy with natural science.

2. "Animal – Wise" by Ted Andrews

Puritan in the Wings

[I'd read Silones's "Bread and Wine" into my present predicament]

My truck broke down in Bowling Green. My sermon had not yet gelled but my engine did. Diesel gelled winter clean freezed I was stranded and swearing near Jimmy Hoffa's hometown just West of the eel river.

Gathering up my small children we walked east across the bridge. The state road was deserted at dawn and we marched into the cold. Above the river my daughter turned and sighed, surrounding our senses in ways of seeing the sun burnished sage; the fields cut clean by the eel. Little Eliot interrupted, " Who in this Bowling Alley bowled the sun?"

"Our Lord," Bethany responded, "who can take this mighty world up in his hand and shake it . . . ,"

". . . like a squitchen!, Eliot added.

"What's a squitchen?" we asked him.

He grinned inscrutably and motioned toward the rain coming in. It cut like a razor through the brush below us, then moved with tenderness up the slope and touched our face.

At that moment my children seemed part of the weather and I loved them as God must love his own issue. It is occasioned by the rain, I thought.

'Occasioned by the rain,' I kept turning the phrase over until it caught with the scriptural reference I needed. (The 38th Chapter of Job)"For even the rain hath a father" "Yeah that's it . . ." I had it! All weeks reading didn't get it. This moment got it. I needed to read Teilhard de Chardin. I never read Teilhard. He was to my spirit what Dreiser was to my brain. My voice would "carry as far as the clouds" while our father "tilts the flasks of heaven til all His children's children cohere together into a solid mass".

I had been reading James Jones and Francis Schaeffer, John Donne, Henry Vaughan, and the Koran. Those times I was identifying with the metaphysical poets and the round heads new model army. I thought of myself as Milton trying to create Cromwell while I still had sight. I would be in full ellipsis as Lord Protector of all that God had given me and no wee mortal, hireling cleric, rube congregant, domestic magistrate, fem flammer, or other modernist degenerate would take them away. My accompanying angels were Amish with guns.

I was building barricades for holy soldiering minds into the next century, over-throwing error into eternity. The absence of moral criteria in church politics was eager to bless everyone except those conscious enough to make moral judgments. If consciousness is virtue, I thought, surely false consciousness is akin to sin. I martialed my categories.

A. Complexity is no less an illusion than simplicity.
1. There is a tennebrae of terror in separating the wheat from the chaff.
2. People become what they think about, but they are ultimately not what they think; they are what they do.
   a. Inversely . . as faith and morals explained in the book of James.
   b. Conversely. . no psycho-babble about sickness as an excuse for evil.
("Look out for the young priest with peanut butter kids! He has a problem. He's not evil --- just sick." My Arse!)

"(1) Sickness is a condition.

(2) Evil is a behavior.

(3) Evil is always a matter of choice.

(4) Evil is not thought; it is conduct.

(5) Conduct is always volitional.

(6) Evil is always a choice.

(7) Sickness is always the absence of choice.

(8) Sickness happens. Evil is inflicted."

(Andrew Vachs – Molested childrens attorney)

c. Subversively . . to the secular order, there is Schaeffers teaching from the Westminster Catechism:

(1) "No opinion can be either more pernicious or more absurd than that which brings truth and falsehood upon a level, and represents it as of no consequence what a mans opinions are. There is an inseparable connection between faith and practice, truth and duty"

(2) John Courtney Murrays admonitions were always to resist the "monistic failure to make moral distinctions." But to do so toward unity, rather than division: that was the challenge. We'd do it and we'd ride the spears of consequence.

My sermon was coming together. So was the weather and so was our weather. The three of us knew God as the devising altogether. (Sura 13-42) During our appointed term we thought in each others mind, acted accordingly, and were endued with understanding.

Another scripture clicked in; "He sends down water, from the skies and the channels flow, each according to its measure."

(Sura 13-17) Rain like thought comes to different channels according to their capacities. There are radical degrees within streams, lakes, rivers, and seas. "So with the rain of Allah's mercy and the knowledge, wisdom and guidance which He sends. All can receive it. Different ones will respond to their capacities." (Ali's Koranic Commentary)

In the natural world, waters are pure; scum gathers according to local conditions on the surface of things, but will not last. Purity will endure.

And there we were in that locale James Jones had known, "beautiful, grim, and frightening", a "spirit locked part of the world;" the broken hearted heartland. Bethany could not discuss Silas Marner or the civil war in her sixth grade without glaring the copperheads down.

I turned to the children, my daughter smiling her wonder, my son skeptically wondering . . . when we'd get out of the rain. Puritans we were who shared adversity and found collective metal.

We'd fought the cavil. We'd fought the Caviliers of enlightened unbelief in those we loved. We'd rode with Covenanters near the bridge. We'd been with Milton for Cromwell against Lauds and stood against them for every single Irish peasant. I taught them and myself to think Arminian and act Calvinist in catholic tradition. We were circuit ridden with John Wesley back to the big picture; the Big Church my grandfather would motion toward the heavenly.

My children helped me to universalize religion. I realized it was a very Catholic thing the Prophet came to complete.

A mechanic was found who heated and revived my engine. The old retired minister of the town called at the garage. He told me his terrier died. He looked like Richard Widmark might in 'A Touch of Danger', the James Jones film that didn't happen. A lone wolf whose sad eyes protested being condemned to isolation. The children hugged him goodbye and we drove away through the rainy tearful timber imagining Epperts Opus 70.

My sermon was delivered and I was censored for it. I wished like Ransom to restore to God the thunder but I knew I was through with the ministry. I yearned to go to mass and/or make jihad but I knew I was through with the ministry.

Like Jones soldiers revulsion toward the military and the persistant loyalty they have to their experiences I was to find that ceasing to be a soldier was as hard as becoming one.

HE IS RISEN

On the sunny side of the Ohio
Indiana rivers are tears sprung to rhythm
dappling all the Jesuit* dreamed about
thought struggling in the light of Easter;
triumphal and fragile at the same time.

On horseback up hills of sunshine
splashing across the glint of springs waters,
outguessing showers by calibrating
the speed of clouds in heaven
to the gait of colts on the ground.

Darkly bright . . Easter is too late for whiskey
and too early for anything else.

*Jesuit Gerard Manley Hopkins: priest whose poetic
style was called 'sprung rhythm'

ERRANT NIGHT

The errant night of our last century
began in the stench
of the trench
the not so silent night
of consciousness exceeding christendom
ends now, not in repose . . . now active
interior curias and caliphates will recall
all the tragic losses . . as so much
white boys' angst.

Lack of hope is not lack of vision
no more than necessity is a virtue
hubris . . . hubris . . .
whether muslim, christian, or socialist
external certitude is but a trusted guide
against ambivalence, pagan
idolatrous... believed only when
the white bull carries off our daughter.
Five thousand years from the shores of Crete
and we're only left with the Amish
idea of civilizations more dangerous
than the naturally improved reality we now respect
paying homage to Nature; Paiutes have called me
Priest of the Trees.

TO ORESTES[1]

(Contra: Evelyn Reeds' matriarchal marxoid misappropriation of ancient history: E.R.: a socialist scholar and feminist leader of the SWP.)

Between the Veldt and the Bush
bad weather builds inside Queen Lovedus[2] Caverns
Gaseous menstruations of moonworship and matriarchy

Where Trekboers[3] bend their brims into environment
pilgrims of the Father's nature
distinct, apart[4] tragically identifiable
holding out on the Cape
for Hope that is strategically beyond them

But for her knee, Frederick[5]
you should have seen her knee
from stirrups in the park
your origin of the family and proud flesh
have cost the Moor[6] his gaze

That shepherds chosen seed[7] awash in historical motility
not worth one tear of the unprotected
Iphigenia[8]; Jenny[9], our lost collective daughter

Notes

1. Orestes struggle ending the blood cult of matriarchy; prevailing against the furies, for patriarchical power, setting the historical stage to get beyond it that we may reach a synthesis of collective care for the unprotected. God's glory beyond personal contagion.

2. Bantu queen believed to be divine with magical powers over the weather, known for inspiring savagery among her warriors.

3. The first Afrikaans, pastoral farmers who trekked beyond the borders of the Dutch and British colonial companies.

4. An original interior apartheid to combat the savagery of natives and the multifaceted alliances of British imperialism.

5. Engels

6. Marx

7. Milton

8. Iphigenia, Agamemnon's daughter whom he sacrificed to the peer pressure of his milieu thus begetting Clytemnestra's vengeance; infidelity, betrayal, and murdering him, her husband begetting her son Orestes' revenge against her and her accomplice adulterer.

9. Jenny, Karl Marx's Iphigenia. The brilliance of marxist framework undercut in the beginning by humanist optimism and the lack of a compleat moral perspective.

Karl and daughter Jenny

THE DIABLO RANGE

'The Diablo Range' designates that chain of coastal mountains in California from the meridian of Mt. Diablo in the north to Priest Valley in the south.

Its name derives from an incident in 1806. According to Vallejo, detachments of soldiers from San Francisco's Presidio engaged hostile Indians near the Pacheco Pass and were soundly defeated. Bivouaced between a willow thicket and Solvio Pacheco's house they were attacked before light, yet held their defenses until an unknown presence entered the battle. The troopers claimed their route was due to the dark appearance of "an unknown personage with extraordinary plumage" whose very presence persuaded Christians the Devil himself was against them.

A minority report holds that it was drunkenness and excuse making; not the Devil. I reckon it was a little of both.

The truly diabolical part has to do with what I was doing there. I'd come to California to get better and to try and make a buck.
Things went badly.

A small truckload of tinned tomatoes, tequila, and I moved into a 12x12 cabin at the end of a place called 'blind horse canyon'. The night terrors returned and my deliverance came accumulatively.

OLD PRIEST GRADE
(for C.P.S captives)

There are deer that run _____
throughout my mind at night. Faster than
notes over a broken fielded plight and sky, keyed up
from pictures of fallen timber. They fly _____
as to last for all seasons.
  And you my little ones, whose eye
and rack mature as velvet rubbed alight
the lamp in rapt cognition. Where is your
habitat defined? . . . the current licks ancestral trace?
a range aligned? a herd to set the pace?
  Sure, we face . . .
an environmental crisis . . . but Love from Him
is bloods honor constant . . .
while human dice is . . . only timely
and annoying.
Hoist the banner when high earth chills
this growing season.
  The scent of dreams instinct distills
untroubling reason in trembling sense to heal
injuries feigning fault line to figure
fawn fugitives should act like veal.
  Hoofclattering to surefootedness now.
Heads up for Nature . . against the nurture mongers
. . against cancerous change.
Strange befrienders is whats wrong here. Heads up
my little ones. Look toward your homeland range.

HUMANIST HAG
(intercepted note to my captive children)

There once was a humanist hag

who was led to carry the bag

for coke dealing district attorneys.

On other degenerate journeys

she calls good parents barbarous warriors

earning funds for herself and the lawyers;

descendant of Emma Bovary

she carries her morals in her ovary

and while Papa does not like to nag . .

Look out! Look out!

for the humanist hag.

WAITING BECOMES SAM BECKETT

First a hum, then an opera in my wall

tending volcanos . . . naught but the cusp

of catastrophe's breath for those with

lungs to dare trajected moments

of great ladies hips apart from

Wagnerian bony prosody; the Red

Beckett in silent reseau as hymnody,

a flight of swallows near the lance

of a moor in Arabic chanted behind

our western door.

Not I, not I, but an object unnameably

still unbroken yon new

sadness . . . singing, swinging

in the last bloody ditch.

CHARGING THE CONDOR

The breathy flute of tierra del fuegan
wind deflecting up for the condor.
His ten feet of wings fly
above sea geese and snow line deer,
yet plummets dumb as death
toward the corpse of a guanacos calf.

Creations drama more wry than Darwins frog
afloat air streams that whore on Mt. Osorno.
Creation more comprehensive than Californians
rafting like torrents duck;
afraid as fire crowns fear of night creatures,
and torrents end of stone fly larvae.

The condor plops on the baby's death.

Bereaved the mother not accepting
such factual tearing of its flesh
keeps charging the condor.

BAD WEATHER

I've always liked bad weather. It is like that feeling
which lays over against an illusive spirit. It introduces a
darker moment to appreciate light. It gathers things up in
order to discern their direction.

Bad weather began to break that morning and I turned to
head home. Crossing the Wellsford Slough I slowed to watch
a pen of llamas await the weather. They could smell it and
they were excited by it and resigned to it. That's always
the way when you appreciate bad weather.

"YOU HAVE SUCH PRETTY BREASTS," HE SAID.
(Proverbs 16:33 On the breast the lot is drawn.)

"You have such pretty breasts," was the line that hurt him. It was not that this was considered a rude statement in California's 1,982nd summer. The pretense of honesty above all was still in vogue. And he had spoken honestly . . . and accurately. The lady described had pretty breasts indeed and the describer sincerely appreciated them.

But, he was a minister. And she was too irrational in her response. Or . . . too responsive to the irrational as his neighbor put it. Part of the problem was he had not been invited. To his neighbor's, that is. He'd just stopped by. Californians are usually casual; without invitations. That leaves everyone spontaneously ill defined.

He was from Indiana and hoosier cool to their lack of convention. But, he was lonely. So, with an intensely casual effort he'd just stopped by. His intensity always attracted interest but rarely trust or ease. There was much insistence on drinking. A reformed Catholic, he held his liquor. "From decades of drinking with priests," he'd say. However, the insistent drink and casual intensity did create a kind of forced relaxation. An ambience he felt favored his lucid force. Drunks talk like old women in a play you haven't read, but an attentive drinker can sometimes enhance a near conscious act. He drank a little tequila in a couple of beers. Western beer tasted thin to him.

Unattended, she wore an old fashioned dress and at first he barely noticed her. His ideological stance, that season, was of an Amish fellow traveler. Long faced and apostolically whiskered he claimed to prefer women in skirts rather than pants. For that reason he now remembers his eyes shifting toward the rustle about her knees.

Freckled and Irish faced her eyes were easy for him to avoid, but not her breasts. They were spectacular! . . . and prominently displayed. He concentrated on the skirt. She grew so animated in his gaze that all conversation deferred to her. An orchestral fade for the solo she played with that skirt. Pulling it above her knees, easing it around them, tucking it at the thigh, patting her own hip, smoothing the material, touching herself, moving that skirt, whisking it about.

He was legally divorced but still faithful to his wife. The lady with the skirt was legally married but in full heat. Resisting uninhibitedness he riveted his eyes above the skirt. And thus upon those breasts. Conformed to perfection and peach colored, they seemed of younger flesh than the rest of her. Not bovine or pugnacious, they were the very poetry of mammary excellence. Full of rouge warmth, they were more of a presence than most of the personalities in the place.

Knowing that his age and station limited sexuality to illusion, lust, or reconnectedness with the mother of his children, he wished to dispel the possibility that at any moment those breasts would speak out loud or in some other magical way claim his life. Images of them now claimed ninety percent of his attention. Every feasible thing that was carnally possible to do with breasts was tearing at his mind.

If he could only reattach them to the Irish girl he might cordially cope with the situation. Otherwise he was going to end up . . . both ends, among them, and doubly sad for measure.

Exhaling he breathed out what he hoped would pass for a California compliment yet still exorcise those mounds amidst his mind:

"You have such pretty breasts," he said.

-Stone larval silence-

A silentness rarely known beyond this lawn.

She and others began to laugh. She laughed so hard it finally sounded like flatulence instead of embarrassment. "Take it easy Reverend," somebody said. The husband was found. He told everybody but the Reverend he wanted to fight.

He never came back. He was never invited back. But, the invite was still out of fashion there. Word of the incident is said to have hurt his career. But he didn't mind remembering it. He remembered it when he thought of California dairies; cows like great ships lumbering out of non corralled pastures, their udders swollen with sweetness and pain.

MISSING THE LOCAL

"I'm beginning to live in my job,"
exclusively along and through corridors
of what others call a career.

Increasingly encased within its cold blooded borders,
it coils and pushes through another day.
With reptilian ignorance of exhaustion it blinks
as the hair on my arms turn gray.

Wrapped around my few and former friends
whose bodies are fallen or dead,
becoming bulbs of passing light.
Impatiently, impatiently our skins are shed.

No matter the sidelong glancing pace.
Danger was never this dangerous; giving
with faith that civilization remains someplace,
as this fast safeness
whose express line
makes no more stops –
- for living.

WARNING* TREES
(JEREMIAH 1:11)

Before the bull bellars

from mithraic depths

Sierran and Coastal ranged horny

handed toasts fallen far in

and far away

the best shot is through the trees.

When they've fallen in regimentally resplendent

and vigilant to the Ides

of March Ravens flying against windows.

Rutting transparencies.

The seasonal angst arrives

in flatbeds with hives, stacked and tiered,

they're trucked through the night, these bees!

Adjutants to the warning trees.

*sheqed: Hebrew name for the
warning or watchful almond tree . .
the first to blossom.)

There are no roots for man:all scarecly rest upon a tremor of rain.
Pablo Neruda, *Song of some Ruins*

DULL ROOTS (αποθανετν θέλϣ)

From blind horse canyon walls
far from my black cattle
and bloods connection;
my foals in far pastures
my faith fractured
I would recall...

All through the night welsh pools suffer reverently along
carriage tracks in muddy light. In their cold community social I've
warmed to its existential chill. Trust me, to use the word advisedly
askew in the clutter of confinement poultry and implements laid
down hard in the muck that brides the tread of Saturdays gone
still closer to the mists of antinomy over fields in far lots for hips
above rough stockings on the road. Those too small eyes that
crowd the bridge will not share würst with me. They are carrying
a five gallon tin sweating in their underwear today. Anabaptist
weather lurks near the lilacs on the stove, mixing woodsmoke that
penetrates their pies; infrastructural obsession of our economic
eyes. Regenerate nevertheless axes have bludgeoned yet uncut
without the camp that voice cries on and on...

The wyrd,...the word in wilderness.

Against the word the unstilled world still whirled
T.S. Eliot, *Ash wednesday*

NO STROKE NECESSARY

We preceeded, no anticipated the switch blades

of hollywood adolescence

by fighting with barlow knives on the playground.

First blood being the final point. Jimmy Casaicas

slightly ambidextrous pivot always caught

me in the left hand or arm. I thought

of that when the ghurkas knife popped

through my forearm. I'd thought about it when

fractured through the oldsmobiles windshield.

The wyrd wants the right side to prevail

over the sentimental, sinister left handed lover.

BYE CHINEESE CAMP

My day and my mood began to treble

like a Gluck opera where pastoral landscapes

betray a heart breaking with cellos going the wrong way.

Burning slightly above and altogether

beside my self I watched more than directed

the driving of my car. 'Anxiety attacks' par broil

our brains normalcy . . . retreating to fret

and spend adrenalin in several considered directions

or compressing into one committed plunge.

ONE PEOPLE

The old republican leaned uncomfortably
on the american table. Shelburn Park*
had bought new plasticy tables and
chairs to replace the worn oak ones
scattered about the bar and saloon lounge.
Gambling patrons as well as racing men
with their greyhounds sprawled less
comfortably on and beside the new furniture.

"You say you're part Welsh then," he said.

"Yes . . . on my fathers side"

"Aye . . and well pay na' heed to the lads at'l rib
ya and say you're half a taffy. We're all cousins
and Celts ya know."

"I know."

"When the Brits first fought our people in
ancient times we were all one . . . the Scots,
the Welsh, us Irish . . . Bretons and Cornish of
course . . we were all one Celtic people. When
some of us fled north to the highlands
turned and won important battles they
became the proud Scots. When others were trapped
and massacred in the western valleys . . . they
became the melancholy Welsh."

"And the Irish?"

"Oh Aye . . . the Irish . . why we're still fightin."

*.   Shelburn Park: Greyhound track in Dublin, Republic of Ireland

THE PROPHET'S ENNUI

My first hour in Palestine,

I sought him out

just as I'd done in Spain, where his wife

served oranges in olive oil.

Here, she was quiet and they seemed very poor.

Time itself was dear. Hurried in hospitality

he spilled paper plates but kept speaking

clearly, solemn in the dangerous sun that

shone through these windows from the Godstones

all around this country.

"Have you been to the Mosque at the Dome of the Rock?",

he asked.

"I came straight here."

"No matter … it .. It is deserted."

BETWEEN MY TEETH

In that shadowed dawn, the Dunker
does chores at the edge of his orchard, near
a canal and that section he sold for
development . . . Modesto's housing infestation
of lost control.

Yet the mornings still safe from
the sound of traffic as he works quietly
among his tools by pilings of French Columbard
up out of the earth along the sun washed
side of his shed.

A shelter above the southern slope is for
vats of home cured olives; cylindrical,
ceramic and salt watered they seep
up the brine of the morning. A hand
lettered sign hangs . . . reporting "This
is a self serve deal – Five bucks a gallon.
Put your money in the rack – We don't guarantee
the sack".

The olive is silvery and tastes of
ammonia absorbing the morning.

I take it between my teeth.

Indian and Cowboys

I'd been reading stories of the White Mountain Apache. I would later hunt bear in that territory with my friend and fellow houndsman Riley Muldoon. Riley lives in Horse Camp, a high point of the Texas panhandle along the last best 100 miles of country road all the way to Magdalena, New Mexico. I'd had to keep moving, but we both dreamed of hunting the White Mountain Apache country.

The White Mountain Apaches themselves are very interesting. Renown for their success in social organization as well as battle. There was a diagram in my book illustrating their lightening quick method of scalping. Like the Sikhs in south Asia and Stockton they believe in never being without a blade for justice and protection.

Does access to weaponry always increase the incidence of violence? I dunno. That was and still is the central issue of the "gun control" quarrels. The most extreme and ridiculous statements seem to define borders of the debate. While Bill Clinton announced 'that high powered rifles should be banned because no one needed such a weapon to kill deer.' G. Gordon Liddy retorts, 'even with a high powered rifle . . due to G-men's body armour, one should always aim for head shots as they bust in your door'. My friend J.C. who kept the hospital going was a fallen away Adventist and G. Gordon Liddy man. My pal and Publisher Ron Pickett was a big bearded gentle fellow. Erudite and civil; he was a poet publisher and mountain mystic who wished all violence would just go away somewhere north of Nirvana. A middle aged Lefty myself . . . left me somewhere in the middle. Opposed to all the gun toting right wing vigilantes I still thought the 2nd amendment secured by The American Revolution was there not for deer hunters but for ordinary people to protect themselves from an oppressive government. In the sixties I loved seeing the Cuban population armed at baseball games.

For my sons fourteenth birthday I gave him a Red Army issued Chinese SKS Carbine 7.62 millimeter, top loading assault rifle with a bayonet. J.C. and I instructed him carefully and comprehensively in its safe and responsible operation. We were planning a hunting trip for wild boar in the Diablo Range come spring. This hunt had to be cancelled after my sons lawyer stepfather turned the SKS over to Modesto's police as an illegal weapon.

A Sinn Feinist'[1] at the Sonora Book Fair slipped me a ballpoint pen with a 3 inch razor sharp pig sticker blade point. "Its for keeping the Engleesh correct", he joked.

The thing looked like a normal ballpoint pen from the outside. I kept it on my desk at home. It was a conversational piece for a while, and then soon forgotten. One morning I mistakenly placed it in my vest pocket, thinking it was a normal pen. Discovering my mistake I changed the knife pen to my right pocket . . putting a bum hospital pen back in my left. The latter barely lasted the shift and I threw it away when leaving the treatment pods side gate. I met J.C. coming through this gate from the service area. We worked the mid-shift. It was 9pm on a Friday evening.

"Plans . . ?" he asked.

"Nope", I replied.

"Myself . . I'm havin' a turrable thirst", he joshed. We both liked imitating Barry Fitzgerald's "Quiet Man"[2] blarney about strong drink and conversation.

"Aye . . it's a nice soft evening", I answered, "lets have a few pints and talk a little treason." We liked to drink tequila and beer at a Mexican cock fighter tavern nestled in the orchards on the road to Turlock . . . but not tonight. Tonight we ran into Ron at my townhouse.

J.C. had followed me home so we'd take only one vehicle. Ron was down from the high country and had just stopped by.

I introduced these guys and they hit it off immediately. I guess opposites do attract. I invited them in for a drink before we walked the two blocks over to 'Mallards' . . a shiny new corporate bar and restaurant just opened up around the corner.

J.C. seemed amazed at the form and content of Ron's language who spoke in quiet eloquence about his Paiute tribal neighbors. Ron was accepted and welcome in their homes and in their austere reservation. His eco-politics matched their nature worship. He spoke of how their headmen had approved his publishing some of their Shamanic chants in the next issue of 'Mindprint Review'. A few of them had attended our last poetry readings Ron had arranged above Sonora. And Ron made my day when I heard him say one of the Paiutes described my reading as "he spoke like a Priest of the Trees".

Ron was intrigued by J.C.'s blood and thunder stories. Especially how he had survived a gunfire fight with thieves while clerking at an ammo store.

At Mallards Ron and I both ordered 'Drunken Cod'. . beer battered fish on Friday tasted good and was full of memories. Both Ron and I were half fallen away and fellow traveler Catholics. J.C. followed suit with the cod and the beer. All three of us remembered childhood rooting for the

Indians against the cavalry in so many movies.

Gaining common ground we also recalled with only faint embarrassment we'd all three been boy scouts . . . with different ranks of course. Ron had been an Eagle Scout. J.C. a Star Scout. And I had flunked out on the first class Morse code test.

J.C. wondered if different military strategies might have helped the Indians. Ron spoke at length how it had been more of a political problem. "They needed unifiers here in the west like Tecumseh had been back east." I wanted to speak of the so-called "Indian Wars" as metaphors for the modern Middle Eastern situation. They weren't interested.

But with more brethrenly banter, and much more beer we closed the place. Filing out . . . a young cowboy got blocked behind us and was irritated we weren't moving faster through the swinging doors.

Outside . . . assisting each others balance we were still walking slowly, three abreast and blocking the traffic on Mallards short driveway. A horn honked. We turned to see that same cowboy pounding the dash of his flashy new truck, flipping us off, and yelling over his loud radio for us 'to get the f. out of his way.'

"F. you", J.C. flipped him back. "Maintain the pace men," I said "the roads not his property." We continued to walk slowly stolidly, and blockingly abreast the next twenty yards to McHenry Streets sidewalk. We turned north toward the Briggsmore stoplight and the cowboy screeched around us, running the stoplight on to Briggsmore circling back into Mallards parking lot.

We ignored him as we collectively managed to get across the wide canal and boulevard. On reaching the other side, what seemed like the far shore . . . we heard a battle cry screaming across the traffic.

It was the cowboy, sleeves rolled up and fists doubled up demanding satisfaction. Quickly assessing our handicap I reckoned only two things could happen. (1) Three older guys were going to be whupped by this youngster or more likely (2) the three of us were going to guiltily beat the shit out of this youth. Neither option pleased me. I drew the ballpoint pig sticker knife from my pocket. Its blade glinted in the streetlight as I assumed what I remembered to be the White Mountain Apache scalping position. "It's scalping time cowboy", I said. Ron then invoked a militant Paiute chant while he and J.C. demonstrably recalled the toe heel Indian dance every Boy Scout learns.

Dancing, chanting, and moving toward him with the knife we evoked a dramatic change in this fellow. Ron's singsong chantry joined by J.C. and my repetitive "scalping time", "scalping time" as we toe-healed toward him changed his tune completely while his facial complexion set pale face records in quickened whiteness. Scared silent he backed all the way across the Canals Boulevard to his truck and was gone.

Fortunately the traffic on Briggsmore had lessened.

1. Sinn Feinist; a partisan of Sinn Fein, the IRAs political wing.

2. "The Quiet Man" John Ford's signature film in Ireland with John Wayne, Barry Fitzgerald, Maureen O'Hara, and Victor McLaughlin.

Tears like heavy bullets have fallen on your dark earth.
Pablo Neruda, *Spain in our hearts*

BURGOS

The first chill of that last year

in cold northern towns

was scimitar light slanting

from ear to ear

of our dreams.

Defeat in Burgos

tastes like

a steel blade.

STALIN IN WALES

I had faded into Wales, like the

apparition of Stalin . . . coal miners wished to see.*

Dark imaginings in welsh history of heroic treachery.

Lost sheep in the streets of Pontypool,

chapels lurking in Blainaven toward that

terminal pub . . . a misted Cardiff conversation

going on . . one meeting after another . . avoiding

audacity . . at least postponing disappointment.

Inexorably drawn to Celtic dreams of

better days which will never be but still worth

fighting for . . .

*Montefiore writes of apparitions of Stalin reported by Welsh Coal
Miners. Much like those of Mary in Medugoria.
Simon S. Montefiore's *"Stalin"*

SECOND AND CHERRY*

She matured to her beauty

but not very . . .

last seen running from duty

past lawyers at second and cherry

*Terre Hautes traditional whorehouse and lawyer district.

FOR LOPE DE VEGA

Like his morning of St. John

all my loves are gone.

But which the greater fear?

Loves frightened off again

or was never really here.

CONSIDER THE RAVEN (or glimpse of the poet as an old horse)
for Ted Hughes*

There was a full murder of crows

more than a thousand cold in the catalpas

at hallows eve by the brewery.

Dark bricked hues of St. Benedicts

infect and slate the tile matched underwings

of the crow hanging up on the diseased

idea of an all souls night viral.

While he was an old horse with west nile

shaking his head at the world

way out there in the weather

where he had stumbled so long ago, under the ravens flag.

Past the papal banner whose promise

is still . . . promising, near the hostile shores

of categorical entities no longer if ever his.

Like William definitely not the Conqueror

on this priory floor.

*Ted Hughes: Welsh poet confused by the Queen

C. P. TIME
(celtic peoples time)

There was snow on the streets of Belfast
and this time I was odd . . out.
I had not slept. Neither had Slattery . . .
if I was lucky. . aye . . the luck of the
Irish . . what a terrible joke that's been.

The outside cold was fighting the fire that
whiskey kindled inside of me. I breathed
like a dragon into the snowfall and
thought of my children . . half hoping
Slattery would find me. Maybe I'd
cut his throat and that'd be the end
of it . . . or he'd cut mine and that
would end things as well.

Slattery found nothing. I found the
ship out . . in time . . nothing
ended.

RAGING SIGHS
(Sura 25:the raging sigh of the eager fire)

The heat upon my temples

craved the cold barrel of a gun.

Pubic hair upon the lip of urinals

is emplaned calligraphy for this age . .

How high must they fly to avoid the depth?

Skywriting distractions are swollen sinuses

of the souls incursive

avoidance of its source.

Humanity held hostage in their hot tubs

cocksocratically;

commercial, personal, sexual interaction

becoming the same F.ing free market intercourse

That talks of Freedom

and causes death

the raging sigh

of the eager fire.

SUMMERS OVER

"Yeah uhuh huh." He stretched out the last sound of that word until it reverberated with the tires on his lane of the bridge.

He needed this Glimpse of the River. Soothing . . . more so . . . even than the canals of the San Joaquin. The Wabash cooled his mind concurrently with what the hell ever else was happening. He hadn't seen Slattery since being mustered out in the far western valley. It had been in a witchy little place called Ceres. Now he'd see him again and he wasn't afraid of seeing him, but the light behind things . . . began to glow and growl.

ROUGH SWALLOW MOON

And her reassuring clouds

reassure no one;

restabilizing insignificant

immensities insists

secrecy consists

of cloud cover

keeping governments in the dark.

ADVERSARY AND ANSWER

adversary: You cannot go from dignity to misery without staying there . . .

answer: You cannot go from dignity to misery and stay the same.

"THE NICHE OF NIGHT . . . *is turned*"
Solomon Ibn Gabriol

Was it Berlin or Terre Haute, this visage did occur? A Jewish center for the hospitals marketing call in last minute assignment they worried my name was german which cued a celtic emphasis in my notes to speak about I knew not what.

My host was quiet and suspicious; his was the anxious semetic dignity of shoe store proprietors in Morocco.

There was a speaker before me sent from central casting; professionally Irish, flat capped, and pissed off this ruddy red Mick spoke into a small mirror with his back turned to the poorly turned out audience whose tattooed hands were clasped upon their shadows.

My ethnic bit suspended I sought for Holy Scripture, The Koran, Gospels, or Torah would tell me what to say.
I was referred to a clear plastic package on the office shelf. Inside the package . . . was only tissue paper. "We only have the Bible here", my host was saying. Aghast, I peered back into the package . . . it now contained hundreds of writ upon index cards I had no time to research or organize . . . . Dismissively my host remarked, "It is a difficult time to be religious."

"A more difficult time not to be" was my reply.

NOT AN ALBATROSS

[Picture a Seagull
thousands of miles from the sea.
The sight of a lone gray gull
on a wintry inland waterway]

Such a one was seen on New Years Day,
wheeling by ice flows on the Wabash;
white and gray as the rivers question
mark against the brackened wood.

I parked off the bridge, my nerves . . .
meandering through the morning haze
to accompany the flight and ways
of natures' otherwise expectation
that gulls should be away in some other place.

Some dumb sub tropical splendor or near Northern Seas,
not problematically here and solitary.
Cold suspect, are you lost or vaguely free
to haunt this unappreciated . . . riverine
heartland of dark contradictions?

The seagull on the Wabash did not respond to me!

Distance is not his problem, I believe,
but the depth and fortune of seasonally
changing dramas. Similarly, yet
strange it is our ancient responsibility!
Passed into climes beyond expectations
to neither value nor respond to surprise.
Into times that are new for the ancient ability
to respond like the gull on the river
.. to be otherwise.

DAIRY HAND

It was like that dairy at dawn near Saint Stanislaus.
The tule fog colors a rotogravure in the mornings sun.
The dairyman stepped through the steam,
gleaming chrome of his clean poor milking
parlor to shake my hand.
Husband, Father, Yeoman Farmer from the
Azores. Emissary from lost Atlantis . . . he and
one hundred like him helped me 'keep from
falling'.

"Blossoms of the Apricot
blow from the east to the west
and I have tried to keep them
from falling" Canto XIII
Ezra Pound

KEEP FROM FALLING

Il Purgatorio past Pattersons intensities solo,

kept fast on the west side of War and Peace.

Intensities beyond Yosemite and the sea,

intensities that are hard light;

glintsome against an armour

lit across the valleys floor.

Not stumbling, nor at march

I keep from falling

simply by recall . . .

astride the fast hard light.

No blossom, but a focused laser

upon the western night.

FADO

Glimpses of the San Joaquin
come like a fado
beside canals
Swept across free stalls
in dusty dueños
toward remote corrals

Mystery spoken in sacral locations

The church quiet bullring near
huge alfalfa fields where
we'd chase jackrabbits with our greyhounds
retiring to the Woolgrowers Rest in Los Banos
smoking Gallois we recognize our
shared recall of wine fresh air

In coastal Malaga

The fado is Cordoba's call to prayer
Hey up! brawn oxen teamed memory
Azores breaking gently apart at sea
Falling guitar sound leaves upon the
fate of her bare shoulders. This fado is there
like the Socialist Camp . . after it has collapsed

Reminding us of Chiapas and ALBA* . . but not despair.

* The Bolivarian Alternative for the Americas

NEW PRIEST GRADE

When I brought my children from Ireland to California
we settled in the Sierras above the San Joaquin _____ where a
fast car and driver can match Sinatra's emotive range along one
hour of mountain road. Up country from Yosemite _____ down
to Valley Home then back up the Priests Grades again I began to
zone that exterior route within my interiority.

In spite of its cold-hearted lakes _____ its highs and
lows, are known unsettlingly. Like in October when seven points
short of a haiku_____

> The fertile earth
> turns in its sleep
> and quakes.

We moved to the valley. The great San Joaquin _____
knowing full well there is a certain mentality that sees the great
valley as a place to endure between the vagaries of the bay and
vertical brush of the Sierras.

The vulgarity of this view has a positive consequence. Middle-
brow hordes of moderns have left the secrets of the San Joaquin
secluded and hidden. The Great San Joaquin _____
stretching from where the prerogatives of Patriarchy, Prayer, and
fighting bulls are still at large thanks to the Portuguese, even
death . . . is held still.

[Spring 1989 San Joaquin Literary Newsletter: Tom Morgan is a writer, now living in the San Joaquin Valley. He is a frequent contributor to 'Mindprint Review' and a collection of his verse and prose, "Not of our Time" is being published by Glenhill Press. "To Hold Death Still" is the titled poem of his non-fictional work on Portuguese bullfights in California.]

Chapter 1   "BRAVE COUNTRY"

a.   New Portugal in the San Joaquin

b.   From the Azores, that last remaining land mass of the lost planet Atlantis.

c.   Culture and Work in the San Joaquin's new Portugal

Chapter 2   "A Pass at the Season"

a.   The Church Calender and the Feshts

b.   Our Lady of Fatima at the Bullfights

Chapter 3   "Sons of Aaron"

a.   Exegetical chapter and verse on the Christian and ancient art of bullfighting

Chapter 4   "Looking for War" (Buscan Guerra)

a.   The Bulls; The fighting bulls type, origin and genealogy

Chapter 5   "Divisias" (Ganaderos)
a.   The World class quality of San Joaquin bull ranches

Chapter 6   "Tourados" (Bullrings and bullfights)
a.   Campo Bravo (Escalon)
b.   Pico Dos Padres (Crowslanding)
b.   Campo Pequeno (Tracy)
c.   Gustine, Artesia, Tulare, and Morgan Hill

Chapter 7   "To Hold Death Still"
a.   The compleat Pega-forcados, cavalieros, and their horses

Chapter 8   "Passion and Place"
a.   Lawrentian "vestiges of blood" and gemeinschaft,
bloodlines and sacrifice

From Chapter 2   A PASS AT THE SEASON

Birch skulled vials of wine hulled skies

pass at the season toward a sonnets darkened eyes

We drove two hours and late through the fog

for a fesht of Fatima and the last taurines in Tulare.

Octobers night reeking a crowds cold flatulence,

Linguica and nutmeg odors that gather

around corralled dairies; that cleave to your boots

and to freestalls of the future in your mind.

We missed the forcados

and Coelho disliked his last two bulls.

The Praca is over but the band won't go home;

playing over and over a seeming mixture

of 'Roll out the Barrel' and some 'Marines hymn'.

Yet shifting its breathy blasts to come together

as one steel pick,

one unitive cusp for the whole

stadium arch as bridge.

Our being played as guitar. It sounds

Pass at the bull; the bull pass around.

Pass at the bull; the bull pass around it.

Pass at the bull; the bull pass around,

Pass at the bull; the bull pass around you.

Pass at the bull; the bull pass around.

While little herds of high hipped heifers

are scattering about; the prettiest stock in our valley

dancing with a few old men,

who hike their leg every third step

and kick away the passing season.

Ezra Pound sought places with "a sort of courage to throw
remembered beauty into an unconquered consciousness."
The Brave Country (Campo Bravo) of the San Joaquin is such
a place. "To Hold Death Still" aspires to celebrate and capture it.

TO HOLD DEATH STILL
(A Serugar Morte Imovel)

Whether Divisia Bourba or Sousa

the bulls of the San Joaquin are getting better.

At Campo Bravo along Escalon's Bellota,

or below their chapel near the Diablo range

The culture of bravery has impaled a certainty

of places safe this side of the Atamount.

To not only pike and pass the Minoan Storm

but risk it's intimacy with injury;

a fighting embrace for driven beauty

the forcados collective arms

arrest intentions of the beast,

controlling not to kill.

A husbandry to hold

        —to hold death still.

CHEERFUL DEFIANCE

"Time is an illusion.
Lunch time doubly so."
Douglas Adams
[The Hitchhiker's Guide to the Galaxy]

The morning was edged with light fog rolling toward Madera. The route to my friend's vineyard took me across the Merced River to Los Banos and then down Highway 33 to Raisin Country. I drove it happily. The river bottoms I called "New Carmague" and I imagined raising fighting bulls there. Perhaps I'd become a new Guardián - Ganadero supplying bulls for all the Portugese bullfights. A new Ganaderia for the Tourados. Forward looking and hopeful, my thoughts flew with fairly sane agribusiness possibilities. I was getting better.

It was a pleasure to see mallards, teal and coot along the way. Once, upon crossing 'Henry Miller Road' (yeah, I've always wondered, too!) into Los Banos, I even saw ducks flying in the town. I particularly liked the pepper trees in that town and a Basque joint there called The Woolgrower's Rest is my favorite place in the Valley. But, it was an odd time and I had to get to Madera.

I hoped Brigham was feeling well, that is, . . . in a good mood. I hadn't seen him since New Year's in San Francisco when I had broken his leg. Brigham, Rolphe and I had left the children with Rolphe's older daughter in our hotel and ended up in some dive down by the wharf.
After scaring Brits who saw us as the last of Oliver Cromwell's gang drinking toasts to the death of the monarchy and long live the Lord Protector, we staggered merrily back to the hotel.

Brigham then developed a wild plan to phone several of his high school classmates he'd heard had moved into this area. While he aggressively engaged the hotel room's phone, Rolphe drew me aside.

"We can't let him drive! He's gonna connect with some

313

body and try to drive out to see them. He's too drunk. We'll have to stop him."

Brigham was laughing and loud on the phone. "Hey Breezy, ol' buddy. I heard you were a judge . . . just give me your address. I know Pacifica . . . (writing down the address) I'll be right over . . . Sounds like a great party."

It was 11pm. "C'mon guys," he invited. "Ol' Breezy wants us over to bring in the New . . . One!"

Reaching out to him, Rolphe said, "I need your keys, man!"

I backed up Rolphe. Brigham didn't argue. He sized up the situation . . . and broke for the door like a bull and was gone. Rolphe did not appeal . . . he ordered me to stop him. Still in the habit of taking orders from both of them . . . I got after him. Down two flights of stairs I caught him in a perfect flying tackle over the hall carpet and we flew to land on the hard tile floor of the lobby. His right knee broke clean in two; he wailed as loud as a bull at bad picadors.

His life dutifully saved, Rolphe and I settled all the children down, then delivered Brigham to the ER. He was hospitalized for a while. It took him a little longer to forgive us. And he walked fine after a few months.

Metaphors of Brigham as a bull were not original to me. It was a common reference to describe his physical and mental strength. I'd seen him pulverize right wing opponents. Comrades in Boston and New York described him as having the devotion of a priest and the guts of a burglar. I was counting on that.

I'd been working as the 'Herdmaster's' man for a DeLaval outlet in Modesto. I knew the dairymen. Feed prices were up, milk prices down. I'd developed a scheme to turn Brigham's rain damaged raisins into cattle feed for a decent profit. I hoped Brigham was done bulling about his broken knee.

He greeted me as brusquely as ever. He walked OK. Speaking about our past usually cheered him up. But not today. I shut up after a few attempts. He motioned us toward his old truck. Climbing in, I knew I would be captive to one of Brighams 'horrible homilies.'

"You hold on to the past," he started. "You can't learn anything new if you keep remembering everything.

Forgiveness is letting go of the hope for a better past." (I could tell he'd been working on that one.)

"You act like an old hound with a bone. Forget it. For get the past. Engage the . . high-tech future. You should hear my kids and their friends talk . . . language has changed . . . on-line, download . . . soft-ware—do you know what that means?"

". . . Nope."

He laughed . . . a little bit. "Neither do I . . . entirely, but I'm learning. I embrace the future and I'm going to make money and be a part of it. You on the other hand, pal, are an emotional if not a visceral reactionary resisting the future."

He hadn't even heard my idea—my scheme—yet and clearly was bent to be against it. I groped for the bottle of tequila (at this hour!) I'd seen in his half-back seat. It lay under some work clothes and it was the kind he liked with a horseshoe on the label. In a mocking toast to our background I drank to the "great socialist reaction, the resistance of left wing reactionaries—to the illusion of a future."

Brigham was done laughing. "You . . . are not being serious! You're on the edge and not daringly, but despairingly. Sure, you've taken some hits . . ."

"Hits hell," I laughed? "I've lost proportionately as much as you've inherited."

"If you settle for that . . . that's it!" He spoke as if he were answering some question I hadn't asked him. "Look," he went on. "You'd built up a life. You got shut of that political youth bull . . . (he groaned mimicking a mindless zealots face) that youth against war and fascism bullshit."

No Marceyite myself, "Maybe Deutscher, Pablo, Canon, Cochran, but I resent the inference. I resent . . ."

"You can't afford resentment, it's the emotion of kept women, he laughed.

Then I laughed . . . and more than a little. He'd been a Neitzschean, down from Wabash College and his old moneyed parents on Pennsylvania Avenue in North Indianapolis. With an instinctive contempt for the middle class and their "bourgeois order" he'd looked for the new meritocracy in that Marxist hangover . . . the supermen of the sixties.

"Gawddd . . ." I gagged. "You are still beyond good and evil and I am the still born American Tragedy."

I'd been a bright proletarian, ambitious to graduate from hard toil and Terre Haute until I met all the liberal idiots and so-called conservatives at university.

The 'bourgeoisie' seemed not only effete and philistine to me, it appeared weak and quite capable of being overthrown. My old man and uncles could run society better than these guys, I thought. We'd whack the corporate liberals and then the olde money would step aside for us. Who'd they have since Hoover anyhow. Even Eisenhower had not been there's and McCarthyism was dead in the water.

Only the soft liberals stood between us and state power. Oh . . . they had the army but we filled its ranks. Then there were the Southern barbarians whom the liberals wished to patiently educate . . . we'd enforce reconstruction completely on those racists and that'd be that! I joined the sixties men after one conversation.

That conversation had been with Brigham. He spoke
about Lenin with an identifiably Nietzchean accent and he
thought I indicted capitalism like Dreiser. Now, like Dreiser,
I'd known the furies and barely survived them. Our thirty something year old conversation had strange echoes in it!

Rolphe had been in the original conversation as well.
And others . . . Rolphe's personal identity was all wrapped up
in the jewish question. Nationality was paramount and the pre-
varications of industrial capitalism had wrought such unjust
confusion that only world revolution by Bronstein would set it
right . . including Israel and the dystonic diaspora.

Brigham was thundering for the mincing middle class
to get out of his way and I wanted my relatives to run the
country. We thought of ourselves as the last bastion of the Olde
Left and the Marine Corp of unborn opposition. Others . . . so
many other new leftys seemed to us, only intent on overthrowing
their parents.

With more contradiction than illusion we nonetheless
formed a solid front against certain sectors of the status quo and
brought a broad smile of hope to our homeland—a smile like
Che's, a smile of tenderness and irony; if critics feared cruelty in
that smile they deserved it. We didn't make the American Rev.
We did end segregation, if not economic injustice. We brought
the troops home even though war criminals were spared. And we
buried McCarthy's redbaiting.

All seemed bust now. Brigham . . . "one of the Left's
best elements" transformed from revolutionary socialist to self-
reliant heir. I was beginning to feel sick again. In a more comradely tone my old friend asked, "You taking any meds for this
depression?"

"Nope. . . It's been a bad dream . . ." I barely paraphrased Holderlin in his madness. . . "the bleeding wings healed . . . hope's line, but to find the great means . . . much, much still remains . . . whoever so loved . . . his path must proceed to . . . God."

Responding sympathetically, Brigham said, "Why don't you cash in on your degree . . . go to the city and make some money?"

"I'm separate from all that now."

"You have responsibilities, god damn it! Are you still hanging out with the Portagees?"

"I'm working as the Herdmaster's consultant . . ."

He interrupted, "Consultant . . . Consultant! That's rich! I heard that's what they call a horny steer or a penictomized bull who detects cows in heat but can't breed 'em. A consultant is one who points out work for others to finish."

That was exactly the 'select sires program' and he'd just described it. It was also close to accurately describing my job in computerized feeding systems. Damn . . . that Brigham, always well informed.

I was committed to life in the country and had decided the mental health industry was a hoax especially after my own had been shattered. That left making a living in middle age difficult. Much earlier, old comrades had condemned my predilection for country life (borrowing the words from Marx himself) as a tendency toward "rural idiocy." A farmer himself now, albeit a "highly technical" one, Brigham was trying to steer me toward making money. This direction suited me to bring up the rain damaged cattle feed scheme so I complied with his rude interrogations.

"Aren't you just playing 'let's pretend'?" he asked.

I didn't answer.

He continued, "You hang out with farmers but you're really not one of them. You're a fake . . . you don't even like country music!"

"Not true!" I spat.

"Name one," he glared.

"Huh?"

"Name two . . . name two of your favorite country music singers."

"Ray Charles and Leonard Chokin' Cohen," I answered. Both of us amused and pissed off. We weren't getting to business very quickly.

"You are terrible," he mused. "How long did you stay in the hospital?"

"Not long. No longer than I had to."

"And you were a terrible patient!"

"I growled a lot."

"You liked frightening the staff. You're sick. You need to stop having so much fun in the middle of a major depression."

"You know I am against that."

"Oh yes, we . . ." Brigham often used 'we' like the Queen of England."

"We forgot you are against . . ."

"Fun! I am against fun. It is no substitute for the finer things of life."

"Whaddayatalk? Fun is no substitute for the finer things . . which are . . . ?"

"Beauty! For one. Beauty, wisdom, truth, justice, a loyal wife, well behaved children, fierce dogs, fast cars and horses. Mad poetry. Ideas. Conversation. And landscapes you learn to love and walk around in . . . maybe ride through. You know, the secret canto of . . . His grace." (Religion was increasingly Brigham's weak spot.)

"What about money?" he snapped.

"Filthy lucre," I shot back. "Mere currency; tickets ex

changed for labor. What you work for to exchange for what you love. What puts you at least one step away from value."

"Forget about it. That's all past now! This old century is going to sleep and you are wailing like a stuck hog in the sixties, full of socialist rhetoric and religion. Things of the past!"

He was coaxed into the set-up; I intoned Eliot.

"And the past is about to happen
and the future was long since settled
and the wings of the future darken the past,
its beak and claws have desecrated
His story."

"C'mon I can't get a word in edgewise here."

"In edgewise is where
one wants a word when
the other persons words
make too much fucking sense."

He was tiring. "More Eliot?" he blankly asked.

"Nope, that was mine."

To get to the rain damaged raisin business, I knew we'd have to reach a kind of ideological truce. Not through mere recollections of our past, but in our recovering the old esprit, transforming failure and changing it into poetic models of action.

"Your rejecting our past," I began again, "handicaps our future."

"Yours not mine," he solemnized. "We no longer share a community of concerns or the same social perspective. Get government out of your head. Political ideas walk

you off the plank while others make the money.
Forget about Marx, think about markets!"

For all his hard ass business talk, maybe because of it, Brigham was being drawn to religious thought. All reconstructed Marxists require a theoretical context. Once before I had introduced religion too directly into our conversation and he'd taken a swing at me. I was riding with him in the air-conditioned cab of his tractor, French plowing the grapevines near Brigham's pool. We talked of Christian marriage vows and his wife's nervous breakdown. Ministering to him that "sanity is overrated" was too much for him to hear. My remark and his sixth or seventh brandy put us rolling around the cab and almost wrecked the tractor. Too much brandy and tractors don't mix. Too much brandy and crop dusters are even worse but that's another story.

This day, I rebutted Brigham that yes, community failed long ago, that society is now shot, that global governance grows in proportion to human gullibility and chaos. And that even the interior order of hope had been sundered, but what remains ... perhaps all that remains is the code of defiance. We can't be classified by the market or the state. New events we engage can fulfill and justify earlier ones we shared. Our new/olde tradition to join with god's grace . . . the secret canto.

Lumbering out of his loss of interest in our conversation, Brigham seriously continued, "Your seeking empathy for all this . . . this secret canto . . . your secret cause and it's consequences . . . I think is simply a fateful personality disorder."

"Nothing simple about it!" was my reply. "Especially the fateful part. Fate is complicated as well as mysterious. Until the days, rather the day of judgment there are rivers of complexity and we must struggle to be as certain as possible."

"That's not fate!" he said. "No sir . . . it is drivel. Yours is a fetid fetish of your own invention . . .
a farrago of fatalism. You are not to be feted.
You are a fatality!"

I knew I had his interest now, and concluded, "All that I am is in the power of His hand . . . that I may note the joy of His dreadful mysteries."

Brigham became pleasantly silent. He was so rarely silent that it seemed like prayer to me. I brought up the rain damaged raisins. The later raisin farmers harvest their grapes . . . Thompson Seedless, French Columbard, or even the famed Black Manuca . . . the higher the sugar content will be. The grapes will weigh more and bring a higher price. It is a gamble. If they wait too long, rains will ruin or damage the entire crop.

Reckless gambler that he was, Brigham had set new records at getting high priced sugar weight harvests dangerously close to autumn rains. Recently he had set records at losing his entire harvest to the rains. Many of his neighbors admiring his former high priced harvests had followed him into the recent disastrous one. He had 'failed crop' insurance. Not all of them did.

Brigham loved the idea of being paid twice for the same harvest and making it up to his neighbors. He felt sure we could get the crop into dryers to mix for cattle feed as the government insurance only forbid processing for human consumption. I had stats as to the number of dairy farms, head of cattle and cost differentials. Brigham beamed not only for the plan . . . he felt sure its very proposal proved his influence prevailed in our argument.

We shook on it. Friends again. Partners in crime. Comrades.

"Hungry?" he asked.

"Yeah."

"There's a new Armenian place I know . . . not pricey but good food and a bar. Let's have lunch. My invite."

"Swell," I actually said. Around Brigham's enthusiasm one regressed to boyhood words like 'swell' and 'neat.'

He'd been driving around back lanes for hours, ostensibly checking vines . . . arguing with me. Now he pulled on to the pavement and drove fast toward the edge of Fresno. His driving and the place always reminded me of Vukovitch.*

On the way I joked how yuppies are said to 'do' lunch and 'have' sex while our generation still insists on having one and doing the other.

"There'll be yuppies at lunch," he said. "A colony of Silicon Valley has landed in town and they always know the new places."

I told him I would prefer the company of Vukovitch.

The restaurant was a non-descript looking place at the edge of a stripmall. There were half a dozen new Cadillacs parked in front. Inside, the Cadillac yuppies filled up the bar area. We took a table near by. They were too loud to be ignored. Young men giggled like girls into the fronts of their suits. We ordered kebob, grape leaves, and two brandies and soda.

Brigham, very fraternal now wanted to talk about his idea to make and market brandy under his own label. I found

*Bill Vukovitch: Renown INDY 500 race car driver from Fresno. When asked why he rarely de-accelerated, he replied.. "When ever I start to slow down, I remember, picking grapes in Fresno, and speed up again.

that interesting and was trying hard to hear his words. Half of the bar crowd seemed to be leaving and a very professional looking female was joining the suits at the bar. She was tipsily and volubly teasing one fellow. . . calling him lunchface. And ol' lunchface was loving it. Every time she would look into his eyes and say 'lunchface' he would jerk like a seizure in his seat and guffaw.

Sitting between them and us was a lonely sad old girl just yearning to join in the young people's pleasure. She asked them something and they ignored her. Never imagining she was being snubbed by these convivial folk she stood and with great civility if not sobriety approached them at the bar. Touching the young woman companionably on the shoulder, she tried to speak . . . but whatever little sound she made was deafened out of the place by Lunchface.

He roared, "No, we don't want to talk to you. We doan' wanna even KNOW you!"

Tears broke on the old woman's face. She turned and tried to balance herself on the nearest chair. His three plus martini blood up lunchface kept yelling at the old tearful woman.

"By god," I said, as Brigham's eyes met mine and he finished the thought, "that's enough!"

We moved toward them, Brigham glancing to the right for me to cover his flank from the other suits as he picked Lunchface up by the necktie and scrotum, shook the shit out of him, brought him down hard and crotch straddled the back of his bar seat. Ol' Lunchface cried like a coyote pup. I stepped aside so the suits could comfort him. Gentleman Brigham escorted the tipsy looker to a far table and we both invited the old lady to ours. He ordered her a drink while motioning for me to call a cab.

The payphone was up by the bar and I could hear the suits behind me muttering about reinforcements. Back at the table, I told Brigham who dismissed it with, "We've got time. Keep giving them the look!" His back was to the bar, mine wasn't. The old girl introduced herself as a widow with a Portuguese family name.

"No, no," she said. "My dear Joe was Portuguese but I'm Dutch." We shared a few Portuguese words and she bragged on her sweetbread recipes. I asked her what island her in-laws came from and she said 'San Miguel.' All Valley Portuguese are from the Azores not the mainland.

The proprietor nervously joined us, not the lunchface crowd. Very much in charge, Brigham, assured all was in order as he nodded permission toward the tipsy looker to leave her seat for Lunchface or the door. The suits were on the payphone now recruiting reinforcements. Looking at them and then Brigham, the proprietor pleaded,

" . . . there's not going to be more trouble is there?"

"Not at all," Brigham reassured him while paying our bill . . . (waitresses wouldn't come out of the kitchen). As we learned that the old girl sometimes worked as a cook for the proprietor, Brigham began interrogating him about her working conditions. All the while, I'm an anxious sentry for her taxi or the reinforcements. Brigham was in no hurry. His back and forth with the proprietor was a stroll on the battlements.

"How much does she make a week?"

"Nine dollars an hour."

"A week?! How much a week?"

"She's never been here a full week. It's figured by the hour."

"By the week! . . . please."

"Nine dollars an hour . . ."

"A week!!"

"About $275 if she's here all week."

"Thank you!!!"

Interrupting his stroll, I announced that her cab had arrived. Grandly now, and very slowly (like a wedding march it seemed to me) Brigham escorts the old lady, her hand on his arm, by the suits at the bar and out the door. Much less slowly, I'd gotten to the taxi and had the door open for her. The suits were glaring at us from the window. They were also looking rescue hopeful down the streets horizon.

Next, Brigham was haggling with the cab driver for a set fee home for her cab fare. Then distressed that she might think he was trying to get her address, stepped clear of the cab and flagged it on.

"C'mon," I urged him toward the truck.

"Easy . . ." he said, smiling at the hostile faces in the window. "You still carry a boot knife?"

I nodded yes.

"Pitch it here!" he said, holding out his hand. I threw it to him, scabbard and all. He caught it over-handed and bent down to puncture the first Cadillac's tires.

"There's no time!" I warned.

"Plenty of time . . ." he responded. "It is altogether fitting and proper that we do this. Just keep giving

them the look!"
Leaving me standing by the Cadillac's' systematic deflation,
I mustered all the mean looks I could toward the window of
jabbering angry faces and especially their man on the phone.
But you know, they never came out as Brigham finished off the
Cadillacs' twelve tires.
Driving away cheerfully defiant . . . I feigned disapproval saying,
        "Aye and you're a terrible man!"
Brigham trumped my day's poetry by quoting Rilke,
        "Everything terrible is something that needs our love."

V Portions of Wrath

Davies County Sale 333

Authority Question 334

Baboon Machine 334

White Man 335

Young Man 335

Old Man 336

Middle of the Roader 337

Designated Clusters 338

Unduly Familiar 339

Little Death 339

Socialist Stenosis 339

The Church is Sold 340

Uncle Time 341

People 341

Lilac Winter 342

Thunder Factory 342

Snide and Credulous 343

Shangrila in Winter 344

Pony Expressions 344

¿Restful Sentence? 345

Laggard Dawn 345

Abandonment Anxiety 346

The Beginning of Sorrows 347

To Celtic Nationalists 348

Wanting Out 348

Legerdemain 349

Remembrance of Rats in the Wall 349

"Guide us on the straight path
the way of those whom thou has
bestowed thy grace
not the way of those whose portion is
wrath and who go astray"
Holy Koran

Libertarianism 350

PZ Pivot 350

A Female for Some Seasons 351

Anti, Anti, Antis 352

Gaza 353

Seasonal Dirt 353

Shades 354

Film Review 354

Coulombs Law 355

Scarcity 355

The Autumn Follicle 356

Exconversation 357

Redoubt 358

Not by Way of Sport 359

A Catholic Child . . . Defiled 360

Anglo Saxon O.D. 361

Collider 361

Even Lincoln had to get over Indiana 361

Anus Envy 362

Campus Banter 362

The Penumbral View 363

Fascinators Funeral 365

Uses of Cruelty 366

Seasons Jostle 367

Emoting Edna 367

Overcomers 368

Diffraction 369

N.Y.C. 370

Collectivist 370

Discourage 371

Manhood In Manhattan 372

Store Poem 372

Mistory 373

The City in Winter 373

Goyopla 374

Kurasawan 374

Meat the Press 375

Wet Ethnics 376

Winter Wren 376

Supermarket 376

Pupils 377

Halloweaned 378

Re: The Question of Women in Combat 379

. . . Or Sense of Comfort 381

Pedro in Outer Space 382

No Signal From Mars 382

Tic Tac Pto 383

Birdwatching 384

Swans 386

Probative Evidence 2 387

U.S.♀ Soldier 387

Hitler's Bridgework 387

Three Positions 388

Comradely Banter 389

Neo Uncon. 390

Geriatricom' on Baby 390

Horse Hauling 391

Anatomical Appreciation 391

Post Blizzard Mud 392

Calendars Disorder 392

Class Reunion 392

Robins in Bagdad 393

The Kindred Shade 394

Friends into Autumn 394

Plowshare 395

Sex vs. Violence 396

Loose Cargo 397

Lionophobic 398

Union Hospital Lobby 398

A Trembling Cup 399

January 399

Les Evans Index and Quote 400

Epigram Against Comrade Barnes 401

DAVIES COUNTY SALE

David held the young mare just outside the arena. She was frightened causing him half circle maneuvers, which angered an older boy with a beard who grabbed her. She threw the older bearded boy-arse, back, and shoulder- blades into the barn wall.

Anger is a very personal attempt to correct a loss of design. Patience is being that design others lack and buffet. Even jihad is a defensist posture against such abjectness. Stay eye of the storm cool, son, and the portions of wrath will waste themselves.

AUTHORITY QUESTION

I saw him on Sunday morning. I'd gone to get gas station cappuccino, and drove home along the side street by the village park. He was there with his sons and two german short hairs. One was dark maroon, the other had that ticing, that snow flecked coat that always arouses a hunter, especially when the scent of autumn lays down on late summer. Last week he'd told me, "I killed her in the shower with a framing hammer . . . but I never struck her unjustly."

In divine sonship, is he my brother or the villain that took her life? Clear as a criminal cousin he is both. The authorities are on their own.

BABOON MACHINE

He imagined her with pubic protuberances and buttock

callosities in brilliant red and blue, the axis of his

inserted lathe revolving cylindricals around which

other metals were merely forged or shaped.

Sometimes he thought of her as a baboon machine.

WHITE MAN

He was pale, blonde and sickly. He looked
hung over, ill, or slightly drugged as he stumbled
out of the men's room. Upon leaving I made a
wrong turn and came upon the unflushed waste
of his life.

YOUNG MAN

The dark sound, trembled
between his close cropped hair and the window . . .
a low rumble that did not rattle the glass,
except in the windowpane of his eyes . . . where
eighteen wheelers, trains, and
Newport's non palpable terror
twisted the peace of his mind.

OLD MAN

There was a remnant of ruggedness about him.

A sweet iron greyness eminent with wisdom, kindness

and the cold weather of violence.

He used to be a knife fighter and a good one.

He still carried a blade in his boot and bedroll.

He liked to cut his opponents in the face. "That

undoes the most steady enemy," he'd say. "Even

a stoic will grab at his own face wound. Then

you can cut his hands and disarm him."

He never walked away from a fight, nor had

he ever sought one. Plenty found him. He would

quote Simone Weil, "You have to be glad things happen

the way they do . . . exactly that way and no

other . . . ought else we wouldn't learn what

we're spose to."

He kept fighting and learning the peace

that passeth expecting anything else.

MIDDLE OF THE ROADER
(failed freudian attempts at moderation)

My vehicle was hurtling ahead just slightly beyond
conscious control. I knew it was too fast but some damn sched-
ule or other kept my foot in it as nuts as Vukovich sticking his
foot in it and never letting up cause he'd remember the boiling
indignities of picking grapes in Fresno . . not the exhilaration of
speed through time and space accelerating into a rounded curve
like holding the hip of your wife as you move into the length of
her entireties, but behind and beside yourself preoccupation that
usually wrecks all direction . . . Vaguely through the shrubs I
saw her move the bulbous Chevy forward . . . tentatively toying
to stop, start, and squeeze past the stop sign into my right away
upon whose trajectories course I rode screaming tires and brakes
trying to miss her. Her big assed S.U.V. filled up my horizon. I
spun left smashing my shotgun side into her engine flipping me
deep into the bean field and spinning her into one opposite the
road.

In the afterglow of lost consciousness, I struggled out
from under the airbag and bent door to try and stand up stumbling over the field across the road to see about her, prying her
door open, finding her covered with blood, especially along the
side of her face, neck, and amply tattooed breast. "God help us,"
I thought and said pulling her loose from the seat belt, then
noticing it had caught on several of her dozen earrings.
"You're not hurt!" I yelled . . . "You're wearing too many
earrings!" . . staggering backwards I thought of myself now and
sat down in the middle of the road.

DESIGNATED CLUSTERS

"Sounds like a cluster fuck to me," said the big Cuban.

He did not let it pass, but waited seconds for the others to join them, putting down his cigar to ask the Cuban, "How so?" as he glared through the smoke; his eyes asquint and far back in his head like caves for some kind of predator.

It made the Cuban nervous. All others waited for the fat mans response. It didn't come. It was the fat Cuban's office. He was boss here, rebutting now with an attempted authoritative silence. It seemed a weaker silence when he was asked again, "How so?"

They had known and endured each other for a year in their respective personaes as Administrator and staff. Staff had deferred to Administrator in order not to think otherwise. In this confrontive moment, they both knew it was terminally otherwise.

The Administrator kept fingering his laptop without images while staff reframed in his mind those pictures he had drawn up from the microfish of Batistianos and their plump sons shot by firing squads with photos of priests blessing their executed obesity.

The meeting coldly adjourned.

Staff stayed in Indiana.

The gusano got his in south Florida.

UNDULY FAMILIAR

The Arab gelding was proud cut and full of himself on the cold
March road. The woman who rode him was no longer young.
Her thighs and rump were swollen but not fat; her riding seat
looked good. I didn't recognize her until she spoke from a smile
that was spread your legs wide and familiar.

LITTLE DEATH

At penetration her eyes, head and neck jerked as if struck
by a shark down there . . . and from her lips came the pre orgas-
mic sounds altogether associated with a shark attack.

Bed sheets blew around like the oceans foam by the
buoys bell tower. The little death? Hell . . .

I was killing her by the time they came in the door.

SOCIALIST STENOSIS

Dx.ed Obstructive Lesions and Narrowing of the Left
Ventricle of the Human Heart.

THE CHURCH IS SOLD

The words *Immaculate Conception*
are still barely there
rubbed out to announce **HOG ROAST**
for full gospel heresy.

Immaculate Conception is closed.
Immaculate Conception is sold.
There's only one hairdresser to serve
the surrounding county seats.

One late vocation left
for larger parishes.
The place seems trashy and two clerically
released black rabbits hop outside the sacristy.

UNCLE TIME

There is kindness in a bullet or blade
instead of that dull heavy leverage
twisting pressure against your very bones.
When you hear one of them crack
you know its uncle time.

PEOPLE

A wrinkled old gal
looks at People Magazine.
She licks her thumb
to turn the pages . . .
of protuberant polished faces.

Lilac Winter

Lilac winter is colder
than when the blackberry cowers
unseasonably dashing
the hopes of spring against windflowers.

Thunder Factory

The thunder factory in Cornwall started this
shit. That McWop Marconis' wondrous
wizardry funded by Jameson Whiskey all the
way to Newfoundland; innocent radio
waves becoming radio activity toward
that ontologically doomed atom of Peace.

SNIDE AND CREDULOUS [1]
(Eulogy for Dan and Mary Alice)

They honeymooned in sleeping bags
high in the Sierras, and read to each other
"The Bending Cross," [2] Gene Debs joined them
as their socialist leaning parents
had read holy scripture.

They were the 'healthiest of elements'; pure hydrocarbons
on the boil from Northfield . . an operon joining
the Dvina and Onegas [3] plunge toward coastal seas,
keeping digs in Oakland I would stay with them
and enjoy the soft rhetoric of their love, laughter, salt air and politics.

We spoke to them in Chicago about their Swedish car and laughed at
the funeral talk of strangers through the cheap hotel room wall barely
noticing her glances at the boss, she left Dan for new jack
city indifferent to heavens frowns and hades maw
this cold adulterous consort in violating . . . natural law.

He suicided in Texas . . .
his handsome head stuck in an oven of unbelief and lies
no birefringent medium measures the refractive power of dead eyes
Asalam, aleikum Daniel, and of course for balast
equal peace to your half baked memory of Mary Alice

1. Suggested by the malice in Jane Austens 'Pride and Prejudous'
2. "The Bending Cross": Ray Gingers biography of Gene Debs
3. Dvina and Onega: River and Baltic Sea Waterway;
part of USSR Volga Canal System

SHANGRILA IN WINTER

The resonance of those Micks* from Indy
formed the urbane embrace of our uncoastal
juke box coloured love.
Alonesome youth surrounds both sides of solitude
High up as Himalayan Winters
in Kashmir.

*Micks from Indy: Flanagan's of Four Freshmen from Indianapolis.

PONY EXPRESSIONS

Orphaned wiry fellows who shoved
the continent behind their hooves
. . . inventing the doughnut
blame the U.S. mail
for autochthonous betrayal

¿RESTFUL SENTENCE?

A snow flurry
upon green swards of grass
make November a strange place
where the night of one season
descends over the color of another
as if rendered to tortures
cold age . . . is less rest
than sentence.

LAGGARD DAWN

Ominous sentiments sensed by the fire
said little in the wake
of next mornings locked horn memory
rattling loud as fence building in hot light.

Not notified about the horse you've raised
is like a son still stolen from you at sixty.

ABANDONMENT ANXIETY
(for Karl Augustus Menninger)

A Breugel painting is not to be dreamt in,
some landscapes are best left alone.
Yet, here I was in such a crowd
sitting beside my own grave,
surrounded by the collective disapproval
of all these beings who'd been buried before.

I recognized them not as souls who had abandoned me
but those who I had sort of abandoned.
You know, you move on . . .
Now they gnashed their teeth and refused me
raucously refusing all helpless requests
for my one shot at survival.

Something about my vitals
they refused and flew away.
Leaving me alone
by my own grave . . sin.

The Beginning of Sorrows

The farmer narrowed his eyes
 like slits across the throat of fawning
 for an illusive future.

"Things are changing now," he said
not meaning anything good.

"The weather and the will of men . . .
you know . . ." he closed his eyes

compleat . . ly.

TO CELTIC NATIONALISTS

My destiny is in the language of ancestral oppression.
I abuse and applaud it.
No muzhik me, to wring the neck of Borzois . . .
Welcome the imperial greyhound!
into the native mind, coursing truly free of grammar,
to wrench, to turn and kill the queens own hare
kidnapping the kings English for our publics uses.

WANTING OUT

She'd achieved a quiet intellectual
dignity; i.e. more subordinate
to me than all the independent
mediocrity she has since enjoyed.

LEGERDEMAIN

Moonlightness at hand is late
October upon a stone cold ledge
As the rains are late
deceits in the look of autumn foliage
When love is late
no less the conjure, less the knowledge
We dinnah choose the fate!

REMEMBRANCE OF RATS IN THE WALL

Rats in the bearing wall
sound Proustian;
gnawing inversions
of well being.

LIBERTARIANISM

Freemarkets of false consciousness
mass in madisonian self interest
dialectically amplify absurdities hymn
and generate a greater idolatry of . . whim.

PZ Pivot

Never knew women could be
priapistic until discovering alack
Paula Zahn putting herself forward
like a disembodied member upon Iraq

A FEMALE FOR SOME SEASONS

"I have not botoxed my butt or anything else.
My plainness is my personae. The people upstairs
have tried to get rid of me. The network clones
are worse . . . but I have my following, My
People, here in the Valley love me. They
love my enthusiasm . . my personality.
I'm told I have a lot of personality . . ."

ANTI, ANTI, ANTIS

She: Paul Newman plays too many proles. He is
       clearly more intelligent than those parts he plays.

Me: You mean more jewish.

She: He's only half jewish.

Me: Half more than a 'Hudson' car and all those
       cowboys and convicts!

She: You are anti-semetic.

Me: I'm not even anti-dentitic. Some of my best friends
       are dentists.

She: You are anti-semetic the same way you are anti-
       clerical. You expect too much from them.

Me: Maybe so, but only if you include arabs.

*"The error that love makes
is likewise yours"* The Bard,
Loves Labour Lost

GAZA

The almost young man spoke to the
almost white woman. "I know your parents
objections became merely an excuse for you.
You wanted done with me.

I also know that since then . . . all
these years you have loved me. And I
take satisfaction and sadness in that
I've not been alone about it."

SEASONAL DIRT

I like em' dirty in winter and clean in summer.
You talking women or horses?
I meant martinis.

SHADES

Hot shade is day witness to night shades dangerousness.
The obscure dramatic glow in a Hopper painting.
The light and heat of what felt like privacy.
Banked fires threatening to cool. Silent thought
in sinister times. Nights and days voiced
over by dark and not so dark angels.

FILM REVIEW

I cried and cussed at the movie **Carrie.**

Then I cried and cussed for crying and cussing

at such a film.

Coulombs Law

The torsion balance
cannot endure more frictional force.
Pale strength and product charge
are intensely proportional
to the square of the distance
between them.

The force of repulsion
drags the dragline.
Like Coulumbs Law
that love dissuade
its closing a single
tawdry page.

Scarcity

Although May it was so overcast
the bloom of black walnut fairly brightened
the day.

Sunshine as scarce as goodness
in a wife gone wrong.

The Autumn Follicle*

According to Poor Wills Almanac in my farm paper, "the Great Square of mid autumn is moving in . . . Cassiopeia lies due south of Polaris; its deepest intrusion overhead."

The first rut of the deer now begins. It will last 14 days. By December 5th the second and last rut will finish their breeding sleekness and go haggard into winter. Settledness in males and females will revive with the waterleaf and red clover as wet hay from the lack of sun increase nutritional needs for all creatures . . . beyond the rut.

Except for that significant sloppy sluttishness that has collected around some female follicles. Such afflicted does and mares stay in season til deep winter. Similarly diseased women statistically leave their men at this time through Autumn.

* An animal disease of pervasively stuck sexual arousal.

EXCONVERSATION

His ex: "No, no ___ no one sleeps their way to the top."

Her ex: ". . . The top . . the top of what?"

His ex: ". . . ?!"

Her ex: "So what position . . the top of what particular shit pile are you chastely lusting for?"

REDOUBT

Reversed slopes of Wellington will not
avoid our Cannon. No cavison of doubt bridles
otherwise. Yet Robert Graves, "goodbye to all
that" is the "that" behind precisely where
we're at.

"NOT BY WAY OF SPORT" (THE HOLY KORAN)
(The preemptive cultural product prior to Abu Gharaib)

Crepuscular as the crowd was hot with homecoming

is chill sweatering unbelly buttoned and bleak

to the point of it all. The Homecoming Game profane

and as coincidental as Warsaw's working class;

the queen candidates gowns providing cleavage

'round their ass.

Globalizing this product will not move it more quickly from the shelf.

Even the Superbowl of sappho and narcissus

is thought to be dismayed,   .

My churchly brothers and sisters it is the very core

of your cultural export back into desert places

remanding attention of His disappearing presence.

Watch the Superbowl and know why

they are more upset than thee; willing

to not only give up their lives to stop it

but take other lives who bring it.

A CATHOLIC CHILD . . . DEFILED

And the tossed black curls
of a catholic child
whose unknown legs
wrap around the fog

her spring grown hip asunder
St Anthony's grey bearded steeple
sighing, on the great damp lawn of the asylum

sidewalk pools reflect
the taste of a screen door
when we all pretended to be kids

Anglo Saxon O.D.

The coroner speaks. No recticular activating
of Winston's legacy. Churchill's legacy begins and ends
with men drowning in the latrines of Galipoli.

COLLIDER

Angular traffic is the meaning left
         near Stockton throughout its motion
             . . . trembling linear in colliding hearts.

Even Lincoln Had to Get Over Indiana

If Indiana were a melon it would make the
hardest greenest thump in the Union.
Hardheaded, half-baked, homegrown hoosiermindedness.
Produce of gentle sun lit rains, and too much humidity.

ANUS ENVY

She looked across our table at the "young people"
sentimentally salivating as Willard Scott might sound
when speaking of Riopan Plus.

CAMPUS BANTER

She: I like early classes to get myself going. And you . . ?
He: I signed up for Skinners psyc. lab once . . at 7:30 am.
Terrible! Rat shit and empiricists at dawn. Too much
for me.

The Penumbral View

He began to notice old broads looking at him. "You know," he'd say, "they look right at you, like females in Jr. High; the look from a brothel window, the way wives look at other men when they're leaving you." "The Old Stoves," he'd fume . . . "blisters!, geriatric floozies God damn . . they should be grandmas by now."

Next he noticed they were usually ten to twenty years younger than himself. For a while he was obsessed as to what this said about his own age. Pointing out persons in traffic or other crowds he'd ask his children, "do they look younger or older than me?" The kids would only giggle. Increasingly came the older looks; increasingly he came to think of them as the menopausal menace.

"You've taken this far too personal", his friend advised. "You're merely experiencing a rather universal end of the century slutishness. These women of all ages look at men of all ages as probable phallic candidates. They're eyeing many guys younger than you and not a few older. It says nothing about you; it says everything about them. They even 'look' at each other," his friend growled . . "in order to case out their collegial cuntingencies."

"You're beginning to sound misogynous", he told his friend.

"Hmm . . that would be an error', the friend replied. "Anyone hating half their own species gets a little weird. Feminists proved that! But, surely you see," he continued, "in this post feminist reality, beneath the ever growing backlash of misogyny. . . is real insight!" The friend's arm swept through the filtered smoke above the barroom floor and theatrically announced, "Observe!"

Observation framed the rectangular barroom as holding approximately twenty tables, the majority held by women, mostly young; some middle-aged. Men seemed peripheral. The patois of pop rock was sensuously pulsing through their pubic conscious-ness. They sat at different angles, slanting into the scene, softly humping the space between their own forms and general vacuity undulating to the discoed sound, simulating sexual gears, coitally coiled toward the empty air as if they passionately knew it was matching what was most between their ears.

FASCINATORS* FUNERAL
(brief tribute to Boyd Popcorn Johnson)

"I never knew Popcorn as well as many of you . . his close
friends and kin. I only knew him through the Fascinators who
are pals of mine. But I'd come to think of him as my favorite
Fascinator . . . not because his voice was big and deep as the
Wabash . . . but because of the stories I heard about him. About
how he fought for his children . . . fought for his fatherhood.
There is nothing more natural or fundamental than being a father,
yet these times have made it problematic. Being a father can
easily slip away, be stolen, or torn away. But not for Boyd. Popcorn fought against all odds for his children and he remained an
exemplary father.

I will always remember Popcorn as this remarkable father as
well as being one of the Fascinators. And the Fascinators for
many of us . . . they are our totem, our archetypal reps . . . out
there being cool in a world and society that definitely is not. I
will always think of Popcorn in both these ways and in both he
has earned our respect"

After this brief eulogy I encountered two attractive blondes
weeping in each others arms. Comforting them I inquired if they
were the deceased's children?
No!, they glared. "We're his ex wives," . . . the very odds he'd
fought against!

*Fascinators: famous do-wop singing group from Terre Haute.
(Don Kelly, L. Fuqua, L. Corey, J Carsey, W. Lynch, J. Calvin, and
Popcorn Johnson)

USES OF CRUELTY

♀ You ok? . . you awake?

♂ I'm awake.

♀ Why are you just sitting there?

♂ I need to speak with you.

♀ I'm late for work & I have a doctors appointment.

♂ Just a minute.

   She approached him between the bed and the door.

♀ This isn't going to upset me, is it?

♂ Not my intention.

♀ Well . . ,

♂ I love you wife. I am sorry for being cruel to you. You don't
   understand as I do how cruelty gets caught up with love. But,
   I am sorry I've been cruel to you. Please don't be cruel to me.

♀ . . .

♂ I think you are vulnerable to the inappropriateness of this man.

♀ Is that what this is about? Come on . . . !

♂ Please. (He touched her lips . . .) What you call my
   cruelty has put you out there past my protection. I know
   the old divils track better than you. You have
   not been inappropriate. He has . . . If I
   thought you responded to him (looking at his thumb)
   that much . . I would not go out like
   Aunt Em (who just died peacefully). I'd go out the way
   I came in. I would kill him for sure if I
   didn't kill you both . . .

   She kissed his brow.

SEASONS JOSTLE

Seasons jostle in freight time . . .

truncated cars . . .

in different hours along a low slung

track of steel. It winds straight in its

intention; metal against hard blocked metal

screech and bang these blocks of steel.

Now carousingly threads the curve of night, hung

over in yards unseasonably unrequited, without

a commonweal.

EMOTING EDNA
(an appreciation of E. St. Vincent Millay)

What lips below

my lips have kissed

and brought encephalitis so

I really need

not to know.

OVERCOMERS

The does were startled in high weeds

they moved vertically as well as away

like the lean . . nude girls we surprised in the shallows.

In too deep . . they splashed away from us.

Taking off our gear . .

we overcame them quickly.

DIFFRACTION
(Diffraction: when light passes by the edge of an
opaque body or through a narrow slit.)

She took off her pants as she did the Charleston.

Dark bands of fringe stuck to the moistness

of her body. Perspiring she poured herself

languidly into the red love seat.

He was all over her. "Where did you

learn all this in the eighth grade?", she asked.

"I dunno," he said.

"Do you know what to do next?"

"I think so, but I may need your help."

"With that big thing you'll not need anybody's help."

Years later he hitched a freight

through the Carolinas, missing her and

those bold diffracted nights.

N.Y.C.

As a stockman . . . I cannot approach this

place without marveling at its phenomenal manure

management. I raise horses, sheep, and goats . .

they'd never survive here . . at this volume of

manure production they'd die on their own

fumes. Hogs or chickens might make it . . .

but it would violate minimum sanitary

requirements.

COLLECTIVIST (for atheist Ayn)

The most selfish thing on earth is pain;

only becoming less so with sympathy

and not always then. We must

contemn individual pain with

collective sympathy.

DISCOURAGE

jr.:   ... discouraging day?

sr.:   Yeah .. a bird shit on my head. First thing out
the door. It got me from the guttering. Doesn't
bode well!

jr.:   Ever happen before?

sr.:   Once, when I was getting rid of a witch.
Seeing her to her car .. she was humming incantations.
I was talking fast about St. Francis.
She looked up and grinned. A bird shit
on my head then .. too.

jr.:   a bad day followed?

sr.:   The truth is son .. good whiskey (God forgive me)
followed in abundance.

Manhood in Manhattan

It is impossible for me to be

in Manhattan without wanting

to be King Kong.

In future remakes and there will be many;

beastial coitus will finally be consumated.

I would recommend a more or less politically correct

albino ape and black woman.

STORE POEM

the weather is not well

she said, since the war

a brown paper sack

clapped open

for the produce I had bought

and we shared a smile

that sadness often lends.

MISTORY

Northern muslims

are like Western socialists.

Moody over losses

of more mistory

than is good for them.

THE CITY IN WINTER

is cold cement

sidewalks and greystone eyes

on our face and tongue.

The frozen spinal marrow

reminder of all those crowded ditches . . and deaths

we've chosen to never think about.

GOYOPLA*

I'm not your goy.

I'm not your shabaz goy . .

or any other kind of goddamned

goy. I'm your Goyopla;

*Goyopla: Geronimos real Chirikawa name.

KURASAWAN

Sparrow flecked fate

drawn witness to the color

of that indescribable sky source of wind

my anger at the privileged pounds

of mouth wagging flack

is digesting me

I could become a pacifist

like Kurasawa

my mind as free of violence

as his movies.

Meet the Press

Our youngest laughed and called it Press the Meat.

We watched it Sunday mornings.

That Sunday morning we watched

and read from the Torah, the Gospels, and Koran

feeling married in the light of those words.

Then fought all the way to the party

passing amish buggies in the rain

who were returning to collective ideas of home

while we were splintering experience

into individual histories,

full of pain and full of ourselves.

We press the meat . . . mercilessly.

WET ETHNICS

Rain refreshes the English

saves the Semites from their sins

and bends the Celtic mind to murder.

WINTER WREN

The details of his August thought

will dart into the coming snowdrifts.

And we will live

like the winter wren

Always ahead of herself.

SUPERMARKET

Coagulated charm at the supermarket

coming along the dairy case

looking like 'Norma Desmond's

post creative close up at the end

of 'Sunset Boulevard'.

PUPILS

The white kitten with grey eyes
rubs up against the clouded glass
separating warmth from the cold schoolyard
whose pupils ignore it.

Two obese and neutered Labradors
accompany giggling girls to the door.
They see the kitten and kill it,
slowly breaking and stretching its head, back, and intestines;

. . . while elementary educators
turn their charges away from
violence at school.

HALLOWEANED

All hallows wind blows rough as an ogres breath phlegming dust
and leaves across this sun stormed world where women wail
and mares act nuts in pastures of the moon. Windswept razors
scrape the earth bound butts of young big assed mothers gathering
their babes ineptly they bump and bully against their own maturity.

There is an insect growth regulator used to poison roaches which
arrests their reproductive intelligence.
It must have spilled into the bloodstream of my
nations adolescence.

RE: THE QUESTION OF WOMEN IN COMBAT

Ali: It is a peripheral question regarding a peripheral state of being much as Mohammeden Ould-Mey writes of peripheral entrapment. *["Global Restructuring and Peripheral States" by Mohameden Ould-Mey]*

Christolf: Might not the spirit of woman take command and call for Peace?

Sam: Blast . . . and double blast.

Ali: Gender politics is as a peripheral state provided cash by those who can then devalue the ability to gain or maintain.

Christolf: Mmm . . You mean like fem-flam family substitutions.

Ali: Like the C.B.I. unnaturally creating command then not supporting it. Recruited and recused.

Christolf: Seduced and abandoned. We fall for the feint and become doubly enveloped by demons. They do what Dan Morgan did to the redcoats.

Sam: Blasts of clitoral clutter. Interior decoration. Bed and breakfast fantasying strangers in the night coming in and out of em' . . . even staying for breakfast.

Ali: We must reconnoiter and decode the clutter of their cystograms.

Christolf: Never again accepting the nature of this command no matter how invited . . . it is out on an unnatural limb to be naturally sawed off.

Ali: As for me . . I'll leave the country.

Sam: If the bitches want to fight . . send them to war, just keep em' out of my house. Hey! Mary Cheney, I'm calling you out! Spend the night with me and I'll make a real republican out of you.

.. OR SENSE OF COMFORT

Or in discomfort . . . at Yale

on tides of disappreciation

'Trucolor' slides as post depression

coed brides move down the hall away

before Bush, Kerry, and Dean

before even I came to New Haven,

before Jack Marsh and me harassed the Harvard Green

I spoke defensively in a paneled room

at Yale without Margaret O'Brians smile

to an audience smaller than the number of my retainers

and met a 'police force pacifist' Professor

and a genius Healyite from England

before all of that, there was discomfort

from Yale as depreciation grows

falling on our failing expectations.

Baa baa baa on the life of the world to come

sadly interfering with our personal effectiveness

. . . or sense of comfort.

*"Proliferation of means brings about the disappearance of ends.
The conquest of space becomes an end in itself, which dispenses
with any need for reflection."* Jacques Ellul, *The Technological Society*

PEDRO IN OUTER SPACE

From the Polytechnic University of Granada
comes News of the ISS Intl. extravaganzas.
Duque in Space.
Decay still on the ground.

NO SIGNAL FROM MARS

The sunny cold waited; an overreach
centrifugally inflated . . missioned out
and overdeveloped. There is no signal
from Mars; polar landering failure
for centripetalist strength.
As Mailer explained to the bitch
two decades ago, "Shut up!",
he explained . . your centrifugal envy
is a Bore Vidal. The strength of
centripetal justice slouches terminally
toward your sly space.

TIC TAC PTO

X   "Look what we want to put on the moon!

Adulterous psychopaths in diapers!!"

O   "Who . . . ?"

X   "The fornicating unisexual U.S. soldiers cum

astronauts. NASA mothers taken away

from their families to fornicate with their

fellow soldiers."

O   "She said it was more than collegial but

less than a romantic relationship . . ."

X   "She drove 900 non-stop miles in a diaper cuz

she wuz clearly getting less than she wanted."

BIRDWATCHING

1963   Kildeer flew in Vaugn white mornings
knowing the fragipan as my hidden sea.

1973   From higher ground outside D.C. I saw buzzards
building nests on the Capital building.

1983   California seagulls fly close around the creamery
inland on Modesto's McHenry Street.

1993   Kildeer, gull, and Condor are lyrical motion
moving muscular in the skies I breathe.

2003   The sky is leaden behind the White House
earth bound lack of flight dulls the american mind.
Until the . . swans . . .

Wild Swans at Shadowgait

SWANS

Wild Swans were with us last year

from cool seasons warm days they came

to my family estate

like Swans of the afterlife;

swans beyond the grave

where my parents were lain

leaving us worse than in testate

they died but months separate

my mother, serene if at strange angles

to the peace I thought not entirely

passeth my understanding.

The fumes of my father twisting

his expression in death as in life

from the darkness as it overspreads

but for the Swans who visited us then

and we look for them this year

we look for them again.

PROBATIVE EVIDENCE 2

bones: We're talking about Cubans man! You know . .
cubanskys. Cut throats without conscience. Gusanos!

cop: They use a Tech 9?

bones: Hell yeah, Tech 9s against a rolled up Sun Times.
He broke both their ribcages with it while they were whacking him
. . . Shooting him . . . trying to shoot him dead. There were bullet
holes all over him and his bookcases.

U.S. ♀ SOLDIER

"A water snake almost swam into my kayak"

HITLER'S BRIDGEWORK

Die Furors jaws and bridgework
were placed in a cheap red box and
assigned to a Russian Lady Dental Officer.
She poured drinks for her men on the 8th of May
in 1945 Berlin while her sisters enslaved
by the nazis were raped by the red army.

THREE POSITIONS

Today's republicans are[1] 18th century liberals who believe in being as "free" with the economy as[2] 21st century liberals are with their genitals.

Even the[3] Marxists,

nobility of intent

their perspectives inherent -

ly undone by enlightenment

in their pants.

Comradely Banter

X: I once was a compassionate comm., now I'm more of a neo comm.

O: You know Hobsbawms "Age of Extremes"?

X: Yeah.

O: Well, his consciousness is out there in those extremes.

X: But, you don't see me as extreme . . do you?

O: Man, you are the very square root of deviance!

NEO UNCON.

I used to go . . . to sleep
now, it comes to me
mounting my receptivity
filling me up with all
that death lacks pride in
being out there in time
running out into nothingness

GERIATRICOM' ON BABY

(" Where their worm does not die nor the fire go out" Mark 9:49)

Damien Hirsts "Physical Impossibility
of Death in the Mind of Someone Living" s'
eight million dollar dead fish
is close to Larry Lee Lewis on Imus in the Morning.
Hardons in Formaldehyde
Geriatricom'on Baby!

HORSE HAULING

A cemetery in dawn light
just out of Marshall
matches the beauty, but not
the breath form of holsteins
up the hill; cornstalks reflecting
the same sun storms that guide
my aging vision . . not to cross
double yellow lines I swear at the
dumbass SUVing around me.
. . . hauling horses is more dangerous
than driving or riding them.

ANATOMICAL APPRECIATION

"I couldn't believe how they carried on
about her arms," the prof. said. A porchfull
of academics chortled agreement. "Yes," I
differed, "that wasn't the part of her
I noticed the most." All chortling ceased.

POST BLIZZARD MUD

 Lights in the cockpit go dark
far, too far from the terminal.
Engines whine against the ice.
In time, the unsubtly keener
sounds of wild geese and flash flood
anticipate the oh so welcome suck
of mud.

CALENDARS DISORDER

The idea of order is outside Indiana,
way outdoors where you can't get home for supper.
Dragging in that regretful morphology
of raggedy ass seasons so fickly overlapped.

CLASS REUNION

♀: I thought you'd be uncomfortable there with all
my classmates. You wouldn't know anyone.
I thought you'd be uncomfortable.

♂: I'm never uncomfortable in any social scene.
I make others uncomfortable.

ROBINS IN BAGDAD
(Vet-Shrink Dialogue)

Shrink: What did you notice most in Iraq?

Vet: Theys robins with long tails in the trees of
Baghdad and lots of lookers in the streets
. . . without veils! . . but wat I noticed
most was em' private armies cloggin the
hospital . . . Blackwaters so called security
squads recruited from right wing militias.
Most of em' westerners . . . those guys
got their own agenda.

Shrink: Yup . . its probably easier to turn
fascists into soldiers than soldiers into
fascists.

The Kindred Shade

No sound

Road

From grazing years, before the grave

Iron bridged but fearing sweetly

The kindred shade breaks softly . .

Splayed hooved and earth pounding

Our nightmare

Rides toward dawn

Friends into Autumn

Late August burns

like a bit into Autumn

turning visceral,

as time breaks the voice of a friend

and we mark our borders

like ill Duce and the old Lynx

like leopards tearing at the tree

of all those tomorrows

we will never be . . .

PLOWSHARE

"The olde ways will save you from the time
I will plow the earth of the Americas
up over these unholy intruders."
Tecumseh's brother, known as The Prophet interprets signs of
The Great Spirit

Northern Indiana was not far enough to be safe from the aid de
camp of Mad Anthony Wayne . . . this Harrison who presumed
to govern and murder native prophecy.
Tecumseh sent General Proctor* packing in his petticoats but
hated torture too late to save the native confederacy. It died but
not his brother's prophecy . . .
"The olde ways will save you from the time
 I will plow the earth of the Americas
 up over these unholy intruders."

*General Proctor: Tory transvestite

SEX VS. VIOLENCE

("I write about love and money; what else is there to write about"; Jane Austen)   She reckoned love and money were the only significant subjects for a writer.

Ed McBain (aka Salvatore Lambino) amended "they've turned love into sex and money into power and violence. The two most important themes for a writer remain sex and violence."

For me it is sex vs. violence. And although it's a late entry I'll give you ten to one odds in favor of violence.

LOOSE CARGO

Cormac: She's wagon room vaginismis. Quaking
pubococcygeus walls more than Joshua
could get over let alone into. Bolt wagon
hard; wide and all too trafficked in. You'd
need calipers to measure that hole into
which so many have disappeared.

Cuckhold: Well . . . he's taking care of her . . isn't he?

Cormac: He . . that wet eared weight lifting
                sissy . . he looks like a start, stop
                and squeeze man to me.

LIONOPHOBIC

Researchers now confirm

African hunters report a certain pathos

in understanding maneless, testosteroneless

male lions who pack together avoiding females

and turn to cowardly man eating

UNION HOSPITAL LOBBY

Cold bleak shades of May

in cowering embrace

hide the sun behind,

over and under the belt of obesity

being less than the plight

of post agrarian, post industrial

loss insite of human souls esteem

A TREMBLING CUP

"Oh ho ohoh oooh, that is so powerful Jack.

Ohooh get it in! Get it into . .

Get it into . . . the mail."

Mrs. Jack Van Impe (Dr. Rexella Van Impe)
Jack Van Impe Ministries
(in response to: ad for "Dictator of New World Order")

JANUARY

Christmas trees burn in trash barrels

around Second and Cherry

Whores squat inside and clean themselves

for the New Year.

McKeon, Edith, 56, 57–58, 63, 67, 73, 78–79, 238
McMoneagle, Joseph, 363–364, 365
McReynolds, David, 210
McSorley's Old Ale House, 139–140
Memories, Dreams, Reflections (Carl Jung), 7–8
Mendiola, Douglas, 48
Mendis, Kamini, 381
Mengistu Haile Mariam, 254
Menlo Avenue, 365–369
Menlo Grammar School, 6–7
Mensheviks, 286
Menuhin, Yaltah, 67, 72, 98–99
Menuhin, Yehudi, 67, 98

Moreno, Enrique (Harry Evans' nicknam 50
Moreno, Nahuel, 197, 257, 295
Morgan, Lewis Henry, 237
Morgan, Tom, 129
    warnings against Jack Barnes, 151–15
Morrison, Derrick, 216
Morrow, Felix, 228, 236, 241. *See also* Goldman-Morrow faction
    as occult publisher, 242, 243
    and Whittaker Chambers, 243
Morse, Linda, 186, 187, 190–192
Mortensen, Mike, 69
Mountain Spring Camp, 107, 119, 278
Moustapha, Imad, 398

(circa 1964) "Tom was angry. But his charges went much further; Jack Barnes is the Stalin of the S.W.P. . . . The older comrades are desperate for successors so they blind themselves to it but Barnes is building a machine just like Stalin did. He undermines anyone who isn't part of his clique and gets them out of the way. He doesn't want recruits who know anything, nobody who was ever in any other socialist organization. All he wants is empty vessels he can fill up with his picture of himself as another Lenin."

Les Evans, *Outsiders Reverie*, A Memoir Boryana Press L.A. As always, Les remains a sensitive, dedicated comrade. Leader of the Y.S.A at U.C.L.A in the sixties he mentored my motorcycle courtship of Anne Dorazio. His memoir records incredible times in Southern California. I recommend it. It is the best of many 21st century revelations of what was bloody obvious 50 years ago.

TGM

Epigram Against Comrade Barnes

Living without the scent of earth
Slick and citified garroting of time
Congenitally arresting conversation,
His imperial self . . . in tragic slime.

Defying gravity is managed
as deformed descent in depravity.
His truncated stump of phallic envy
an Adlerian phenomena to cripple others.

His eyes probing actuaries
for targeted advantage.
Out the side of his mouth
perspires a twistedness
not easily untangled.
His rictus, their gaping sycophancy
chats up his cheering sections
to feel less empty as his vassals.

Transtrotskyists in leather, souls shod in Kobas boots;
marxist thought massaged then metastasized.
Homophonous homunculi; fruits of the womb
fear nothing but not to be asked or told.
They follow his prowling flash of heat
lightening up the marginally undefined.
Scorn as corn in collaborative alliance
with lumpen synanthropy. He's not askance
to print the scabbiest in union defiance.

Immunity of his org. within the Org.
accounting organizational critiques accrue cover
for political disloyalties. Retail agreement
required for wholesale theft,
this businessmans banal
and primitive accumulations
lies in his bullet bald brains
Imperious Liquidations;
Integrity bereft...
Genius spent or subsidized
he is...Liquidator of the American Left.   401

"… man has lost all contact with his natural
framework and has to do only with the organized
technical intermediary which sustains relations both
with the world of life and with the world of brute force
… man then finds that he cannot pierce the shell
of technology to find again the ancient milieu to which
he was adapted for hundreds of thousands of years."

Jacques Ellul *The Technological Society*

"For a mans words flow
out of what fills his heart"
Luke 6:45

VI   A PROPER CALIBER

A Proper Caliber 409

Anno D. 412

The Comely Widow 413

Love in the Environs of Lee Avenue 420

While I Wait for Her 423

Our Time 423

Adumbrare 424

Turkey Run 425

Crazy Eights 426

Love is not a Reality Achieved, but Endured 427

From my Window 429

Barnswallow 429

No Place to Die 430

In Clover 431

Caress 431

My Foals in Far Pastures 431

Fledgling 432

Teamstering 433

Tender Pastures 434

The Shepherd Boy 435

Womb Envy 436

Teen Time 437

Factions 438

Outside Modesty 439

The Death of Stallions 440

The Black Hem 441

Heather 442

Funeral Rain 443

Boiler Plate 444

No Surprises 445

Nearer the Dust 446

Death of a Wren 447

Wreath 449

The Pentecostal Bomber 450

Breeze at our Back 459

The Greatest Elengeness 460

Green on the Ground 461

Ozark Coffee 463

Egyptian Wells 466

Optical Allusion 472

Locking the Doors of Darkness 473

November Sun 474

Not so Little Deaths 477

Gently Stupid 478

Indian Giver 478

Gray Pudding 479

Plain Justice 480

Prairie Minded 482

Amish Prisoners 483

Heavy Water 486

Everything Matters 487

Yonder 487

Sycamores 488

Pollack 489

Olde Brush Wolf of the Wabash 490

Brave Kid 491

Injured Buck 492

Cold Conviviality 493

Mules on the Road 494

Aposiopesis 498

High Denial 500

Coldstream Guards 500

Van Gogh Yellow 501

Koranic Haiku 502

Comely While Leaving 503

Pathetic Fallacy 504

Two Kinds 505

Beyond the Pale 506

Bison 507

38th St. Smoke 508

New Made Bed 509

Mexican Frowns 510

Three Jakes 511

Ancien Regimes 514

Clouds on the Ground 515

Breaking Severities 515

Red Grey Evenings 516

The Furthest Turn 517

Holy Saturday 518

The Full Loaf 519

Permutation 520

Imperanent Pasture 522

Winterior Seiche 523

Calico Coyote Hounds 524

Sluice of May 525

Fist of the Moon 526

A Natural Smile 526

Brother Hounds 527

The Other Time 528

Into the Rain 529

Dying Men Don't Drink Beer 530

Long Johns in June 536

Sprung 537

Consolidation 538

Truth and Commotions 539

No Gnats in Goshen 546

The Authority of Failure 548

Firewake 549

Need for a Neo Comm. Manifesto 550

Ballad from a Still Pond 551

The Talking Pond 552

Stables 554

The Yearling Mule 555

Sweet Furlough 556

Embalmed Evening 557

A Hearts Tack 558

Wholly Holy Picture 558

A Muggy Day in Manhatten 559

Revolutionary Recluse 560

Sunsigns 564

Hope for Audacity 566

Negritude 570

Hard Light 571

Synchronicity 572

Rain not Fallen 573

Terre Hautesprit 576

Les Vestiges de Terre Haute 580

Conditional Love 582

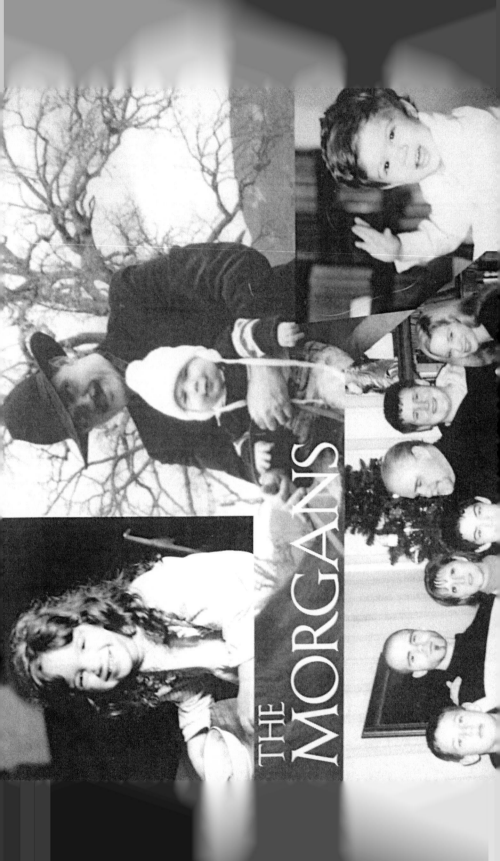

THE MORGANS

A PROPER CALIBER

Monday morning after the first weekend

of deer season,

he pulled up the long rock grade

to the docks of the packing plant

and found a pile of dead deer

on the ground.

A still life of hooves and horn

no longer thrashing but still . . . on the cinders

unhappily expressed in death . . . half seemed

biting down hard on their tongues

as if choked to death, rather than from

those shotgunned holes in their chest.

He came for the lamb he'd roped and wrestled live

from field to shed then violently on to the truck.

A 140 lb ram lamb of Cheviot wildness,

it fought hard against capture.

His knuckles had bled on the wool

and into the wild frightened eyes of the lamb.

Worn out . . . with his forehead on the brow of the young ram

he yelled, "You're dead already, quit fighting!"

Then guiltily asked God's forgiveness for

being so rough with the beast

whom he loved and made sure had water

when he left him in the holding pen.

Now, he put sixty some pounds of chops, and roast

into his car and turned to look at the deer again.

A whole dead herd of twenty to thirty bucks and does

. . . he never counted them,

but thought about the trio of disoriented

not yet yearlings seen in the meadows.

He remembered the last time he saw herds of deer

was in the Sierras just below the snow line. . .

nearly a hundred blacktail

picking their way down the slope

ahead of bad weather.

Mountain mice some Westerners called them

and complained of driving hazards.

These hoosier deer may be the biggest white tail in the world;

corn and soybean fed to maximum size and antler point.

He loved seeing them in the field, forest

and jumping over fence lines.

He didn't like traffic any more than they did

and stayed when he could in the back country.

He hated deer season when they'd run up to the farm

or your car on the road;

eyes bulging with fear and panic

like the ram lamb he'd dragged to the butcher.

No pink cellophane packaged denial,

no humane disrespect for reality

that beasts need to be loved and slain

occlude his heart felt hatred for the killing.

He ate venison but usually disliked deerslayers.

He butchered his own beasts he'd bred, raised and loved,

but it bothered him.

He thought of his old neighbor the quail hunter

who kept Pointers and taught him the mystery

of wing and shot; about how to love everything about the quail

including the shooting of them.

Old Taylor raised quail, released them, visited and

talked to them out of season, before shooting them

in season.

His was a proper caliber.

Anno D.

The crescent
        cuts into the November cold
        opening narratives again;
        a slender grasp
        on fat reality

Harvest hawg ass loud
        the din . . .
        false faces that cause
        children to hold their ears
        and consciousness breaking wind

Honesty militant,
        and temperament remote
        convene the very weather
        giving thanks to what has been
        otherwise . . . when . . .

Not then, but yielding
        now existent
        our old years weather
        is never new nor worn
        it passes beastly thin

        into the damned old dirt!

THE COMELY WIDOW

My life was grinding to a halt. I could hear it . . . like a lame horse in heavy gravel. A second divorce, a second beginning . . . shot.

She'd taken my young son with her . . . all the way back to the West Coast. My first ex had my oldest son and daughter on the East Coast. She had bitten the big grimey apple of feminine careerist ambition decades ago. For half that time I wandered in the opposite direction until she (my first ex) formalized her adultery in legal union and I wed my second ex on the basis that I had denied myself beauty too long. She was the prettiest "girl" in the hospital.

"Girl" being the operative word. After four years and one issue of our union she left at 25. I was 52. She returned to a succession of pot smoking beaus and poor investments.

"Heed the Spark or Dread the Fire"; more their problem than mine. I would stay in my broken heartland and leave them the adulterous coasts.

As per my sainted mother's advice, I worked at three jobs during the week. . . then collapsed on the weekend. Soon my wages were being garnished by the last ex . . . calculated on my triple job income.

I needed counseling!

Stumbling over to my Amish neighbor's one Sunday I received it! Jake Hostetter heard me out, reframing my trouble

413

into more work to be done. He asked how I was sleeping?
He said God honors work and Love turns work into rest.
Demonstrably he shared some light work around his dairy barn
with me before we sat down and drank whole milk from its stain-
less steel bulk tank. "There will be a way," he'd say. "You have
to wait on it to open up. Faithfully leave it to God . . . don't try to
help him. He does not need us. We need him!"

"I'll say!" I tried to end our talk. He continued seriously,
"In His own good time. Sometimes that's a long time. Sometimes it's . . . before suppertime", he grinned and tugged at my
arm toward their kitchen door. He didn't always do that on Sundays. I was glad when he did. That evening supper with Jake
and his wife, Annie, I began to notice on Sundays none of the
children were around. Weekly, I would walk past their NO SUN-
DAY SALES sign and since I wasn't buying or selling anything .
. . didn't bother about it. That Sunday I was beginning to get it.

There were no kids around. Other days there were always
kids around. After I asked about them, Jacob glanced at the Sunday sign and looked at me.

The Amish are like that. Instead of hitting you with a
thought they'll just look at you until you hit yourself with it.

Damn, it hit me . . . Sundays are Mom and Dad's intimate
time. I got it. Jacob saw that I got it and never said a word; I never
visited on Sunday again. They always seemed pleased to see me
on all other days.

On one of those days, there was sadness in the Hostet-
ters household. A young cousin of Jacobs had died in Wisconsin.

They'd been especially fond of him. Also from Lancaster PA, he'd chosen to settle his family in the north country instead of Indiana. He had eight children and their families were close. He'd reached over his buggie's dashboard to adjust the single tree. A fluke accident . . . his green driving horse kicked him right between the eyes and he was dead.

"Leaving his Rachel with all those children . . . " Jacob paused, and looked at me. It was a serious look. He spoke very slowly, "She is a comely widow . . ." Annie came in to look at us both not speaking but looking at each other over this matter.

I couldn't think of anything else, the whole next week . . . and the week after. (Jacob, Annie and their older kids had gone to the funeral in Wisconsin.) "A comely widow . . ." I swear that Jacob sounds more Elizabethan than Amish sometimes.

I'd planned to ride the bay mare with a bad eye over to Jake's on Saturday. She was a standard-bred but never raced . . . and more than a little spooky. I was trying to desensitize her to deer and traffic. Regular weekly exposure to the same was working, but I decided to forego horse training and sped over early in my truck with some special coffee for Annie.

We sat outside with our coffee mugs . . . Annie trudging from the kitchen and children to wait on us. Jake spoke right up to where we'd left our thinking last week. "Somethings are meant to be," he said, "My cousin, Chris, seemed to know . . . he was about to go. He'd just finished clarifying his will and talked to the family about it. He reconciled some old quarrels in community and spoke to the minister about dying. Rachel, (the comely widow . . . I was growing accustomed to her name) said he'd become especially affectionate with the children just before the accident."

I asked about every child . . . all eight of 'em . . . their names, ages and what they were like. Jake responded in detail with extended anecdotes.

Impatiently, I broke in, "How soon can I petition for courtship?"

"Give it a month," he said.

I found myself saying, "Allahu akbar." Jacob beamed. We shared mutual Muslim friends, but that's another story.

I'd have to join the Amish community first, but Jake thought I could do that concurrently with my petition for courtship. I'd have to speak with the Bishop while Jake would carefully woo Rachel's approval for the courtship. She could always veto the proposed match at any time.

I was more concerned about . . . a wee bit worried about . . . if I was tough enough to become Amish. I knew I could be a faithful husband, father, and provider. I was ready to go without car and truck payments. Lanterns and gaslight wouldn't be so bad . . . going to bed and getting up with the sun. Yeah . . I was ready to get rid of wires and electrical bills...but plumbing, that is, the relative lack of it might be difficult. Mainly I didn't like the idea of doing without music, movies, and TV . . . Hell, I'd tough it out. Small sacrifice for the return of family life. I yearned for a loyal loving wife, children to fill up my lonely, big old house. I could hear the wheels of Providence grinding out a new straight path.

I could always steal away to Mass and the movies.

A month passed. Jacob spoke to Rachel and to the Bishop. I got a lot of encouragement from the former and an appointment with the latter.

This Bishop's home sat 200 yards back off the pavement. A straight lane cut between cultivated crop ground and pastured meadows for dairy cows. A sign out front advertised fresh eggs, Jack Russell puppies and of course, NO SUNDAY SALES. I'd sold the first Jack Russell years ago to the Amish community. I wondered if these pups were related.

Bishop Stoltzfuss received me in an open room adjoining his large kitchen. In his early forties, I guessed; he was younger than I expected. He was Amish hospitable, but in a reserved, bespectacled manner.

First, I tried to josh we might be related through the canine line of Jack Russells. He seriously didn't get it. More seriously I tried to inquire about the breeding of his Jack Russells. He didn't know!!

My cordial attempts failing, I got straight to the point. I told him I wished to join the Amish Community and church under his bishopric and to petition for courtship of the widow Rachel Riel in Wisconsin, with her permission, of course.

He asked how well I knew her children? I answered I did not know them, but knew of them . . . then spoke at length about each from Jacob's descriptions. He asked about my children. I lovingly described the issue[1] of both crops and railed against how contemporary no fault divorce was unique and horrible in the

417

history of human contracts.

This young bishop then smiled a bit and seemed sympathetic about my divorces. He asked how I earned my bread and how separate I was living and how separate I could live in the future. I described my private practice and my livestock farm. He didn't ask me to quantify income, but I could tell he was interested. Carefully he asked me to describe not my previous divorces, but my previous marriages, i.e. my wives. I did so in detail.

After some more questions regarding my sheep, goats and harness horses (I never mentioned my hounds), he seemed satisfied and I expected him to say he'd get back to me or to set another meeting. Instead, he said (rather hushed and almost hurriedly for an Amishman), "We'd love to have you join us, but you would have to reconcile with your first wife and come in as a family."

I couldn't believe it! I had given him a detailed account of my first wife's betrayal and how she was "out there somewhere to the left of whoopee." He knew fully of Jacob's sponsorship and Rachel's encouragement.

Involutionally and volubly I heard myself blurting, "Are you nuts!?!"

Decades later, those same steel wheels of Providence have delivered a seasoned and successful marriage to me, reconciliation with all my children and the greatest reputation and stock possible with the Amish . . . because I'd wanted to be one of them and since they always bump heads with their Bishop, they have the highest regard for anyone rejected by him.

In time, Jacob would josh in merry scorn . . . "With your mental health credentials, you shouldn't have challenged his!" Then we laugh together. We laugh together as only Amish can. In sudden joy these venerable Patriarchs . . these free holding farmer fathers laugh, "whenever confounded good thoughts strike their laughter loving brain".[2]

1. Horseman's term for offspring

2. From Washington Irving's Alhambra

"Love in the Environs of Lee Avenue"

Terre Haute in the cold is a dreary ass place. Its dark and wintry soul succumbs to the shades of an old noir film. Sinister, sore and still ashamed with a wanton working class preference to be insane, never inane.

That was my department and the occasion of my first seeing Lee Avenue. It was her block dead-ended against Lost Creek between Carosis cuisine and Stop Fives drunkenness. Three generational home place for her family, grandparents, aunts, uncles and cousins.

It is a strange strange place when seen through a map of the minds metabolism and her people's history of pain. Divorced parents still associated through decades of hard work and scrimmage in a dying culture. His gun fired earth beside the head of a thief who threatened his daughters. Their mother broken upon hard surfaces intoxicating paralysis preferred to betrayal. Far from Corinth their unchurched love abode with faith and hope . . .but the greatest of these was sacrificed in struggling, suffering years . . . they bore and reared her forth. She did the rest. . yet what's in a life . . ? . . but a story you write. . choices created . . and/or dissipated sometimes simply waited . . for . . like the sum total of film internalized in matinees of mortalities vision . . . played out in projected dreams near the finish line; hope on the homestretch looms nowhere more than in her eyes.

The armatured slip of the beast pervasive was persuasive but against those odds she was still protected . . a petal redolent yet pierced by thorn. From ragweed to milk white phases of the high-grounded heart broken moon she ascends from Lee Avenue. The color of sin in contexts desirably drawn . . . wan heat advisories and softer afternoons made safe for a lifetimes licit countenance. The taste of Chardonnay in refracted hotshade for those August lions still roaring in my loins.

She changed the seasons all around. Even April had been spitting snow . . . you know the kind seen in refugee footage; a pasts cold flack in the face of hopes future. From Lee Avenue she brought mayflies out from under where the sun and foliage come together, subtly healing what I thought was my last long season . . . maybe a couple of them mucoidaly coughed together where the very idea of promise had vaporized. Life as a stream drawn up from multiple sources of possibility had withdrawn from me. A solemn body of water, not stagnant, but no longer, coursing any-where with finite shores became my sign for some other terrestrial angle.

Yet here she was to suffer not Lee Avenue or the rifle shot shattering her cars back window . . . the suns crossing within her being with tidings so unfamiliar, her tone a child's first expectant Christmas in a mine shaft so dark the countenance of hope appears so innocently unfamiliar its sound evokes unknown timbres that aspire from somewhere in my soul to be the wise man bearing her gifts.

And when inside across the woolen carpet of previous flocks, the border collie rebounds to her cue. She claps hands and cheers a Chardonnay laughter. It is akin to the clap of an angels wing brightening all cloud cover.

Off, but moving on to perfect pitch, our bluesy nights and patch of days lay skiff like . . . snow imagined in a cold marred sky. The grid of our being came tenderly back to Lee Avenue where cocks crow in the city limits.

It is a community of kinship and brave in-laws banishing the shades of unutterable injury the straight path of our generative canal in liege to the child. The new princess of Lee Avenue where babes are tragically unborn next door to brides with cancer we bury one step ahead of the predatory poor spirits who never know . . .they imitate central castings desolation row.

Ancients remind us, these shades were sadnesses too dark for the howling light.

And she remains a summer night

not far from May

that keeps the howling, howling light

. . . at bay.

While I Wait For Her

The sound of a train
while I wait for her
precedes the cold spring sleep
that plumbs our roots
as if we were an orchard
robins find in the morning

Life's gale force ebbs
like the sound of the train
then returns, with the birds
on the ground,
of our being.

Our Time

After winter in Granada under fascist scrutiny I returned
and watched 'Coop' play Robert Jordan on my folks old black and
white tube, moved in my room as dark as the tresses and
bourgeois heart of my pasts bedeviled beloved.

Pilar said, "All our lives die in the time that remains."
Spring firing into cedars and colors of life before death our love
came true as we read together and the bell tolled for us.

I revisit the book and picture in our home-light graced by
love that survives all earth splitting offensives. "This time is our
time and will always be . . ." My dearest one takes care of me.

(Past Christmas Dagnets grave at the old catholic cemetery E. of Armiesburg)

ADUMBRARE

When we hit the near ninety degree turn north of Mecca, I coasted into it ... the engine quiet to surprise a group of wild turkey who scattered in rough flight and refracted running between blonde corn and the deep wooded gorge .. mostly mature pullets half the size of their parents with beautiful blue heads so lovingly frightened it was as if for a moment we were one with them;our directions spangled upon the dawn side of darkness.

Turkey Run

On my sixty fourth birthday, just before getting a speeding ticket

on my way to court ...

I turned up the old road, north of Hillsdale;

a mile ahead it bends around a pioneer cemetery.

As I banked the curve, a band of young and wild eyed turkeyhens

ran into the graveyard like homely nuns or plain Amish girls

carrying their skirts as they ran through the graves

of forgotten folk whose worldly consciousness

is gone but, maybe, just maybe they feel

the flutter of those fright breasted birds

spooked into beauty by me and dead souls.

Like us, they run between traffic and death.

CRAZY EIGHTS
OR
(TOMS IN HARD RAIN)

Hard rain surrounded us before dark
in streaming walls
south and west of that 'Snakey Bend' on the Wabash;
not swirling our way,
settling into the Prairie . .
leaving our foliage on dry ridges
rustling . . toward fall.
Underleaf yearning appeals
the Silver Maple reaches
and kneels; a supplicant
in gray gloves
harbinger
for stressful loves . . .
The next day breaking
in drowning skies.
In vast seas of all that rain
I'm driving through on the bad road to Terre Haute.

They appear now as Indians who were not there before.
Eight big Toms . . wild turkeycocks
heavy with authority across the wet glade
safe in their sense I wouldn't stop in such weather.
They strode . . slowly and sure of themselves
like chiefs breaking camp
in hard rain.
Phantom Octaves
of Gods Dark Grace.

LOVE IS NOT A REALITY ACHIEVED, BUT ENDURED

It had a class traitor atmosphere of bourgeois imitation; the house spic and span clean without a sign he'd ever been there. An old family dog was kept out in the cold.

"I'll take the tallest," he said. They were in the Toasty Shop when two country girls from the Beauty College came in. He took the tallest and was true to her for the next half century. Three daughters and twice that many grandchildren followed him across the continent . . . four or five states and at least that many economic fronts.

He aspired to a career in music but settled for what he could get with grand performances in everything he did; every conversation he had. His vitality was legend. He kept a Wurlitzer Jukebox in the basement and performed for his children. He was Father Flanagan's Whitey Marsh* in "Boys-town." He seemed . . but was not indestructible.

I saw him last year and he was so depressed I feared for his life. Separated and fearing divorce betrayals he was on the lam. Suffering multiple stents and sexual deprivation he fretted about his last laps, repeating several times. . "all those years and she never let my dog in the house."

This spring he phoned in good spirits with good news, he said. "They say I've got terminal cancer, but I'll whup it. It doesn't matter because I've got my bride back." He'd reconciled his marriage. He had six months to go.

We finished his funeral with great memories recalled by words, photos, and friends. We followed his family home for the reception where his old dog preyed at the door for scent of warm food and fellowship. This frail Australian Shepherd was taller than average (He'd not been) and unique in many ways (as He'd been). No rodeo poodle like much of his breed but a serious, slightly failing kind of a fellow, locked outside of realities he only wished to improve.

* Whitey Marsh; Mickey Rooney's character in Spencer Tracey's movie "Boystown."

FROM MY WINDOW

I awake in mornings of tulip tree presence

When foliage or cold branch is home to the hawk

Who hunts a squirrel

on its ledges

BARNSWALLOW

The barn swallow built her nest

in close to my eyes.

She hops off, falls ... then crests

before she winge'd flies.

NO PLACE TO DIE

This is no place to die!

His thoughts and daydreams would always return anchored to that one sullen realization. It was a bad place to live but he could take it. He knew though as his mind continued to settle and rest on the things of his being; the where and how of it. The where seemed almost more important to him than the how or why. If he could find the right place to die he felt sure he would grasp the how . . maybe even the why of it.

Sense of place for him had been primary to the eighty some years of his life. It was why he had traveled early, why he loved the valleys and the sea, and even the prairie, why he had batched for years in a shack on the river and why he had settled in the Heartland to raise his family. It was probably why he thought so much about the next place or if there was one. It was also why the first paragraph of his clinical chart at the 'home' read: [Thomas Moon; Senile Dementia: exhibiting obsessive conceptual preoccupations with schizophreniform avoidance or delay in dealing with technical details of the present]. The 'home' was also a sloppily run place so that the old man got hold of his chart and read it. "F. the present", he groaned and added the chart to that category of technical details of which he had no interest in dealing.

He knew the old divil really is . . . in the details.

IN CLOVER

Barefoot, with four to five beers full of feeling good

I strode out across the cool beds of clover

. . . Extant!

CARESS

A heron flies through the foliage

the way a squirrel hunters eyes

caress the leaves.

MY FOALS IN FAR PASTURES

require a brave and pastoral fear of spirits

in the glade. Like bull calves in cold pasture;

their defiant cheerfulness when mice

built a nest in my desk drawer and snakes

ate all the ducklings up.

FLEDGLING
(counselors lament)

It sat alone on the bars of our iron gate, a fledgling baby

black bird with parents flying somewhere alone; their slicked

back green heads athwart with worry why? . . .

this youngster would not fly?

I opened and shut the gate slowly 'round; the little one

did not fall or fly until its mother coaxing from across the road

brought it down to be runned over and not yet die.

I held it in my hand, caressed its head and tried to perch

it back upon the gate. It tightly gripped my thumb with claws

and would not let go; little fallen one of the many I've failed to

get across the road.

The damned ol' traffic's not worth one dead bird.

TEAMSTERING

The idea of a matched team, by the mammoth jack, out of hafflinger mares brought me across the big walnut into Putnam County. It's Satidy night and old 40 is still the least crowded 4 lane highway in the world. A small Nissan truck pulls ahead of me. It is gray … hauling 4 large tractor tires and a young Newfoundland as black as the tires with the wind lifting his hair.

The dog has a serious look which is encouraging. I found the mule farm east of St. Thomas Mores, where they'd just finished harrowing their garden. We brushed the mules out and bedded them down.

The farmer and his wife were parishioners and spoke of Fathers Briggeman, Colentis, and Eldred. Vocations cashiered, deceased, and newly started particles of life, and time.

The idea of a team … on the Putnam County line.

TENDER PASTURES

Cool September. Its breezes bring us back

to ourselves. As a dark colt jumps through the

catchweed, black field crickets settle into new

shoots of waterleaf and we recognize where we've

been before. In relief from summer heat; still

safe this side of the killer frost . . . content as the clover.

THE SHEPHERD BOY
(Tanner's Extra Credit)

Tanner in grade school was learning a young shepherds responsibility . . . unevenly. He resisted being accountable to me. He also resisted handing in his homework assignments. He asked for extra credit. He wrote the following paragraph. I added the last line.

There once was a young shepherd who tended to the sheep at the end of the mountain. He was very lonely up there. So he decided to play a trick on the people so he ran down the mountain yelling wolf! It worked and some people even stopped and talked to him; he was very happy with this. So a few days later he did the same thing and it worked. After that the wolf did come and he ran down the mountain yelling wolf; it didn't work nobody came this time.

Then the wolf ate all the sheep for a meal. And . . . this was not a happy meal for the shepherd boy *when his step dad found out.*

WOMB ENVY

I am raising boys again

whose second decade turns their being

toward that from whence they came.

Envying the fetus and the phallus in the womb

envy I share in memories of every altar shade.

Ducking into churches the way,

I ducked into brothels in their decade.

My souls yearning libidinally confused

with getting laid.

I yearned to be in church, that place

they dream of comforts conquest made;

repose and refuge in our Mothers sheltered space.

TEEN TIME

He was seventeen that summer. Sexually
active . . an average American adolescent
without the civilizing influence of a mate
he'd become all hard on and appetite driven
to fuck or fight in hormonal negligence
 of previous parental and childhood values of
love and work.
In short, he took a break from being
human.
He found his way back along a peculiar
route. His father was 2,000 miles away. If he
could purge the remnant influence of his fathers
propaganda he would be free. That is, from the idea
of a loving, wrathful, judging Father in heaven.
He turned to his atheist mother for help.

      "Whaddaya bleeve, mom . . happens when we die?"

      "Well, I think its simply someone else's turn," she answered.

      "Gak!" he blushed. "No purgative here!" Libidinal
selfishness itself converged with the protection of
Providence. He began returning to the path that
restored his being.

FACTIONS

(VOICE OVER) . . . prompted by a picture, I think, and a growing strategy . . . He'd begun to counsel others to factionalize their many forces and faces of identity to protect their fundamental thou. The ideas of Martin Buber haunted his memories like a spectral thread that tied them all together. Through school, politics, work, olde places, the land, beasts, and loved ones.

To fight factionally is to ally with some against others. To do so in a principled way is to ally with those whom you agree are right against those whom you think are wrong.

Otherwise in an unprincipled way you ally with some for your personal advantages against those who oppose your advantages. From kindergarten it goes on . . you tell yourself the former, sometimes you slip into the latter; most of the time everybody lies or denies they do either.

Catholics, Muslims, and Protestants do it. Jews do it. Capitalists and Communists do it. Corporate goons and Union thugs do it. Parents and their issue start it. Shopkeepers and lay abouts live it and even working stiffs succumb to it. It is the very breath of bureaucracies and the saint and criminals problematic path.

Alls fair or unfair in love and war; the former being the latter conducted libidinally and/or the latter being the libidinal result of the former. It is the root of all evil and the praxis of all-good. Divine chaos in ancient mythologies and pagan cliques. Especially since Abraham's struggle has been recorded toward or away from Gods Peace.

And if this peace exists somewhere it truly is a place and a peace that passeth all understanding. If it lies within us, it has one hell of a lot of company.

Outside Modesty

Way out west in the San Joaquin,
my son's friend Sean is watching late night TV.
Outside Modesto he's watching Conan O'Brian after midnight.
    When lo and behold his childhood chum,
my son Eliot appears on the screen
in a mock fight with Conan.
    Both redheads throw a few punches
then my son takes the dive,
pretending to be K.O.ed by a comedian.
    People across the country saw this skit.
Many phoned.
I never heard from Eliot.
    Months later when we met
he sheepishly remarked, Pa, that O'Brian
guy is a lot bigger than he looks on T.V.
Our eyes met as we shared
a modest moment of immodesty.

THE DEATH OF STALLIONS

My father loved horses and music yet advised against both. "Pay no attention to horse people or music people," he'd say.

"When they have the horse, know the score and . . you won't, they'll pretend they know the secret . . . and you don't. When you have the horse and know the score . . and they don't, they'll be all envy without respect."

Pride in milieu always trumps respect.

Dad's dead. He died years ago. I think of him on Fathers Day as I bury my stallion, 'Forrester', my vicarious virility kicked in by resistant mares . . his ribcage caving into his heart he followed me from the yard as I moved from room to room into darkening hours. I found him dead this morning.

No music today.

April 24, 2006 Pope Benedict will don a pallium not
worn for a millennium.

THE BLACK HEM
           of his garment represents the hooves of sheep.

The cold front came down on us
like geese upon a pond.
My niece cannot speak for the chemo's
metal taste and nausea.

We fight "infectungin" with Ratzinger
and face the black hem
of seasoned hooves tracking
life's own Sceadwianum.*

*Sceadwianum: OE secretive shadows suggesting what is to follow

HEATHER

My dear niece has died.

Grief has nearly

slain my daughter.

I sit with my head

in hand and think

of my sister when she was

nine . . . cantering

in the south yard . .

playing like a filly

with her friend across the alley

. . . named Heather.

Sadness near silently sung

for one so very . . . very young.

(Marcus Wolf and Ed Bradly died this week. So did the
husband of my oldest living cousin who would
not leave his coffin all night long.)

FUNERAL RAIN

Firemen pallbears stood alert . . . wet

leather visors and a piper on the hill

played 'Going Home' to endure

southern Baptist rhetoric;

eating at church with the children

knowing death is not the end . .

"None of us will get off that easy!" *

*my Mother's profound remark and theology

BOILER PLATE

Silver ribbons stripe the nights

rain water ditches and low places vein

out like silver does in the deep earth.

Silver also stripes the darkness and

lateness of my age; reflective patterns . . .

in the collapse of light . . . better than

boiler plate steel from inside the furnace.

NO SURPRISES

No Prisoners!
    No Surprises!
        Death Notices
        do not recall how Faulkner described
        the light in August, or
        if it surprised him.
        The last shades of summer
        appear serious
        in surprising light.
        It suggests the end of things.

        The end of summer
        provokes a radical priority,
        a possibility
        that life can end well. . .
        however abruptly.

NEARER THE DUST

Soaring forth in significance
the mass for my aunt
achieved a space and time
greater than . . .
all finite tedium.

The farm on the hill
my mothers blood,
Aunt Mary's hearthen table
and the altar of the Christ's
ancient resoundedness.

My cousin said the mass
and spoke to me as St. Francis
addressed olde Suleman.
Grandpa Abe and I
belong to the Big Church,

my Grandma Kate would sigh
then signify toward the arc
of undenominated Hymeran skies
from a City in Egypt
to a town around here.

"Einis und Alles", "Enough for the Hellmanns",
mother would note plenitudes excesses.
Love not requiring comprehension

but 'bildung'[1] an approximate integrity;
we battle on . . .

In step with Abe's beloved hymn, [2]
we become partly Him . . marching on
to end the mass doors breaking open
solemn light to soaring light
of seraphim outside our inside
. . . dim coherence.

1: 'bildung': moral consciousness formation
2: Battle Hymn of the Republic.' My Grandfather Abe's favorite tune.

DEATH OF A WREN

Jenny Wrens funeral is over . . .
spartan, sapphic . . slightly suburban
and southern baptist at the same time.
God gently judge her living the lie
of other lives struggling for her own.

The Lady Ministers' were mostly on the money,
but joined denial that Jenny's remaining sister
was really her daughter adopted by her parents.
Baptist guilt and American law converge in unreality.

How many years did Jenny yearn
for the love of a dutiful daughter
yet settle for a sisters sympathy?
Or maybe after burying their (grand) parents
they changed their roles at home,
moving to a different town with different Baptists.

Public sisters avoidant of extended kinship;
typically modern women with an unnecessary burden
of untruth . . . it and they grew heavier.
We sat miles away and rarely called them.

And yet they toughed it out
through too few factory jobs
and too many male predations.
Jenny Wren kept on course
caring for her adult child
no matter what the world thought
or how many Baptists
cloned Trent Lott.

She paid her dues and daily prayed

she prayed for peace and peace . . . delayed

Jenny Wren in a closed coffin;

little bird again . . . like the night

she first flew from the nest . . to

the back seat of her beaux's convertible.

He was a honker who never came to the door.

She bore . . him a daughter and he never came "round

yon infant so tender and mild."

We loved them and denied

they were mother and child.

Consciousness is not property.

It is a radically collective phenomena; in the way

it is gathered, developed and expressed.

Its very significance depends upon others

and yet it is mutually more radically dependent

upon the solitary company it keeps with ones own Soul

along that lonesome valley we all got to walk

by ourselves alone.

WREATH

      The downed down is whiter than the
snow that held it. A whiter wreath of down
. . . feathers skiffed and funereal the bird
I brought to earth was torn apart by aging
speed, hit low by the ash from high in
 the spruce.

      The old red tail hunted the edge of
our yard killing sparrows and game fowl before
I brought racing pigeons to the loft;
before my Morgan Grey fought off her last
brood of flyers reared along gales above
the road . . taught between the forest and
meadows. Not settling for carrion she
retired to our yard.

      Meeting in midair, the hawk and
the squab grew toward one another.

THE PENTECOSTAL BOMBER

The Pentecostal Bomber was what they called him. A lay minister and middle weight boxer who could hit as hard as heavy thunder . . . they said.

He studied Kid Gavilans' bolo punch the night he knocked out Chuck Davey forever. I can do that he decided. What Gavilan had developed with a machete in sugar cane he would do with a corn knife. And he did.

After years of practice on the farm he made a name for himself in the ring. "Cuz when he swung that stalk cutting arm on 'em they'd go down husks and all" a fan reported. He preferred those early knock outs. If the fight dragged on he didn't like hearing the other guy whimper after he'd hit him . . . after he'd hurt him.

He did not remember going down. He said he heard something . . that's all. We saw it all from ringside.

We heard something too. First muffled gloves grazing, then a sharp gym shoe sound. All the while Dave is stumbling forward as the other fighter seems to catch him and then rise up striking him from on high like a nor-easter. It hit Dave like a lance through his chin and sternun, the length of his frame falling away from where he thought he was.

Afterwards he smiled as he always smiled . . like family glad to see you. He smiled like he smiled at horses, calves, and children . . . and his worst enemies. Then he would speak in silly aphorisms . . little sermonettes that always sounded stupid. Worse they reminded me of Arabic folk sayings delivered in bad English; those no one ever understands. Still we seriously suspected the very spirit of Christ moved through him.

Handicapped as a husband and father like he was handicapped as a boxer; he didn't like hurting others, so he was sure to be divorced and depressed about it. His children grown, his wife left, he kept working as he'd done for two decades as a millwright. He was a UAW union man.

I counseled him to do something for himself.

"Like What?" he answered less with his words than with his eyes . . all hazy and puzzled up.

"Well" motioning toward his old beater of a truck,

"why not buy yourself a new pickup?"
He smiled but seemed indecisive.

"Can you afford it?" I asked.

"I reckon", he answered, with words, eyes, and presence drifting off . . and was gone.

The next time I saw him was in his new truck. A big new body styled Dodge Ram; clerical black with lots of chrome. Happily, he beamed with pride about it. Pointing to everything from the hood ornament to the 4 wheel drive mark he described how he'd been visiting his extended family from Indianapolis to Louisville showing off his new Ram Truck.

"They all love it! My cousins, nephews, nieces, old aunts and uncles think it's the best truck they've ever seen. You'd think getting it was my greatest achievement."

It was a nice truck, a brand new looking kind of truck but I figured Daves family was hyping him a bit about it because they were so glad to see him getting over his depression. And I told him as much. "Your family loves you man. Its their love for you, not just the truck." "I dunno," he replied, "even stranger's carry on about this truck."

One stranger who "carried on" so was a large young woman Dave met "just outside the factory gate."

"She flagged me down near the execs entrance," he began. "She was a big girl, but real prurty . . . and young too. I'd pulled up along the curb and she stepped right up and into the cab of my truck . . her eyes sparkling at its interior, her hands touchin' the dash as she went on and on complimentin how its body style and color made it look 'strong' and . . he laughed a little embarrassed. . . 'sexy', she said. After she looked in the back seat . . why, she just sat for awhile talking to me and complimentin my truck."

The big girl finally got out of the truck and Dave got on to work. He drove in the second 10th St gate carefully parked his new vehicle and greeted several pals before they punched in for the swing shift. Excitedly he began telling them about how everyone bragged about his new truck -- even strangers! How today (he inflected "today" like Neal Diamond plays an audience) a young woman had just (he used the word just unlike an evangelical but close) flagged him down in traffic to admire his new truck. His pals seemed only half interested until one pulled him up and said, "Dave where did this young admirer get your attention?"

"Over there by the maples, before the turn lane . . you know where traffic slows done."

"Yeah I know Dave . . . said the one pal, shaking his head at the others.

One of the others said, "Dave . . Reverend Dave . . you are a pure saint innocent or . . . . . the others talkatively joined in "ignorant beyond belief!" Dave was truly both, but he had to sit down on the service room bench when they began to taunt him one after another.

"That's a streetwalker man, don't you get it?!"

"She's a hooker!!"

"That fat ass in a mini skirt is a whore, Dave!"

"She got in and admired your truck for a fast chaste 10 buck fuck."

Their taunts turned into derisive laughter. Dave couldn't believe it. That nice young woman who spoke so well to him about his truck . . .a whore? The entire shift he thought about her. He thought about her eyes. He gave himself permission to think about her hips.

The next day he said his prayers, found a "Christian" J.P., "ministered and proposed" to the big girl by the 10th St. gate consummating their business that night. He married her, took an early retirement from the plant, pals and criticism, moving 60 miles west to a river farm near mine on the Wabash. She stayed with him until after her baby was born. The child was as strong, beautiful, and black as his truck. She claimed she'd been raped by a jailer. Dave didn't mind. He loved and cared for the child before and after she left. He loved and cared for this child the rest of his life.

The big girl returned two years later. She was pregnant again. She said she wanted to give Dave the opportunity to raise his adopted sons' sister (sonograms had sexed the unborn child), who after she was born and weaned was abandoned by the big girl just as her brother had been.

Dave reared them both with love and discipline, if not much extended family or community. We invited them to what few events we convened. Dave and I attended Amish sales together. We both admired the Amish for holding out for a life we'd lost. We respected the Amish authority and community we could not join nor had to put up with. I counseled Dave to develop his farm, fence in his bottom meadows for hay crops and cattle. He invited me over to train. We could jog, walk, and talk down the tree line where he planned to fence pasture. I was flattered by the invite. Somewhere in my mind I was still a 14 yr. old wannabe golden glover and Dave was an ex champ contender. Plus . . I was dog tired of my old upstairs treadmill.

Early one morning I joined him to train. We did not spar but shadow boxed a bit, weaving around in grass and gravel convincing his curious cattle we were crazy. Then we jogged off downhill toward the river before turning north along the section to be fenced. I heard he'd sold a small acreage of uneven eroded ridge ground on the northwest corner of his property to the Police. "Whaddaya doin with the cops on that ridge over there?," I asked, nodding ahead to the east as we huffed and puffed along the timberline.

"It's the F.O.P . ."[1] he said. "I've always supported em. They were Indy's first sponsor of golden gloves. They're putting in a firing range."

I was tiring, not eager to talk and focused on the uneven ground so as not to stumble. I'd forgotten 'firing range' as soon as I'd heard it. Whing! whing! I was quickly reminded of the phenomenon as galvanized bullets whinged and whirred into the trees not ten feet above us.

"Keep your head down!" said Dave, "and don't run away to the west. That flat land is slowly elevated. We'll keep straight on this trail. It's the lowest point around here."

"Around here . . hell, that's the problem. Let's get the hell out of here", is what I said. What I felt was a great impulse to hit the dirt and lie still.

"Those shooters haven't got their bearings yet," Dave continued. "They're shooting over and west of the targets. We're probably alright. Just stay with me on the trail . . . and (he said it again) keep your head down."

Too out of breath to cuss, holler, or even think straight I ran on following Dave to the northern boundary behind the shooters. As he turned, the gunfire seemed sent more rapidly and louder. "They'd never hear us" I thought as I followed Dave back south again . . .keeping my head down. We plunged into and charged hard under and beside the spray of their bullets.

After fear sprinting all the way back and up the hill we collapsed by his watering tank. Later he'd joke I ran as fast as he did on the way home.

Dave was not comfortable taking his children to any of the several surrounding 'Assemblies' in our area. He knew their racial history. "Mega church patter will not pass for true religion," he would say. I referred him on to a United Pentecostal Church in the Illinois country and at first he seemed satisfied. Buxom church ladies with beehive hairdos in gingham dresses like our mothers wore started appearing all over his weekends and not a few weeknights. They "ministered" to him and his children whose health, hygiene and schoolwork improved accordingly.

Yet in some abscess of Dave's consciousness; in his quest for the sacred in doctrinal schizogenesis looping back through his head injuries past the synaptical Malabar coast to the Council of Ephesus he had this terminal instinct for heresy . . trumping the

Nestorians by one to announce he was not united but apostolic, that is, Apostolic Jesus Only Pentecostal. Separating from the United Church ladies he bought an old church building in Saint Bernice painted it and presided over a new congregation of five. The church building had stood idle for years, its previous congregation not surviving the U.M.C. vs. EUB[2] merger.

His dreamy vision seemed punchy but profound. He swore on a bible in front of me, and I have absolutely no idea why, that he would never evangelize for membership on the cheap grace of emotional belief. He would evangelize only for the teachings of Jesus. He winked and said, "see, I'll be a behaviorist like you." Later he'd add "and by god they will behave! . . . cuz they'll know I won't enforce it and they'll be responsible whether they feel like it or not."

Of course I was struck by these kinds of Anarcho-libertarian flaws in his rather totalitarian schema but more alarmed with my own feelings of responsibility in having recruited him to certain concepts in counseling he was now theologically applying to his life.

Rev. Dave was so scrupulous against coercion he felt compelled to preach ad nauseam about his doctrinal positions on everything without inviting or attempting to persuade or prevail upon another. A young couple who were neighbors of his, admired his parenting and were seeking a church home had started attending his services. Sunday after Sunday Dave preached on his own doctrinal takes of Jesus Only emphasizing that these positions were valuable to him and they were all welcome to them now or sometime later but it was not his responsibility whether they took them or not. It was theirs. Such emphasis was designed not to recruit membership. It could also not sustain membership. The young couple, his neighbors, left the congregation. Dave came to me depressed again. "I've lost almost half my congregation", he seriously said. "It's just me and the kids now."

The next Sunday I attended Dave's church with my children. He was delighted to greet us and so were his kids, but he turned somber for the hour and half sermon. Not even Nestorius himself could liquidate the future faster. He opposed any reference to God separate from Jesus and any reference to Jesus separate from God. It seemed the Jesus cult without human sacrifice. A perverse Unitarianism turned inside outside of itself. I was about to pray, "bring on the tartars"[3] when Dave called on me to pray for the congregation, him and his kids, me and mine. I referred to "the prayer that Jesus taught us" and prayed alone the "Our Father."

Confounded silence followed. His kids looking at him; mine at me. Finally Rev. Dave's smile spangled all over the place; he laughed and said, "Hey lets talk about it—eats are in the kitchen."

We shared a fine wholesome meal (without drinks) and returned to his place for pie and coffee. Conversationally Dave was easier to understand. I talked late into that night with him after he allowed me a little brandy. 'Fathering' to him was the other side of being fathered by God and his 'Jesus only' heresy wouldn't hold up to the lords prayer. We talked mainly about fathering rather than being fathered until he brought up his death notice.

He had less than a year the doctors said. He said it was something everyone has to do alone and he knew about that. He said that's what's been on his mind ministering to others. "The aloneness", he said "is how God has set it up. Not for us to like, but for us to learn from. It's how he fathers us."

About fathering . . we agreed you can't be too strict with children in modern culture unless you are strict beyond your means to enforce it. Dave objected to being strict beyond the grave. "The test is when you actually croak", he'd say! "Not only to die well but to die in a way that frees your heirs to get credit doing right or reap their consequences for doing wrong. Fathers who couldn't discipline their offspring while alive try to do it with wills when they're dead. There's no transfer power in wills; no will power after death. You can't enforce morality when you're here let alone after you're gone. Lawyers will tempt you. I'll not take the bait."

Old Dave, the Pentecostal Bomber; (like his lord) he died intestate.

1. Fraternal Order of Police

2. United Methodist and Evangelical United Brethren

3. The Nestorian heresy was finally overrun by Tatars in the fourteenth century.

BREEZE AT OUR BACK

The soft light of summer
fell apart . . .
under pathetic building blocks of personhood.
The child reaching for those frail particles
that enthuse a five year olds false hope
for life beyond the shatteredness
of Mother in prison and Daddy gone away.
She holds forth in school clothes
bought by church ladies who blink
on tripod canes with blank . . compassion
and stare . . .
at the air . . between us;
held forth by the child who dares expect it so.
Displaying previews too plump by far
for pedagogical and peer review;
little obese angel
heading toward all those lives . . with knives
for her delicate condition.
She's armed with shells of church basement socials
and sincere illusions of collective heresy.
Duds against the greater Evil.
We worked in His paddock that afternoon.
The heat of the day tempered by a breeze at our back;
foretelling the cool of evening
and the coming cold night.

THE GREATEST ELENGENESS
(at my cousin's death bed)

is the elenge of ones own

solitary dead ended road.

More or less a love object

plopped on a mattress

where elengeness vs. privacy mutually self destruct

in the glowering pleas of pain

"actively dying in terminal restlessness",

with caring fingers pushing pills

like poop in ones anus.

No thank you. Without the stupid will

of selfish suicide I nonetheless maintain

my plan to go that last short road

in active terminal recklessness.

Drinks at my deathbed; not suppositories!

GREEN ON THE GROUND

Green leaves are falling
cause the drought has leveraged autumn.
Cold clouds clasp the morning pond
and caress the god damned cockleburs.

Dawns gun fire wound the geese
that fly from the 'nuisance season'
and my neighbors ditch back to the covert
by four acres of water close to my heart.

Pumping life and pummeled death
is the order of things.
My old game cock, Zorro, is found dead
near the corpse of a young cockerel contender.

Their blood sport may have excited
 my hound pack to take the life
of a ewe I found in the horseweeds.
All hounds were sold and I miss their canine company.

Combined and uneven is the development
of time around discernment of my fathers'
presence, his calm ghost and photograph in Labor Days' paper
standing tall and flat capped near the stamping mill.

Supporting 'The General Strike', which ruined
the town, framed far too much of my fate
from the peoples finest hour degenerators deny
the failure of our collective consciousness.

The madness of my sibling
I commit to no bad thoughts or feeling
and revere my fathers serious fix
on the racing seasons.

I hear his voice in hoofbeats
the way horses speak drawing out the sound
without sound requiring effort
from senses; perceived from the beloved.

Interpenetrating work and value
lives that were lost, in love are found.
Life's consciousness like seasons overlie
green leaves upon the ground.

OZARK COFFEE

Woke to a soft rain in north Arkansas.
Set for awhile on the stoop with
Gideon and the Sunday papers. Still
couldn't read much from the
August thump to my head. Jest
set there enjoying the warm September
rain, that was the tip
of a cold hearted hurricane in Texas.
If that mule hadn't bucked
and broke my back, I'd of never
discovered Missouri. Left her at
the sale in Columbia and drove
south on 63 through the Ozark
hills and meadows of Ralla, Vichy,
and Kabool. What country! Just
six hours west of the Wabash . .
gone past it in the past but
never into it.
Best livestock country in
between the blue grass and the Pacific!
Affordable quality jack-stock,
hoof stock and fox trotters
hours from my front door.

Rancher friends met us for breakfast
. . . cured side, country fresh
eggs with flaky biscuits and gravy.
Then black coffee as strong as
the eye of the storm we loaded
our stock and headed home in.

Morgan Hunter

Welcome to the Annual

MIDWEST GOODMAN FOXHUNTERS ASSN

Black Gold

Premium Dog Food

Black Gold

PRO PLAN

"Dice" With Breeder Thomas Morgan (right)

Local Foxhound And Breeder
Honored At National Field Trial

A Parke County six-year-old
black and white foxhound named

unprecedented 745 points on the
first day; hundreds ahead of the

Egyptian Wells

Somewhere between Paris and Walnut Prairie the night first speaks of Egypt. This Egyptian country is southern Illinois and has an earthen, swarthy, almost hirsute likeness; a melangian[1] mood and manner we imagine with Abe Lincoln and Elvis Presley. Arabia in foliage is stark as Sweden in the desert. Wild strawberries in hot sand. From pale burning flesh to dusken light absorbing hidden waterfalls.

Driving into new country with hounds who'll cover its terrain is a great pleasure to me. I've raised these calico youngsters just as I whelped and raised their mother. Confident of their conformation and hunting skills, I am certain they will do me proud.

I arrived at field camp 'round 4 a.m. Hounds were to be cast at 5 a.m. sharp. Had time to register, kennel my pups and prepare for the first cast. At five . . . seventy hounds of the Goodman (old Irish) strain packed and flew from the camp paddock into the 500 acre pen. Rolling ground with an even balance of meadow and woods with hillocks, draws, and ponds in each quadrant . . four judges and the master of hounds were posted and patrolled the place on mules and A.T.V.s.[2]

Nose down my two braces[3] of two-year-old calico pups ran behind the smaller speed and drive bitches and dog hounds with shrill voices. These weedy looking front enders offended my aesthetic sense of foxhound conformation. Anorexic appearing yappers they sped with their heads up drinking in the quarry's scent . . only if it was in abundance . . which it always is in a penned trial, not like on the outside where hounds have to actually hunt their prey before giving chase. In this 500 acre pen there were twenty coyotes and ten foxes. If one gives them the slip, they'll run on to another line in minutes, not hours. Not really hunting . . . but a good safe place for field trial competition in a beautiful secluded setting with a kind of natural community in the camaraderie among houndsmen, hounds and predatory beasts.

The pen keeper has imported several yellow foxes from Wyoming. Bigger than our native reds they run and look like a coyote. They are as yellow as the pair that denned directly across from my gaze at the kitchen window years ago, when I was first thinking about foxes and hounds. They say foxes will den near farms with foxhounds. It is my experience they den near those who just think about them.

The coyotes here were less impressive. Wintered on "Black Gold" dog food, their coats shone but seemed smallish, running too close to the ground. . . not the big hundred pound brush wolves we chase back home. Many of them were bob-tailed . . the pen keepers own sign or brand . . his way of keeping track of purchases from volunteers. He said it also "keeps their tails from freezing up in sub zero weather." A veteran brush wolf hunter . . . I think like a coyote and know better . . . We (i.e. me and the coyotes) prefer a full rudder and brush regardless of the weather.

My big boned two year olds were admired but they were not properly conditioned. I'd been afraid to hunt them all winter . . because of a 'Deputy Dawg' who'd moved in a mile up the road. Swaggering up my porch steps from his squad car, pulling at his holster . . making it squeak he'd announced the baying of our hounds was costing his wife her beauty sleep. Studying him I reckoned she needed all she could get and almost said so, but he was a neighbor. I explained they were cubbing i.e. chasing the young foxes up in the woods near his place in small tight circles rather than the long wide ones they'd soon be making after coyotes down by the river. He softened a bit and told me his wife was pregnant.

Expectant parents can be irrational and deserve special consideration. Indeed . . . this bad deputy in the long run became a good neighbor as he became a good father and also . . . as he became free of the Sheriffs Department. The short run degenerate who was Sheriff at the time inspired him a week later to rudely cry into my message machine with full guvment intimidation "You're foxhounds are up here chasing a fox!" Later formal charges came in the mail.

My attorney advised me not to run the hounds around home until the conflict was resolved. A few times we hunted away from home but mainly my pack languished for six months.

467

In spite of this we scored twelfth, fifteenth, and seventeenth at the end of the trial. Hard running big ol guys "Truce", "Dice" and "Sacre Bleu" had badly bruised feet and I doctored them . . getting ready for the evenings bench show.

The bench show judge was not a 'Goodman Breed' man. He was a slender man with cowboy shirttails sticking out of his pants wrapped tight around his haunches. A darkly disheveled and attractive wife tagged along looking as if she'd been rode hard and not put away. Her husbands judging matched his own skinny ass view of himself. He dismissed my big hounds out of hand. "Big enough to saddle," I heard him chirp . . . placing every scrawny miniature in front of me and other big Goodman's in every class. After the Derby, all age, best brace and best pack classes I kenneled my hounds and turned in . . discouraged. Not since I'd had PenMaryDels had I been dismissed by an idiot in a show ring. The PenMaryDel hounds would be leading in a trial and some peckerwood show judge still lacked a category in their heads to include them. They were used to seeing sub grade Walkers, Triggs, Julys . . . and Goodmans.

My first Goodman I thought was a July. (July hounds are a sort of cousin strain to Goodmans. Julys also come from Irish hounds; all other running strains come from original English and maybe some French stock). My pal Red Bedwell had given me a big white hound with one merle eye and no registration papers. We thought he was July bred and I named him July Johnson. At a training meet in Green County a man approached me and said, "I raised that hound of yours as a pup, how do you like him?" "I like him fine," I answered, "I like his deep bawl voice, his being true to the line, his biddability,[4]" and . . I liked his size.

"Well that's what I breed for in most of my Goodmans," he said.

"Goodmans?" I questioned. I hadn't seen many . . didn't know much about them. This man was tall with an intelligent brow and a gentle manner. Succinct and soft spoken he explained the history and qualities of the Goodman . . from the Old Irish, through the Maupin breeding up to the big white hound on my leash.

Sold! I became an enthusiast for the Goodman. And this

good man, Mr. Colliflower advised my fledgling breeding program. I like the big Goodman, with big voices (bawl or chop), big hearts, and a big stride but tractable within a decent distance . . . hunters who stay within range from horseback not speeding into the next county out of sight and sound. I want them pale in color to see at night and calicoed distinct to please the eye and identify in daylight. And above all, I think the ancient art of venery[5] requires their scenting ability be superb and their mind sharp enough to moderate it. That is, superb in distinguishing the quarry directed to hunt; moderate in resisting cold trails and not insisting on multiple hot ones. Discerners!

Savvy breeders of all sorts of performance livestock would do well to study that species with the most rapid generational turnover. I speak of the game bird or game fowl, the contemporary ever-controversial fighting "Gamecock". I've found the best hound breeders keep or are knowledgeable about game birds, have a sub to 'Grit and Steel' and follow the different strains and breeding programs. They know that a champion-fighting rooster closely bred to female issue produces improved fighting stags (young males) and fertile hens. The trick is to never use these high performing stags as terminal sires. Talk circled 'round the fire how this simple fact of husbandry could save race horses, hunting dogs, and production livestock dynasties a lot of grief and disappointment.

One old timer in by the fire, as gnarled as his cane added,

"It'd be good advice for Presidents families too!"
There was more conversation and quiet laughter with hunting tales from Missouri, Kentucky, and Illinois . . of famous foxes chased season after season, of record sized brush wolves brought to bay and also of hounds hunting boar and bear always within contextual ideas.

In town women gossip about people they know and don't know while men converse about things they tinker with or want to in the garage, shop, or office. Out here conversation runs still and deep as the sacred night. Young and old speak quietly, relaxed, agreeable and informed. Conversational remnants from another time.English hunting and/or American imitations of it has been likened to high liturgy compared to the simple chapel and homespun hymn of hilltopers who hunt and come to field trials in their trucks, sitting in the shade or by the fire, never really riding to hounds. To me it's more like reading Trollope or Hemmingway. Not that some of those Tories can't ride and hunt but there is an incipient Anglo-Saxon snobbery in all of them. The worst only want a urine dragged[6] Easter parade with Champagne breakfasts. The best want to risk your neck, theirs and everybody's horse in extreme equine heroics. I've enjoyed both but prefer the good men who sit still by the fire and speak wisely of many things, occasionally mounting a mule or horse to get closer to the music.[7]

I turned in early, the wind dying down in the darkness and no longer discouraged by the bench show. I lay my bedroll out in the long grass between two clumps of trees so I could see the sky full of stars. There was a shimmering quality to this sky that was new comfort. I'd never looked up at this sky in little Egypt before and it seemed anything but little. All of Southern Illinois, indeed all of Illinois seemed bigger than Indiana. Like Sandbergs big shoulders . . broader than hoosier mindedness . . big timeness from Chicago's Lake to Cairo's river . . . the country side seemed to sigh with the plangent sound of cicadas.

And I awoke from the well springs of this Egyptian night, rested and ready for the next days cast. Like the cicadae my exoskeleton darkened against any minor distractions from purpose. Ted Roethke said that, "Art is the undoing of haste. It is what everything else is not." That second day was what all my worries were not. Soft breezes and sunlight sent the hounds out over the dew and they maintained a fast pace until noon. Everyone spoke of "the hounds" or "the pack" rather than their own particular dogs. I never heard a single sour remark. Voices were relaxed and easy . . like they expected the rest of the day to be good or get better . . like baseball radio announcers. The weather seemed to lime the very fields of our being. The difference between human community and pathological togetherness was reached and we helped each other with the kenneling, feeding, watering, and pick up tasks. Then there was time for town, white squirrels in the park, beers, a big salad and getting back to camp for a nap by trees before the awards dinner. It's been seventeen years since the cicadae have sounded like this. The females low hum at dawn joined by the evening buzz of the males orchestrated together at dark into pulsing white waters that get to the blood in your veins.

I drove home in this song of cicadas . . . one hundred decibels of what everything else is not, and thought of my wife's eyes . . as deep as egyptian wells.

1. "Melangian": an ethnic group of unknown origin, theorized to be Turkic or Arab muslims shipwrecked into the southern gene pool and responsible for the good looks of Lincoln and Presley.

2. A.T.V.s: All Terrain Vehicles

3. braces: pairs

4. biddability: obedience in a hound

5. Venery: the ancient art of hunting wild game with scent hounds

6. Urine drags: Urine scent dragged around to chase instead of a live beast.

7. music: the baying of the hounds

Optical Allusion

A suddenness of sunshine
surprised us, as the Old Girl set
enlarged and blood red
west across the river.

It made the flock and sheds more white
against a winter green that would not die;
brief comfort from her thermidoran sigh.

LOCKING THE DOORS OF DARKNESS

A soft Faulknerian whiskey night
of buttermilk sky . . . curdles low
over the dark meadows
bare branches caught in cold autumn light.

My hounds bawling in the distance
between my terriers and me
leaving the Great Pyrenees behind
with the Border Collie at the boundary line.

Lord Protector of my holdings;
if it were not
for my numb hands and cold legs
I should stay here forever,

locking the doors of darkness.

November Sun

The dark night of November was falling all around.
It had been falling on Henry Stoltzfus for some time. He was a
schizmatic Amishman who'd grown a moustache.

Years ago he'd brought a mare to my stallion. Slow to
pay the stud fee, he built fence for me and traded in Boer goat
stock. Before that his older daughter had been my patient.
I liked Henry and he confided in me. A big middle-aged man,
not quite modest of his strength with an intermittent gleam in his
eyes. He was imaginative. He was not well.

He told me he'd figured out there was more than one
God. He kept company with Indiana militiamen[1] from Vermillion County and would spout their party line. His eccentric
views were ignored and endured . . . tolerated would be too
formal a word . . . by the Amish community.

He refused to pay his FDIC loan and lost his farm.
He had eight kids. The community and his brothers bailed him
out, bought him a new place north of the Narrows and started
building him a barn. Henry ran off to a militia training camp in
Oklahoma.

Six weeks later a chagrined Henry returned home. "It
wasn't what they claimed it was," he said. "Things rarely are,"
I told him. His eyes lit up and we shared laughter in light rain
finishing our fence work. I'll bet those Baptists feinted when
they heard his thoughts about their being several sovereign gods.

I'd see Henry at seasonal sales but never spoke at length-
with him for years. I heard he'd hitched up again with a splinter
group. He had three more children and seemed to be questioning
"The Tradition". I also heard he was standing a Haflinger
stallion.

Three weeks ago on a Sunday he stopped by, driving an
old tan Ranger truck. "What the hell you doing in a truck?"
I joshed and scolded him. He seemed got for a moment. Vic
Lash had brought company to watch our border collie work, "It's
not even the right color," I continued. "Tell you what, I'll trade
you this black truck (pointing to my 15 year-old's truck without
an engine) even steven for your black buggy."

"Even . . .," he thought barely saying, "even?"

"Sure I said cept this one [pointing to the truck] has no engine!" Henry and all of us laughed as he met the company. Henry was proud to show us his driver's license. I wasn't approving to look at it. He said he had a job driving a truck and trailer.

Today we buried Henry. Two days ago he'd gone to sleep and drove the truck and trailer into a tree. Vic called me about it, that is, the viewing Sunday and the funeral this afternoon. My youngest son Tanner and me went to the funeral. It was in his home. We brought his wife a shoulder ham, some sausage, and mutton steaks.The funeral sermons and recited poems in Pennsylvania Deutsch went on for two hours. I kept dropping my hat and Tanner almost slept off the bench. There was kneeling and abbreviated genuflecting, reminding me how the Amish never suffered the alienating effects of the Reformation.

After several long-winded sermons the reception was tense. This was an Amish District some distance from us and I didn't know half the people there.

There were also two charter buses from Lancaster, PA but the tension came from the several dozen auslanders[2] that nobody seemed to know and some suspected we were a part of. They were evangelical recruiters and evangelical turn coats from the community.

Amidst the uniform old order Amish were some non-uniform half grown moustaches, some prayer bonneted gals driving a van and one ex-Amish family in flagrant un plain-attire. The most interesting auslander I met was David Cohen . . a Messianic Zionist, that is to say proselytizing Protestant Jew. An exceptionally handsome and timid fellow, he dressed Chasidic, as did his wife who seemed attractively terrified to be there.

Tensions and differences faded however when we all walked into the woods. It was mid afternoon and the November sun was perfect. The sun rarely shines right in November but today it shed light on the just and the unjust alike.

A grave had already been hand dug here in the forest and four long handled spades lay on the clay pile beside it. First his wife, children, and grandchildren then everyone filed past Henry's plywood coffin. It looked like the black paint had just dried on it. It had no handles. His pall bears closed the lid and toiled to kind of slide him in the hole. He landed with a gentle thud. Men lined up and shoveled the wet clay on top of Henry.

His wife and eldest son wept. Little grandkids looked big eyed down this hole in the ground as it filled up on top of their grandpa. Closure!

The reality of death and love in its losses shone as uniform in every face that knew him as the line of buggies shot by the sun drove home along side Percherons in his abandoned pastures.

1. "Indiana militiamen": Maverick chapel Baptists (in the main) of a reactionary populist bent. Deciding during the Clinton Administration that liberal upper class immorality, the U.N., and the black helicopters of the federal govt. had usurped the constitution and their "Sovereign Gods" authority. They preached not paying income tax, federal bank loans, and getting drivers licenses or plates. What they preach is more often followed by their new recruits than by themselves. Ideologically they are close to the "Western Patriots" and those thousands of crypto fascists recruited into private corporation armies e.g. Blackwater.

2. Auslanders are sometimes called Engleesh i.e. non-Amish at Amish gatherings

NOT SO LITTLE DEATHS

The French call it little deaths.
I dinna want to hear about it.

Himmler's curiosity of crows and executions.
Ike's commitment to liquidate the German officer class.

Grandma Kate's announcement that Divorce
is worse than death . . "it is a living death,"
she said. And all the injured shades that call
for me at Shadowgait. Bad shades speak and tweak
this side of Purgatory as Tracy Congeals
snakes in her pubic hair at the Ghost Bar
in Nevada. Shades that speak collective treachery
and contingencies of betrayal spake in the shade
of shadows gone away in the darkness of fears
in darkness of hope, in the darknesses of years
that plumbed the darkness of all the hopes and fears
convened beside their bed coming permeable
to personaes in all those beds; the little deaths
and living deaths in white and not so white bed-
sheets over the heads –
of a lifetime like . . .
the "snow over all of Ireland"*

* James Joyce "The Dead"

GENTLY STUPID

The dark night of November
occludes my vision.

If hope is what sustains us
why does it seem so gently stupid.

To know better is to know less
of what's required

in the home
of hearts defiled.

INDIAN GIVER

They were as orange
as a mick protestants heart.
Almost hunter orange
but not nearly so pervasive.
Just . . here and there
they fell from maples and oak;
clutching the ash
late into November.

Indian Summer is the way
a big weanling moves.
Overgrown, and happy about it.
Gait extended beyond the conventions of growth
and the measure of time.

Giving it his all
yet not giving it up.

"con el gris repartido; graying divisions and the
rage of days full of daggers" from Pablo Nerudas
"Woes and Furies of Quenedo"

GRAY PUDDING

It was a dark and wintry day
barely gray by the sun which only shone
sideways around the damp humid dome
of a day more gray than wild turkeys
or the brush wolf that stalks them.

My neighbor Levi and his sons
stirred a cauldron in their yard,
making "pudding" they explained
from the head, legs, waste, and bone marrow
of the hog they'd butchered plus a little venison.

Flecks of bone floated in the gray pudding
they stirred it with welded steel bars
then lifted its grayness toward my lips in an old spoon.
It tastes of ground pepper and garlic,
but it still looked gray . . .

As the dawn and evening sound in my senses
breathed and choked on the grayness
of the pale Yorkshire pig's resistance and the wrench
of the buck against shot as both of them close their eyes.
No wonder my species over decorate this season.
Denying the dying
of the light.

Plain Justice

Levis' son Beniel shot and killed the deer. He found it nosing amongst turnips in their garden. Beniel and his brothers hitched their team of half Morgan-Percherons to a sled and hauled the deer carcass up into the woods. They hung it from a tall hickory, gutted and skinned it out. Engleesh neighbors called the cops. Deputy Bolinjerker dutifully responded. First he consulted his accomplice, D.N.R. officer Suchasin, then drove straight to the Riel family farm.

Announcing to the Riel men at their barn that it was against the law to shoot a deer on their own property unless they own forty acres or more. He was coldly received.

"How big is your farm Levi?" the deputy inquired.

"Thirty nine and one-half acres," this Amish father answered.

"Did you shoot a deer this morning?"

"Yes I shot a big one eating our turnips!" Levi answered, nodding to Beniel.

Nervously adjusting his holster and looking around at all eight Riel men, the Deputy droned, "Well, I'll not arrest you this time if you'll haul that deer to town and purchase a tag for it. Otherwise I'll have to take you in." And then . . . "by the way, where is the deer? I'll have to inspect it."

Levi, like most good men has no innate problem with authority, that is, unless the authorities are wrong. Having the state pull rank on you in front of your sons on your own place did not sit well with him. And when aroused Levi can be a forcefully concise fellow. He explained this episode to me later as, "When people fear the state there is tyranny, but when the state fears the people there is liberty." The Riels knew Bolinjerkers reputation.

Levi began, "Now officer, you do, what you've got to do

and I'll do the same."

"Huh . . . !?"

Levi continued, "Our deer is hanging up there in the woods to bleed out. We will not be putting it in our buggy to drive to town. You arrest me and put me in jail if that's what you got to do but I will not be taking our deer to town for a tag."

"Damn!," the deputy thought, "I wish Suchasin was here. He'd know what to do. Why just last month he'd shot and killed a suicidal man in a cornfield for the Sheriffs' Department. The man had been out of his mind and threatening the Sheriffs' relationship with his wife." The Deputy did not like these Amishmen glowering at him so peacefully.

The stalemate defined, Levi waited a full minute before nodding to his sons toward the house. They preceded him on to the porch . . leaving the deputy all alone in the middle of the barnyard. Dazed for only seconds, the Deputy now militantly strode uphill toward the deep dark woods.

From the porch steps, Levi called out to Bolinjerker, "Oh and Officer . . one more thing. We cannot be responsible for your safety in those woods. The officer turned and looked back up the ridge. Then turned clean around to look at his well-appointed squad car. With two major leaps, he sprang downhill to his car and drove away. Levi and his family never heard from him again.

PRAIRIE MINDED

Over two thousand and redwinged
they fell;
over two thousand black birds dead
from a high down draft
they fell on the Illinois flats
near the swine farms lagoon.
While a barren ground caribou
by the Great Slave Lake
lifts his head and ponders it . .
far north of the prairie.

AMISH PRISONERS

The sons of Ezra King sold them all around Fountain, Parke, and Vermillion Counties. They sold them as . . . more precisely, the buyers purchased them as 'white King nestlings'. White King pigeons are desirable. They make full bodied squabs . . . they are great flyers . . . and they look magnificent flying out of barn lofts, past white sheds and porches. In spring and summer skies they are as ornamental as the foliage that enraptures Indiana's countryside.

But these . . . these particular white birds were not white kings! They were homers! Technically, they were really "prisoners". Homers are only called homing pigeons (or homers) at their place of birth. When they are kept any other place in the universe their correct nomenclature is 'prisoner', and upon escape these 'prisoners' will fly home to their place of birth.

So did these prisoners fly home to the Ezra King farm no matter what auction they were sold from or from wherever their new owners/captors released them. Then rather than decorously gliding about, making picturesque their new home, they sped directly to Ezra King's place located near the West Union Bridge.

And they did so many times! For as soon as they returned to their home coops, the King boys gathered them up for a new auction the next weekend.

Ezra did not really know about his sons' recyclable bird

sales. That is, he chose not to think about it too long. He had
some suspicions but he had so much more on his mind. There
were the produce contracts and keeping track of all those damn
boxes; the addition he had promised to build on the house for
the babies, Pam, his lead mule's chronic lameness; and the daily
nuisance of ol' Red (his main family horse) tying up after only
ten miles pulling the buggy. He should've stayed with Standardbreds from the track; he'd scold himself, with miles of trotting
behind them. But he'd liked this chestnut Morgan colt at auction and did the training himself . . . probably too fast and too
much, he'd scold himself again. His father-in-law had warned
him the horse would tie up if he pushed him too much and now
it was happening . . . he'd figure it out, that is, what to do about
it . . . he needed to talk to the vet and some veteran horsemen .
. . he didn't wish to talk to his father-in-law. And in the mean
time the horse had to be driven to town, to church and in the
other direction, to the creamery and feed store . . . next Spring,
Noah, his second oldest, would want a courting buggy—his wife
had been gently reminding him, Noah had an eye for the Miller
girl . . . Levi Miller's daughter who lives clear on the other side
of Bellmore . . . a 30 mile round trip . . . he'd be courting her
with lanterns on his buggy, and on the state road so late at night
it troubled his Dad to think about it. He couldn't trust ol' Red
tying up on state road 36 at 3am with the risk of being run over
and he could not yet afford another buggy horse. His own mind
would tire like ol' Red's gait on the 7 hill road. There was so

much to think about. He would give it all to God . . but he felt quietly that he still worried . . . that his worry was somehow a lack of faith in his maker, his community, the tradition, and even himself. With such thoughts, Ezra would sigh, reprimand himself, say a little prayer and get back to work. After all, his main task to think about these days was a pleasure to him. His Sarah, his first born was to be finally wed and it pleased him so . . . to think about it. The district teacher, she'd become entirely too particular . . . too picky; even her mother said so. And then, that Lapp boy, their nearest neighbor, had gotten her attention. Praise God and what a good lad . . . Ezra had always liked him . . . watched him grow up . . . worked with his Dad in the field and at carpentry . . . his Dad was a master carpenter . . . he'd grin in the wind at that thought . . . carpenters were going to be handy soon!

[Mudding in 2000 my sons and I discovered
the heavy water structures of 1952]

HEAVY WATER

From Telemark to North from Terre Haute
Norway's night vermilllion wounds the Wabash
where heavy thoughter frumped the shore
with secret pilings masking waters War.

Nucleic acid nurtures but does not
denatured elements assault
the new mown eyes of the world
against the razor of corporate malice.

Heroes blew up the corridors to Berlin.
To do no less .. will depend
on how our memory sustains
the senses and census of sin.

EVERYTHING MATTERS

Matters in art, in life . . . entireties
mural still, or in motion night and day
lunar shadows do not eclipse neuroaestheologically
rebonding futures that differ; contending
tears matter entirely . . . in the incandescence
of detail.

YONDER

Promise was what youth held in English movies
I never noticed much until its absence;
its fading coal an exemption from my ages reference.
For the dialectique of becoming
presumes beingness.
Theres no becoming if being has been.
Beingness broaches beyond all present possibilities
and yet . . it is the very capacity to be
Yonder . . that brave promise which
prescribes lifes focus . . how you
move toward moral surplus value.

Sycamores

We rode up above the Wabash, heading east toward home. The new mule had been a bit balky, but better than the white one who'd broke my back last summer. Riding into the river bottoms vast and harvested bean fields, the old mule became nervous in this tundra of unspecified direction. In all these miles of open space with the cold prairie wind from Illinois at our backs, he naturally inclined toward the northeast, while I needed to ride due east toward the Old Lafayette Road.

I aimed between his long ears, his forelock as crosshairs toward a grove of sycamores less than a mile ahead of us. At the edge of the forest, pale and speckled in the darker wood, they reminded me of my wife under the covers. I urged the mule straight on toward home.

POLLACK

Pollack amid sycamores at night

would spare the image

and get the colors right

like caucassian and non caucassian

not really black, nor brown, nor white

but subtle variations to soothe

our partial sight.

Olde Brush Wolf of the Wabash

I've seen 'The Wabash', like

Lew Wallace did. Crossing at night

in the rain. Headwaters strong-

arming from the North to grab

the Southern Ohio.

For Western fire and glades

of the East are its boundary waters.

The Heartland held in all the

compass of its powerful promise.

BRAVE KID

The door of the shed was stuck

to hard black lumps of mud in the ketch pen.

As I kicked it open I heard her scream.

The baby doeling's foot was caught under

cold boards of the door.

I pulled back the door and she limped around it.

Her hoof was mashed in the frozen mud.

She limped for the next few days but never cried again.

Brave kid.

INJURED BUCK

The injured buck

should be let out tomorrow.

South African strong, he became sick

and was no match for the big horned Dall Ram;

who broke his stance and the entire pecking order.

This Boer buck is named

Nelson Mandela

and he will regain his power and position

if he doesn't run out

the open front gate.

COLD CONVIVIALITY

When the cold moves in, you know
you're not as tough as the Amish.
You can work in it as long and as hard, but
not stay out in it to talk about it . . .
not in the barn light or barn lot and
not in the first light to dark at community sales.

Conviviality is stuck in my craw
as something warm.
Conviviality in the cold
is something which
I am stoker coal
calibrated otherwise.

MULES ON THE ROAD

Stampede sounds. Hard hooves on the pavement, and lots of them.

The woke!, woke!, woke! of our alarm faded to the echoing hooves of stampede east of our bedroom. My wife at the window gasped, "Our horses are on the road and disappearing into the North."

"Damn! into the north .. what the . . . who the hell left a gate open. They never go north!," I blurted still struggling into my boots and stumbling outside. All gates looked secure as I jumped in my truck and sped toward the pavement. Driving into the north I couldn't see anything but heavy winter fog and darkness. Then suddenly there they were. Looked like thirty of them. Not our horses. Not horses. It was the biggest herd of mules I'd ever seen. Big long eared draft mules; out of Belgian and Percheron mares by mammoth jacks. It was spitting rain and the steam off their backs and huge bodies mixed in the morning mist. There were a few blacks and grays amongst all the big chestnuts. My headlights forced them into a faster trot. A mule doesn't move like a horse. Their gait is different. Leg action is mostly from the knee down. It makes for a smoother ride, and moves them like pistons across a plowed field, or like this morning with a uniformed power down the tarmac.

I tried to get around to their side so's I could turn them back to my place. If they'd go in my gate I could hold them for their owners. I remembered Faulkner's' "Mule in the Yard" and figured all these mules could tear up ten acres of pasture let alone a lawn .. still I couldn't leave them on the public road .. not at this hour. Soon traffic would be speeding deadly along all the county roads racing to work.

They slowed a bit going down hill past Doc Murphy's

lane. I pulled around two groups of mules lagging behind the
leaders. They stopped completely and I drove ahead after the
leaders. This lead group of mules filled up the width of the road
from one side of the woods to the other. No way could I get
around them. I followed them for another mile to the edge of
West Union where they scattered off the road into an open field.
Turning my truck around I went back after the slower mules.
They were nowhere to be found.

I drove home and whistled for our border collie. She
came round the house and jumped in the truck beside me. Her
specialty is sheep and goats. She'd do her best with cattle and
horses but lacked confidence with the larger beasts. She could
be confident however, herding any sized beast that would allow
her to do so. I doubted these runaway mules would allow her,
but we'd give it a try.

I headed up hill toward Jonathan Bielers. Of all the adjoining Amish farms he had the most mules. I found him in the
lantern lit darkness of his large dairy barn. He and his sons were
finishing up the mornings milking.

"We've got mules out, boys!" was my greeting in cold
alarm. Seriously unalarmed, Jonathan replied "How many?"

"Seemed like thirty", I answered.

"Couldn't be ours," Jonathan said as he walked out the
barn toward the mule pen, "We're down to sixteen head."

I bought my first farm near Freedom, (Indiana) north of
the Amish in Davies County. I'd visited Amish farms in Arthur
Illinois with my father and several in Northern Indiana with
Standardbred horsemen but these Amish neighbors of mine were
different. They hailed from Lancaster County Pennsylvania and
they were mule men. My friend Red Bedwell asked one of their
elders once why they had mules and none of their brethren to the
south, north, or west would keep them. At first he mused about
some obscure biblical verse...then in epiphanous dismissal threw
his lead line up over the breeching of his own magnificent red

chestnut team and said, "it's probably cause they can't appreciate a really good span of mules."

And what spans of mules these Amish have. Eight to fourteen wide,they'll hitch and pull tractor-sized equipment across God tended fields.

When Jonathan and me reached the rear mule pen my flashlight found a gate down in the darkness. "Guess they're ours," he grinned. "Can you help us?" "Sure." Still, I seemed more worried than they did as we piled in the truck together and sped the entire 4 miles back to West Union. The slower mules had somehow caught up with the lead mules.

My border collie bluffed the entire herd now back on to the road and I followed them close with the truck. "Not too close . . ." Jonathan kept reminding me. I've never known an Amishman untempted to be a backseat driver.

The mules moved east with us behind them all the way to the ten o'clock treaty line road. Turning south they charged off toward the general direction of home. We nodded in the faint light.

"A mule doesn't like to be alone," Jonathan announced like he was sure they were going straight home. I wasn't sure. These back roads were better but there was still traffic and more rain now. Jonathan's eleven year old son smiled at me and said, "they sure picked a rainy day for their picnic."

Despite the wet I cracked my window to hear their hoof beats, and thought how mules are the most existential of creatures. With no pride of ancestry, nor hope of progeny they engage life with a robust if hybrid vigor. A mule won't injure himself or overeat I'd heard as a boy, and loved reading about Indiana's 27th Mule Brigade in 1863 which struck deep into the south breaking the very idea of southern compromise. The year I was born, 1940, a Marine Corps publication, "The Small Wars Manual" emphasized the mule as vital for Insurgency and Counterinsurgency. It describes how a mule "withstands hot weather better, and is less susceptible to colic and founder than a horse . . how the foot of the mule is less subject to disorder and how a mule takes better care of himself, in the hands of an incompetent driver."

I slowed down more carefully as yet again this herd of mules made the correct turn west this time. There were only sixteen of them. Sure had seemed like thirty. They trotted slowly now under the scraggly second growth branches over the narrow lane. One more turn to the left and they'd make it home to their own lane. The Bielers were all beaming proud of their mules. Jonathan had been concerned about his mules but had even more faith in them that they'd get back to where they ought to be. "The Restoration Of Peace and Order" is what the "The Small Wars Manual" said every peasant hopes for.

This year (2004) the US Army has just replaced "The Small Wars Manual," with the F.M.I. 3-07.22 or "Counterinsurgency Operations" for waging, "asymmetrical conflict" that is, bullying weaker armies. It mentions women and children as enemy combatants.

It doesn't mention mules.

APOSIOPESIS
(From Coleridge: *The Funeral Guest)*

The funeral ends.

Presumptive host
D: You bowed your head in there. Are you
religious now?

funeral guest
T: You know many sixty year old atheists?

funeral party: Laughter becoming silence.

D: Too bad it takes a time like this . . . Anyhow
its grand . . us all being together . . huh?

T: Wasn't always so . .huh!?

funeral friend
J: (Quizzically for everyone) Yeah . . Whys it
changed?

T: We're all a part of each others story now . . And
what better time . . . communitas comes together
to fill the gap.

D: Now you're sounding a little bit like
a Commie . .

J: (interrupting) and motioning toward L. and his wife.
They've had a storybook life; one marriage,
children . . prosperity . . . but he may have
missed a lot.

D: I don't think so. Remember his youth.

real time host
L: (joining the group) . . but you guys had more wives, he
laughed.

T: A man who cannot be satisfied with one
woman has no imagination.

J: Hey . . . say now, I like that, (repeating) "A
man who can't be happy with his
woman is without imagination" . . . naw
lets see "A man who cannot be satisfied
with one woman has no imagination"
 . . . Yeah!

L: I dunno . . I sure thought about it . .

T: Thinking about it will not hurt you.

L: I dunno . . .

T: Thinking about it will not hurt you;
obsessing about it will hurt you.

J:Hey . . ! [unquiet laughter] Ode T.
has a lot of 'em . . . dudn't he?

D:They may not be his . . .

J:Whose then? . . . to whom do we credit
the spirit of these remarks?

T: Vladimer Illich Lenin

D:(to L so T can hear) There it is again . .
what's up with this comm. . .

L:Aw, he's not anymore . .

D: The hell . . he's no . .

The funerals begin.

HIGH DENIAL

The gentling sun
in middays February
encourages my old heart
that harms way
cannot hold against the seasons
even for a day.

COLDSTREAM GUARDS

Rainbows along against the steel

of rainmakers plumbed deep in the aquifer

below wheat straw . . gold

as Van Goghs beard.

Van Gogh Yellow

Van Gogh has come to Western Indiana

. . . Yellow!

against the heart aching foliage

cold springed canola

partially and perennially

joins new fields

to brighten the yearning

deep in the breast

and breadth of the season.

KORANIC HAIKU

The red tail hawk

flies off the lines

out across the corn.

There is some utility

in watching this

and much instruction.

COMELY WHILE LEAVING

Aye the burnished wood!
Taupe and maroon as tannin
a wine dark wood in this light
which is the last light
of an early winters day
caressingly so long . . and
comely while leaving.

Sure, and its more
than fires on the sun.

"PATHETIC FALLACY" (JOHN RUSKIN)

The glare is eaten

by the prairie tiered night,

the neon glare from batteries, generators, and

power plants flicker, in pure and cheap light

under its overspreading maw

quenching tapers is the law

for souls outside

their destined selves.

TWO KINDS

There are two kinds of dog;
1.the kind humans have improved from the wolf
2.and the kind they haven't

There are two kinds of meal;
1.the kind you feel better from
2.or worse

There are two kinds of women;
1.the kind that leave you
2.and the kind that don't

There are two kinds of life;
1.the kind you live
2.and the kind you don't

BEYOND THE PALE

"Wildered and dark"
(Coleridge)
in the time it takes your watch to stop

While a woods cat
can break in your screen,
raid the kitchen
and scare the shit
out of your house cat

You may wonder
whether it is bravery
or the brute
in you that yearns
for that wild
in the bison's eye

Large-lashed and luminous
a massive pool
of dark consciousness
which hates my paleness
across the fence
Ancestral trace of ancient breeds

BISON

It is weather for bison
to be born in
and her contractions instinctively
lead her away from the herd.

Separate she is . . .
a dark clump facing
the eastern sky, a brown rock
amid the grassy sea.

Unshed, her early summer coat
is worn
like an old carpet
for bison prayer.

She breathes . . .
into the coming night
whom she allows to take her
reflecting such resignation in 'Cow Eyes,'

so feminine, so fine
unlike the bulls
her eyes do not hate mine.

38TH ST. SMOKE

Wintersmoke, the black man laughed
barrel chest rumbling like an old furnace;
"When the near north side of all our memories
lay out in coal and woodsmoke,
we lived in those smoky days ..."
As in an old photo
without the subtlety and falseness of colour
autumnal thoughts of spring are endured . . . for
if there is no winter to endure,
what's the sense of summer?

NEW MADE BED

Crossing the low hills at dawn I had the illusion of meadow

bottoms heavenly aflame. It was an optical illusion.

The first ribbon of light from under the cloud covers made it so.

I liked being illuded in that way and wondered about the light in

Fatima and Medugoria. Perhaps the greater

illusion is winter morning meadows in 'normal' light

appearing stable and neat as a woman's new made bed.

MEXICAN FROWNS

My God! . . . I loved the Mexicans in California.

Pissed off and Catholic, they all

seemed as hard working poor as I was . . .

Except the guys would frown at you in traffic.

It was a rude but comradely frown. The kind that Soviets

would give you to cover their lack of hospitality.

The only appropriate response to such frowns

is to frown like hell right back at them. That

response will get you apologetic

and embarrassed smiles on

McHenry Street in Modesto. That same response

however will get you a qualitatively different

reaction if you are the lone gringo dancing

with a Senorita in a Firebaugh Cantina.

We skedaddled out the back door.

*"The sun rarely shines
what with the dust and confusion"*
Thoreau

THREE JAKES

Saturday conversation was sunshine by the barn door. It thawed the last of winter laying skiff like in our soul.

I called on Jake Miller at midday. His daughter Rachel rode and waved from her spotted pony. Jake's a stallioner, farrier, and general horse dealer. I'd come to get supplement for my expectant mares. As Jake prepared it his Dad, Chris walked across the road to speak with us.

"How have you wintered Tom?" he asked. "I've wintered fine," I lied, then explained how we'd been sick. He did the same and sat down on an overturned bucket. We laughed at the Ides of March.

William R., the trotting stallion I'd helped Jake acquire was noisy in his stall. He knew the nearness of his third breeding season. Three years ago he'd been crippled in an Illinois racing accident. I told Sean Fitzgerald (at Hidden Hope Farm) if anyone could save and rehabilitate him to stud it was the young Amishman Jake Miller. William R. was given to Jake who worked with him from September on. He bred six mares that spring and the next. He enjoyed his work.

Jake Hostetter pulled in driving what is called in Ireland . . a trap. It was a two-wheeled cart on rubber.[1] Jake noticed me noticing the rubber and shook his head smiling like I was his very own bishop. "We're not going far," he laughed. His ten-year-old daughter sat beside him. Their cart was hitched to a two-year-old green broke gelding. "Your new Morgan?" I asked.

"Yep, he needs some work, but he'll make Mary a fine horse," he said beaming at his daughter. We all liked looking at Mary in her black bonnet. They'd come to the Millers to get this new Morgan shoed. He was a bright red chestnut I guessed to be of the Jubilee King line. Jake said he'd have to check his papers.

As the two Jakes busied themselves reshoeing the Morgan, a third Jake drove in the lane. Three Jakes! This third Jake was Jake Hostetter's twenty-four year old son Jacob. He lives across the meadows and was driving a lanky Standardbred hitched to a grey and black prairie buggy. This last Jake was alarmed his wife's mare aborted her foal this morning. Chris was standing now and said the Miller family had lost two foals as well.

The third Jake and Chris both looked at me inquiringly without speaking. Looking at his son Jake but directed at me Chris asked, "Should we have the vet out to check these mares?"

It was a delicate question; Equine abortion is usually caused by the Rhinovirus, which is a form of herpes. If the aforementioned mares were bred to William R. it was him . . . Jakes stallion the vet needs to check. Trotting mares now coming to Jakes stallion used to come to mine. My stallion is a pacer but trotter bred on his dams side

I waited for a minute. Jake Miller straightened from his farrier work and looked my way. "Were these mares bred to William R?" I asked. "Yes they were," he answered, "and the David Stolfuss mare too . . she aborted last week."

"Better check him," we nodded to each other. Both Amish fathers comforted their sons. Jake, the son of Chris helped his daughter off her pony. Jake, the son of Jake touched his dad and sister before taking his leave. Jake, the father of Jake and Mary handed her the reins and waved goodbye.

Left in the sunshine, I missed my sons and daughter.

(Proverbs 14:13 Even in laughter the heart finds sadness, and joy makes way for sorrow.)

1. Amish Bishops enforce the ban on rubber wheels as a temptation people will drive too far from home.

ANCIEN REGIMES

Last week at Judson's Harness and Saddlery there was a mixed crowd of Old Order and New Order Amish plus some modern quarter horse folk. The latter were confused by the 'Old Order' orthodox Pennsylvania garb and the 'New Order' improvised and slightly disheveled look. I was wearing my old black hat and black denim jacket. A young woman asked, "Excuse me Sir . . . are you 'New Order Amish'?"

"No mam, I am Ancient Order Irish."

CLOUDS ON THE GROUND

The March sky has not a cloud.
Cold winds cannot blow away the sun.
It alights the flock;
becoming clouds on the ground

BREAKING SEVERITIES

The old porch swing
barely moves in the breeze
safe from the south wind
severely breaking into the yard.

Sheltered by our homes foundation
the base for breaking severities;
spousal spirit for unyielding directions
of the dream.

RED GREY EVENINGS

Red grey evenings
after bright afternoons
with Belgians, olde government Morgans,
and Jackstock the knowledge of dreams.

Four hours of my Saturday
discovered new families along Parke Counties eastern ridge.
They must have arrived last summer
laying out lime rock lanes
into the hills and rolling ground.

Not developing the land, but saving it,
working it with little Haflingers
or with Spans of Mules
bigger than most horsemen can imagine.

At the end of the day
children put bag balm
on the great teams harness sores
and tend the tame black lamb by the beehives.

At the end of the day
with over sixteen hands of longitudinal being
the grace of latitude is shown.

"Cement stuck to human dreams!"
P. Neruda, *Ruinas*

THE FURTHEST TURN

Upon a winters lawn
with sidewalks the texture
of a hearts unknowing . .
the ways it would be
'round the top of decades . . going
to the pace in the frosted breath of darkness
both before and after the light of knowing
sequence in His attempts
to kill me in all
but the seventh race.

50ˢ   First stoned in Sugar groves
60ˢ   lost in the great banks of grandest error
70ˢ   I returned restored then torn asunder,
80ˢ   wandered the wilderness out west to reconnoiter
90ˢ   dead folks and the job of Jobs reward.

2000   He tries to break me in the furthest turn
before the homestretch and the finish line
I am Saddams face
in the spider hole unsafe
from missed appointments in Sammara.

I dream the cold lawn, the concrete complaint
but taste the sweet iron bit
that is compliance, that is constraint.

WH~~O~~LLY HOLY SATURDAY

The sun did not rise all day
it's been that way for weeks
on the wet late winter roads
I wheeled from farm to farm.

Yet light in the eyes of my neighbors
beat the risin' of the dawn
when pilgrims claim He's Risen
beats the risin' of the dawn.

THE FULL LOAF

A January thaw can tackle you clear up to your calves,
cling to your boots all season, track on to the wool carpet, and
seem permanently plastered along the long porch.

First week I got my truck stuck in the yard where this
week it refroze into trenches we trip over. Then I remember all
that, out west dust in my eyes and how, I longed to be home and
never complain, about mud again even in acres of quicksanded
lanes and lots which grab and hold us close to the core of the
earth holding still great wheels strong enough to pull your boots
off especially at Spring sales it spatters the knees of sleek trotters
as admiring draft teams charge through muck and the laughter of
communards lifting up above the mud we glimpse a muddy peace
on earth goodwill to kin at least.

I bid on the last remaining loaves of bread.

Any of the different arrangements
in linear order that can be made
of a given set of objects.

The hoosier spring is fickle; a wife returning
unrepentant and unreconciled to be so.
Glimpses of spring . . . phone sex for the real thing.
Silvery cigarette cases of hope
for comfort getting cancerous retirement.
The old mare and me were buffeted
by cyclone force wind knocking us both . . down
on the hard ass ground.

My cousin whom I'd put up with a lifetime of rumors
he was my brother strode into the February thaw
slipping on porch ice, slid down steps,
 legs caught calf deep around his knees
twisting into wrought iron railing
he floundered, breaking his nose, jaw and elbows
struggling against dumb random destiny.

With Uncle Charlie drunk and dead in Chambersville,
his sainted mother Daisey died. Named after her father's horse
we called her Aunt Peggy . . . she saw both his brothers die.
Devoted to sisters, this World War II gunners mate
tin can veteran of the 'Perry' and 'Isabel'
midcentury trucker of Bedford Stone for Rocky Mountain
churches drove a fast red Hudson and married a cheerleader.
A ringer for Gilbert Roland I'd introduce him
to neighbor kids as my cousin the movie star,
they'd say, "goodbye Gilbert" as he left wondering why?

For hours his concussed spirit railed against
cold concrete; frame reduced to a limpid
lady in cement with mini-strokes he froze
fighting seizures for three more weeks and quit.

Loving issue gathered 'round; four sons and one daughter,
Masons and Legionnaires code
color guards against my mythic weather.
A nephew appears gender bendered beyond
their acceptance and my approval.
I invite him to join us. He refused,
hanging back to the rear.

Sartre thought they'd have to think of themselves
as the Proletariat or they would not be so.
Rivalries whether sibling, fraternal, or fratricidal
are beyond the object . . and abject borders of identity and memory.
We imbricate attention differently,
permutating time and space
beginning endings and ending beginnings.

Leaving the funeral pyre,
I kiss my kin goodbye
While his youngest (my favorite)
in the spring of his youth that is over . . frowns at me.
And yet there will be robins.
I will rage at the gales
that knock us down
but, there will be robins soon.
Too soon for some dying in the memory of warmth
huddled on cold pavements
before, after, during or otherwise sung
to broods that brave all fickle seasons.

Imperanent Pasture

Not even the seasons

are as permanent

as our ideas

about them

There are new colors

darker, deeper, dawns

not darkened at noon

but nooner – evening er

a gloaming coverlet

for the catholic day

a bold black and white print

from the front

rotagravured

brown sectioned bright

beyond technical colors

when the night

won't let go

of the morning

and evening is a gentler surprise

WINTERIOR SEICHE

February, 2005: *a Timber Wolf*
is run over on I-94.
Wisconsin lifts its no kill policy.

The heart of Milwaukee bears no seiche; no Sue Nami nor

Goddess Dominatreix. Yet no one remembers Father Grappi at the

shoreline of thawful winters sett, by the paintings pointer bitch, the

Wallachian Post, Hotel Pfister or the County Clare.

Quietly affording our region of neglect, an elegant

Palermo precedes my gathering of wood as another granddaughter

runs toward the frame...forgetting LePage in her pinafore of time.

Milwaukee, do not scold my sighs.

Milwaukee, I've swam your rusting skies.

In the last year of the last century corrupt county officials and degenerate DNR types attempted to outlaw running hounds in Parke Co., IN

(courting trouble with ..)CALICO COYOTE HOUNDS

He could still see his breath but, the evening sun warmed him. He stood in one of those russet gloamings that come in mid March, when the lion and the lamb romp in cold sunlight.It pleased him to watch his young calicos cast in and out of the thicket. They were hell after the brush wolf who'd left but a handful of hair from the missing doe. Then they hit the line hard and bayed accordingly. His own hair stood on end and he was ready for sport or court again.

SLUICE OF MAY
(Gwalchmar becomes Gwalchaved)

The sluice of May into June rain . . .
is sliced . . . 'as good as rain'. . they say.

Tulip poplars blossom the last of the
rite toward the slower aspect that
 stretches out like a child's country road
and lays gentle as a dark warm night
to cover recollection of the hunt
in homecoming thoughts; lovemaking
the light come on time.

FIST OF THE MOON

Schooling the hound pups near the pond and northern pastures
a blue heron, more black than blue
winged low from the willow breaks
Crossing the pond in tandem with its own reflected image
as our pickets that night
made a fist of the moon

A NATURAL SMILE

Farmlands smile at the end of summer
their corn crop yellowing toothy stalks
spread like an aging grin
from ear to ear it spreads
cutting the throat of this season

BROTHER HOUNDS

It was a cold spring day. Yet, the season
seemed bravely edging out winter. The
sun barely shone. A canvass of grey sprawled
over the green seas of new grass. Past the
rip rapped retaining wall I saw my three
young hounds standing by the stream. They
stood beside the stone piled wall with a kind
of serious vanity; elegant as stallions or
bull elk. They surveyed the forested hill
and yonder meadows. The stream flowed
from the hill, then disappeared
beneath the meadows. The pale July hound
drank from the cold stream while his saddle-
backed brothers stood guard beside him.
It is the way winter passes between
the warmth of our attention.

THE OTHER TIME

I watch my hounds in wooded light

and see them as Hemmingway saw Cavalry in Spain;

dappled through the trees

soft petitioned leaves have stayed

fleet shadows of the other time

hide the sacral glade.

They come like quiet thunder

in quickened canine pace

the night gives up a glimpsed repose

in beauty well beyond the ridges reach

of rolling contradiction.

Hunt em' up brave songsters.

Hunt em' up!

INTO THE RAIN

Three grey heron match the sky
flying over a field of large English Whites
flying south east into the rain

They will stop at the lake
Two will mate and nest near the bridge
The third will not be left for long

For it is Spring, and the force of nature
more than quantifiable turns of the planet
becomes a builder in his old bird brain

to complete every single thing he's started.

DYING MEN DON'T DRINK BEER

The blood was all around. It covered our clothes. It
covered our faces and arms. It flooded the senses. It must have
smelled like this in ancient battle, I remember thinking . . . thick-
ening in chain mail, caking on the horses manes and tail, sticking
in your teeth and theirs. Human blood in battle stings sweet and
scary. You're always quantifying whose it is. But, horse blood
when your will is struggling to save a great beast is different. Its
scent is heavier than a 'Destrier'[1] in armour and dull . . . it hits
you like the back of a manure shovel. Not a violent smell tempered by anger but the dull, heavy tug of death.

Her colt was dead, its head and right fore leg severed;
its left carpus still caught between the pelvis and the main vets
chain. The lady vet had another chain and the three of us pulled
against the smell of death. For the mare was dying now, unless
we could remove her overdue foal. And then ... there was more
blood ... from my butcher knife episiotomy . . .

My son, Zach had been the best sentinel. He charged
the porch steps to yell, "The colt is coming!" I jumped out of
sickbay, without clothes, gathered on my robe, forced my bare
feet into new work boots and caught up with him, running to the
barn. We found her lying down in back, not in front where we'd
prepared clean bedding. She was lying down for the first time
in two weeks. I'd been up with her every night 11 PM to 3 AM.
She never lay down. But now she did . . . thrashing in pain and
dystocia[2]; teeth barred and already with dead looking eyes. I
phoned the vet and Zach fetched my britches.

A huge dystocic colt was presenting upside down, his long ears sticking out of her, forelegs and shoulder snagged behind her pelvis. As Zach calmed the mare, I went into her. According to the book, I pushed the colt's forehead back as far as I could, attempting to turn it so nose first he might be born. Her contractions exploded him back against the vaginal wall in the same impossible position. Again, again, and again I would push his head with not enough space and/or strength to make the turn. Thud would come the back of his skull. I doubted he was alive. I knew she was dying. Time . . .

Zach cauterized the butcher knife with a lighter he'd hidden and I attempted the episiotomy. Another inch and I might get him out upside down and all. I remembered episiotomies in women, but not in horses. I remembered them as vertical instead of diagonal or horizontal, as they should be. To the south was bone, to the north was her rectum; I cut north and then away from the rectum. More blood. The knife sawing through the gristle of live flesh. The mare in so much other pain, she barely noticed my hacking through her vulva. Now I would grab that ill presented head and pull against those powers opposing this baby's birth.
I prayed that if "it is written" for them to die, 'Please God, rewrite it!'

The enlarged vulva opened enough to the world for his head to come half way out. His little poll and larger skull then stuck just below his eyes. They were glazed and I could see that he was dead, and far too big to be delivered. My knife work was in vain. The mare could only be saved by caesarean or the colts dismemberment.

The vet arrived and we decided the latter. Encouraging and hurting her at the same time, I managed to provoke her to stand and stagger out of the barn on to clean grass. The colt's head and forelegs then dismembered by a band saw shot through a half-inch pipe to protect the mother's viscera . . . and still its shoulders stuck. There was no reaching the other leg . . . more chains and pulling as we sweat in the cold May light.

The mare was going fast, so the vet in charge recommended we risk the calf jack to remove the remains of the foal. It had to come out fast for her to live. The risk was probable injury to her internal organs. Worse, she might need sedated to relax and lie quietly.

I'd seen jacks whirled around like lethal missiles by unruly mares . . . but not this mare . . . she was doing all she could to help us with her situation . . . she was just holding on and too weak for a sedative. I unhooked her halter and encouraged her forward. She wobbled and within ten feet lay down perfectly still. They infused her with fluids and applied the jack. Her breathing was labored and she groaned at its pressure, but she kept still. The carpus and legs emerged. It was out of her.

The lady vet then sprang upon the task of suturing up my butchered episiotomy. For one hour and a half, she tediously sewed the ragged wound. Finally, too much for this weakened mama, the mare began to fight us. Still too weak to sedate, she was too strong for us to restrain completely. I sat on her neck and held her head down. She'd garner up her strength every ten minutes or so and try to rear, her front hooves flying near my head. Worn out, I failed to duck and one hoof grazed the bridge of my nose while the other impacted the side of my head. The latter popped like a muffled gunshot. The vets ran to me. It knocked me silly for a second and I said something stupid like, "It's a kick in the head!"

In minutes, my wife was there. Radiant with new energy she serenely calmed the mare. She also scolded me for being too rough with the beast; she hadn't seen the head injury. Slowly now, this beautiful but bedraggled black mare rose to her feet; breathing hard and still weary. She would live! The blood on her black coat matched the color of her dismembered dead colt. He was a blood bay…my favorite color to hitch a sulky to racing silks. He was the color that Walter Farley[3] chose for the son of his black stallion who became a harness colt. I had read all of Walter Farley's books as a boy and preferred that harness racing story. Mine had been, after all, an Indiana boyhood, but this blood bay Indiana eligible colt would never race . . . would never pull a sulky to the pace of my boyhoods imagination. And his mother's brood mare career was also finished. She'd been the first filly I ever got to the track. She'd set a record in her maiden race at Balmoral and made a lot of money. In fact, she was one of the reasons I was thought to be a successful racehorse man in my bachelor years. After marrying my accountant wife, she not so gently pointed out that all equine expenses had to be subtracted from racing profits. That viewpoint I considered petty at first, but slowly adapted to reality, got out of the racehorse game and concentrated on broodmares and being a stallioneer.

This mare had been born in April, a decade ago and we named her "Cruelest Month" after T. S. Eliot's verse. Most people thought the name referred to taxes. She lost her first foal. Now, she's lost her second. She must never be bred again…

healed up she'll make an Amish buggy horse or family pet. She's been our favorite and the most beautiful in our band of mares.

I was exhausted and time was slowing down as I helped the vets wash up at the watering trough. "We soused our face and arms in the cold hard water of the horse trough."[4] I offered them cold beer and was glad they refused. They were tiredly celebrating the end of this job . . . and the end of their day. I was grieving losses and the end of this mare with me. She had about as many years left as I did. The evening's dying light disturbed me. All life dies . . . it just takes a while and the time it takes is our test . . . to care enough about the right things. I was glad again we didn't drink beer. It's not that dying men don't drink beer . . . but not while they're thinking about it.

Ideas about death mainly reflect mere attitudes toward organization. Life is messy and never complete. Death threatens us with completion whether we want completed or not. Most of my work was done yet I was too tired to take this dead colt to the "tiger man" . . . who runs a zoo farm where most of the dead calves and colts in our county are taken.

Instead it seemed reasonable to load this dismembered deceased little corpse into the truck, drive to the thicket in back of the farm, and unload it for the coyotes. They'd clean things up by dawn.

By the time I drove back to the house it was dark. Within an hour the coyotes were singing and yelping over their feast. The mare heard them. She was in the foremost part of the four-acre yard, on point with the scent less than 200 yards away from her colt and the coyotes. She keened and neighed in a grief stricken low whistling like alarm, making horse sounds I'd never

heard before. I took her into the barn, tried to comfort her . . .
even tried to cover her ears. She wouldn't have it and struggled
to get outside. I let her gallop back into the yard. I'd of brought
her into the house if I thought it would help, but there was no
consoling her. She stayed on point throughout the night for the
last of the life we had lost.

1. Destrier: medieval war horse.

2. Dystocia: abnormal labor in birth caused by obstructed muscle fiber of the partrurient uterus

3. Walter Farley: author of the Black Stallion series of boys books. Basis for Francis Ford Coppolas acclaimed film, *"The Black Stallion."*

4. From *Among the Cornrows, Main Traveled Roads: Stories of the Midlands of America*, by Hamlin Garland

Long Johns in June

Cold springs the sadder

for its lack of sunlight.

Winter seems more cheerful

than the chill of foliaged darkness.

"Those we've loved and lost
are now . . . wherever we are"
St. John Chrysostom

SPRUNG (PER G.M. HOPKINS)

Dark winds blow at the brightness of May;

shadows entangle sunlight

after night trains call retreat from the fields

for the next noonday.

Young Amish farmers scrape the mud

from their boots on weeds reaching green

toward the seasons reflection

of falling, falleness, and the fallen . . .

We may not remember those who are wherever

we are in overcast lenten orthodoxy

that paradox of color lit darkness . . .

the virtue of obloquy.

CONSOLIDATION

It was still dark in May, but warming

as sunlight began . . to bring in bugs.

The outside mares stood in the slope of locust shade

their tails practicing . . . to fan off the flies.

Rising from prayer I saw them as a sign

of all that's given but seldom seen til summer.

Big rough amish mares; over seventeen hands

whose black and chestnut bodies

could pull us through consolidation.

TRUTH AND COMMOTIONS
(Compression and Displacement)

> *"God has given the human mind*
> *awareness of duration; he has*
> *endowed them with the power of*
> *reflecting on sequence"*
> Ecclesiastes

> *"I think that comedy is the quintessential*
> *human reaction to the fear of death.*
> *A diabolical shade of suspicion behind every*
> *proclamation of truth."*
> Umberto Eco Paris Review Summer 2008

Are animals bereft of humor? Eco thinks so. I don't. Packs of hounds will grin, smile, and laugh especially when their sense of impending punishment, danger or death is relieved. That is to say, hits someone other than themselves. I've seen dairy cows in California, and human pedestrians in Moscow do the same. Surviving a collective disturbance with its turmoil, confusion, and excitement is always funny. Wit is based on recognizing, appreciating and reframing that moment.

Eco's right about the rest. Suspicion behind fearful facts is that suspense in life best relieved by humor. That brave humor is the essence I think, of what the ancients meant by faith. That sixth sense of light at the end of dark tunnels; a way out of all the commotion.

And commotion can pile on quite suddenly. Especially when careful preparations are made to avoid it. One cannot ticket oneself. It requires others. Similarly commotion requires assistance.

My first assistant was Fred from up the hill. A strong

strapping lad, the oldest son of my secretary. We liked working together. He knew I loved the Amish, but today he was "pissed at them". Christopher Weiler, an Amish Bishop had developed a large dairy and produce farm surrounding the smaller freeholds of Fred's family. "The Weiliers are fertilizing their fields with raw manure from their dairy barn . . . its stench is terrible and its legal . . cause he has less than 300 cows! Today I hate the stinking Amish."

Later I would argue that raw manure stank no more than the corporate chemical shit that all the other farms were spreading around . . . poisoning the earth, for their ethanol crop . . . but time was short . . "Lets get the sheep up," I said.

The 'sheep' were of the Dall breed. They are basically an undomesticated, that is to say 'wild' animal. They cannot be herded by my border collie unless joined with the more tractable domesticated goat herd. I'd acquired about fifty head. I first discovered this breed while visiting an Amish friend in Wayne County.

We were inspecting some mares he'd just retired from the track when I noticed big horned rams in his lower pasture. With horns bigger than Rambouillets[1] and conformation smaller than Dorsets[2] they looked like wild sheep from the Rocky Mountains.

"From farther north" Eli explained, " and there is a high market price for those horns." "You market the horns and the meat?" I asked.

"Mostly the horn," he answered. Puzzled, I pressed, "For what? Is there an Asian market for the horn? Is it considered an aphrodisiac?"

"No . . . no," Eli replied "it's for the shooting preserves."

Eli . . !," I scolded, "you mean to tell me you raise these farm sheep for some rich b.- to shoot and put on his wall?! Isn't that kind of degenerate?"

"Well I get $350 to $500 for a really good rack."

. . . "Hmm. I guess its not that degenerate" I thought and said.

I started my 'Dall' project that day . . buying an unrelated pair from Eli's flock. Buying, trading, and mostly just breeding I developed a large flock very quickly . . selling exceptional mature rams and less exceptional young rams at the annual Autumn Exotic Animal Sale in Cape Gerardo, Missouri. A few buyers came to the farm. Our farm was listed in the regional Ag papers 'Breeders Directory' for Dall Sheep, Savanna Goats, and Standardbred horses.

Several 'stock buyers' were scheduled for today. Even though it was Saturday my secretary had conceded two clinical appointments as well. Prepared for the former I had forgotten the latter entirely.

The first of the former to arrive was a big Mennonite from Kentucky. Dressed aggressively plain he drove a new Dodge truck with a cab full of pretty daughters. Right behind them came two car loads of rough necks from across the river who said they were interested in the cross bred (boer x kiko x savanna) goats I'd advertised. They quickly became more interested in the Mennonites daughters. Next came the two clinical appointments together in the same van from Hendricks County. Excusing myself from livestock work I walked up from the barns to greet them in the parking area.

The driver of the van was a young mother who'd brought her adolescent son. In the back seat was an older lady and her "adopted" grandson. They'd come together "to save gas". I settled the first patient and her football player fifteen-year-old into the parlor. Terri the second older gal was one of my favorites. She'd been named after St. Tehresa and had been a daily communicant until very recently. Severely disabled and childless she had reared her husbands' grandchildren for years until their mother could resume her parental responsibilities. Their visitation became difficult. Terri became depressed. This appointment today for the youngest was a very important event to her. I encouraged her and her seven-year-old "grand-son" to wander about the yard but not over the fence.

Returning to the barn area I found my border collie and most of the men worn out and panting. The men couldn't properly instruct the dog so they over compensated by running around after the flock themselves. Sheep and goats scattered apart to barely regroup way north of the pond. The dog followed suit but couldn't count on the men to coordinate accordingly. I re-ordered the stock dog north and instructed each man to a proper coordinate in the field. The Mennonite girls joined us now and were directed to coordinated positions.

Even then . . when the border collie and I brought the joint flock south . . the sheep and goats charged past the peopled positions like a champion football squad.

Once again . . . the same thing. The third time was worse. The country boys were pissed and cussing loudly. The big Mennonite looked grieved his daughters were hearing such language and smiling about it.

The fourth time I go-wayed and go-byed[3] the flock around both sheep and goats tired and turned readily into the ketch pen gate. The boys were jubilant, the girls cheered, and

the big Mennonite suggested his daughters wait in the truck.
They didn't. Next he suggested the boys go first in selecting
their stock since they seemed in a bigger hurry. He didn't say
hurry for what . . but they had been looking at their watches a lot
in between cussing and flirting.

The boys noisily selected six cross-bred does I helped
them load into their trailer. As they paid me Terri's little "grandson" petted the goats through the bars of the trailer. I had him
stand back as they drove too fast out the lane waving and honk-
ing good-bye to the Mennonite girls.

A half hour had passed. Terri patiently asked if her
"grandson" could accompany me back to the barn. She stayed
in the yard. I walked with the boy back to the ketch pen finding Fred and the big Mennonite in deep discussion about all that
was wrong with Old Order Amish. Alarmed at such Anabaptist
betrayal further bending Fred's bigotry . . I jumped in.

"The Old Order Amish to me are the best people on
earth. They are holding out for a life we've lost entirely and the
Mennonites are losing on the installment plan."

This poor Mennonite father had just endured the rough
neck boys. Now . . shaking his head he thought he'd have to endure the crankiness of an old conservative farmer. "What is your
religious background?" he politely asked.

"The same as your Founder," I answered. "Catholic.
The same as Father Menno[4] and his revolutionary brother!"
Reflecting on this before replying his attention jerked away
toward his daughters we heard exclaiming alarm as they pulled
Terri's "grandson" out from under a horse. My black Albatross[5]
mare had wandered in close and he was petting all over and
under her. I went over to assure them and the boy regarding the

safety of the mare. He could have swung on her tail or tackled her legs and she would remain protectively tractable and still. That was not true however of the other horses I pointed out in the far southern pasture.

Then we all set to work loading the selected and marked ewes and ram on to the Mennonites stock paneled truck.
The ram was not cooperative. I went over to help with him as we heard the hoofbeats of horses cantering in from the south.

A large black Park Place[6] mare with her colt paused near us just long enough for Terri's little boy to run out to pet her flanks. Annoyed the mare kicked not to kill but merely shove him away. Her hoof struck him below the sternum in the pit of his stomach. He went down and lay still. The girls tearfully alarmed were all over him. I coaxed them away so he could breathe and be examined.

"The wind had been knocked out of him," we all agreed and carried him into the yard. Terri was at his side immediately as was the young mother who'd been waiting in the parlor.
The ram escaped and was trying to rejoin the ewes in the ketch pen. Fred and the dog easily caught him up again into the truck. I stayed with the boy until I was sure there were no further injuries.

The big Mennonite was more than ready to go. He paid cash $100 shy of the tallied bill. He had misunderstood the price of the ram and had no more cash. I apologized if I hadn't made it clear.

"No, no, no", he benignly objected. "There has been much commotion here today." Commotion?! I guess . . what a perfect word for it. Fred, me and the big Mennonite all laughed so hard we had to sit down on the cathartic ground. I fraternally cut the $100 to $50 if he'd mail me the balance.

I took care of my patients. The boy was fine but has yet to return here. And the big Mennonite never sent me the fifty bucks.

1. Rambouillets: a large breed of sheep originally imported from France.

2. Dorsets: a smaller breed of sheep from Thomas Hardy country.

3. go-way and go-bye: stock dog commands to the right and left respectively.

4. Father Menno Simon: Roman Catholic Priest who founded the Mennonites after his brother was slain leading Peasant revolts against princely priviledge.

5. Albatross: a famous pacing Standardbred Stallion and his breed line.

6. Park Place: University of Illinois Standardbred Stallion and strain.

NO GNATS IN GOSHEN
(ode to drosophilas)

They were at the wedding . . . old comrades I'd studied in
'60 . . . swarming about the mimosa and around the old groom's
head; genetic pilots and precursors of wrath.

I had not met that hope with her father, the brides father
we buried two winters ago drilling the frozen earth with machinery for his grave and our prayerful loss in a cold hard hole. Taps
touched his daughter's tears and tore off past fallen graves away
from the mine ground and over the rolling land his life had loved,
worked, and welded into the flesh of evening.

They're around the bride's head now; a cloud upon the
veil led by the cyclic ampresponsive element binding protein
through thirty-day life cycles since I was in school and knew their
four hundred eightieth predecessors. Insect intelligence like a
forty-year old man remembering one hell of a shock at twelve.
Harrowing home-centered hope his cousins rabbits could have
seen from their upland hutch triangulated to the point of her
murdered husband our grandfathers gray countenance drawing the
line in winter field deflecting one and accepting another into the
ground of our being as more than old snow transmitted clear by
his cycle ampresponsiveness . . . elemental as the woods grain on
his radio.

His issue dying now . . near evening also far . . in the city of angels going to Mass in Spanish since they changed it from the latin . . preferring aesthetic non communication to infantile patter; particles of labyrinthine infrastructure driving the megapolis model of life without centers I longed for my fathers bar where they could still translate gezelligheid and dream of gemeinschaft. I feared the bulbous fracture of gimme – gimme – gimme mien shaft bent over and rapacious gezellschaft degenerately peddled by the heirs of heretics in pervasive propaganda.

The goldfinch is now in the showery rain, gripping the green branch of a berry tree submerged in the summer shower and bright presence of the sun's promise to shower tomorrow. As time goes by for the goldfinch my fathers fathers enjoyed this wild canary.

If we are the entire cast of our dreams . . why aren't we the all of the waking dream of consciousness; the bird, branch, and gnats of our ancestors cyclic ampresponsiveness.

The Authority of Failure

If good judgment comes from the experience

of poor judgment; our species

may yet exponentially evolve.

By the authority of ultimate failure

man has failed God

and blamed Him for it.

From the silent night of our epochs

blood battling butchery

to our . . . sour dreams of tyranny and decay.

FIREWAKE

There is a relationship between the fireflies
on my lawn
and the fireworks I see across miles
of meadows in toward town.

The sound of distant explosion is barely audible;
a faint thud.
The life behind the light of fireflies barely imaginable;
a slight bug.

Both celebrate their source on the fourth;
. . . obliquely understood.

NEED FOR A NEO COMM. MANIFESTO
(a conservative case for communism)

For I am a failed revolutionary . . . content

here and now, like now and then

to tend my flocks and bands,

herds and hounds; to counsel

and console those wounded

by the ever fragmenting free market

that still sounds like freedom, but

increasingly . . . smells like death.

BALLAD FROM A STILL POND

A harmonic moment
has to do with the waters
turning over in the universe.

Clear moments upon the surface
of a season changed
perpendicular to the sun-shot
arc of the vernal equinox

lay undulating
beneath what's up
in the thermocline.

Prescient still
pond,
and lake potion

not fanfared
nor vulgar
but still.

THE TALKING POND

At first it murmured.

We paused and its sound leapt across
four acres of frozenness to moan at the far end.
We turned to look at it and the sound bellared
deep and distant to us like a great
heart breaking as its ancillary nerves
sporadically reported pain in muted
shrieks and groans with an increasing
irrational rhythm.
       Tawmp . . . Thawmp . . . towmp . .
tomp towmp the sound transforming to
an eerie erratic drum whose message
the three of us perceived differently.
Pilar, my Great Pyrenees was frightened;
growling as she ran this way and that . . .
both at . . and away from the scattering sounds.
My sixteen year old step-son charged strongly
up the dam . . . muscular minded to make
sense of this matter. "What is it?" he frowned
as the ricochet sound was joined by low
chanting along the willows chantry.
"You mean what's the matter?" I teased
as we laughed together.
I'd heard the crashing thaw of Soviet rivers
in my youth. Much older now my own thermidor
lamenting like a landlocked heartlanded

chantry pond in bluesy hoosier sounds.

"The matter and its meaning," I said, "is
of its accreted history and our momentary
thought about it . . . a glimpse of . ."

"Of what?" he protested . . .

Tawmp, Tom, Tawm Tomp aiee the
pond sighed.

"Probably the ghost drums and
chants of the Shawnee who worked this land
before we did," I said.

". . . Thought you said they were
massacred upriver at Battleground?",
he spoke less protestantly.

"Most were," I answered, "in
ghost shirts with the Prophet, but many
were saved by ol' Christmas Dagnet and
the Catholics who helped them escape to
Slavery in Oklahoma. Some stayed and died here."

Tomp sigh tawmp sigh Tawcum sigh . . .

At sixteen this son sometimes thinks like a
man and acts like a boy. Sometimes he thinks like
a boy and acts like a man. It's hard to coordinate
and I always thought St. Paul more than a little
self congratulatory about it.

While tempted to smirk he left the pond respectfully
with a grown up smile. Later he was overheard to say,
"It's a good thing olde Tom is only crazy part of the time."

Pilar patrolled the pond for hours.

553

STABLES

There is a sadness about the stables

of the Standardbred.

Days late and dollars short

on the dreams that wed

racing men who love horses

to racehorses who've loved men.

Confusion in collective mien.

THE YEARLING MULE

He'd had a wild winter. Running wild with his pal,
a same age standardbred stud colt pal .. they'd run through
wooden fences and over wire ones. Imprinted at birth he was occasionally tractable .. when he wished to be .. but usually "too
smart for his own good," we'd say. Last fall he was haltered to
his mama, a large quarter mare; to prevail upon his lead, that is
to say .. drag him around the yard. He'd wait till she paused
then pull her the opposite way. Within an hour he had prevailed
and was leading his mom around the yard.

Tied to an iron post he would not lunge against the
chain. Rather, he would study it like an army engineer .. walking slowly around the thing until he achieved the proper angle
and leverage. Then he'd pop it by bolting straight backwards
.. .turning to trot toward us with a satisfied smile so that we
might remove the remaining chain from his halter. He would
lead when he wanted too, but not otherwise. He had effectively
outsmarted us. Us .. being my sons and me. My main horse
stockman son was my youngest. Together we tended the herds
and flocks of the farm. We suspended attempts at mule training
for the winter.

Chris Zook is the most admired young mule man in our
Amish community. An expert horseman or whisperer is not a
mule man. Horses have a fight or flight response to what they
perceive as danger. And they imaginatively misperceive danger as often as a loving wife or alert deer. Mules have a more
restricted fight response to what they think is necessary to keep
themselves safe. A mule man doesn't soothe as much as clarify.
Chris is a clarifier. Our yearling mule needs clarified . . . we
thought.

SWEET FURLOUGH

flying low over
slumber . . .
not high
between the boundaries
of the bardic columns
but low. .
low as the landing gear
of geese
and quick as their calling
for sweet furloughs
repose that settles
that does not spread like sumac
but settles in
between the waking heat
and summer rain.

*"Utopian dreams come to little because
no civilization can spend what it
has not earned."*
W.B.Yeats

EMBALMED EVENING

Two pair of teal fly close to the thicket

and birdsong brings down the evening.

I've followed the track of both flocks

in from the north, and a soft rain

is falling on my horses

all the way home from here to the Jersey shore.

Distance is only a virtue

when you choose it

from where you are to where you want to be.

Fates destrier a lie from context or contagion

sweetly embalmed in the reliquary

stench of so-called sainthood.

A HEARTS TACK

Gunstocks, saddle, and tack
red and white bird dog, terrier, hound and bay hunter
are the colors that crave
fasthold hope and yearning
for dignity
within my heraldry of seasons

WHOLLY HOLY PICTURE

Goldenrod moons
the corn in mid August
the crop still green, but drying.
Its husks will drum against my horses knees
in September, looking for the hound pups
cubbing near the river.

We'll ride to the furthest season
falling to the winter setts,
spring firing back to Summer.
We ride the roll of the Seasons
as time accelerates its hiddeness
and holds . . . the picture.

A MUGGY DAY IN MANHATTEN

Summer can be a foundry
from my daughters quarters by the flatiron
autonomic thoughts staying home to hold
hot shade and foliage olde
enough to cool in

Near her third world village
a muslim cabby smiled
and shook my hand
"must be your daughter," he waved
at her waving good bye.

If Mark Rudd is the
"perrenial activist"

I have been a . . . <u>**REVOLUTIONARY RECLUSE**</u>

Comrade 1 "He's not a revolutionary . . . he's a recluse."

Comrade 2 "Maybe he's both . ."

Comrade 3 "There is nothing more pathetic than a revolutionary in non revolutionary times . . . except perhaps . . a non revolutionary in revolutionary times."

Comrade 1 "Yeah I know he always said that. He managed to be both. The 'left wing reactionary'being a 'rural idiocy tendency' against two centuries of informed consensus."

Comrade 2 "He stood against that consensus as 50% rotten."

Comrade 1 "Yeah, yeah he wanted it both ways or he rejected both ways."

Comrade 3   "Naw, he pressed to converge the best of both ways displacing the worst of both. The wheat from the chaff converging both paths."

Comrade 1 "He hid out his whole adult life . . burying

brightness into obscurity on farms in Indiana and back valleys
in California with time out for whatever the hell he was up to in
Ireland."

Comrade 2 "He lived in Berlin, and in Spain. He studied
in Germany and Mexico."

Comrade 1 "Yeah . . . yeah his was the worn out trail of the
hoosier hicks grandiosity toward hollywood . . . like Charlie
Manson and Jim Jones."

Comrade 2 "Don't forget James Dean and the other James
Jones."

Comrade 3 ". . . Cole Porter."

Comrade 1 "Uh huh . . While years in the San Antone and San
Joaquin Valleys an hour from San Francisco he never engaged
a single urban issue."

Comrade 2 "Huh! when the Left in the city of St. Francis
shifted their base from longshoreman issues to libidinal
ones . . . he wasn't interested."

Comrade 1   ". . . Since he was too busy with greyhounds, jackrabbits, dairy cattle, and bullfights."

Comrade 3   ". . . he was single parenting two children fighting madness in the courts, hospital and broader culture."

Comrade 1   "and keeping himself out of jail."

Comrade 2   "Barely . . . but what about the Amish and Communist Cuba."

Comrade 3   "He was the first to make the connection."

1939 ➤

1939: The new Deals Farm Security Administration set up
nearly 2000 acres of federally supported collective farms in
Indiana. The Deshee Unit of the Wabash Cooperative Farms was
named after a creek running south of Vincennes between
the White and Wabash Rivers. "Eleanor and her comrades'"
enthusiasm for the project raised rancor amongst right wingers
who referred to the farms as "Little Russia".

Jonas Raber was a Bishops son. Tall and patriarchal he stayed remote from the Engleesh. He had diagonal and high horizontal ropes rigged like a come-along on the rafters of his barn. How his daughter and mine would squeal with joy when he'd whoosh them around on their toy horses.

Jonas kept bird dogs and a flock of sheep. Unusual. Even more unusual he had friends who were "New Order Amish" i.e. schizmatics who wanted their cars and buggies and drive them too. Jonas visited us at "Gloryville Farm" near Freedom several times. He bought a border collie pup from us and I helped him train it. This pup's stock dog ability was much admired by neighbors, cousins, and friends of Jonas. Over the years we sold them many a stock dog. To this day most of the black and white canines in Davies County trace back to our kennel.

Some of Jonas's 'New Order' friends accompanied his visits and loved the surrounding countryside. Years after I'd left for Ireland they started a settlement just north of our place and south of the west fork of the White River. Monroe Hochstetler still serves as their bishop. He and Joseph Stoll had been leaders in multiple attempts to found new collective communities.

Joseph Stoll's book, "Sunshine and Shadow" narrates their Amish attempt to convene a new community in South America. The plan was to settle several families in South Honduras near the Nicaraguan border.

After multiple internecine struggles and day after day of that hard celebrated toil that mark the Amish as Gods greatest sign for the post global planet he reflects on the opinion "that there are only two ways a communal society can succeed – either from shared religious convictions ("as among the Hutterites") or by authoritarian force ("as in communist nations")".

The Old Order Amish, at their best, do fine in both categories.[1] The communist nations fail in the former.[2]

When Joseph visits the New Palestine Collective farm across the Patuca River he discovered both categories doing fine there. Its people were devoted to their shared religious values instructing sacral stewardship of their marriages, families, toil and the fruits of their labor in strict principled discipline. Justice prevailed over personal complaints for freedoms sloth which was shown the door or denied provisions. Acts of the Apostles inspired catholic and communist solutions to unemployment and welfare. "From each according to their ability to each according to their needs"[3] and "He who does not work does not eat." [4]

More signs the south's "Alternatives for the Americas"[5] will survive the northern break down and instruct the broken future.

"Capitalism is the worst enemy of humanity. Capitalism is irrational industrialization and is destroying the earth. We're trying to think about ways of living well, not living better. Living better is always at someone else's expense. Living better is at the expense of destroying the earth. Things that capitalism destroys are things that cannot be saved with just money. We have to resolve problems of life and humanity. That's the problem that planet earth faces today. And this means ending capitalism."

Evo Morales, President of Bolivia

December 17, 2009

1. Mary and Joseph Josephson "Man Alone"

2. Eric Hobsbawm "Age of Extremes"

3. The Communist Manifesto

4. The Holy Bible

5. e.g. ALBA (The Bolivarian Alternative for the Americas)

> *"To realize the relative validity of ones convictions*
> *and yet stand for them unflinchingly is what distinguishes*
> *a civilized man from a barbarian"*
> Joseph Schcumpeter

HOPE FOR AUDACITY

My parents were New Dealers. My extended blue-collar family spoke reverently of F.D.R. and Eleanor. Dad thought Truman was a "weak sister" until he fired McArthur. Me and all my peers at school liked Ike while Dad wore the only Adlai Stevenson button I ever saw. The Irish Catholic Kennedys would have been appealing to him if they'd been less eager to bludgeon the Teamsters Union and Socialist Cuba. Johnson seemed so much better than Goldwater except he led the bloodiest unjust war of the century. That he "passed" Medicare-Medicaid and the Civil Rights legislation we understood as merely concessions to leftward pressures from the street, farm and factory. I never voted for democrat-republican presidential candidates.

Like the majority of Americans I rarely voted at all . . abstaining to not endorse the system. I only voted twice. Once for my cousin Robert for congress. Once for my friend Ralph Levitt on the Socialist-Workers ticket for Indiana Governor. The latter caused some trouble as the "secret" ballot was published in the newspaper according to township.

The protest socialist vote seemed increasingly silly as U.S. socialists were fragmenting from Parade Marshals into several sexual support and police spy grouplets. The old Gene Debs condemnation of the two party system as that of tweedledee and tweedledumb still made sense to me but when his traditional appeal to my forebears in western Indiana coalfields began to flag,

Debs would appeal to socialist thinking but democrat voting coal miners that their pragmatic 'lesser of two evils' criteria was wrong. "It is better to vote for what you want and not get it than to settle for what you don't want and get it," he'd say.

Yes . . . I agree there should be unity between theory and practice, prayer and behavior, but . . . then . . here comes Obama and his "Audacity of Hope."

There had been an especially capital W weak decade of amnesiac political decline. A strong rebound from backwardness might occur even beneath the decay of the bourgeois establishment. Fanatical certainties were further emasculating any nuanced capacity for moral judgment. Reverend Wright and Barak Hussein Obama versus The Clintons!?! I got on board for Barak inspired by the young multi racial staffers at Obama Headquarters.

I started receiving social security. John McFall and I ambled over to its second and Cherry offices from Obama Headquarters after a quick drink at the Saratoga. Then we walked back to John Hochalters Esquire barbershop. McFall told Hochalter, "We've just revisited Second and Cherry[1] but now we're getting money instead of spending it."

Social Security was achieved by the New Deal under CPUSA[2] influence. In the seventies I'd turned my "Militant"[3] subscription and its sexual politics into the post office for violating Indiana's pornography laws. I now subscribed to the "Peoples World"[4] as I was feeling more grateful than revolutionary. It's sycophancy for Democrats was always excessive but I was backing Obama now . . . and receiving Social Security.

I canvassed my nearby village door to door and was

greeted with great hospitality and encouragement. I left literature i.e. Obama Propaganda at the Fish and Game Club that had
solidly backed electing my cousin and at the convenience store
gas station. At the latter there were problems.

The proprietors gave me permission to stack my literature beside the "complimentary", that is, free real estate, auto,
other advertising sheets and magazines. I did so. Returning the
next day I discovered all my Obama literature gone. Suspicious
but charitable I hoped its quick disappearance was due to my
candidates growing popularity. I left more literature and came
back two days later. Same thing. All the Obama propaganda
gone. The other free literature did not seem significantly
disturbed. I knew the local lady clerks. They all nervously
claimed ignorance. This time I left the last of my literature and
drove to Terre Haute that evening for more. Returning late that
night I noticed the gas-mart . . . deserted but still open.

Inside there was only one night clerk and someone moving equipment around in the back. When the clerk noticed me
she looked worried toward the back room. I went straight to the
shelves where I'd left the literature. No literature. The same
bleeding phenomena in only hours.

Respectfully, but with enhanced volume I asked . . "Who
is taking the literature away?!" The clerk was pretty, younger
than my daughter and I knew to be a witness . . a Jehovah's Witness. She wouldn't register to vote and she wouldn't lie. She
just looked away . . embarrassed, I think. I turned back to the
free literature looking for a clue . . . I guess . . when up from
behind me roared a loud simian sounding voice. "We doan
wanna have anything to do with that nigger!!" I turned to con-
front a great white ape taller and broader than me with his sweat-

shirt sleeves cut off to publicize his armpits . . . axilla askew
whose whiskered vulgarity seemed palpably voluble with the rest
of his racist wrong-headedness.

I quickly surmised he was too big to whup. But I could
not and would not retreat from this encounter. Ambush surprise
with no strategy in mind . . we just stood there staring at each
other . . when I spied a pencil and note pad on the cash register
counter. Grabbing them up toward him I demanded, "I'll need
your name."

He defiantly spit it back.

I wrote it down . . then,

"And your address."

He looked at the clerk . . who was smiling.

"Fifty nine something Jefferson," he answered.

I wrote that down. Studied the writing for a long second,
looked up . . my finger poised like a school marmish stiletto I
aimed my words straight between his eyes.

. . "When "that nigger" is elected we're gonna come visit you!

The clerk burst into laughter.

The hulk looked ridiculous.

I still savor that moment, and the majority of Montezuma voted
for Obama.

1.Second and Cherry: Notorious Terre Haute brothel district
until the free market closed it.

2.CPUSA: Communist Party United States of America

3.Militant: Venerable newspaper of Socialist Workers Party (Trotskyist 4th
International)

4.Peoples World: CPUSA newspaper – previous Daily Worker

NEGRITUDE

The cold woods look black

at the edge of despair

black as the coffee

that used to console me

black and beautiful as negritude

survives the snows of disaster

HARD LIGHT

Indiana; you can enjoy spring all summer here
if you get up early enough for it.
After dawn you begin to feel heat behind
the cool of morning, like the hot dry muzzle
of a hound with fever.

Indiana at points is greener than Ireland
humid cool, damp, cold, or scalding
its haze of humidity precedes the sun
in this world; conserving the ancient
mist and cloud of those awful regions

Into hard light.
Weeping brawn
chords resound a hardened site;
"hard thread that will
uphold the dawn"
Pablo Neruda, *Canto to the Red Army*

"All those systems or tendencies which appear to be inherited in the constitution of mind due to experience of the past [are those] in which responding to social inheritance from our predecessors wakens into activity the potential of our nature. In such collective experience, that larger whole from which what we know as the self has been differentiated and remains with us as the sense, latent or active, of a greater power." M. Bodkin "Archetypal Patterns in Poetry"

(A Jungian Study of Collective Consciousness)

Synchronicity

Re: J.B.s Forthcomings or "A Flat Tick Is Still A Tick"

Finally the old sectarian genius is poking his nose into print. His socialist perversions of bourgeois gains reveal the central contradiction of his life's work.

Supra class phenomena and the parasitic existence of surplus value skimmers is not new . . so what's he so on about. That the "non-productive, bell curved caste of house rich, cash poor, ironic," bourgeois wannabes have contempt for traditional values? Those values "held by broad sections of the working class" and "promoted by the upper classes as essential main stays of social order". Is he suggesting in geriatric reflection the truth that no revolutionary force without a modicum of those values has prevailed for long?

Jack Barnes has maintained a life's work in acrobatic avoidance of turning his marxist analysis upon himself and his own relations. Can he not see the bell curved "Bolshevik" existence he's lived curating communism in sectarian ghettos as insular as any cognitive elite. Privilege rich and responsibility poor non-productively skimming off what little surplus value could be sold or sucked parasitically from supra class and Proletarian hosts with lumpen contempt for moral and traditional working class values.

Over the years it has been tempting to think of J.B. as a probable police spy. The only recruit of Peter Buch in three decades he brilliantly behaved as an inside liquidator. If he turns out to be a stooge we'd all be in the historic good company of Lenin. Unlikely. His projected and covetous contempt for the cynical parasite is too revealing. He still hunts for hosts of the marginally undefined.

A flat tick is no less parasitic than a fat one.

Thomas Morgan to Olde Comrades

Shadowgait Farm

March 15, 2010

In response to: Thomas Morgan accusing the national secretary
J. Barnes, of "dishonesty, incompetence, and sexual promiscuity
with national office members."

"Morgan has always been a disturbing factor and I very
much doubt whether the removal of Barnes would in the least
change his attitude. Morgan is able, has a certain kind of honesty, possesses to a superlative degree the cunning of a fox, revels
in the spotlight on occasion, and is the deadly enemy of any
man that does not accept his views unequivocally. Of course, he
will continue his attacks on Barnes; Morgan never forgets, nor
forgives, and he is unrelenting in his hatreds . . ."

Theodore Debs to Adolph Germer
March 15, 1911
Terre Haute, Indiana
page 410 Letters of Eugene V. Debs
Volume 1, 1874 – 1912

T'was ever thus. Personal identity is not private property.

RAIN NOT FALLEN

I hit the pavement before first light and liked watching
the sun come up. It was March but getting warm in the morning.
I stopped at a gas station and had cold deviled eggs and hot coffee for breakfast.

It was going to be a good day.

That old gentle on my mind sound comes from the radio,
becoming more what and whom I think about. My memory an
engine in overdrive . . . a song, a leaf . . . a look deploy panoplies
of vision . . .
As I scent the rain that has not fallen.

TERRE HAUTESPRIT (High sprited high groundedness)

City of our Valleys heart . . Desiderative[1] . .

Desires the Parthian Shot[2]

Thornhill[3] could play it hot, even with Frenchorns but
not. . . memorably. Yet man, when the Claude T. sound was 'a
breeze' off the Wabash or 'Snowfall', Ellington, Thelonius, Bull
Halsey and Gil Evans prophesied Miles achieving 'The Birth of
the Cool', a note resolving discord before the chord was played,
a reverie so riverine our native river riffs through time and place
and scene . . Notre Dame to Cayuga where Nicole's brother
found her body in the logjams, downriver to Montezuma falls
and Vermillion islands while piranhas hunt hot water ditches by
power stations above the bridges and viaducts of 'The Haute',
my nephews fish ranching and spooks of Valentine cattleheads
afloat over channel cats as big as sharks in the shallows north of
Vigo's treatment plant, the Federal Prison executions draw crows
and flies from fair banks of fishing camps on stilts near Hutsonville and Graysville ghost lovers . . her rear revolving like a sail
before the mast of democratic eyes. Prayers repair and prepare
us for the flavor of departures.

    Our heart cures nothing. Love dissuades closing a
single tawdry page. To yearn and grieve through river bottom
darknesses occlude our heart where light is shorn from life, end-

shear insures the taste of gloom. DeVegas 'Morning of St. John' suggests my loves were gone. Which the greater fear? Loves frightened off again or was never really here. Hung up as Ted (dark bricked) Hughes[4] by the brewery, a murder of crows, more than a thousand cold in the catalpas diseased ideas of an all souls night viral while I am an old horse with west nile shaking his head at the world way out there in the weather, my foals in far pastures I looked for a sign in the rivers question mark. It was New Years day. Auguring the flight of a lone grey gull wheeling by ice flows on the Wabash, I parked off the bridge, my nerves meandering through the morning haze to know the ways of natures expectation that gulls should be some other place, some dumb sub-tropical splendor or northern seas not here solitarily. Cold suspect! Are you lost or vaguely free? The gull on the Wabash did not respond to me. Distance is not his problem but the depth of times fortune similarly strange ancient responsibility. Passed into climes beyond expectation and the ability to respond like the gull on the river . . to be otherwise . . like the little city of the big General Strike . . bravely otherwise. Retreat to home centered sources found love in 'the environs of Lee Avenue' . . dead ended by Lost Creek between Carosis and the Stop 5. Northend avenues clasp Lafayette like a weapon as our pickets back then made a fist of the moon. Yet here she was to suffer not Lee Avenue or the rifle shot shattering her cars window, suns crossing her being with tidings so unfamiliar, her tone a child's first expectant Christmas in a mine shaft so dark, hope appears innocently . . its sound evoking unknown timbres my soul aspires to be the wise man bearing her gifts. She changed the seasons all around. Even April had been spitting snow . . you know, the kind seen in refugee footage; a pasts cold flack in the face of hopes future. From Lee Avenue she brought mayflies out from under where the sun and foliage come together. And when inside across the woolen carpet of ancestral flocks the border collie rebounds to her cue she claps hands and cheers a chardonnay laughter. It is akin to the clap of an angels wing brightening all cloud cover. Tenderly the grid of our being came to Lee Avenue where cocks still crow in the city limits of morning. She remains a summer night not far from May that keeps the howling, howling light at bay.

Collective sight then commands an older light to discern the spirit of our city. An older light that streams through St. Benedicts and the fallen sites of olde communal taverns like Brocksmiths up Hulman Street from the switchyards, that shadowed light by wooden stoops at the Bent Elbow. A red pony light on 17th Street, flaxen maned remote from fires at the coke plant and Flaming Pit. A Gene Debs porch light where letters from Lenin were read, where Cannon covered his funeral for the Labor Defender; a dimly celebrative light dining at Louise's and the soft shoe Kelly and Carsey did.

The faltering light around fir trees decorated with annual financial abandon; wintersett never quite going out in cold hope for better light that will not come til Spring except . . otherwise . . in the laughter and kindness of reckless and careful smiles that bravely banter in the old cold light.

Terre Hautesprit.

1. Desiderative:from *Desiderata* world famous poem of Terre Haute's gentleman poet Max Ehrman. (circa 1920) *Desiderata*, was stolen and published worldwide by enterprising hippies in the 1960's claiming it was obscure medieval wisdom.
2. Parthian Shot: tactical gesture of cavalry in strategic retreat.
3. Claude Thornhill: Terre Haute band leader who began the cool sound. Duke Ellington: recognized it. Thelonius Monk: respected it. Admiral Halsey: admired it and Gil Evans: arranged it for Miles Davis to play 'The Birth of the Cool'.
4. Ted Hughes: hung up Nobel Laureate welsh poet. Author of 'The Crow'.
('Terre Hautesprit' did not win, place, or show, in the 2011 Max Ehrman poetry contest)

Les Vestiges de Terre Haute

Les Vestiges de Terre Haute, come in the hour that's blue
L'heure bleu for Hoosier Robochaya Marselyeza
Came the cove of my own presence
Ashore, above the mists of democratic sewage

High grounded spirits collective their mass
Martial gray within the haze
The Wabash holds the depths of nineteen thirty-four
Its banks remember striking avenues

Refracting moons in minds of drinking, praying men
Catch the glow of saintly worn down curbs
The county's railroad hard to fate's near western border
They come inside the steel, apocryphal tradition

«РАЗДАЙСЯ, КЛИЧ МЕСТИ НАРОДНОЙ!»

(Ring out the call of the peoples' vengeance!)
Forward old paraclete for dignity's dimension
This place needs a poet, Max
Who works for a living.

Beer glassed, stained glass Gill-frescoed remembrance
The sons of St. Joseph have shone
On the banks near the high ground
Against stamping mill bayonets and soldiering strike breakers

They fell near the Wabash, the Seine, and the Neva
Holy labor in the river's depth
Commute the sentence of great gluttonously starved grandchildren
Hour of freedom within the hour that's blue
Immunity to Death

"*Love one another*, ought to be balanced by a colder

saying . . '*Turn away from each other*' (a guide not a rule) – to that

Great Presence of which humanity is only a squirming particle.

'Love your neighbor as yourself', that is, not excessively if you are

an adult but 'love God with your heart, mind, and soul'. Turn out-

ward from each other so far as need and kindness permit to the vast

life and inexhaustible beauty beyond humanity. This is not a slight

matter, but an essential condition of . . . sanity."

Robinson Jeffers The Double Axe

CONDITIONAL LOVE

*"The reality of the thesis
is almost a condition of
its unconditionality."*
J. H. Newman

*"O pass not Lord
an absolute decree
or bind thy sentence
unconditionally."*
John Dryden

*"The form of time in which we always find condition
beyond condition, cause beyond cause, and never
reach the unconditional; the causa sui."*
Immanuel Kant

Like everybody else in this new century I have a lot of business with females. In my business it is female equines as well as female humans. I keep a band of Standardbred mares with my stallion at public stud. His stud fee is $1,000 for approved outside mares payable upon issue of a live foal who stands and sucks. Most Standardbred people are men, the few times they've not been . . . it's been a disaster.

I am not unacquainted with women. My mother and grandmother were the closest human beings to my growing up. I have many dear aunts, cousins, and friends. I have raised a lovely daughter as well as four sons. I've had three wives; a good one, a good one gone bad, and a barracuda.

I see mostly women in my practice. In fact, I had come to think of myself as an expert on female mood disorders.During the hubris of that thought I succumbed to the challenge of two nearly fatal females. The first was a spectacularly built large and beautiful black mare aptly named Shark in the Water. Her sire was the celebrated Cam's Card Shark and when she only brought $75,000 at the Harrisburg yearling sale everyone knew she was trouble.

A fellow shrink of mine bought her and sent her to a trainer in New York State who announced her untrainable. Her intermittent explosiveness cost the owner thousands of dollars in breakage and she'd attacked the trainer and all his staff. Quarantined to her stall, this sullen creature aroused pity in the trainer's wife who tried approaching her one day. The lady horse grabbed the lady trainer's arm in her mouth, breaking it at the elbow, dragging her into the stall and according to the trainer, "She tried to kill my wife! Get this bitch out of here by the weekend or I'll shoot her. I don't care if she's worth $175,000." I bought her for the board bill of $3,000. At the time, I thought I'd made the best bred bargain horse deal in recent harness racing history. The issue of Cam's Card Shark were racing for millions of dollars and never sold for less than $100,000.

As soon as she arrived in Indiana, my Amish pal, Jake Hosteter, and I stealthily approached her. Jake was a lot less stealthy than me. In every speed barn in the state Jake was known as the hoosier horse whisperer. I'd learned to breathe like a horse from him. His reputation had spread from the first Hoosier Classic sale in Indianapolis. The State Fairgrounds had filled up with horse trailers full of green broke yearlings that no one could lead to the stalls or arena. Jake was called on. He matched breath forms with each big colt and filly for a while then he'd lead them easy as you please, to where they'd belong. This caused such a sensation that the press came and wanted to report it. Jake obliged them (to the consternation of other horsemen) by leading the green broke yearlings out of the barn and back into their trailers. Then he'd laugh and put them back in their stalls again. The Indianapolis Star said, "Not Since Houdini" had the Hoosier state seen such a performance. Much hoopla, but Jake just kept chuckling as he worked, and declined his photo taken.

This day as he approached Shark in the Water, her handlers who'd just unloaded her all looked worried. Slightly to her left side, at about a seventy degree angle, Jake was slowly, gently extending his hand towards her shoulder when precisely across that same angle, she struck him with her left front leg right in the gut! Knocked across the barn aisle, he was trying to catch his breath and examine his own rib cage when we got to him. Catching his breath, he announced, "No breaks," as we helped him to stand. They put Shark in a stall and now we all approached her. Peering through the bars of the dark stall, it was hard to believe our eyes.

On the one hand she was the biggest and most beautiful pacing mare I'd ever seen. Her general confirmation was huge and muscular like a stallion but with a delicately refined, very feminine head, neck and legs. She was like the olde Morgan idea of equine countenance . . . to look like a Percheron and move like an Arab. She stood sixteen hands with perfect pasterns, massive quarters, strong bone and correctly sloping shoulders ending upward at her withers ever so slightly below the angle from her croup forming what Ullysees S. Grant called the porch of power in the harness horse. Long barreled with an ideal width of chest and straight line placement of both front legs, with strong knees, her hind legs were also classically conformed, that is, not set too forward or too far back.

Yet she crouched, no . . . rather coiled, all that classy confirmation into a threatening viperous form in one dark corner of the stall, making gutteral sounds like the chuff of a mad tiger. And then she sprang at the stall door, biting the steel bars, striking its wooden panels with her front hooves and ass kicking the side wall with her back ones; all the while screaming this hysterical equine scream. Jake and I looked at each other, presuming precisely the thought of the other. We both thought and almost said together, "Hormones!"

In New York they'd been treating her with Regimate to avoid pre (and post) menstrual syndrome. What they'd achieve was a kind of perpetual menstrual syndrome. When I got her home she was turned out alone in a small six acre grassy paddock. A 'Beware of Horse' sign was attached to its front gate. We worried about the children and warned them to stay away. I studied her every day. No more Regimate. She naturally came in season and . . . by god, I'd guessed it! . . . . She got better when in season.

I'd seen something similar when I was a kid. My pony

mare loved my father. As we grew older she only tolerated me and my friends. In season she became particularly cooperative and affectionate; nuzzling up to us . . . especially to my father. Out of season she was more diffident and sullen refusing our attention. In season she was receptive, even down right inviting to Dad the alpha male and a little encouraging to us lesser studs. There was no stallion around. She related to us as equines.

In spite of my warnings our youngest boy made friends with Shark in the Water. When she was in season he'd talk with her through the gate, and feed her apple treats. I decided to keep her in season. Regularly medicating her with an anabolic estrogen concoction our vet prepared, she stayed in season and became halfway biddable, although a permanent distraction to my stallion two fences away. Before that she would charge you like a bull if you entered her paddock.

Over the summer we halter broke her to lead, groom and stand to be harnessed. She was no pet but she was ready for training. I syndicated her ownership and we were all counting on winning the Genesis Series and stakes races the next summer. She was clearly the best bred, most impressive looking race horse in the region.

We chose a trainer carefully. Howard Mathis, a retired basketball coach and school teacher from Terre Haute Wiley, he lived in Montezuma along the Wabash with one small pasture. He'd buy colts every three years at the Lexington or Springfield sales . . . "Keep 'em over the summer, send 'em to the race trainer over cold months, race 'em as two year olds, sell 'em at three." He'd won the Genesis series twice. He was a wise and solid Standardbred man. He'd turned the legendary Tim Wilson on to harness racing in his typing class, discussing articles in Hoofbeats magazine. Tim went on to become the highest ranked driver and trainer in Chicago.

Howard had read all 1,054 pages of James C. Harrison's Care and Training of the Trotter and Pacer several times. I'd read sections of it. He'd speak of the section writers Fred Erwin,

Stanley Dancer, Bob Farrington, and T. Wayne Smart like he knew them. I bogged down in Harrison's "gametic range" analogies with "suits" and "decks" of playing cards. The main thing I got, which was not Jim Harrison's primary intention was a warning against inbreeding. To cut down chance in the shuffle, top performance racing families were getting too closely related. This shark mare was unrelated to my stallion and every blood line on the farm. As she was aristocratically far above them on the food chain of anything I could afford.

Howard recommended one of his favorite trainers who had his own farm track. Shark would have to be "put on the leader" or "trucked," that is, hitched to the back of a pick-up once gaited and forced to faster speed. "Pulled along to the pace," horsemen would say with sinister smiles. That would not be allowed at any of the public tracks. The first time Shark was "put on the leader" she resisted for a full half mile. Then she laid into the breast strap with such power and speed "she practically pushed my truck over the curb," the trainer bragged.

Later that winter we watched him train her at the state fairgrounds mile track. She was pacing under 1:52 and getting stronger. While congratulating ourselves on owning and training a superhorse, we still walked wide arcs around her front and back end. She was still surly but not assaultive. It seemed we'd turned all that lethal destructiveness into speed. We stabled her back at the trainer's farm for the last leg of Spring training before summer's racing.

And Spring came early that year. Whether it was global warming or some weird storms on the March 3rd high beating up the equinox a pussy willowed moon warmed everything up and laid a precocious long light over our days.

That night the trainer and I shared thoughts that maybe we'd exaggerated Shark's dangerousness . . . maybe all this time she'd just been bluffing.

The next morning he phoned only to say, "Well, I'm bluffed! Come git your mare!" Due to the radically changing light we guessed Shark's behavioral remission had terminally failed. She had grabbed him with her teeth by the nape of his neck, slammed him into the corner of her stall and went for him with all four hooves. He was severely bruised on his cheek, shoulder and groin. He was alive and meant to stay that way. She had to go.

She was then tranked to the hilt and shipped to the Delaware sale. We were honest about her condition. Everyone admired her looks. Nobody bid on her much. She sold for killer prices to an Australian outfit who said they still planned to race her. Aussies think they can train anything . . . but I suspect when light changes over the Outback she will be feeding the dingos.

I keep fifteen head of horses. That's counting colts through Spring, Summer and early Fall. I sell the weanlings before frost. A mare's gestation is eleven months. Older mares' will go a year or more. Five months of the year my mares are nursing their babies or too heavily in foal to be ridden. They can be driven after foaling. I used to do that with the foals running prettily along side the wagon or jog cart. Now I worry too much about traffic.

All these horses and none for me to ride or drive through most of the year. My stallion may technically be ridden any day of the year, but he's a handful; impossible during the breeding season and not exactly a pleasure ride year round. Years past I rode a Morgan stallion in New Brittons Hunt Field and all around open mares. But . . . that's a Morgan . . . with a racehorse you're always one mistake away from being off to the races.

I considered getting a gelding. After all my stallion had raced along side geldings and mares for ten years. But that was before he'd become a breed stallion. At stud he was territorial, possessive and patriarchally preoccupied with the breeding business. Horror stories abound about studs tearing down fences to get to geldings and mutilate or kill them for even looking at mares. Stallions are definitely anti-clerical.

Cowboys claim a mare's main purpose is to produce more usable geldings. I've never agreed with that. I am partial to mares. Moody as they are I love them. Working with them is a conversation where most of the time you just listen. Theirs is an on-going narrative about what's wrong with their life. You can't tell them anything directly the way you do a stallion. And you certainly can't allow them their own way anymore than you would a stallion. You just have to lovingly, albeit forcefully encourage them in the way you've thought out to be the best. Geldings are less interesting. Yes, I guess . . . a bit like clergy.

I needed a mare to use year round. Like a modern woman more focused on work than being female. I needed a mare that would not foal. I decided I needed a mule.

Mules and mule lore! The most intriguing of all animal husbandry. With no pride of ancestry or hope of progeny mules are the most existential of creatures. Horse and pony lore is shared with children, especially pubescent female children. These children and geldings seem to share a mutual appreciation of each other. But mules have historically been a thinking man's stock of knowledge.

If a mule gets caught in barbed wire, old timers would say, "They won't thrash around and cut themselves to pieces , , , they'll think it through, figure it out, and find a way to calmly extricate themselves." At the blacksmiths off 17th Street in Terre Haute I had watched the old men move their fists and arms simulating a mules hoof and leg being extricated from a tangle of wire.

Mule talk would always include . . . "They're not gluttonous like a horse and less likely to founder. And they won't work themselves to death like a loyal horse for an idiot." Mules were always described as smart enough to share one's command in teamwork. Yet there were contradictory 'Mule skinner' remarks, too. "You can't punish a mule a little for a little thing.

You have to damn near kill them for big things." "Horses have fight or flight instincts; mules only have the fighting one."

The way I've heard mules described made their collective personality sound like my uncle's. My favorite, Uncle Tom, earned an extra dollar a day for driving 'Killer Mules' in Sullivan County coal mines. "Mules were financially more valuable than miners to mine operators," my uncle would explain. "Once they'd killed a man, they still kept them, and you could earn a little extra for working them. First thing in the morning, I'd take my Barlow knife and cut a small thin splinter out of the overhead beams. I'd stick it between the killer mule's teeth so they'd worry about it. It wouldn't hurt them, just distract them. Twelve hours a day or more, they'd concentrate on that splinter instead of killing me." Early on I'd figured to be a mule man was a slightly higher rank than even that of the honored horseman.

In 1948, Marilyn Monroe's first movie came out. It was called Scudda Hoo! Scudda Hay! I can't remember her in it but I can sure remember the mules. My mother and my Aunt Bernice took me and my cousins to see it. They wanted to see it because they thought it was going to be French. Walter Brennan, June Haver, and Natalie Wood are also in it, but the true stars are Moonbeam and Crowder, a matched red team of draft mules. Clearly they were from the finest Belgian mothers and Mammoth jack fathers. When Walter Brennan says, "A man 'at's got a team of mules knows he's in business," I knew it was true.

Of course it made no sense in my modest suburban neighborhood. But something in my ancestral memory or prescient pastoral future clicked solid. I have loved mules ever since. If my mother would have allowed pin-ups, which she didn't, for me it would not have been girls or baseball players, but them mules.

Seventeen years later, my parents took me to see the Hamiltonian. Those days it was still held in DuQuoin, Illinois. Considered the greatest event in world harness racing and named after the foundation sire of Standardbreds immortalized by

Currier & Ives in their famed lithograph of the great progenitor and his owner William Rhysdek. And yet . . . that great race was not as exciting as the mule exposition and show afterwards.

Teams and ten to twelve span of yearling and two year old mules (Belgian X Mammoth just like Moonbeam and Crowder) were shown by the hundreds. Lithe as deer and powerful as engines their legs moved them around the arena like pistons. A mule's gait is from the knees down giving them a smoother, straighter more direct line of action. And the mule men handled those multiple spans like liberty horses in a circus. You could tell they loved their mules. Liberty and love . . . a dangerous combination. Unconditional love of any kind always trumps wisdom.[1] [See The Grizzly Man] Notes.

The men of the 51st Indiana who led The Lightening Mule Brigade [2] in 1863, may have loved mules and the union cause but not without discerning requisite conditions. Indiana State Archives record Field Orders No. 94 issued by chief of staff General Garfield that Colonel Abel Streight of Indianapolis was to command an independent provisional raid into Northern Alabama raising insurrectionary forces within the many union sympathizers in the Sand Mountain region. They were to destroy the railroad between Chattanooga and Atlanta, somewhere in the vicinity of Rome, Georgia. The 73rd Indiana, 80th Illinois, and 3rd Ohio would join Streight's 51st becoming 1,700 dragoons requiring 2,000 mules. There was no return or escape plan. They intended to break the back of the confederacy so that Grants army, still west of the Mississippi, could drive into its heart.

Easier keepers, more sure footed, and generally tougher, mules were chosen over horses to hold up better for the three week, two hundred mile raid across the mountainous terrain of Northern Alabama. There was also a shortage of horses.

Only 900 of the required 1700 mules were issued. "It was the plan of the high command that the rest of the brigade find mounts as they passed through the areas of the expedition, supposing that the friendly hill people would provide animals in profusion." It was also suspected that the high commands ambivalence dicated that sound animals not be used in case they should fall into confederate hands. The regimental historian, Theodore Scribner, complained, "The issue were 900 broken down mules which had previously been condemned and pronounced unfit for service." [3]

The old unfit mules were put on Navy boats at Cairo, Illinois and the brigade shipped south. They disembarked at Palmyra, Tennessee to procure more and better mules. "The majority of the brigade taking the land route to Fort Henry on the Cumberland River was to concentrate on mules: confiscating, breaking, training, catching, riding, and feeding the braying, bucking, uncooperative beasts." [4] Colonel Streight himself reported, "I discovered . . . these mules were nothing but poor, wild, and unbroken colts, many of them but two years old, and that a large number of them have distemper, some forty or fifty too near dead to travel; ten or twelve died before we started and such of them as could be rode were so wild and unmanageable that it took us all that day and part of the next to catch and break them before we could move out . . ." [5]

Theodore Scribnner futher remembered, "These animals, though lean and scraggy, when mounted went off on what the men called a sheep gallop, jumping stiff legged with head down and heels up sending their riders flying into the air as if shot from a bow." Sergeant Michael O'Connor of Company H, "drew a mule that bucked the very buttons off my coat, threw me forty feet above its head and then devil that he is, shot at me with his heels while I was in the air." [6]

Worse than a circus was this thousand head of obstreperous unbroke equines sheep galloping across enemy occupied territory. They were also very noisy; plaintively braying away any possible element of surprise. A horse is a beast you can train and with whom you might have a relationship. A mule is a beast with whom you can have a relationship and you might be able to train.

591

During its three week life of "noisy desperation"[7] this raid of never more than 1,000 mounted dragoons . . . nonetheless significantly encouraged the pro union families of Northern Alabama, scaring off the confederate home guards that terrorized them. Getting as far as Georgia, they burned the iron works outside Rome and then succumbed to the lies of Nathan Bedford Forrest. That old psychopathic slave trader was almost as big a strategic liar as Reagan with Star Wars blarney.

Abel Streight, the farm kid from New York who'd become an Indiana abolitionist and publisher (he owned the Railroad Press) never got to blow up the Southern railroad, but he did divert old Snake Forrest's attention from the gathering strength of Grant's army. While Forrest was busy bullshitting Streight about the size of his forces and fretting about pro-union Alabaman's being traitors, Grant was already coming down to cross the river and take Vicksburg from the East and South.

Historians I think have been too quick to blame the defeat of the Lightening Mule Brigade on the mules. Instead of the conditions that men provided them or rather the conditions that men failed to provide.

Sometimes we only understand our own condition when spoken to from the condition of another. In another part of the war, the historian of the 7th Kansas recounted this episode of human and equine conditions. "A shell landed in the earth directly under a mounted dragoon. Where it exploded, it blew him up in the air some distance and tore off his leg at the ankle. The hind leg of his beast was torn off also. The poor creature in its agony hobbled up to the man and called out to him for relief."[8]

Responsibility in war and love is the ability to respond in principle to the other's changing condition. Conditions always change, principles do not. Principles reside in the mind. Changing conditions primarily affect the nervous system.

And the autonomic nervous system can function autonomously. That is to say, all mammals can spook. When an equine spooks there is a particular terror in it. A horse in full spook is like an individual woman . . . hysterical, frightening, dangerous, restrainable and ultimately . . . tractable.

A spooked mule however is a qualitatively different phenomenon. There is an unearthly collective compression in it. The very earth, heaven, and hell swirl around in it. A hybrid heterosistic terror that threatens to haul off the landscape in its wake. It is more than the sum total of a previously calm beast. It seems nature's rage against the denial of ancestry and progeny.

Last summer I bought a mule after admiring her from afar. She was elegant! Snow white with dark eyes and pigment. She was the thirteen year old issue of a Thouroughbred mare and Mammoth jack from a ranch in Montana with a slight brand on her lovely left hip. Her owner had paid over $3,000 for her and said she was not for sale. He hunted elk with her in Colorado, bear in Canada, and coon in Indiana. Next to his large mule barn was kenneled several red tick tree hounds, mountain curs, and a few hunt terriers. He fired high-powered rifles off her back and claimed she did not spook. Most coon hunters want a little mule, short enough to ride under foliage and brush. I wanted one tall enough to see over the Savannahs crop ground when running coyotes. This mare mule, her name was Chris, stood over sixteen hands and would stretch out like a show horse in block and bridle. She seemed perfect. I rode her and my sons did. Fast and tractable. I couldn't think of getting any other mule, yet she wasn't for sale. "Not that I could afford her if she was . . ."

The truth is, I'm a terrible horse trader. I prefer to believe people and expect them to believe me. I don't like dancing around. I usually violate conventional horse trader's etiquette . . . which begins A.) seller: says all positive things about horses to be sold B.) buyer: negatively critiques horses presented C.) compromise is reached with a sale. When it's my horses, it goes something like this A.) seller: I say all the positive things about my equine children I've bred and reared, their ancestry, present virtues and future promise B.) buyer: critiques presentation and nitpicks about potential flaws C.) seller: I ask them to leave the farm. I do better at auctions. When the price gets too high I quit bidding. When it is too low for mine I take them home. No dancing. Months later, the owner of Chris came to my place. He had a terrier bitch he wanted bred to my old stud dog. I told him old Nick Kelly was probably over the hill but we'd try. We shared cigars, and talked about Fox Warren bred Jack Russells. He knew of one in Montana whose owner called it the one dog bear pack. He admired my terriers. And then we talked of mules. He said, "I was telling my wife we should sell you Chris since you like her so much . . . ." His silence at the end of his sentence was a clear invitation for me to make him an offer. I didn't.

"Can't afford her," I said.

"Too bad . . . ," he answered.

We walked back to the kennel and talked terriers. On two separate occasions I'd see him and he'd say, "You just oughtta buy that white mule from me." I'd shake my head and mosey on. But . . . he'd got me thinking about it. Finally he phoned and said, "I'll take $1,700 for Chris, the white mule."
Deciding to stay cool and pretend to be a cautious livestock trader . . . I found myself blurting out . . . "SOLD!"

I brought her home that weekend. My sons and I were jubilant. My wife, much less so. My youngest son, Tanner, wanted to ride her just then. I thought better of it. "Let's get her used to the place," I cautioned. We didn't saddle her for a week. During that time she was kept in the six acre enclosure with a bred companion mare. Two fences and ten yards away, our stallion showed her only mild interest. She showed more than a mild interest in him. My wife was unimpressed. "I don't like the look in her eyes," she'd say.

Chris had an almond shaped, powerful eye. She would lock onto your gaze and stay in it as long as you wished. That was creepy to my wife. To me, it was like the gaze of my first eighth grade girlfriend, that is to say, one of rare privilege and fondness.

My first thought every morning was to get downstairs and look at my mule. From the porch I'd call her name and she would come to the fence. We'd greet each other with that long gaze and I'd be ready for the day. I'd breakfast then go out to freshen her water trough and feed her apple treats. Throughout the day I'd take breaks and peck on my north window to get her attention and enjoy that gaze. God forgive me, I think I was a little bit in love with that mule. Now I know that "in love" expression is pretty much a woman's point of view. Most men know that love, like work, is a verb, it is something you do, the quality of which cannot depend on some subjective state of mind. (The common excuse of most homewreckers is that while they love their spouse they are no longer 'in love' with them.)

I prefer to view this chemically. Phenolthylamine is the brain chemistry of arousal, romance, and being "in love." Oxytocin is that of contentment, commitment, and "being loving." The latter you can build a life on. With the former, you can't even see straight. With Chris, I was enjoying the emotive gaze but not seeing the beast clearly. The next weekend she badly threw Tanner. He had eagerly, perhaps hurriedly, saddled her Saturday morning. Just as he'd done at the seller's place, he rode her down the road and into some open meadows. He was headed toward the river. He didn't get far. A new machinery farmer had planted a corn crop over the old bridal trail. As Tanner turned back and rode up the embankment home, Chris went into a frenzy of bucking. She threw him so high, he scraped tree branches before thudding to the ground. She came cantering home, saddle sideways and the crupper torn off her tail. I resaddled her without the crupper and went looking for Tanner. She handled perfectly. We found him crippling up the embankment. He was bruised and banged up, but still game to ride this mule. I helped him on her and led Chris home.

After settling Tanner in with his Mom, I rode Chris

back to the scene of her crime. Nothing. No spooking. No bad responses. The crupper lay on the muddy embankment. Dismounting, I fastened it to the pommel of my saddle and circled the meadow looking for a way north across the granny branch to get beyond the new corn crop. Satisfied I'd found one, I rode home in a fast walk, trot, and gallop. Again, Chris handled fine. Sunday night, Tanner and his older brother by six months, my son Michael and I took turns riding her to hounds along the riverbank. We cast our three braces of calico coyote hounds just above what is called the Snakey Bend. I had driven the dogs over in the truck to meet the boys on the mule. We got several coyotes up and it was good hunting for hours. All night Chris behaved herself. When the hounds made a late run south out of hearing distance, we left my jacket[9] by the trailer for their return then drove and rode home. We decided a bad fitting crupper was the culprit causing Saturday's bad behavior. It must have pinched her into bucking, we decided. I secretly thought it was because she was more bonded with me than the boys.

For the next month I rode Chris almost every other day. What a pleasure. Riding her fast walk behind those floppy, relaxed long ears, I covered the territory. Her fast walk covered more ground than most horses do at the trot. She was unafraid of heavy traffic, dark trails, thick woods, or steep ridges. I actually rode her up the East Crypt ridge by the waterfall that has to be slanted on at least a 70 degree grade. She could jump little fences mounted and five foot fences dismounted. The fenced heartland became open range for us. I also decided the high withers she'd inherited from her mama meant I could saddle her like a horse not bothering with the crupper. Most mules have too flat a top line to keep the saddle in place without one. All seemed perfect but for her increasing preoccupation with our stallion two fences away.

Toward the end of that first month I was saddling Chris to visit an Amish family who lived near Bloomingdale. Evangelical missionaries had got to them and in schism they were leaving the community. I was asked to counsel reconciliation to them. Jake Miller, Christian's oldest boy, had described for me a way of riding through the back country to get to their place. Years before he'd blazed such a trail while courting Jonathon Bieler's daughter. I still wasn't sure of parts of that trail, and kept going over it in my mind as I started to mount the mule. At which point, she went into a forty second frenzy of bucking. When she stopped I blushed to see the tell tale sign of her lifted tail. Now when a female equine lays her ears back, squeals, and lifts a hoof, threatening to kick, let alone goes into a bucking frenzy, she is clearly saying, SCRAM! However, the same behavior plus raising her tail may mean "come hither." Two or more diametrically opposite messages may be included in what appears to be the same expression. This not only includes the phenomenon of a female's right and ability to abruptly change her mind, it also reflects her capacity to maintain contradictory points of view with slightly fluxing emphasis at the same time. This is commonplace with women. When men achieve it they are considered genius.[10] In animal husbandry, like the other kind, if a man responds thoughtlessly to such double whammies he will get trampled. Rather he must remain in the dialectique to synthesize a new mood and/or consolidate a prevalent one.

I left her tied. In the tack room, I put apple treats in my pocket for the positive and found a stout broom handle for the negative. If a mule is to be punished it must be straight away. All mule men counsel against being dominated by the beast's anger. Punishment must be prompt to be effective. It will not be effective if you wait until you come home from the hospital.

Returning to her with treats, I made over her for minutes until she became calm. After loving on her, I prepared to mount again. As soon as that idea transferred to her, she began the bucking all over again. At which point, I sternly applied the broom handle to her buttocks.

Trembling under a dozen whacks, her eyes implored me to stop. I then hooked her to a lunge line and ran her up and down the yard until she was quite exhausted. A tired mule is a tame mule, I reckoned, preparing to mount for the third time. No trouble now, I rode her out the front gate and south along the border fence. She ignored the stallion as he ran the length of the pasture beside us. A full days riding followed in sunshine and the glory of good weather synchronized in the saddle. My beautiful white mule behaved as beautifully and admirably as she was admired by the many horse farmers I stopped to call on. A great day in the saddle all around except I never reached my destination. We jumped a low iron gate and meandered along a wet weathered ditch into unfamiliar country. Past a deserted property with clumps of Ash trees, some of which were unseasonably red already, I rode up a bluff near a pine grove covered with ground ivy and mint coming on to an old quarry on the eastern slope. Its stones massively blocked further passage. We were way off Jake Miller's route. Riding back, enjoying the smells of mint and pine, I laughed thinking how a friend of mine spoke of the journey being more important than any destination.

Weeks followed where required activities kept me from long rides. I enjoyed several short rides about every other day. Some days when I'd call on Chris and time was particularly short, I'd just swing up on her without saddle or bridle. She'd walk calmly around the paddock and we'd both enjoy the ride. One evening my friend John McFall came by with his two grandsons, Kevin age nine, and A.T. seven. Both so admired my mule they begged to ride her. My thought was to put them on Chris, one at a time, bareback, and lead her around the yard. We put Kevin on first. No sooner had he sat gently behind her withers, when up she went with a forward buck that sent the slender boy ten feet in the air. He came down on her soft rump only to be bucked forward to her neck. Shaken up but okay, little Kevin clung to her mane. John and I rescued him and I scolded Chris all the way back to her paddock.

Later that night I spoke with Chris again about the whole thing. I speak to my livestock. They seem to like it whether or not they understand any of it. I think they tune in on the tone of human conversation. And careful perception of animal signals of communication within the context of specific conditions becomes quite like a conversation. Around 1948 when I was still in grade school, I saw a motion picture with Butch Jenkins and Peter Lawford called . . . , I think, "My Brother Talks with Horses." A few years later when I'd hang out at the Vigo County Fairgrounds, I would attempt to converse with racehorses. More scientific than Butch Jenkins, I'd devised a fool proof system. If my equine conversation indicated a winner, it confirmed the genuineness of inter-species communication. If I reached a null hypothesis, that is, a sleek pacer indicated to me a loser, it confirmed that horses like humans are not clairvoyant and can't bat a thousand.

Always guarding against sentimentality, which I learned at school was called anthropomorphism: i.e. 'endowing animals with human characteristics' . . . I went the other way . . . I didn't expect the beast to think or communicate like me . . . I tried to think like the beast.

Half a century later, I would read how Alex Kerr, the lion trainer in his book No Bars Between would warn about the boundaries of such wisdom. He was asked if he would allow his daughter to train big cats. He answered, "No!" Asked why he said, "To do it successfully she must think like a lion or tiger, and if she thinks and acts like a big cat they will look upon her as one of them, and that would mean when she came into season, as human beings do just like other mammals, the cat would know. And since the way a lion denotes affection is to pick the female up by the scruff of the neck, that is what he would do. And he would break her neck."

I explained to Chris with tone and manner that since she was special to me, I expected her to respect my whole herd, that is, all my family, friends and anyone I helped on her back. She stood aloof and inscrutable. I've been criticized for allowing my stock dogs to eat dead lambs and placentas. People think that will give them an appetite for lamb. (What are intelligent canines to think of some dumb master who would scold them off such good food.) It is far better to let them know the live sheep are yours and not to mess with what is yours.

I was telling Chris that live children on my place were mine and not to mess with them. I felt confident I could demonstrate this lesson if John would return his grandsons for the event. Grandfather John protectively declined but I think his grandsons were still game.

More full scheduled weeks passed and I had not called on the schismatic (Amish) family. I did not wish to call on them in a motor vehicle. Amish sense of time is closer to the weather than the clock. They laugh at mechanical farmers fussing about the "fiscal year." They measure time more by the fiscal generation . . . yet I was pressuring myself to complete this task to "git 'er dunn" as mule men would say.

Then I found Chris horsing along the fence line for the first time in what I could see was 'full heat.' The stallion roared and squealed in full display across from her. Now . . . the hybrid mule is not always completely sterile. They are 100% incapable of conceiving from another mule, but once in a million times they may conceive if bred by a stallion or jack. I think the odds would be considerably better if tried more often. Chris tried all day, then all week . . . up and down the fence line trying to tempt the stallion over two fences.

My stallion, Styling, is a very sensible fellow. He earned nearly $400,000 racing 52 weeks a year for ten years at Chicago tracks. Chicago horsemen called him 'old iron legs' because of his soundness. He rarely came up lame. And if he did . . . he was back racing in a few days, not a few weeks or months. Alex Adams, his owner / trainer in those years, knew then as I know now, it wasn't his legs . . . it's his brains. He is too smart to foolishly risk getting hurt at the race track, breeding shed, or open pastures.

Styling will signal me loudly when he is ready to breed

a mare, but will not engage her without my assistance. One kick from her and he is finished until I apply the kicking hobbles. My previous stallion Forester would breed mares whether they were ready or not. It was rape city with him. At the end of the breeding season, he was one great hematomae, covered with cuts, bruises, and kicked in scarring. He got the job done but at too great a cost. While serving a mare in pasture, another jealous one donkey kicked him in the ribs. His rib cage broke into his heart and he was dead in fifty hours. The vet said there was nothing to do. I brought him into the yard near our house and he would follow me from room to room, pathetically looking in the windows with his pain ridden eyes. He is buried on the place.

One must allow at least a five day window for a mare to be bred, from the onset of her heat cycle to her passing out of season. After more than ten days, Chris was still horsing and as mule men say, "hot as a fire cracker." A few more days passed before the weekend with slight change. By Saturday morning, I thought, "Enough's enough!" and saddled up my white mule. She squealed a little when I tightened the girth. She squealed again and side stepped a bit as I held the left iron to mount. Instead of mounting I leaned over her neck with half my weight imitating the reassurance of a companion equine. I placed the palm of my hand behind her ears to suggest the pressure of another horse or mule. All the while caressing her with the tips of my fingers, simulating a mother's nuzzling to reassure her foal. Still, I didn't think she was ready to ride. Her eyes indicated otherwise. I left her tied for an hour. Her history included being tied for days in camp on Colorado hunting trips. After an hour, she seemed fine, but still reluctant to ride. I left her tied for two more hours. Then unbridled, she was turned loose, though still saddled, to graze around the yard. I kept an eye on her. She began to express curiosity as to what was next. I hooked her to a lunge line and she sighed in disapproval. Her expression told me she was ready to ride. Rebridled she submitted easily to remount and we trotted out the front gate. Her long fast walk made good time up the graveled county road, but it had gotten too late again to ride to the Bloomingdale area. I needed several hours with the family and I didn't want to ride new territory after dark. I rode south and east of the old quarry, finding a trail in the strange wood until I reached a gate in the southwest corner of another wood lot. It seemed to be the gate Jake Miller described as opening up fields all the way to the Lapp family's neighbor and the Clay Plant road west of Bloomingdale. It would be the return point of my next ride. I turned the mule northwest toward home.

About a mile close to home, Chris's gait picked up in speed. Never barn sour, but she did seem anxious to get home. Her fast trot was tending toward the gallop. I turned her off the road into a hilly alfalfa field and gave her her head. She went into an easy gallop uphill that quickly turned into a slight buck. Then into a gut wrenching, jack knifing, hard buck. Staying on, I pulled her head clear back to the side. But we still sailed through the air in angles. I glimpsed the bluff ahead. We were seven feet above the road by now. "That ought to stop her," I thought, and headed her straight toward it. She slowed for a mulish millisecond and then bucked off the bluff. Bang! . . . we landed . . . she was trembling and still as I climbed down her neck to sit in the saddle again. With soothing words I stroked the side of her neck to further quiet her. She responded by bucking again. The second buck was a doozey. It threw me up out of the irons and down hard on the rocks in the road. She galloped off and away toward home.

I limped home. The pain of being thrown is like that of a car wreck . . . only more personal. More like a bar fight where every pain has a personal referent. Every hair on my head and bone in my back hurt and I was taking it very personal. Neighbors phoned my wife when they saw a saddled mule run bye. My wife became very agitated. Equally agitated my mule had run into our yard and kept running up and down as if the sky was falling. The mule feared retribution. The wife . . . circumlocution. "Don't say a word," she explained. "I've warned you about her. You're getting too old for this!" Such jealous alarm was not exactly the sympathy I required, so I said nothing and stationed myself in the center of the yard and waited. My wife came to me affectionate and solicitous. The mule followed, wary but anxious to see if I had treats in my pocket.

My wife asked me to "please not get back on that mule." I told her it was necessary to correct the behavior just suffered. Shaking her head she went silently back in the house. I rubbed the mule down, walked and cooled her out a bit before re-saddling her. All the while talking to her about what she did wrong and how we were going to correct it. On the remount she seemed calmer than before, almost grateful I wasn't punishing her. We rode slowly back to the alfalfa fields; her ears floppily indicating how relaxed she was. Entering the field from the west, we came downhill 100 yards to precisely that point where she began bucking before. As I turned her around to face uphill, I caught in her eye one full moment of impacted emotional information. She immediately recognized the place with myriad associative cues, pushing her panic button to do precisely the same thing again. "Oh my god, this is where I bucked you off before! Oh my god, I am compelled to do the same again!" The bucking was faster and less vertical this time. I decided to jump off rather than get bucked off. When I shifted my weight to do so, she gave a little lurch up, arching her back just enough to sling shot me into the lower ground below us. That broke the second, third and forth lumbars of my back and gave me a not so slight concussion.

Unable to stand erect, and half out of my head, I was stumbling toward the road when a small pick-up slowed to help. It was Elwood, great grandfather of friends of ours. He suffers extreme Alzheimers. I fell / sat into his little truck and the two of us sure made some duet of conversation coming out of that hill country home.

Almost home, Elwood pulled into a place where Chris was being held by a young couple in their front yard. I got out and Chris came to me directly. I tried to thank the young couple, before realizing they couldn't understand a thing I was saying. Nor could I understand them. All speech becoming an on and off cacophony of confusing pulses. I walked home with my mule, unsaddled, and turned her out. Waking around midnight, unable to sleep, I knew my back was broken before I drove to the ER. I also knew that the conditions of my conditional love for Chris had radically changed.

There is altogether too much talk these days about unconditional love. Especially from politicians[11]. . .and daughters. Love is limited, that is, conditioned by time, space and other factors as much as anything else. Even the idea of god's unconditional love for His creatures is conditional upon the consequences of its relative acceptance. Love, no less than other spiritual gifts, should be done with propriety and in order.[12] Conditions of the heart are less critical than their behavioral expressions. Chris, like Shark, would have to go. I let go of my behavioral love for them.

The seller and his wife helped us prepare Chris for a mule sale in Colombia, Missouri. Chris preferred this lady and traitorously treated me like an abuser, trembling and spooking when I came near. She never acted this way unless this particular lady was present. This lady, I think, was fem- flammed entirely and probably still thinks I am a mule abuser.

At the sale I positioned myself close to the auctioneer when Chris was brought into the arena. I told him, "I love this mule. I have loved her over long rides and rough country. She's out of a Thouroughbred mare by a Mammoth jack in Montana. She's traffic safe, will go up a seventy degree ridge where you wouldn't put a horse, and can jump a five foot fence flat footed. The bad part is . . . approximately once a month she will . . . try and kill you. I wouldn't advise her kept near a stallion."

The auctioneer covered the mike with his hand during my last two sentences. After she sold for $1,200 he beckoned me over. "Keep that bad part on the farm, son, here . . . it's Caveheat Emptier."[13]

Notes

1."Grizzly Man" Werner Hertzog's documentary film on how young Mr. Treadwell's libertarian and unconditional love for Alaskan Grizzly Bears on the artic slope enabled him and his girlfriend to be eaten alive on camera and full soundbyte.

2. "The Lightening Mule Brigade" (Abel Streights 1863 Raid into Alabama) by Robert L. Willett author of "One Day of the Civil War"

3. IBID Robt. L. Willett

4. IBID Robt. L. Willett

5. IBID Robt. L. Willett

6. IBID Robt. L. Willett

7. Walt Kelly's Albert the Alligators spin on Thoreau

8. "The Lightening Mule Brigade" by Robert L. Willett

9. Trained 'running hounds' will return and stay at the point of the cast

near the scent of their master.

10. "The test of genius is if a man can maintain contradictory points of view at the same time" F. Scott Fitzgerald

11. re: Pope Benedict XVI Encyclical "Deus Caritas Est": commentary on same.

The magisterium of the church, I think, is at its best giving hope to this desperate world when it sets forth teachings of Jesus in a catholic form applied to the dynamics of human life and the problems of evil. Not . . . when it merely peddles ideals or factionalizes with one set of Konkret historical forms against another.

In part I of this his first Encyclical Pope Benedict achieves the former. In part II he succumbs to the latter. "Deus Caritas Est" first draws on sacred scripture and tradition to address the most central concept in Christianity and also the most used and misused word in all human languages . . . love.

He scholarly notes the etymology of words defining and connoting different dimensions of love developing the thesis that Gods love and human love are profoundly interconnected. That love between human beings is only fully developed within Gods will. And this "communion of will increases in a communion of thought and sentiment", never finishing, but faithfully maturing in destiny "through a unifying process, it makes us a we which transcends our divisions and makes us one, until in the end God is all in all". Yeah!

This promise of loves definitive goal requires mutual, practical and demonstrable commitment (Idem velle atque idem nolle) not to be "reduced to a generic, abstract, and undemanding expression of love." If one semantically insists on saying 'unconditional', it must be an 'unconditional with demands', that is to say, conditional love. 'Unconditional' requires 'conditional' development.

In part II of "Deus Caritas Est" we get an echo of the company he keeps with the likes of Marcello Pera in the Italian Senate and the idealized personae of underpaid Catholic Charities workers. The former is transparent, the latter so inflated with ideal gas that if such personnel were ever realized they would all join the union with liberation theology.

Unconditional love begins to sound clinically and behaviorally like the old free love arguments did sexually. At the first plenum conference of the C.P.S.U. in power Alexandra Kollontai argued that like material goods, sexuality should be collectively accessable. "Sexuality is like water," she said. "It does not matter what glass is used to slake ones thirst." Lenin replied, "Yes comrade Kollontai, but who would wish to drink from a glass greased by the lips of the multitude."

12. Corinthians (Paul epistle to) 14:40"Let all things be done decently and in order".

13. Caveheat Emptier: Caveat Emptor-Buyer Beware

"We thank thee for our little light, that is dappled with shadow"
T.S. Eliot

SHADOWGAIT (east)

VII Epilogue:

Editorials, Articles, Political Action Report, Ads, Five Funerals and Farewell

Editorials to the New York Review of Books and The Terre Haute Tribune.

March 1997	Re: Philotyranny 613
March 1998	Re: Fintan O'Toole 614
April 1999	Re: Columbine 615
June 2001	No satisfactory retribution 617
January 2007	Defunding War 618
September 2008	Re: Hillary and Geraldine 619
Easter Week, 2009	Re: Ideologue Bayh 620
February 2009	Re: Guantanamo 621
September 2009	Re: Obstruction of Health Care 622
October 2009	Re: McGenerals 623
January 2010	Re: Obama and the Banksters 624
June 2010	Re: coke bottle 625
December 2010	Re: Recent Supreme Court 626 Decisions, Elections, & Deficit Commission Reports
January 23, 2011	Revisiting Facts of the Rotten Tree 627
February 2011	Re: D.A.D.T. repeal 630
August 2011	Empire, Indeed 631
Spring 2015	Letter to Editors Re SAE racism 632 Terre Haute Tribune • Indianapolis Star Indiana Daily Student • Bloomington Herald Indiana Statesman
January 2016	Trump Check 633

Articles

Restoring the Traditions (Midamerica Harness News) 634

Abortion & Bourgeois Feminist Debate (IN Center on Law and Poverty Review) 645

Political Reports & Ads:

Loves Labor…Intent (Not Lost Nor   Unspoken) 653

'Swimmer', Shadowgaits Standardbred Stallion and Issue 656

American Night: Response to Allen Wald 658

Leroy McRae: Obituary and Responses 664

Five Funerals . . . . and Farewell   667

TGM 2013

MARCH 1997
NEW YORK REVIEW OF BOOKS

RE: PHILOTYRANNY

To the Editor:

The Lilla case is only the most recent example of how the antinomian philistine, whose love for the radically moderate has declined into philotyranny. Under cover of the Phaedrus Lilla would drive his Chariot lower than the tyrants he does not name as sycophant for the same. His hubris in dismissing Heidegger, Lukács and Sartre is only matched by his imagining "sharp divisions among intellectuals over Algeria." I remember how earlier gutless wonders imagined sharp divisions among intellectuals over segregation, and the holocaust. Heidegger indeed may 'not have began to understand his unpolitical' debt to evil but what is Lillas excuse. He defends the death of consciousness.

Thomas G. Morgan

Re: Fintan OTooles reviews of Taylor and Adear NYR
2/19/98

To the Editors:

    Who is this radically moderate Mick; and who is he to
judge generations of irish political morality?!
    The NYRB is known for information and insight.
Otoole offers neither. He is undoubtedly a part of the 79% paean
to American dick head democracy.

Thomas G. Morgan

Thomas G. Morgan L.C.S.W.
Daseinanalayse
Marriage, Family, Child &
Individual Psychotherapeutic Counseling

APRIL 30, 1999   RE: COLUMBINE
TERRE HAUTE TRIBUNE

To the Editor:

Media attention on the recent school murders has been
politically correct and intellectually bankrupt. Educational, clinical, and religious spokespersons are once again camp following
the propaganda of pressure groups rather than honestly address-
ing causes of this unprecedented behavior.

Mainly, we've heard about a) "too available guns and
firepower" via the gun control lobby. We've been warned
against b) "raising boys with guns" and c) "calling outsiders fags
and wimps" via the gay and women's lobby. All this suggesting
that more legislation and sensitivity is the solution for children
massacring children at school.

Nonsense!

A) For almost 200 years every frontier and farm kid in America
had a rifle and/or shotguns, which was readily available as were
explosives at the local hardware store yet they were not taken to
school and there were no massacres.

B) Toy guns and weapons precede these current massacres by
thousands not just hundreds of years.

C) There has been cruel child and adolescent name calling since
pre-history. What is as unprecedented as the massacres themselves is that for the first time in history we have a generation or
more who have not experienced the violent discipline of corporal
punishment and boundary setting by their parents.

Too many educators and clinicians continue to carry on
about "violence in the schools" never distinguishing between the
violence involved in bullying a child and the violence required to   615

defend a child. All this unreality compounds into highly budgeted child protective services which rarely prevent or prosecute monstrous violence but daily inhibit, intimidate, and harass parents from using reasonable violence to discipline their children.

I have to counsel parents that they must be willing to go to jail for the children they love if they properly discipline them.

The perverse hypocrisy of crocodile tears in the media over school massacre is that they are shed by those who are its probable cause.

Thomas G. Morgan

June 13, 2001
New York Review of Books

No satisfactory retribution

To the Editors:

Professor Deaks' compulsive balancing act (Heroes & Victims" NYRB 5/31/2001) beats the bureaucratic acrobats of Budapest. He finds no satisfactory explanation for anti-semetic-anti communist violence in an area of time and space drenched with these dual themes of fascist power and propaganda.

This cartoon of political correctness dishonors jewish sensitivity and the truth that thousands of brave 'heroes and victims' were jewish communists.

Thomas G. Morgan

JANUARY 27, 2007
TERRE HAUTE TRIBUNE STAR

DEFUNDING OF WAR ONLY PROPER OPTION

To the Editor:

Historians will record a great similarity between the
Weimar Republic and the U.S. Democratic Party. Obsessed with
sexual rights and other secular fantasies they failed to protect
their people from the jackboots and war profiteers of the extreme
right.

President Bush, like Hitler, has announced his intention
to march both east (Iran) and west (Syria) to widen his unjust
war. The Democrats' insipid response to create an "unbinding
vote" against it is unprecedented cowardice.

"To chain the dogs of war," Thomas Jefferson wrote,
"Congress must defund the war-makers." Anything less is hot
air. Defunding troops on the ground is not taking away support
for them. It is putting them on a plane home where they belong.

Democratic no less than Republican "leadership" is
beholden to and clientele of global corporations (Haliburton,
Blackwater, et al. in Riyaddh, Tel Aviv, New York, and Houston.)
They will be held responsible, no less than the corporate
profiteers for every casualty and war criminal they create.

Thomas Morgan

RE: Hillary and Geraldine

Dear Editor,

The Hillary Clinton Campaign has become the Franken-stein monster of bourgeois feminism. For years certain liberals and closet conservatives sat out the civil rights movement and then attempted to vicariously claim it by elevating their gender confusion to equal or prior importance. Gender-bender giggles replaced the radical call for equal pay and equal rights. Now Geraldine Ferraro howls misogyny because they can't change the rules that include an equal opportunity to lose.

Respectfully,

Thomas G. Morgan

Easter Week, 2008
Terre Haute Tribune Star

Re: Ideologue Bayh

Dear Editors,

Re: Senator Evan Bayhs announcement he is splintering to the center and that he is "not an ideologue"

Not an ideologue! In a pigs eye! Everybody's Evan is a knee jerk moderate who would take the middle of the road in terminal traffic. He lacks both the grit of opposition and/or the courage for loyalty. He would take the luke warm middle between Pilate and Caiphus-Jesus and Judas: (Rev. 3:16). Time for the electorate to spit him out in 2010. We need a Senator from Indiana who fully supports our Presidents program to change the privileged past.

Respectfully,
Thomas G. Morgan

FEBRUARY 3, 2009
TERRE HAUTE TRIBUNE STAR

Letter to the Editor:

Re: The Conundrum of Guantanamo and its Detainees

Why not donate the entire area back to Cuba from who it was stolen in 1904? No one has demonstrated better than Cuba the ability to put people to work and process criminal emigration.

Thomas G. Morgan

Re: The Obstruction of Health Care

Blue Dog disease is more pathological than any red state of inanity. Its aetiology stems from these running dogs of lobby money overdosing on millions of Insurance Company dollars this summer in the development of the bogus Baucus bill. Diseased Blue Dogs have so degenerated as to claim this legislation, which is seen by the insurance industry as their "Protective Profit Enhancement" bill as a great moment in history for Health Care. It should be the Blue Dogs last moment.

It is time these diseased blue hogs were voted out of the publics kennel and off the taxpayers trough. They especially should be quarantined from our regions electorate where their deception infects innocently ignorant citizens and naïve newspaper editors.

Thomas G. Morgan

October 2009
Terre Haute Tribune Star

Re: McGenerals

Letter to the Editor:

Remember McArthur.
Fire McCrystal!

Thomas G. Morgan

December 16, 2009
Terre Haute Tribune Star

Re: Obama and the Banksters

Our President has expressed his concern that our Bankers "just don't get it" as to their responsibility for helping or hurting the economy. Could it possibly be that our President doesn't get it? In the U. S. free enterprise system, Bankers only serious responsibility is for profits and usury. Corporate welfare only helps them do their thing.

Historically, the only Banks responsible to a nations economy are Banks who have been nationalized. Stop giving money to freebooting banksters! Nationalize the Banks!! Respectfully,

Thomas G. Morgan

JUNE 2010
TERRE HAUTE TRIBUNE STAR

Re: billion dollar coke bottle

     Mark Bennett has once again given Tribune-Star read-
ers insight into our local history and culture. His June 6 article
vindicating working man Earl Dean's invention of the Coca-Cola
bottle discreetly dismisses millionaire Chapman Root's exploita-
tion of same.
     Every working-class kid growing up in Terre Haute's last
century learned from their parents the lesson of the coke bottle
story , . . "Big shots steal the credit and profit earned by working
people."

Thomas Morgan

In re: recent Supreme Court decisions, elections and deficit commission reports

"I see in the near future a crisis approaching that unnerves me and causes me to tremble for the safety of my country . . . corporations have been enthroned, an era of corruption in high places will follow, and the money power of the country will endeavor to prolong its reign by working upon the prejudices of the people until the wealth is aggregated in a few hands and the Republic is destroyed." Abe Lincoln-1865.

Since Reagan, Republicans have been dismantling the 'New Deal' benefits for working Americans. Since Clinton, blue dog Democrats have cravenly capitulated to same. Since 1979, working American "middle income" rose only 0.7 % per year. The poor (bottom 20%) fared even worse at a sickly 0.3 % growth per year. Whereas the rich corporate upper class throughout this time including the so-called recession saw their incomes soar 260% from an average $337,100 per year to $1.2 million. That's 9.6% per year, ten times faster than the rest of us and light years faster than poor people. Since money is power, this degree of economic inequality makes political democracy impossible. The free market has never worked for working people and is threatening again to return the 12 hour day with minimum raises and maximum unemployment. The free market only frees 'Big Business' to exploit everyone else.

It's the corporations . . . stupid. Not the government. The government is simply the corporation's speakers bureau. Working families must fight to conserve the New Deal and Public Sector against those destroyers of the Republic: the corporate sponsored right wing Republicans, cowardly blue dogs, and terminally confused tea bags.

Respectfully,
Thomas G. Morgan

Revisiting Facts of Rotten Tree

Please thank D.R. Phillips for publically "letting go" any serious "challenge" to my November, 2010 letter regarding corporations. After lamely accusing me of dreamed-up facts, being "consumed by the liberal drumbeat" and that no knowledgeable union leader would agree with my premise, he then concludes with a retroactive and exclusive claim on the Constitution.

My facts: "Since 1979, working American middle income rose only 0.7 percent per year. The poor (bottom 20 percent) fared even worse at a sickly 0.3 percent growth per year. Whereas the rich, corporate upper class throughout this time saw their incomes soar 260 percent from an average $337, 100 per year to 1.2 million. That's 9.6 percent per year, 10 times faster than the rest of us and light years faster than poor people," were taken from the last compiled Congressional Budget Office Report of the George W. Bush administration.

D.R. offered no counter facts, just his opinion approving of the corporate take because he felt it was less than the governments' postage stamp and some Union wages. He reports that "U.A.W. at G.M. had a wage scale in 1970 of $4.30 an hour and in 2008 it was $28.12", and that the 1959 5–cent stamp is 44 cents today disproving that the "rich corporate class" is at the bottom of outrageous increases. Come on, D.R. you're comparing pennies at the post office and hundreds of dollars barely for a working family to make ends meet to the billions of corporate gluttony.

In these last 90 days, as almost 20 percent of all Americans remain unemployed or underemployed, corporations earned profits of $1,659,000,000,000 in this third quarter of 2010. It is the highest quarterly figure ever recorded. So despite their protracted whining about big government taxes, rules and regulations corporate bosses can still make a buck – make that 1.7 trillion bucks in just 90 days.

There are only so many pieces of the pie. Corporate gobbling of so much of the pie leaves not near enough for national prosperity. Not even a fickle trickle down, D.R. The rich are getting richer, the poor are getting poorer and working people are getting overworked and underpaid. President Lincoln's fears regarding same were followed by Republican and Democratic Roosevelts' efforts against free market monopolies and for New Deal encouragement of the workforce to unionize. The resultant post-war prosperity significantly increased the tax base from wage earners without corporate tax dodges. Pay scales at non-union plants were kept up by the threat of unionization. And decent wages were achieved by strikes and/or the threat of them.

Today, a larger part of the work force is not unionized, a significant part of industrial work has been outsourced, and global corporations have increased their power. The recent B.P. (British Petroleum Corporation) episode demonstrated that global corporations have more authority here than our own federal and state governments.

As to "the liberal drumbeat", Emerson noted we may all march to different drummers, but mine is certainly not a liberal one. In these failing economic times, mine, no less than the rest of the country, is a conservative mood. Working Americans wish to conserve what they and their ancestors worked so hard to achieve. A living wage (for themselves and their children), their own home, the eight hour day, Social Security, affordable health care, education, retirement and the right to organize against corporate greed. Million dollar "liberal" bailouts to failing business managers and billion dollar right-wing tax cuts to billionaires are mutually destructive to the Republic. Both are initiated, bought, and paid for by the excessive profits of corporations who spent $6 billion in buying this last election through campaign "contributions".

As noted in the columns of my conservative Farm World Newspaper, "business policies have flooded benefits upward" not trickling "sideways or downward like the thirty years of academic, business, and political baloney has promised . . . The biggest lie in American politics for decades: for all to do better a few have to do fabulously better."

So spare us, D.R. your lesson re: people's capitalism, R.O. I.'s, individual stockholders, 401K's, and pension funds (most of these last were lost by nonunion workers this year in Indiana and throughout the country). What you (we) were taught in school was a lie. It was a lie then and is demonstrably a lie now. Look at the reality around you. Not a few bad apples. The tree is rotten.

This September, the same corporate banksters our tax money bailed out who still refuse or resist lending to small businesses and working families took over 102,134 homes; 820,000 total in 2010, and 1 million more face foreclosure, not just from deadbeat homeowners but from bank frauds of deceptive assets.

D.R.'s response is worse than apologizing for the above. His version of the Tea Party is to give such inequities constitutional authority . . . Bring in the violins! D.R., the good planters on horseback, who framed our Constitution, like you, knew nothing about corporations or their behavior. They didn't exist then. What is your excuse?
Please reread my letter's quote of Lincoln re: "Corporation Enthronement."

Respectfully,
Thomas G. Morgan

TO THE EDITORS:
TERRE HAUTE TRIBUNE STAR

Re: D.A.D.T. repeal in U.S. armed forces.

"Asking" or "telling" is not the issue. Behind liberal and right wing rhetoric is the future wholesale outing of the military.

Soldiers and sailors have been sodomizing each other both before and since Julius Caesar celebrated it and Roman legions spread the practice throughout the west. The U.S. military is no exception . . . except in its evangelical denials.

Single sex segregated, under willful and confined authority, licentious (i.e. necessarily privileged to disregard normal laws of morality against violence and to commit 'necessary' brutalities), required to endure physical hardship and personal sacrifice shared with 'buddies' and 'leaders' forming deep, emotional, physically comforting friendships. Whether being supportive to each other on their ancient shields or in the back of their modern headquarters or helicopters military love is a very queer phenomena.

Readers may recall seventy-five some U.S. mercenaries and security guards filmed last spring in Afghanistan passionately partying to the offense of native families by publically drinking vodka from each other's rectums.

Most such practices are overcome in post-military lives. Some are not. Some are brought into the military where it has been officially discriminated against but so very accessible. There is no evidence it detracts or distracts from military operations. There is historical evidence it enhances devotion to the cause. And Patriots, of course, must always celebrate and support applause for the cause!?

What bleeding cause?!!

The bankrupting Bush and Obama bullroar invading Iraq and attempting to occupy Afghanistan. If liberals wish to end sexual discrimination they would be calling for an end to Obama's as well as Bush's wars. Otherwise, they appear like pathetic civil rights drop outs dithering about trying to integrate fallout shelters and fraternities. If right wingers really wish to restrict the "Sins of Perversion", they should do the same or bear guilt for being supportive of a substantial part of its cause.

End the wars. Restrict the military budget, authority and influence.

Thomas G. Morgan

August 2011
TERRE HAUTE TRIBUNE STAR

EMPIRE, INDEED

London, the capitol city of little England is aflame. The fruits of "austerity", unemployment, and teenage criminality all beating up those anglo-saxon sissies in uniform, the London bobbies.

We have as much evidence here as we had or will have in Libya, Yemen, Syria, Egypt, and Iran . . . to invade the place. Adding to that, the recent crimes of British Petroleum and the long history of Royal oppression throughout the world we might as well indulge our corporate CEO's envy for empire and invade the place. Indians, Africans, Arabs and the Irish would support us.

Any socially conservative or socially conscious objections could be met by quoting Prime Minister Maggie Thatcher, "that society doesn't exist." Only Empire, that corporate imperialism clothed in democratic veneer.

The problem with Empire is it always creates an undertow of rot. If we'd invade England, our largest and most expensive armed forces in world history, larger and more expensive than all other nations' armies combined, who cannot seem to conquer a city block or country town of Muslim Warriors, might do well against English bobbies.

Like the olde British Empire as our corporate expenditures to attempt profitable dominance grows, our people, like the Brits decline into further down-gradedness.

TGM

Spring 2015 letter to Editors **Re SAE racism**:
Terre Haute Tribune • Indianapolis Star
Indiana Daily Student • Bloomington Herald Telephone
Indiana Statesman

I pledged to the SAE fraternity at Indiana University in 1958. Within months, that same national office, now boo-hooing innocence of racism on TV, called on local chapters to explain its internal racial restrictions. They were dropping their foundational "Aryan race" clause; substituting the words "socially acceptable." The national office wished to reassure its members that the code words "socially acceptable" still meant the same Aryan white racist thing.

Their present dishonesty exceed their past deceit.
They maintain "that isolated individuals in the last three or four years" are to blame for the SAE racist chanting at the University of Oklahoma. I am sure there are individual SAE members and alumnae who are non-racist good men but their organization is racist to the core like all the other Greek lettered lily white 'temples to Minerva' and the ancient slavocracy. Racism is fundamental to their origins, history, and present day policies and practice. An insult to our communities and country's religious and secular morality. Abolish them!

Peeking out from under their white sheets of identity, the Ku Klux Klan has more integrity then these people who hide their bigotry behind the business façade of bourgeois respectability. Such gangs and fraternities are not allowed at our public high schools. They should be abolished, i.e. not allowed at our public universities. Or ... University and government officials can admit they condone racist policies and practices if it is accompanied by significant U$ influence.

Thomas G. Morgan

P.S. The eternal dialectic at work interpenetrating opposites it should be noted that the Indiana Gamma Chapter of SAE
produced more anti-racist, revolutionary marxist and civil rights
activists than any other Greek fraternity of the last century. Don Smith of Chicago, Jack Glenn of Los Angles, Mike McNaughton of Mexico and San Joaquin, John Dittmer and Tom Morgan still in Indiana—to note a notorious few.

Terre Haute Tribune-Star
January, 2016

$\mathfrak{S}\mathfrak{h}\mathfrak{a}\mathfrak{d}\mathfrak{o}\mathfrak{w}\mathfrak{g}\mathfrak{a}\mathfrak{i}\mathfrak{t}$ $\mathfrak{F}\mathfrak{a}\mathfrak{r}\mathfrak{m}$
Racing & Broodstock

TRUMP CHECK

(Trump's definition: a playing card elevated above its normal rank in trick taking games.)

It is clear that Donald Trump; his countenance, face and hair constitute the funeral wreath of capitalist deception. Underneath official "liberal" whining and "conservative" growling he is the reality of our corporate managers. Vulgar selfishness from central casting.

The highly manipulated billions of dollars subsidy of provocateurs and fratricidal destruction for oil in the Middle East is now an expanded war. Such are most effectively administered by a Nobel Peace Prize liberal democrat, which confuse and dilute anti-war efforts. The democrats are quantitatively the largest membership party. That membership support is growing cold. A majority of Americans no longer believe in fakey professional wrestling, even when it is entertaining.

So here comes a new wrestler with a sinister cape, strange hair and wild illiberal rhetoric. Guaranteed to bring every hesitant or abstaining democrat to the polls for Hillary. And if that's not enough, Donald's Corporate peers will have him run on a third party thus enabling Hillary and her chief of staff Weiner into the white house. So called republican opposition and democrat campaigning required for the appearance of Democracy.

Thomas G. Morgan

Walnut Hall

Restoring the Tradition

RESTORING THE TRADITIONS
By Tom Morgan

Restoring the traditions of Walnut Hall and beyond is what Meg and Allen Leavitt are all about. The Leavitts were wed December 17, 1994, joining two historic streams of the Standardbred industry.

Meg Leavitt is the great granddaughter of L.V. Harkness who purchased four hundred acres for horses and the grand paneled mansion known as Walnut Hall in 1892. In 1906 Harkness innovated the idea of marketing the entire produce of his broodmare band as yearlings. The start of this century saw Walnut Hall producing, selecting, and standing legendary Standardbreds such as "Moko", "Fereno", "Walnut Hall", "Guy Axworthy", "Peter Volo", and "Scotland".

Meg's grandfather, Dr. O.F. Edwards, was a scholar of bloodlines and known for horse sense, i.e. his prescient appreciation of a horse's potential. "Guy Axworthy", for example, was bought as an inexpensive 14 year old; no one realizing his sire potential except Edwards who produced twelve of the first fourteen Hambletonian winners with him. "Scotland" was also a horse everyone overlooked except Edwards.

Meg's parents were Colonel and Mrs. H.W. Nichols. Her mother, Katherine, drove "Margaret Castleton" to her record of 1:59.9; the world record for a trotter driven by a lady and amateur. Meg's father was a director of the Grand Circuit and Chairman of the Board of Tattersalls and The Red Mile. During her family's stewardship. Walnut Hall produced world champions "Best of All", "Flower Child", "Impish", "Nardins Byrd", and the great "Abercrombie".

Allen Leavitt has more suddenly made history. In the mid-sixties he founded the famous Lana Lobell operations with a small New Jersey farm, a few broodmares, and his sister Lana's name. Lana Lobell quickly grew to become one of the largest equine operations in the world. Under Leavitt's leadership it expanded to 4,000 acres, in three different states, with 250 broodmares and standing eighteen stallions. Allen has syndicated and/or stood such modern giants as "Speedy Crown", "Speedy Somoli", "Noble Victory", "Overtrick", and "No Nukes".

Lana Lobell was the site for giant human achievements as well as Farm Manager, James C. Harrison collaborated with Allen on breeding programs. Readers will recall the same Jim Harrison compiled and edited the holy writ of harness horsemen, the 1054 page classic "Care and Training of the Trotter and Pacer". Harrison himself wrote the section on "Bloodlines and Breeding". Trainer greats, Jack Kopas and Howard Beissenger, are part of Lana Labell's history. Allen has served as President of the North American Harness Racing Marketing Association, Trustee of the Hambletonian Society, and a director of the U.S.T.A. His greatest achievement, however, he credits as finding, in August 1989, the love he had lost 20years previously.

There have been many losses, but, since Allen and Meg found each other again – history is being made and traditions restored. The Leavitts are located literally in the very center of where the world comes to Lexington to look at horses. Bordering "Kentucky Horse Park", the new-olde Walnut Hall Lmtd. is 440 acres of tree-lined pastures being reseeded, miles of fences being repaired and painted, huge barns rebuilt, and venerable lawns reclaimed. In less than two years the Leavitt's Walnut Hall Lmtd. has acquired 78 new broodmares and are standing four stallions. The stallions are: "Victory Dream" 2.1:59.2 3.1:53.2 ($1,016,537), "Cambest" p. T1.46.1 ($1,349,835), "Esquire Spur" 2.2:03.3h 3. 1:56f ($551,336), "Garland Lobell" 3.1:55.3 ($345,689)

VICTORY DREAM

Allen's philosophy is to make Lexington World Class Stallions affordable as never before. "Cambest", the fastest recorded harness horse to date, with the world record time trial mile, has a breeding fee of $2,500. Twenty-seven of Walnut Hall's twenty-nine pacing mares are bred to him. "Esquire Spur", the million dollar racehorse, has a breeding fee of $1,500, and is advertised as the best trotting value in America.

It is "Victory Dream", however, that Allen likes to speak of most. This winner of last year's Hambletonian has inspired his intuition. Syndicated in 1994 with Frank Antonacci, this horse became the highest money winner of all trotters last year, well after his syndication. Not since the bravery and stamina of "No Nukes" has a horse so captured the imagination of Allen Leavitt and the wisdom of Frank Antonacci.

Indeed, the very look of "Victory Dream" would stop some Standardbred men in their tracks. His appearance recalls the thoughts of Jim Harrison that the Standardbred is still achieving the Standard. That is, we have not yet established a definitively conformed type. It is evolving.

On the track, and especially the farm, can be seen a vast and sometimes odd assortment of conformation types. Neat little Morgan types, big-headed Narragansett types, rangy running horse types, and huge carriage horse types – all part of the evolving standard for Standardbreds.

And, while speed will always come before beauty and type, the latter is definitely the means which determines the end speed. In order to establish characteristics of speed in gait, free of knee-knocking, shin-hitting, and crossfiring, Jim Harrison wrote we must further probe for type.

In the here-to-fore mentioned classic on bloodlines and breeding, Harrison envisions the development of a beautifully refined and long-barreled trotter/pacer with graceful clearance between the legs. The challenging aspect of the art and science of breeding trotters and pacers is that every mare researched and every stallion selected this Spring significantly evolves the Standardbred. Present breeders are on the cutting edge of its history

GARLAND LOBELL

ESQUIRE SPUR

and development not mere curators and customizers of the past.

The speed, gait, size, and conformed beauty of "Victory Dream" may well auger toward the future standard of the breed Allen Leavitt believes. Standing 16.2 hands tall, his finely chiseled head lifted toward the breeze, he resembles the regal thoroughbred type. Allen also reports that he possesses great determination, manners, and intelligence with an exceptional willingness to please.

Next to pride in his horses is Leavitt's pride in his staff of equine professionals. Walnut Hall is staffed by the "best team of people I've ever been able to put together", say Allen. His loyal friend and Executive vice-president is Steve Katz. Steve has been both Marketing Director and General Manager for Lana Lobell. Prior to that, he was producer of the cable television program "Racing from the Meadowlands" and was harness racing editor for "Sportseye". His Farm Manager is R.L. Turner, and wife Judy, have brought their dedication from Lana Lobell to Walnut Hall. Serving as Foreman and general assistant to Turner, is Pete Foley from California. Pete's wife, Lynne, a previous resident of Calumet Farms, is in charge of the stallions. Roger Birch, who served his apprenticeship with Carter Durer at Peninsula Farms, is in charge of yearlings. Lorrie Locke is Office Manager. She was previously a manager at Meadowlands. Walnut Hall's attending veterinarian is Lynda Rhodes-Steward D.V.M. She is assisted by her husband, Robert, who is also a trainer at The Red Mile

Tradition and innovation continue to converge with the staffing and care of horses at Walnut Hall. The old method of regularly ponying the yearlings has been reinstated along with new methods for foal safety. For example, foals are not allowed to run loose when mother mares are led. Every foal is handled and led with the farm manager and foaling attendant present.

Allen intensively hovers on mastering all details. He meets at 5:00 p.m. every evening of the week with his farm managers. He developed his hands-on attention to detail in the heydays of operating the Liberty Bell, Bedminster, and Lana Lobell Select Yearling Sales. He also conducts daily comprehensive and informed conversations with Steve Katz. It was a pleasure

CAMBEST

to share conversation with these men as we drove past old slave quarters and stood beside the stature of "Guy Axworthy", in the equine cemetery. Most recently buried there, in 1993, is "Silent Majority", "Yellow Belle", and "Walnut Hall" were the earliest to be buried in 1910 and 1911. Other notable equine graves include "San Francisco", "Scotland", "Volomite", "Peter Volo", "Her Ladyship", "Margaret Castleton", "Nedda", and "Cedar Frisco", dam of Volomite.

An atmosphere of creative energy and classic landscape envelop this place. It is grand to spend an April morning here amidst nearby bird-calls and the buzz of wasps.

Tattersalls has just refused to do business with Allen Leavitt. They erred similarly fifteen years ago with Bill Sheehan. Their last mistake opportuned creation of the successful Kentucky Standardbred Sales. Who knows what opportunities might follow this last spite-ing of the establishment face.

The middle of America is the heartland of the Standardbred. Indiana especially is returning strongly to her racing traditions. And, the world still comes to Lexington to buy horses. Could that world be interested in, say, Indianabreds who will race for increasing purses versus only regional competition. Midwestern, particularly Indiana, horsemen may find a real friend and ally in the genius of Allen Leavitt. With a bloodline of the biblical prophets and like the rod attached to the second oldest oak in America (located in his new backyard) he is bound to draw the lightning.

Luminosus vs. Moribundis

The restoration of Walnut Hall is a sign of faith for our sport and industry.

STEVE KATZ & ALLEN LEAVITT

WALNUT HALL BROODMARES

Contents:

NOVEMBER/DECEMBER 1977

LAW AND POVERTY REPORT

LEGISLATIVE PREVIEW 197

LAW & POVERTY REPORT
NOVEMBER/DECEMBER 1977

The participants in this issue discuss the question,
Should the State of Indiana Provide Medicaid Funds for Poor
Women to Obtain Abortions? Ms. West is an attorney active in
women's rights movement, and Mr. Morgan has been a long-time
advocate of social justice in Indiana. The views expressed by the
authors are their own, and do not necessarily reflect the views of
the Indiana Center on Law and Poverty.

YES
by Martha S. West, Coordinator of Women's Rights
Project of the Indiana Civil Liberties Union

The right to an abortion is guaranteed to every woman by the
U.S. Constitution. Five years ago the Supreme Court ruled
that the right to privacy allowed a woman to decide for herself,
without government interference, whether to have a child or to
choose abortion. But today the right to choose has been inter-
fered with, and in practical terms, belongs only to those women
who can afford to pay for it.

Last year, one million women exercised their constitutional right
to have an abortion. Of these women, 261,000 were too poor
to pay for their abortions. So the government paid, just as it
paid for all of the other health needs of poor women, including
childbirth. Another 600,000 poor women in this country wanted
abortions but could not obtain them. Their communities had no
public facilities, or their states had restrictive and unconstitutional laws against publicly funded abortions.

This year the situation is worse. The federal government, instead of correcting the unequal treatment suffered by poor women, has taken away from the poor the right to an abortion altogether. The Hyde Amendment, passed by the House and Senate in varying forms, bans Medicaid reimbursements for abortions unless the life of the mother would be endangered. The Supreme Court has ruled that this limitation on funding does not contravene the constitutional guarantee of the right of privacy.

Because of the recent Court decisions, a poor woman's right to an abortion has become a political question, rather than a legal one. By its restrictive decision, the Supreme Court has, in effect, said that it is up to each state to decide whether or not poor women in that state should be financially assisted in exercising their constitutional right to choose abortion.

The funding of abortions for women who cannot financially otherwise obtain them is primarily a question of human dignity. President Carter's recent remarks in the summer of 1977, dismissing the plight of poor women by saying, "there are many things in life that are not fair, that wealthy people can afford and poor people can't" reflects a surprising insensitivity to human needs and problems. During his campaign, President Carter deplored certain injustices in our present economic system, and gave hope to many that he would work to relieve those injustices. In what we hope were uncharacteristic remarks, he has indicated an indifference to the stark reality facing a woman with an unwanted pregnancy and has taken a stand against giving the same choice to poor women that is given to middle class and upper class women.

There is no reason the people and government of Indiana need be as insensitive to the constitutional rights of the poor as the President and Congress. The Supreme Court has said it is up to the states whether or not they will provide the necessary funds for poor women. We would hope the citizens of Indiana would support those individuals in our society who are seeking the right to make their own choices and to gain greater control over their own lives. It is easy for the Supreme Court to say that under the Constitution women must be given the choice as to whether or not they want to bear children, but it makes little sense to give women this choice and then take it away from poor women who do not have the means to exercise it.

We hope the people of Indiana will not so lightly dismiss the plight of those who are poor and who are women. We urge the Indiana General Assembly to make full use of the latitude given to the state by the U.S. Supreme Court, and decide not to condition the exercise of a woman's constitutional right of privacy on her economic status. All women who find themselves pregnant, whether rich or poor, should have the opportunity and economic means to make the decision whether or not to bear a child.

For women already faced with an economic crisis, this decision is not one of convenience, but of vital necessity. Mr. Justice Marshall said, in dissenting from the recent Supreme Court decision on allowing federal funds to be denied to poor women: "I am appalled at the ethical bankruptcy of those who preach a 'right to life' that means, under present social policies, a bare existence in utter misery for so many poor women and their children."It is interesting to note that those who were in the majority on the Supreme Court in not recognizing the fundamental rights of poor women, and those in the federal and state legislatures who deny the funding of abortions for poor women, have never been poor themselves, and more particularly, have never been women and faced with the risk of pregnancy. Why should these "high moralists" and self-righteous, comfortable, male Americans be able to impose their narrow opinions and puritanical judgments on others? By their self-interest and insensitivity, they are sentencing many women to death through high-risk pregnancies and attempted back-alley abortions. Unless legislation is passed in Indiana, many women in our own communities will die because they cannot afford an abortion. Most will be young, many white, many black, and all will be poor.

NO

by Thomas G. Morgan
Director of Social Ministries for the Archdiocese of Indianapolis

A federal versus local rights dichotomy has long existed in Indiana. Many Indiana families fought a civil war in order to insure federal protection from local satraps and fiefdoms. On the other hand, the anti-federal tradition in Indiana began with the "copperheads" who opposed the Republic throughout the 1861-65 "War of the Rebellion." From the time of opposition to the Civil Rights Act of 1868 to present day resistance to federal regulations, the "copperhead" mentality defies the public's jurisdiction on its private turf.

Advocates of social justice on behalf of poor people in Indiana have battled "copperhead" thinking for over a century. I would think that most readers of "Law and Poverty Report" would be veterans of that battle. I submit that work for a human life amendment to protect unborn children from the abortion peddlers is an important part of that same fight.

Currently, the authority of the state may make no regulation which would overrule the private doctor's private judgment to perform an abortion. The aborting doctor has nearly unlimited license to (*) = ("kill," "terminate," or "medically remove from an unwanted situation" – I ask the reader to choose his own term, as one faction's verb is another's euphemism) the unborn child. This allows the commercial abortionist to accommodate affluent ladies' control of their own bodies by (*)ing their unborn children. Many of the same people who are shocked that middle and upper class ladies can so easily purchase an enterprising M.D. to (*) their unborn child in order to control their own bodies for social, career or cosmetic reasons seem tempted to think that the poor should have equal access to the same (*) ing thing. They sometimes reason that, since poor women are disproportionately represented in the late abortion cases and that since doctors charge higher fees for late abortions, there should be government funding available to (*) the unborn poor. It is an argument reminiscent of the desire to integrate fallout shelters in the nineteen fifties. Equal rights for oblivion has little to do with social justice.

Behind the present deadlock in the House of Representatives over the Hyde Amendment to the Labor/Health, Education and Welfare Appropriations bill for F.Y. 1978 looms a bizarre spectre. Bourgeois feminists with their slogan, "Keep Your Laws Off My Body", lead the cheers for politicians as they speak of "hardware" and "a quick scrape" for dilation and curettage of impoverished pregnant women. The "copperhead" mentality is insidious and serpentine in its penetration of the American mind. The bourgeois feminist cant about control over their bodies is merely the warmed-over argument of sanctifying private property. An argument whose moral power I find to be stunningly inert.

It was the argument used to lock our grandparents out of the factories and mines they worked. Nelson Rockefeller (whose credentials with poor people are as well-known as his plans for their future) had a grandfather, John D., who, in 1900, said to the Federal Anti-Trust Commission, "Keep Your Laws Off My Physical Plants." The libertine and laissez-faireist converge. The "copperhead" mentality reasons that if it's under one's private and personal domain, the public trust be damned. The nation, our community, shares a public trust in the welfare of every child. It is a trust not arbitrarily deflected a few moments, or a few months, before the M.D. proclaims them whole. This season an Illinois man is charged with murder for the shooting death of a seven month unborn child. The mother survived the shooting. Some would have us abandon reason to think that if the mother were poor enough, public funding should encourage her to have an M.D. perform the same service without a gun.

Advocates of social justice on behalf of the poor, the frail, and the powerless should be calling on the federal government to increase its protection of the poor, including their unborn children, rather than asking the government to subsidize the doctors in aborting them. Effective opposition to the government's deregulation of the abortion business will, in the long run, go farther to raise the total social justice demands than any efforts to depopulate the poor. Comprehensive National Health Insurance, National Health Care facilities, Child Care facilities and the abolition of unemployment are needed and will be increasingly required if we are to welcome all children and not abort them.

Dick Gregory, Erma Craven, Jesse Jackson and others have developed impressive arguments pointing to corporate conspiracies "to depopulate problem populations" over a period of time through abortion. I do not pursue these arguments because 1) I doubt their validity and 2) I fear their validity. I prefer to think that all this "jive" encouragement of abortion simply stems from people without much imagination. We've all seen that glassy stare of certain suburbanites when they are around poor kids. It's the look you see in dog pounds.

This week (the week of November 26), the head of the Carter Administration's study group on alternatives to abortion disbanded her group after concluding "that the only real alternatives to abortion are suicide, madness and motherhood." From our limited knowledge of these options I propose that we work for a sane, just society and choose the last alternative.

LOVES LABOR . . . INTENT (NOT LOST NOR UNSPOKEN)

"Democracy ceases to exist when resources are taken from those who work and given to those who would not" Thomas Jefferson

March 10, 2011 Indianapolis: Thirty two thousand union men and women assembled with fists raised against the state house whose inhabitant regime was threatening 'collective bargaining'. Every industrial, agricultural, and craft union in Indiana and surrounding states was represented.

The night before governor Walker of Wisconsin had pushed through late night legislation eliminating 'collective bargaining' rights of 179,000 public employees. Governor Mitch Daniels of Indiana has proposed the same plan plus his desire to take 47% of Indiana's horse racing purse into his general fund. The former threatens 'complete' union busting, the latter undoing of small scale horse farming and thousands of supportive jobs.

Intended words (unspoken) from the speakers' platform: [Silence] "Greetings Union Workers of Indiana (crowd roars) 'Union workers of the entire mid-west region' . . . may all 'The Working People of America' note your action this day [Crowd roars . . . then Silent]

'Workers of the World Unite'

'You Have Nothing to Lose But Your Chains' connected to the cretins in this Statehouse. You have more to gain than waiting for months to elect more of them! You have solidarity with brothers and sisters in the public sector. Do not fear thinking or speaking the word STRIKE!
[Crowd roars]

Do not fear thinking or speaking the words General Strike!
[Crowd roars. Extended cheering and jeering at the Sons of Mitches looking out the Statehouse windows.]

After four hours standing in spitting snow, prayers led by black
Christian and Muslim ministers, cheering Union Power, listening
to too many speakers, adjourned to union songs
'Solidarity Forever', 'Which Side Are You On Boys', and
Woody Guthrie's admonition . . . 'Take it easy, but . . . TAKE
IT!', we all retired to the nearest joint . . . which was the back bar
at the Marriott. The place packed with union men, I was gathering drinks for my I.B.E.W. relatives, remembering lyrics from
a Willy Nelson duo I'd heard on the radio this morning, I raised
our glasses against evil forces, loudly ordering more whiskey for
my men...and beer for my horses.

The whole place laughed aloud, lifting their glasses,
toasting UNION POWER.

Then a peculiar thing happened . . . dozens of young
union men began surrounding our table asking if I was "one of
the speakers?" They hadn't seen the platform clearly. "Your
presence and voice seem so familiar . . . don't we know you?"
was asked collectively and repetitively. The young masses hungry for grey bearded elder leadership!

Denied the speakers platform only factually, I now began
to speak . . . of the too limited undertowed theme of electing
democrats or "better" republicans. I mentioned the latter because there were Teamsters and Miners in the group. I encouraged them to think of STRIKES as labors ultimate weapon.

We talked together of how we liked the Steelworker
who spoke and had recently led strikes in Canada. I pointed to
the many letter I's of the word International on their union titles
was only because they had an office in Toronto. Unions would
have to truly organize internationally to address global corporate
outsourcing. Beginning in Canada there is much to learn. The
Canadian N.D.P., New Democratic Party, was formed forty some
years ago as a labor party, a third party to their Liberal and Conservative establishment parties.

And while not able to win national presidential elections, its regional alliances had won real national health care and solidly secured its social security and public sector. And . . . if Governor Walker and the tea bagged republicans do more than merely over reach the corporate oligarchy but actually and con-jointly begin to implement free market fascism . . . unions and left caucuses in labor parties would be required to stop them, nationalize corporate monopolies and run them for the public good. Like olde Debs described the "Cooperative Commonwealth."

> Cheers! and Hurrahs!
> against corporate forces
> More whiskey for the men
> I spoke about the horses.

'Big Fellow,' first yearling colt by 'Proud To Swim Home' with TGM, on the way to Deleware sale, and racing career.

ROUD TO SWIM HOME

uscles Yankee (sire of 177 $100,000 winners)
f sister to TOM RIDGE ($886,144)

PROUD TO SWIM HOME

is coming of age. His exceptional breeding, temperament, intelligence and conformation producing foals gaining attention in **Illinois, Indiana, and Ohio**

Ill. Steve Searle: "My filly by **PROUD TO SWIM HOME** (Charming Mary) out of Hot Flash Hanover) is the best trotter I've trained."

Ind. Tom Simmons: Filly by **PROUD TO SWIM HOME** (Light Upon Light out of Tuflilskirt) top Springfield qualifier, now racing at Hoosier Park.

Ohio Ben Miller: "My 2yo filly (Flight of Deer) and yearling (Habemus Papam) by **PROUD TO SWIM HOME** (out of Shades of Grace) are showing extraordinary desire and speed at the trot."

Longshanks: Full brother to Steve Searle's filly out of a mare by Lindy Lane whose siblings include Heyworth Hanover 1:51 ($143,000) produced Janos Box 1:53 ($291,000) and Hialeah Hanover 1:55 ($162,300).

Trotsky: Full brother to Tom Simmons' filly out of a mare by Agogolauxmont who won her division of the Reynolds Stake at Pocono, placed third in N.Y. Sires Stakes at Saratoga, producing colts at 1:59, 1:55 ($177,797).

Summers Review: out of Triumphant Review and maiden mare with excellent conformation.

Powerstroke Swimmer: filly out of GL's Katelyn, excellent conformation, the Muscles Yankee X Vaporize cross, the ideal nick.

Shadowgait Farm
Racing & Broodstock

765-245-1413

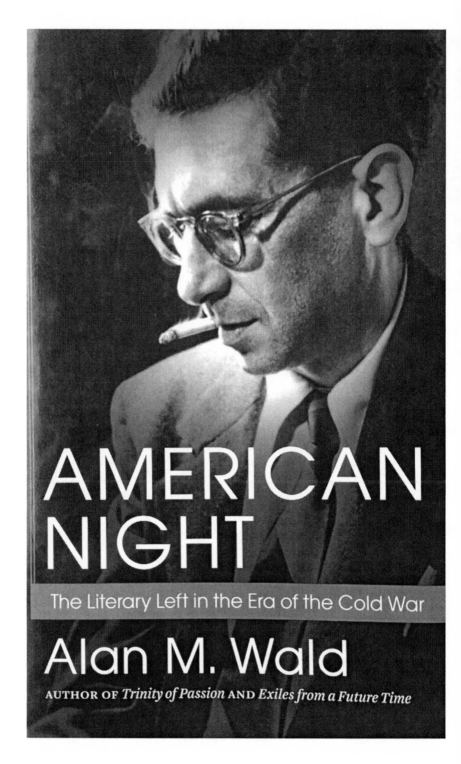

AMERICAN NIGHT

The Literary Left in the Era of the Cold War

Alan M. Wald

AUTHOR OF *Trinity of Passion* AND *Exiles from a Future Time*

Shadowgait Farm
Racing & Broodstock

April 12, 2013

Dear Alan,

My late congratulations on American night. It became an important part of my nights this winter. Masterful, how wide a net you've thrown to recognize and appreciate the brave writers of the American Left. Authoritative...hell magisterial yet comradely. Never knew Thomas McGrath or Ann Petry, or enough about Kenneth Fearing. I suspect Vincent Ray Dunne and I may be related to John M. Cockeyed Dunne. The Dunne's were my mother's clan.

Yesterday, Ralph sent me your (draft) essay on Blooming Three Case. Months ago, you mentioned working on it. I have been working on finishing a second manuscript where I detail my experience of it. Rather than a prompt and respectful reply to you months ago...I kept thinking I'd finish the whole thing and send it to you. Still might if you're interested. In re to your draft, please note (1) I was with Bingham when he signaled we go ahead with the demonstration. By fluke, Jack Marsh had driven into the mob before we could get to him and was passing out picket signs. The mob turned on us and Bingham signaled we defy them proceeding with the demonstration.

(2) Never heard any 'great legs' talk.

(3) I do not recall George Novack as playing the significant role in the Bloomington Case. Barry Sheppard was the leading YSAer; most diligent worker and bridge to the SWP. Peter Camejo was as well. The entire cadre of the SWP and YSA showed us the greatest solidarity, across the country working hard for our case;

consistently generous with their time, family homes and general camaraderie. Jack and Betsy Barnes typically opposed us and any phenomena not viscerally their own. Besty a.k.a Besty-Wetsy by Don Smith, served as den mother to the cretinous cubs Jack was spawning. I remember one named Bob Ernst who suffered a nervous breakdown when too abruptly weaned from Jack's side. Novack was already dithering about as a subsidized geriatric Barnesite. He "advised" and I thought pressured Don Smith into divorcing his wife Polly, while as comrades we were trying to reconcile them politically and maritally.

(4) We also were (as the SWP-YSA was nationally) opposed to the use of illegal drugs including marijuana. We were disciplined not to use nor associate with anyone who did. We especially avoided the Nancy Dillingham incipient hippie crowd.

(5) Every writer desires accord between his convictions and his constituency. One must be careful not to impose this desire where it does not belong nor exist. Liberal values on sex which now prevail in so many so-called socialist or leftist circles did not prevail with us. And only from such circles would we appear as "hyper-masculine or WASP". Indeed, we only had one Anglo-Saxon member. The image I think we successfully presented was that of traditionally serious, modest students, who looked typical of the sons and daughters of ordinary working people throughout the region. During the winter of '62, YSA and Y.P.S.L. convened several fund raising events and ran canned goods and groceries to the striking coal miners in Harlan County, KY. Hoadly accused us of "conducting a running gun battle with the Commonwealth of Kentucky." Jack Marsh or Jim Bingham of the YSA and Charlie Lineweber of YPSL were shot at while making runs to the miners. It was this issue that brought my family around. When Tip Kendal of Channel 10, Terre Haute (later Sacramento and an NBC talking head) phoned my father

aggressively questioning him about our politics and indictments, Dad kept repetitively saying only two sentences. (1) "They are against the war and for the miners." (2) "I believe everything my son does." The latter more loyal than informed.

Right after we were indicted, IU's Faculty Senate met and Professor Gus Liebenow reported their unanimous position that "the YSA and Prosecutor Hoadly deserved each other." The typically liberal position against those "extreme" to the Left or Right.

Within a month Prosecutor Hoadly announced that after cleansing Indiana University of Communists he was going after homosexuals and wife trading faculty members. The faculty senate immediately reconvened and proclaimed solidarity with the YSA. We contemned their moral cowardice and degeneracies.

Jacques Maritain has complained that Communist and successful Leftist Revolutions are usually led by men and women of conservative temperament; what one would call today social or cultural conservatives. Twas ever thus. From Lenin and Trotsky to Raoul Castro. Kollontai was tolerated not celebrated.

You have wisely noted in your books conclusion "The paradox of Marxist wisdom is that it becomes folly when it does not know its own limits." The velocity of socialist thought is best calibrated by the limit, the constraints of bringing the Proletariat to power. Not indulging the Enlightenment's arrogance opposing nature. Lenin could not get the rivers to flow backwards-Lysenkos' winter wheat was as impossible as it was logically impeccable. As the Libertarian Party of Indiana's ideals inspire and process a disproportional amount of "transgendered patients" into $100,000 surgical mutilations in North Indianapolis does not alter a single chromosome.

Gerry Foley was a good comrade. Leonard Boudine, a winning leftist lawyer. Their plumbing and sexuality was none of our business. Not then, not now; to disapprove or approve.

Where significant gay and lesbian presence did occur was with the University Administration which expelled us. President Herman Wells had been recruiting and perpetuating such presences for two decades since WWII.

In the Spring of 1962 several Bloomington YSAers: Jim Bingham, Jack and Tom Marsh, and I think, Ralph Levett were leafleting the commons with pro-Cuban Communist literature. They were confronted by an Administrator and several disturbed gay male graduate students who were effeminately exasperated and enraged by the leftist leaflets. They squealed and squalled right wing bigotry against us. At one point, they blocked Jim Bingham from a public bulliten board. Slowly and politely, Comrade Bingham, our maximum leader informed them if they did not get out of his way, he would injure more than their ideological ovaries.

That's the way we were. In fact, The Indiana YSA was closer to the Hasidim and Amish than to any present day gay or GLBTerian Left. In principle, you, of course, disagree. But please respect the reality of our integrity at that time. We were consistently—politically and emotionally disciplined to not discriminate nor celebrate, worry or waller around about any-one's privates or private affections.

P.S. I forgot to mention what is too often overlooked re: the Bloomington 3 case. The support we received from the CPUSA was significant. They provided us with multiple contacts, speaking engagements, financial aid, and press coverage.

In Chicago I worked at Republic Steel; on the weekend comrades Joyce DeGroot and Peter Buch were extremly resourceful reaching out to others for the CABS. Jack Barnes and his henchpersons were not. SWP locals in Detroit and L.A. were especially skilled and cooperative in working with the CP and their west coast press. Detroit's annual CP sponsored 'Buck Dinner' featured CABS with SNCC, and Carl Braden's other allotted southern civil rights groups as deserving recipients of funds raised. Michigan hunters contributed many bucks they had killed during deer season for dinner and many more bucks for the featured groups.

The Bloomington 3 case went far in reducing the chill between SWP cadre and the C.P. The chill returned after the founding convention of DuBois clubs where they viewed our (the Y.S.A) role as divisive. We had called them out to clarify their identity instead of posing as left Unitarians.

Comardly,
TGM

Damiano Funeral Home
191 Franklin Ave.
P. O. Box 567
Long Branch, New Jersey 07740
OBITUARY

"The end may justify the means as long as there is something that justifies the end."
-Leon Trotsky

LEROY RICHARD McRae was the bouncing baby boy of Thomas T. McRae and Cora Belle Boyd Cummings born in Freeman's Hospital, Washington, DC on December 30, 1940. As the eldest child, Leroy was the proud leader and organizer of his three siblings, Diane, Eric and Barton. He attended Motts Elementary School and was valedictorian of Langley Junior High School during segregation. Leroy's religious instruction was received at Tabor Presbyterian Church in Northeast Washington, DC where he served as an Eagle Scout and Vacation Bible School Teacher. He spent his summers on the tobacco farm in Croom, Maryland, of his paternal great aunt and uncle Ruby McRae and Charles "Buster" Holland. These summer experiences had a profound effect on Leroy, and he would often reminisce about the "real" education he received from his time spent working on the farm and enjoying Aunt Ruby's delicious meals with fresh fruits and vegetables from her garden.

An accomplished academic, Leroy was offered and accepted a scholarship to the prestigious Windsor Mountain School in Lenox, Massachusetts. He was President of the Student Government, a member of Student Council and Student Court, played soccer, ran track, was an avid ping pong player, and a star basketball center. Leroy received many awards for scholastic achievement, athletic excellence and citizenship during these high school years, including the "Max Bondy Award", the highest award the school bestows on the student who exemplifies not only scholarly achievement, but outstanding service to the school community as well.

Following his Magna Cum Laude graduation from Windsor, Leroy was one of fourteen African-Americans to enroll at the University of Pennsylvania's Class of 1962. A political science major, Leroy was motivated by the Trotsky movement, and joined the Young Socialist Alliance (YSA) of the Socialist Worker's Party (SWP).

Representing the SWP, Leroy ran for New York State's Attorney General in 1962. That same year, his eldest daughter, Deanna Lyn, was born to him and Virginia Louise Faller of Corinth, New York.

Leroy and Ginni met through mutual friends in the summer of 1961, when Leroy worked as a waiter for one of the Tanglewood resorts in Lee, Massachusetts. Together they relocated to New York City, and lived on the Lower East Side of Manhattan and in Philadelphia until separating in 1964. Leroy continued his work with the Socialist Workers Party and various aspects of the Civil Rights Movement throughout the 1960's. He is noted for his speech at Indiana University on March 25, 1963 where he promoted "Negro Civil Rights". His speech led to a protest in which three students, Thomas Morgan, James Bingham and Ralph Levitt, also known as "The Indiana Three", were arrested and charged with violating Indiana's 1951 Anti-Communist Act. The prosecution stated that Leroy advocated "the violent overthrow of the governments of the State of Indiana and of the United States" in his speech, "Black Revolt in America". This court battle would last for four years and become one of the catalysts for the civil rights movement.

TGM response

Leroy McRae has died. Comrade Leroy McRae; African American National Secretary of the Y.S.A. (Young Socialist Alliance) in 1963. His civil rights speech at IU that year was the prosecutors "evidence" to indict us (Jim Bingham, Ralph Levitt and me) for conspiring to overthrow the government. Prior to his death, our attorney, Leonard Boudin, outed Leroy as an FBI informant. His obituaries nonetheless included Leroy's high regard for Socialist Revolution and the S.W.P. Alan Wald, esteemed literary historian of the American Left, queried his old comrades re the contradiction. My response:

To: Alan Wald
From: TGM
Re: Fallen Comrade Leroy McRae

    He clearly held Trotsky and the S.W.P. in higher regard than the cliques who encouraged – indulged – discouraged and drove him away with God knows what processes Ed Heisler* should be interviewed about.

    Time in Tennessee with Leroy McRae, David Fender and John Lewis…some of the best times I remember of the sixties.

    Mikhail Sholokhov wrote (The Don Trilogy) of the bravest Red Cossacks riding miles with the Whites in fractured pain and the moral chaos of civil war.

---

*Ed Heisler: working class Y.S.A. er who was ad-hominem gossiped down into disloyalty and betrayal with the FBI.

Deacon Elias   Preacher Morgan

The poet carries death within him like a
good priest his breviary.
                    Heinrich Böll

FIVE FUNERALS . . AND FAREWELL

1.   Eulogy: for a murdered woman child
2.   Homily: for the mother of my bride
3.   Homily: for Uncle Bob, Peoples Mayor of Atherton
4.   Homily: for a Union Man
5.   Eulogia Antidoron: for Buddy
6.   Davids Death
7.   Farewell: for my friend Mike's wife (a love embattled)

Like Eugene Debs the Elder I am asked to preside at weddings and funerals. Debs did so with a series of toasts (several toasts I suspect) that their communities honor their fallen and protect their brides and grooms from the old divil dollar; that their homes not suffer the lack or excess of dollars; that they be blessed by plenty of work and time to rest from it in all the loving struggles of their lives. Old Gene preferred weddings. I prefer funerals.

TGM
Pastor to the Proletariat
Priest of the Trees*

*See previous Paiute honor.

(After days of searching a 15-year-old female inspired by the oral history of President Clinton's culture was found date raped, drugged and murdered in Cayuga's Bend of the Wabash River. A dear old welsh Methodist minister and I were asked to do the funeral. He was the good cop, I was the bad.)

EULOGY: FOR A MURDERED WOMAN CHILD

Dreams are a visual aid for our unconscious feelings. I don't know if Allah dreams but I've always felt weather was like His dreams. It is a sad overcast day, I am here . . we are here because we have cared about Nicole. We have had an active concern . . . We've loved her and her family.

And when our minds turn to the dark log jams along the nights slow moving Wabash our hearts are filled with a glimpse of the grief her parents must be enduring.

A daughter is a precious gift from God. To lose a daughter . . have her life taken away from your expecting her to come home in the doorway and know your expectation is like an amputated limb that still aches and yearns to be whole but will never in this life time heal is a greater burden than I can imagine bearing.

Her parents are a brave sign for all of us. We must help them comfort their family and finally each other . . for behind this grief there must be anger and regret that such a thing as this has come to pass.

Nicole's mother knows . . . believes through her faith in the ancient religious traditions that a martyred innocent goes straight to God and remains there as her parents angel. This mother seemed to know a year ago when she sat in my parlor and said,

"Nicole if you don't listen to us a year or more from now we'll be dragging the river for you."

Please understand, like you I've come here to bury Nicole not to scold her. And I'd like to think . . . Nicole that you're with me on this our last session as you are with your mother.

So, friends, parents, so-called teenagers lend me your attention for Nicole's last will and testament, I think, is for her peers . . . her friends whom she loved, counseled, befriended, and whom she could not imagine not loving her back; in short she denied evil. She loved people not reality. She wanted to be pals and friends with others; she could not imagine others hurting her. She was drawn to magic not morality. She moved the fulcrum of authority in her life from her family to her peer groups and grouplets . . her friends imagined or real. She believed in the universal adolescent nonsense in pop music and on T.V. She didn't want to be in Indiana. She was a bright, smiling good-hearted kid who just wanted to be loved. She was a budding young woman struck down by stupidity and evil. She was the quintessential American teenager.

Nicole use to laugh at my stories about Ireland. I lived there for a while. She'd laugh especially when I'd tell her how teenagers are against the law there. Adolescence of course, is the normative life passage we all have to get thru – but 'teenager' is considered a British-American marketing term to sell young people special products, special music, special clothes, special food, special hair and just an over all sense of being special. Believe me – for Nicole – being a teen is not very special.

Now we know peers are very important - all the schools tell us so – but like a lot from the schools we should take it with a grain of salt. I ask you (of whatever age) what'd you ever learn from a peer?

Young people they say are especially vulnerable to the herd mentality called peer pressure; a wee term that doesn't grasp the greater phenomena. I would suggest instead the term 'peer contagion' to describe so-called teenage culture.

An Indiana sheep farmer I know once likened his teenaged daughters to his flock of Suffolk whose care was his livelihood. "A sheep's worst enemy is not stray dogs, disease, parasites, or brush wolves; a sheep's worst enemy is another sheep," he'd say. "One of 'em infects the rest. A lot of 'em infect a lot. More of 'em magnifies all magnets of destruction." So much for peers.

Now, I'm sure there'll be much talk again about how "there's nothing for us (young people) to do in our hometowns." That is the most worn out complaint in the country and a terrible excuse for Nicole's death. I've heard it all my life. I even talked that way once when I was sixteen. I remember it well as it was the occasion of my first experience with 'police brutality'.

After we'd take our dates home us guys would 'hang out' wasting time together along 'milk shake row' which was a couple of restaurants on Wabash Avenue. At midnight after the restaurants closed that spring we'd still hang around our cars for hours shooting the breeze; killing time. Dozens of us, then hundreds of us . . we were spilling out into the passing traffic when Terre Haute's finest pulled into the parking lot. My less articulate peers pushed me forward to talk to the cops who were telling us to 'clear the area'. "There is nothing to do here and no place for youth to go at this hour," I patiently explained. "Just where would you have us go?," I rhetorically questioned the officers.

During the question I noticed officer Crockett's right arm reaching way down past his knee toward his ankle. What is he doing . . adjusting his socks? . . what is he doing I wondered til I saw his fist coming up from the pavement – a haymaker! – it jacked me under the jaw lifting me three feet off the ground barely caught by my shrinking peers. "You can go home!," he answered.

And that is the direction for all of you. Go home! Go home after the day is done. Go home to your God given elders who are there to help you care for yourself. Go home! . . and if they're not there for you – at least you've done your part.

If Nicole had gone home she would have lived. If she had lived, I think, she would have found her way. So many errors (hers and others) have prevented her from living.

Learn from her brief life, build on it . . struggle in the cause of God whatever your tradition. Build patience, restraint, fortitude, faith and bravery so you can endure every hardship and loss, facing every adversity eye to eye like Nicole's family and all of us now have to do.

HOMILY: FOR THE MOTHER OF MY BRIDE

Kay, I know you wanted this to be short and . . . light hearted. I'm sorry I don't think I can be very light hearted. I'll try . . . by telling all how I was especially fond of Kay in my active concern . . . my love for her . . . because she was the only mother-in-law I ever had who liked me.

That's about as light hearted as I can get today. But I am encouraged when I look out at all your family, friends, and loved ones who carry bits and pieces of you around with them. I see you in the eyes of your daughters mothering their children.

I see Kay in the defiance of anything other than a fierce pride in her sons, their wives and children, her daughter's husbands, her nieces and nephews, her dear brothers and sister and all her grandchildren. She even immediately claimed my lost and found son Michael into her brood of grandchildren and he responded trustfully in kind.

Her youngest grandchild Spencer Ravelette after being told Kay had died . . . awoke the next morning telling her parents that when "grandmothers die they become angels that comfort grandchildren in their sleep at night."

. . . And that's as good an explanation as any of us need. You don't have to believe it. At my age I find it hard to believe anything. The weather mans report, the politicians promise or the theological construct. The Anglo-Saxon word belief connotes in our time something you can positively empirically substantiate. Put your hands on and prove beyond the shadow of doubt. Whereas the venerable Biblical meaning was closer to how we still use the word trust or faith. I frequently counsel married couples to not lose faith in the best of their partners . . . the best of their children, and to not lose faith in the best we know of Our Father in Heaven . . . through Tradition, Holy Scripture and the lives of people around us if we'll take a real close and brave look.

More important than the good woman of the Proverbs, I see Kay's life as the good woman of the beatitudes whose ten virtues Nicole has read for us and I would abbreviate to one . . . that happy are those who do good whether or not it works, who give and do not complain or be surprised they do not receive what they deserve from destiny or anybody else. Whereas the modern clinically informed stand at the foot of the cross and ask,

"How's that working for you Jesus?"

It clearly was not working in any conventional sense.

And not wanting this olde cup,

Christ regained his composure.

In crucified failure of His goodness

. . . that with Him we [may] know happiness

in not being surprised when goodness doesn't work. Seeing pictures of Kay as a young woman full of beauty and promise; then still a youngish mother devoted to her five children; and then all the tragic stumbles, and soul bruising losses and falls she grew to never justify her flaws or condemn others for theirs . . . she struggled on with respectful camaraderie for her co-workers, gratitude for the help of her brothers and sister and how they've pulled together inspiring ways I've not known or thought possible. She struggled on . . . right up to her final struggles with terminal pain, storms, power failures and that old oxygen machine. Her struggles have been beatific . . . a life's moral struggle. What the Koran not the politicians call Jihad. Her jihad, her moral struggle is over. Ours continue . . and we would do well to draw near to her spirit as it stirs in the lives of her grandchildren and thank God we have known her.

Let us pray now the prayer that Jesus taught Kay and the rest of us Our Father who art in Heaven, hallowed be thy name;

Thy kingdom come; Thy will be done on earth as it is in heaven. Give us this day our daily bread; and forgive us our trespasses as we forgive those that trespass against us. And lead us not into temptation; but deliver us from evil. Amen

HOMILY: FOR UNCLE BOB, PEOPLES MAYOR OF ATHERTON

Graveside.

We gather today to bury and pay homage to Bob. I recommend everyone read his obituary in the Terre Haute Tribune. It is a wonderful piece about a wonderful man... written I think, by Sheila with brother Bob and sister Linda that records his work, friends, extended family, dear wife Maurine, children, grandchildren and great grandchildren we join in avoiding that commonplace heard so much at funerals (usually by remote cousins) "that isn't it too bad that it takes something like this to bring us all together". What better to bring us all together!

A great space has been left in Bob's departure, which brings us together to fill that space with comfort for all those who loved him. ...And to reflect together on the limits of life and death. Those very limits St. Paul addresses in prayerful words to the Ephesians. In short: Blessed be God the Father of Jesus the Messiah and all of us. He has blessed us with every spiritual blessing in all the heavenly places. Before the world was made to live through love in His presence, for His own kind purposes. In Him we have redemption through the richness of the grace He showers on us in all wisdom and insight. He has let us know the mystery of his purpose, the hidden plan he so kindly made from the beginning to act upon when the times had run their course to the end. Amen Before noon this New Year's day, Robert Lee Pruett's life on this earth ran its course to the end. Those of us who loved him... still love him. And in that love there are multiple prayers of praise, thanksgiving, petition, and caring. That dialectical witness of God's holy spirit.

Reflecting on Bob's life helps us trust (Ephesians 1:13) God's word and seals us within the "Holy Spirit of Promise". And what is this "Holy Spirit of Promise"? Verse 14 states it is the guarantor of our inheritance until the redemption of the purchased possession. (Repeat)

Sounds like earnest money to me.

????:"What is earnest money?" (call)

!!!!: "Good faith money!" (answer)

You betcha . . . good faith money. In purchasing a horse or a home, the trust and dignity of the deal is not in carrying on about how certain we are about the final payoff, it is based on holding on to the promise that's in the earnest money.

Faith is not some test as to who can imagine certainty the most. What authority would be taken seriously let alone trusted who could bring innocent life down to earth, turn it loose in this olde world full of snares and evil and then after fifty to one hundred years test their faith as to who can imagine certainty the most.

Faith is not some test as to who can imagine certainty the most. It is the natural common sense to recognize and pay attention to God's investment in our lives. To how the Holy Spirit, the Holy Ghost, the Barraka works in our life and the lives of others. How in Bob's life his home-centered, love-centered labor, produced value for seven decades all around him for all of us. For these youngsters of this new century who are inheriting not so much the world Bob worked for but one messed with by others we would do well to recommend his life to their attention. Robert Lee Pruett. Family man, true husband, father, grand and great grandfather, working- man, stockman, skilled mechanic, the People's mayor of Atherton. As his parents, wife, daughter, and many friends welcome him.

Thank God he will be there to welcome us.

One sort of comrade takes advantage of his friends' good
fortune,but in time of trouble turns against him.
Another sort of comrade shares his friends' hardships out of
concern,when it comes to a fight, he springs to arms.
Do not forget the friend who fought your battles.

Ecclesiasticus 37:2-6
The Jerusalem Bible

HOMILY: FOR A UNION MAN

Ah Gib . . how you've suffered this last time. And how those who love you (and are left behind) still suffer.

It is written in the book of Job 14:7-22 that there is hope even in a tree that moans.

In Gibs last days and hours his flesh knew pain (he wasn't a stranger to it) and his soul within him did moan. – But minutes before his death his daughter, Ronda reports a different countenance. She saw his breathing difficulty cease as he clearly looked toward heaven and then into his daughters eyes . . . peacefully . . and then as we say he passed away.

We trust that Gib found the peace and now rests in the peace that Jesus taught "passeth all understanding."

We pray now with the Psaltery for all of those who grieve his passing; wife, kinsmen, friends, union brothers, sisters, sons, daughters, and grandchildren . . . all of us whose flesh still know pain and our souls not free from moans and mourning.

For life is messy and impermanent. Sure like always the rich get richer but now more remote and insulated; the poor still get poorer but now more synthetically stimulated and finally wasted. All things being equal in an increasingly unequal land of economic swamps and sheer emotional cliffs . . all life, all value seems so impermanent it doesn't have far or very long to go. Now is when we need to look toward the only permanence, our only ultimate refuge . . . Our Father in Heaven.

Forest Wayne "Gib" Puckett was an individual and significant part of the post World War II, last half of the last century's working class whose measured steps and productive work created and maintained what we use to call prosperity. We are all learning to miss that. And we will miss Gib Puckett. More importantly we will remember him. After the homily there will be some music and an open invitation to come forward and share with us your distinct memories of Gib.

My first memory was meeting him and Ruth with Wendi at a Legion Post way out in the sticks near Riley. It was his eyes. Those Cherokee Nation eyes he gave to his children and grandchildren. I pointed to Wendi's eyes and looked at his. He didn't say a word but acknowledged the thought with that slight, lucid, knowing smile of his.

Next I remember him standing with me in knee deep water I'd caused by breaking pipes I was trying to fix in Wendi's basement. Things had grown even more tense because I'd just thrown a bucket of water over Zach who'd come down the basement stairs as a plumbers critic and said, "Neener, neener, neener – Way to go Tom." Gib fixed the plumbing and explained to me how. Before we came out of the basement I asked him for his daughters hand in marriage . . . which again brought on that lucid yet remote clear moment look in his eyes which said without words . . "well . . it won't be for me to decide." Fortunately his daughter did decide for me and we've shared many a Gib story.

My favorite was how he decided to discipline a thief who'd broken into his house on Lee Avenue where his children lay sleeping. Disciplining error is increasingly difficult in a society which basically forbids it . . yet to indulge misconduct or excessively punish it always compounds things making them worse. So later when this thief approached Gib at the Stop 5 tavern and tried to sell him his own stolen handgun the situation required moral discernment.

Gib politely invited the fellow into the back alley, deposited him on the ground, pointed the loaded gun between the thief's eyes and quickly fired two shots beside both ears into the earth. Moral Discernment! Never hurt the man but put the fear of God in him discouraging future crimes. Gib would tell this story with that lucid clear look in his eyes.

The lucidity that Ronda saw in them as he took his leave. A lucidity that constitutes his suffering at the same time crowned his victory. There is no fate that cannot be surmounted by such conscious sorrow. It always and ultimately becomes accompanied by joy.

We all have our nights in Gethsemane. Gib had his. We all have to roll that rock up the hill with Sisyphus. Descend and do it again over and over. Through our higher fidelity to God the sorrowful descents can also be joyous for we know our work up the hill creates value and will be rewarded.

Marxist categories are the child of ancient religious devotion. Their rigor is to implement what has been revealed. Marx began his development on the labor theory of value at Lutheran grammar school.

All value including its perception is created by effort. All economic value is created by work. It logically both precedes and follows that moral value is created by moral effort and work. Judgment and eternal reward for this mans life of effort to provide, love, screw up and be forgiven is based upon the mutual assurance of Gods fidelity to our hard work, to our struggle . . what the Koran calls our jihad. It is as solid as a union contract and that much better than anything else. Amen

Gibs with God. Now its up to us.

EULOGIA ANTIDORON: FOR BUDDY

for the desolate and the brave

Welcome. Our meeting today is to be a very solemn occasion. And it can be . . . if we collectively will our prayers in that direction.

Let us pray: the prayer that Jesus taught us.

Our Father,

who art in heaven,

hallowed be thy name;

thy Kingdom come,

thy will be done on earth as it is in heaven.

Give us this day our daily bread;

and forgive us our trespasses,

as we forgive those who trespass against us;

and lead us not into temptation,

but deliver us from evil.

For the kingdom,

the power,

 and the glory are yours

now and for ever.

Amen

It may be impossible to imagine this party room of the Marine Corps Club as a church or chapel but we can imagine it as a gravesite . . . which in reality it has become for Maurice Buddy Puckett.

The circumstance of Buddy's death at 49 years old is so harshly dark it eludes conventional attempts at expressing it.

So let's return to those most pristine and ancient words regarding darkness, darkness and light, and our only light in such darknesses. Buddy's Uncle Donny will read from the book of Genesis.

Genesis 1:1-5 In the beginning God created the heaven and the earth.

Now the earth was a formless void,
there was darkness over the deep,
and God's spirit hovered over the water.
God said, "Let there be light, and there was light.
God saw that light was good,
and God divided light from darkness.

Uncle Wendel will read from the Gospel of John.
John 1: Prologue   In the beginning was the Word;
the Word was with God
and the Word was God.
He was with God in the beginning.
Through him all things came to be,
not one thing had its being but through him.
All that came to be had life in him
and that life was the light of men,
a light that shines in the dark,
a light that darkness could not overpower.
And last . . .Buddy's only son Alex from the first letters of John,
"God is love"

Buddy died with his blood and brain full of cocaine and lethal amounts of liver killing alcohol on Thanksgiving eve. Thanksgiving morn his girlfriend Amy Engels was found dead by her sister from an apparent . . . errant effort to join him. And the grief all around is compounded.

Seventy years ago after enduring multiple deaths, fickle waste, and wars destruction, Dylan Thomas refused to yet again conventionally mourn the death of a child, by fire, in another London bombing raid. I've appropriated some of his verse for our situation today.

(Appropriated from: A Refusal to Mourn the Death, by Fire, of a child in London.)

Never until the mankind making
Bird beast and flower
Fathering and mothering darkness
Tells with silence this last light breaking
And the still hour
Is come of rivers tumbling in harness

And we must enter again the round
Zion of the water bead
And the Synagogue of the ear of corn
Shall I let pray the shadow of a sound
Or sow our salt seed tears
In the least valley of sackcloth to mourn

The majesty of life and wretchedness
Of this adult child's death I shall not murder
The mankind of his going with a grave truth
Nor blaspheme down the stations of his breath
With any further
Elegy of innocence and youth
Deep with this death lies his son and daughters

Robed in the love of long friends and family
Grains beyond age, the dark veins of their mothers
Secret by the unmourning waters
Riding by the Wabash which itself has wept
After this last death . . . there is no other.

It is one of the qualities of darkness . . of sin and all evil
that it wishes to drag down others in its own camp, and rejoices to
see them humiliated, disgraced, and dead just as, in the
opposite case, the good [in God's light] rejoice to help and honor
others and make them happy wherever they are: if we recognize

and respect the one and only eternal Reality, that is God, Allah, Our Father in Heaven, and through His infinite Mercy and Forgiveness all things are possible on both sides of the grave.

Holy scripture teaches us to not return evil for evil, and not exactly good for evil . . . but to foil evil with love. In so doing there can be a descent of Angels upon and within our prayers for the fallen. That in moral and spiritual affairs, seeming opposites may by Gods love be made to sub serve the purposes of good . . of darkness into light. That lost souls through this light attain the position of guests to Host, receiving unnumbered gifts out of all proportion to their . . . to our own merits. Heaven is no meritocracy. And there are no (as her Aunt Tanya told Tori) addictions in heaven.

The intent of a soul is important. If one intends good but behaves otherwise one is accountable for that. But if one behaves well or OK without good intentions . . . how is that
better?! We will remember Buddy's handsome face, wit, grace, and injured love for his family. I think Buddy's short life intended good but behaved and ended badly. Worse . . . he will not be here to help, to guide, to work through, and make right so many things with and for his children Nicole, Tori, and Alex. Our love will have to help out here just as our prayers of love become Gods light for him and us out there: Eliade, Romanian theologian: spoke years ago (similar to the way physisists speak now of Parallelograms) . . of a dimension he called the 'Hyrothene' where the sacred eternal and profane mortal can meet in a kind of ceremonial space. Where . . . (through our prayers) we are there for him. As the passage Alex read from John . . . 1 John:4:8 My dear people, let us love one another since love comes from God and everyone who loves is begotten by God and knows God. Anyone who fails to love can never have known God, because God is love.

Please conclude with a prayerful lyric I've learned from
the Amish, 'Gutes Geselle, was sagest du mir?
Good Friends, what do we say? O good friend I tell you –
I tell you   one thing, God alone.
He who lives and He who soars.
And He who leads the faithful
In Heaven and on Earth.

Let us pray: Praise be to Our Father in Heaven,
Cherisher and Sustainer of the worlds. Most gracious, most
merciful, Master of the Day of Judgment. To thee alone we pray,
thine aid we seek. Guide us upon the straight Path, the way of
those You have bestowed thy grace whose portion is not wrath
and who go not astray.

Allow our prayers to be there for Buddy; to be there for him.

Amen

No more . . . no other funerals.

DAVIDS DEATH

For the Sons and Loves of David Gerwe

The unsettled thoughts of yesternight
are but sparrows, in a tear;
they punctuate regret in flight
for the crash I could not hear.

The Whack! those whacks of glass and steel
that killed him on the pavement
his smirk lugubrious as still . . . genteel
extreme now unctuous, sheltered, and sent

beside lanes of hurtling mortgaged steel.
Our Warner from the Pisgah Forest Swift
above all motives gathering lift
as on and in our wheel.

Corridors of civilized affection
we did con-celebrate; and hereabout anon
I will truly speak of thee . . .
so perhaps from where you'll be,
you might speak so of me.

Read by my son Eliot at Miekija's Funeral.
Dear Miekija, wife of my friend, Mike

FOR WE HAVE KNOWN A LOVE; EMBATTLED

A baby girl was born near European War

brought across North African weather

to cold peace in America.

And She's Been Heating It Up Forever!

From the battlements of her heart

all nuance less than it ought to be

trembled . . and yet was so befriended

never dispassionate, always athwart

loves inexorable dreadful endedness.

"I'm going to marry him," she said - it has to be

she loved our Michael . . . and she loved thee.

Fighting the elements underground

she bravely rescued her son

endearing her to us like the very frame

of the landscapes she's become.

Rescued he was and rescued he had to be

she loved our Sean . . . and she loved thee.

She had a knack for the languages.

preparing her daughter for the ages

of innocence, strength, and beauty.

Tough loving tenderly.

she loved our Jennifer . . . and she loved thee.

Half a lifetime the hideous threat

of cancerous death hurt and harassed

with brave laughter, work and wit.

Her very essence fought it.

She fought on for her life

for her family,

and I think, it was Providence

that sought this exemplary woman's loving battle

for all of us to see.

For us to know. For us to have known

such love embattled as Miekija abrasively

loved her friends and family

And by God

Beloved is she!

"The only kind of fights worth fighting are those you are going to lose. Because somebody has to fight them and lose and lose and lose until someday, somebody who believes as you do wins. In order for somebody to win an important major fight 100 years hence, a lot of other people have got to be willing - for the sheer joy of it - to go right ahead and fight, knowing your going to lose. You mustn't feel like a martyr. You've got to enjoy it."

I.F. Stone

from UnrepentantMarxist.com